MW01147897

COWBOY ROUNDUP

COWBOY ROUNDUP

EDITED BY DREW HUNT

jms books

COWBOY ROUNDUP

All Rights Reserved © 2015 by Drew Hunt

Cover design by Written Ink Designs | written-ink.com

These stories are works of fiction. All events, locations, institutions, themes, persons, characters, and plots are completely fictional inventions of the author. Any resemblance to people living or deceased, actual places, or events is purely coincidental and entirely unintentional.

The stories herein are copyrighted by and remain the sole property of their respective authors.

No part of this book may be reproduced or transmitted in any form or by any means, graphic, electronic, or mechanical, including photocopying, recording, taping, or by any information storage retrieval system, without the permission in writing from the author and publisher.

"Roughshod" © Dale Chase. "Taming Brooks" © R.W. Clinger. "The Spring at Sloan Pond" © Lee Crittenden. "Rogayo" © Landon Dixon. "Cowboy Therapy" © Hunter Frost. "A Change of Pace" © Drew Hunt. "Firefly Ranch" © Rebecca James. "Wild Ride" © Kassandra Lea. "Guy Walks Into a Bar" © Georgina Li. "Nephi Takes a Husband" © Bob Masters. "Flyboys and Cowboys" © Michael McClelland. "Wild West Show" © Rob Rosen. "Riding for the Brand" © J.D. Ryan. "Daniel in Distress" © Feral Sephrian. "Save a Horse" © J.D. Walker. "The Good, the Bad, and the Ojete" © Salome Wilde. All published in October 2015 by JMS Books LLC.

JMS Books LLC
10286 Staples Mill Road # 221
Glen Allen, VA 23060
www.jms-books.com

Printed in the United States of America
ISBN: 9781517158132

CONTENTS

INTRODUCTION

IT'S PROBABLY MORE than a little odd for a guy from the north of England to have such a fascination for cowboys. Is it the boots, the jeans (usually Wranglers), the chaps, the thick heavy belt, the flannel shirt, or the hat? Yes to all of the above. But each of these articles of clothing serve a needed purpose on the ranch, enabling the cowboy to do his lonely and often dangerous job in all weather and harsh terrain. The cowboy is usually depicted alone; it's him against nature. Therefore he has to be tough, resourceful, and able to make his own decisions—all very desirable qualities in the ideal man. At least, *my* idea of the ideal man.

I remember watching old western movies on TV with my grandfather and taking more of a shine to the bad guys dressed in black rather than the hero, who usually ended up with the girl. That last certainly didn't hold an appeal for me. But given that there were so few women back in the Old West, I think it's a pretty safe bet that there were quite a number of men sneaking into the bedrolls of other men, just to feel a warm body next to them on a cold desert night. Although history is fairly quiet on the subject, I'd be willing to bet quite a number of cowboys set up housekeeping together and lived their lives quietly and privately out of the prying gaze of history. Wishful thinking? Perhaps, but then the imagination is a powerful thing, and it has been employed to great effect in the stories in this collection.

These sixteen gay erotic and erotic romance stories take the reader from the wild frontier of the Old West of America in such gems as *Nephi Takes a Husband* by Bob Masters, *The Spring Sloan Pond* by Lee Crittenden, and *The Good, the Bad, and the Ojete* by Salome Wilde. We ride into the present with the likes of *Cowboy Therapy* by Hunter Frost and *Wild Ride* by Kassandra Lea. There are plenty of interesting stops along the way, such as visiting a *Wild West Show* courtesy of Rob Rosen and a pretty unique rodeo in Landon Dixon's *Rogayo*.

Whether it be herding cattle, chasing down outlaws, or taking a dip in the water hole, you're guaranteed a thrilling ride within the pages of *Cowboy Roundup*.

Drew Hunt
West Yorkshire
September 2015

ROUGHSHOD
BY DALE CHASE

I WAS DOING well at poker in Tombstone's Oriental Saloon when the young fellow sitting to my right started going on about the dealer cheating. It annoyed me that I couldn't assure him he was mistaken because doing so would reveal my fine array of cards. I hoped he'd quiet down so I could claim the pot, but this was not to be. Damned if he didn't keep on ranting at the dealer, gaining in volume as he heated up. When he jumped up and drew his pistol, I jumped up too and knocked it away. This sent him reeling for a second before he sprang at me, fists flying. I put an end to this with a serious gut punch, then turned to the game and laid out my hand. When I'd scooped up the money, I bowed out and saw to the kid on the floor.

He was dazed, but took the offered hand and let me pull him to his feet. I located his weapon, but didn't give it back to him. Into my belt it went. And outside we went.

"You'd have killed that man," I said once we were out front of the saloon.

"He deserved it," replied the kid who couldn't have been even twenty. "He was cheating."

"You ever stop to consider you're maybe not so good at

poker?"

He lit up with fresh anger that I found appealing. "You ever think to mind your own business?" he returned.

"You'd be in jail about now if I hadn't stopped you. And I had a winning hand, so I don't believe the dealer was a sharp. I stopped you because I didn't want the game overturned which it would have been had you continued acting trigger happy."

Now he blazed. It was a warm July afternoon and he lit up like the sun itself, going red in the face, breathing heavy, fists clenched. Goddamn, I wanted to fuck him, but I settled for buying him a drink. When he bristled at the invite, I made light of the situation. "Calm down," I said. "It's too fine a day to be upset about anything. I'll buy, seeing how I won."

He drilled me with a look, and I saw he was suspect of good gestures. "What's your name?" I asked as I guided us up the block to Hafford's Saloon.

"Ben Wylie," he said. "You maybe heard of me?"

I pondered a second, then said no. "How are you known?"

"Killed four men."

He was slight of build and stood maybe five foot eight so he didn't come off as a threat, though I knew from experience that men of small stature were often the most deadly. I wasn't too much bigger, being a lean five-ten. What I had on him was about ten years. And I'd killed twelve.

"You on the run?" I asked.

"My trouble was in Kansas so I came west. I'll take no guff from any man."

"I'm getting that, but have no fear. I'm an easygoing sort who appreciates interesting company. Name is Cal Decker."

We reached Hafford's just then, but I found as I entered that I'd lost Ben. He stood fixed just outside the door, people pushing past. "I've heard of you," he said when I went back for him. I put a hand to his shoulder and drew him inside.

"No doubt you have," I replied.

He downed two whiskeys before he spoke again, and I let

him stew because I was enjoying him gaining new perspective. I also enjoyed my dick getting stiff. As I sipped my liquor, I considered how he might come two or three times before I wore out.

"You've killed a dozen," he finally said.

"That I have."

"Then what right had you to stop me from plugging that gambler?"

"No right, as you put it. More common sense. I felt you heating up and, as I said before, I wanted to keep the game going."

He threw back his third drink and got a fourth. "Best you slow down on that whiskey," I counseled.

"Best you not tell me what to do."

I liked his fire, misplaced as it was. He seemed angry at far more than cards, and part of the attraction was considering the source. Too often a wronged man holds tight to the wrong and it starts coming out in other ways. Like shooting people, although not in my case. Every one of my dozen was ruled justified by the courts as every one had drawn on me. My crime has been pissing people off.

"How about I buy you supper?" I said and I saw he had to decide if this was an intrusion. When he said okay, I felt we'd bridged a gap, though maybe not with the most sturdy of bridges.

Five whiskeys rendered Ben somewhat pliable and over supper he told of his Kansas upbringing on a cattle ranch. "Learned early on to ride and shoot," he said.

"That your work? Cow punching?"

He cut a bite of steak, chewed, and swallowed it before answering. "I left that life at fifteen. Been on my own ever since."

"How old are you now?"

"Nineteen."

"Why'd you leave?"

He cut several more bites of steak and ate them slowly, occupying himself rather than answer so I attempted to backtrack. "I know how it is," I said. "Sometimes you just have to break free and find your own way."

Still he didn't speak and I got that he'd been driven off by recall. I wanted to apologize for stirring things, but held off as it might make things worse. We finished the meal in silence.

It was when I picked up the check that I caught Ben's eyes on me with such intensity that it crossed my mind he might want to kill me so he could claim my dozen men with his four. Not a clear type thinking, but one I'd run into before. It was a deadly look, and blazing hot. Gone the effects of his liquor. Whatever I'd stirred, it was dangerous, so I moved with caution. I paid the check and we walked out into a fine sunset. When I turned to go up the block Ben fell in beside me, and as we went along he said the damndest thing. "You want to get up to something?"

I almost laughed, such was my relief. Before I could speak he added, "I've got a room at The Grand."

We walked to the hotel in silence and by the time we went into his room, I'd decided my gunslinger reputation was working in my favor, that and my being fine looking. Soon as the door closed, Ben stripped. I wasn't so hurried and enjoyed watching him as I slowly shed my duds. He brought back memories of that early urgency, of getting hard at every turn and coming all over the place. By the time I got down to drawers, Ben was standing naked, stiff cock in hand.

He was a beauty, lean and still filling out. Dark haired, but fair skinned and near pretty. It occurred to me, as I gazed upon him, that the anger he carried was indeed likely due to a man having wronged him.

He watched me finish stripping and when my hard cock was freed, he stared at it. I got how he wanted it up him, how he needed hard riding, and I was the man to do it. "You surprised me," I said. "The way we started out, I didn't figure to be in such favor."

"You figured wrong."

Here he fell to his knees and drew my rod into his mouth, then set to proving himself an expert cocksucker. I stood with hands on hips, looking down at him going at me. I hadn't been worked so good in some time. Finally I eased him off. "You keep on, you'll get my load in your throat and I'd rather put it up your ass."

I gave him no time to comment, just pushed him to the bed, got him on all fours, wet my dick with spit, and drove in. He let out a yell at being speared, while I got from the very first that this was more than the usual fucking around. Something about this hotheaded kid captured me, and I set about enjoying that fact while taking pleasure in fucking hell out of him. The great surprise was him being a talker. Soon as I set to riding him, he began to spew. "Fuck me, fuck my ass, choke me with cock, fuck my shit hole, get it up there, fuck me."

It drove me crazy and I went full out which got me to come way before I wanted. But come I did, giving him a load that I attempted to drive up into his mouth. I pounded his sweet ass until I ran dry and went soft. I then rolled off onto my back, gasping for breath.

"You come?" I asked between gasps.

"Hell, yes," he replied. "Puddle under me."

I opened my eyes as he rolled onto his side and there it was, thick and white, a goodly amount on the bedding. I blew out a breath and ran a hand down to his cock, feeling stuff on the knob. "One fine fuck," I declared and Ben leaned in and replied, "Need more than one."

"Sonny, I'll fuck you raw if you give me time to recover. We got all night."

He issued a sigh, rolled onto his back, and we lay quiet for a bit which I didn't mind as I liked his company. Funny thing was, he'd run his mouth with a dick in him, but went the other way once it was removed.

Too often I've fucked and run, taking pleasure, then done with the fellow. I'd almost forgotten what it was to linger with a man and savor the promise of another go. I took pride in knowing I could handle this, though I'd seldom put it to practice, at least with another party. A man such as me, having no fixed home, often finds his hand the sole companion. I've been known to come two or even three times when bedded down alone beside a fire on the open range.

After a time I got up and washed so I could get dirty again, and when I found Ben watching me clean up, I made a show of it, handling myself while his dick rose up. A fine sight, fellow coming up hard at no more than the show you put on. I decided I'd suck his cock, seeing how mine needed some rest.

Once clean, I sat on the bed and played around with him. He was most willing, and once I set to sucking him he started orating again. "Suck my dick, suck me good, Cal. Take it all. Drink my come then eat my ass. I want that bad, Cal, want your tongue up there where your dick's been." On and on he went until he shot a load into my throat amid much squealing and crying out on what he was doing. When he went quiet, I rolled him over and had me a filthy meal.

I'd only eaten ass a couple times as it was downright foul, but with the right man, especially one who begged it, I was willing to descend into the wallow. When I parted Ben's butt cheeks, his hole winked at me, and I ran a finger over it which got more prodding. "Eat me," he said. "Eat my ass."

I licked like some dog, working myself toward the awful thing I was about to do. Putting a tongue up an ass is as filthy as you can get, which Ben reminded me. "I want it nasty, Cal. Goddamn, get in there."

He was pulling his cock and that, plus his demand, got me moving. I stuck my tongue in and started giving him a little fuck. This not only fired him to serious jabbering and faster dick pulling, it drove me near crazy. My spent cock announced itself resurrected far sooner than expected, so I tongue fucked him while doing much growling and snorting. Then he called out he was coming and I kept at him until he settled. Soon as my tongue withdrew, in went my prick.

I wanted to tell him what he'd accomplished, but had no words. I was gone on the fuck, single minded now, pumping away, and knowing the rise might be distant. The spunk in him served me well, a wet slap our sole accompaniment once Ben quit talking. Sweat flew and my breathing became labored with the long ride, but there eventually came the drawing up and firing and I cried out on this. Ben returned that he wanted me to fill him. I rode to exhaustion, then fell off, and recall no more because sleep got me.

It took a minute to fix on where I was when I woke, but once established I sat up to find a new day and not a trace of the man I'd bedded. I got up and stood in the room's middle, turning round and round in search of a clue that he remained. When I got none, I sought the piss pot where, floating in soiled water, I found the sole evidence of Ben Wylie. Before I let go a stream, I stood wondering if a man leaving you nothing but shit is sending a message.

It was not the day I expected. The night's excess had led me to believe I'd wake to find Ben beside me, dick hard, and I'd fuck him and then get breakfast. Now I moved about uncertain which annoyed me no end.

"Fool kid," I said to the mirror. I then laughed, catching just who was the fool.

I had no plans, being recently arrived in Tombstone, so I sought the day as if there had been no disturbance. I'd simply enjoyed a longer version of the usual sex. I'd get breakfast, walk around town, then settle in at cards. And if I found another agreeable fellow, I'd fuck hell out of him.

I wasn't looking to find Ben Wylie which, of course, set him in my path. When I came out of Pearl's Restaurant, full bellied and feeling lucky, I'd gone not ten feet when the kid all but ran into me. He was going along with way too much purpose, head down like a charging bull. "Hey," I said as I pushed him to one side. "Watch where you're going."

When he slung an arm at me I grabbed it and twisted him around to pin him against a post. "Easy, sonny," I counseled as I held him fast.

"Get off me," he demanded.

"You settle down and I might. What's got you so riled?"

"None of your business."

I laughed, then leaned in and put my mouth to his ear. "Look here, Ben, I'm the fellow who's had his tongue up your ass, so you leave off saying I've no business. Now what's got you?"

"Let me go and I'll say."

I backed off and he turned around, showing more of that fire he carried. I waited while he silently fumed and when nothing came forth, I prodded. "What is it?" I asked. "You lose at cards again?"

"No," he snapped. "Fellow owes me fourteen dollars and won't pay so I went after him, but others stepped in and he got away."

"You wave that gun around again?"

"I was ready to draw if he didn't come through," Ben explained, "but his friends pulled him away, making excuses for him. I'll not be put off. I mean to get my money."

"Honest money?"

"I'm no thief. He borrowed and won't pay me back."

"Fair enough," I declared, "but try to stop short of killing him. You had breakfast?"

"I have."

"Why'd you run out on me this morning? I expected to get another taste of you."

The flush of his upset deepened as he searched for a reply, and I almost wanted to take back the question, seeing how it cornered him. "We was done," he finally said.

"Fair enough," I replied. "Of course, that doesn't mean we can't start up again."

I could see him wanting to flee and took it as a compliment that his manly occupations overpowered whatever worry he carried. Why some men couldn't shed those objectionable parts of life was beyond me, but I'd seen it before, this unexpressed moan, this ache that made itself visible. The trouble this time was Ben had an itchy trigger finger. Also that I was too much taken with him.

"Did you check out of the Grand?" I asked, wanting to fill the silence.

"I did," he replied. "Took my things down to the livery. I'm leaving soon as I get my fourteen dollars."

"Where you headed?"

"North," was all I got.

"I've got a room at the Cosmopolitan," I said. "How about we go over there and have us another go. Give you a sendoff, seeing how you're leaving."

I hadn't engaged in such pursuit for some time as I'd been content to fuck in alleys and barns and wherever opportunity presented itself. Quick and dirty works well, but when a fellow such as Ben Wylie steps in and stirs parts too long neglected, a man presses on because the reward is truly fine.

Ben considered me and I liked him taking my measure, so to speak. I sport a good head of dark hair, close cut beard, trim mustache, and eyes one man said near made him come. My mouth has also proven adequate in dick sucking and there have been no complaints on my equipment, beyond a couple fellows staggering away while saying they'll not sit comfortably for a time. I was confident Ben would give way once more. Which he did.

While I like a kid coming all over the place, I also want him to learn the pleasures of slower practices so once I'd fucked Ben good and he'd sprayed his stuff on the floor, because I did him standing, I laid him out and proceeded to lick and play over his every inch. He resisted at first and I almost asked who'd ruined him because it was clear I brought on powerful recall. But even though he retreated in some way, he gave over at the same time, and I'll give myself credit on that. I sucked his tit nubs at length, nibbled his neck and ears, got my tongue in under his arms, and worked down to his toes which I sucked. He whimpered when I went around his privates and I lay my cheek on his thigh and told him how fine his body was and there was more to sex play than just dick and butthole. "I like the whole man," I said. "Like your every inch and I'll get to your bottom in due time. We've got all day if we want, and I do want."

I enjoyed his hands on my back or whatever part of me he could reach as I quietly devoured the whole of him. And he soon stopped his squirming and settled into the play, near floating on the bed as I licked his calves and in behind his knees. When I rolled him over he began to beg me to eat him again, but I didn't do that. I ran a couple fingers up him while nipping his bottom and he got a hand under to work his cock. Knowing he wanted pay dirt, I reamed him until he cried out and came, and when he was done I kept the fingers working to show him I meant to keep on going.

I finally licked my way back up to his ear into which I declared him a tasty morsel. He was so undone he simply purred. I then rolled him over and kissed him. I could hardly recall the last time I tasted a man this way. Nobody much bothered with it, but then most cared only to unload and move on. As my lips met Ben's, the idea of his moving on was far distant.

He responded fully, tongue going after mine, and I got he was well practiced at intimacy. I was unexpectedly stung by a moment's jealousy of the man who took him so fully and wronged him so badly, but this jealousy quickly gave way to pleasure in the present.

I purposely didn't let this kissing become urgent as the satisfaction I sought wasn't a passing sort. I wanted to possess Ben Wylie, keep on with him long as I could, never mind he said he'd move on. With encouragement such as presently undertaken, he might not go.

Parting my lips from his, I looked into his eyes where I found the blue of the sky. He met me on this, but what he brought wasn't what I'd sought. Absent the fire, his gaze bore a touch of sadness that I couldn't chase off, no matter how hard I stared. Still, I pressed on. "You've captured me, Ben," I said. "You may not have meant to, but you have."

I gave him no time to reply as the last thing a man in my

spot wants is an argument. I kissed him again, gently, tongue exploring, and when I eased up on this I kissed his cheeks and forehead and eyes, kissed on down his neck. Funny how quiet intimacy can rouse a man. I sometimes forget that as I'm too often thinking with my dick. Then, on these rare occasions, I slow down and savor a man and feel a rise that begins not in my nuts, but in a place deeper, heart maybe, though it feels more gut. My whole body stirs, muscles tensing, skin pulling taut, and the slumbering dick can't help but wake and go along. So, after a period of this gentle intimacy, I had my cock good and hard.

Ben was now fluid in my hands. Gone the kid looking to make tracks, and I couldn't even imagine the hotheaded trigger happy fellow I'd first encountered. He lay with arms at his side, willing to give whatever I wanted, and I feasted on the sight which led to the need to fuck.

I lay out beside him, on my back, and pulled him over onto me. "Sit up," I said with a little push. "Straddle me."

This he did, his expression that of a happy drunk. He sat on my chest, my stiff prick behind him. "Climb onto me," I said. "Raise up and drop down on my cock. Fuck yourself with it."

He grinned and did as told, plopping down so hard I let out a moan. He got what I was about and set to rocking on me. It was now my turn to display the want. I reached up to take him at the waist, urging him to raise up which he did and when he dropped down I ascended to heaven, surely I did.

Soon he was riding me at a good clip, bouncing on my dick and pushing away my hands when I tried to keep hold. He resembled a man astride a bucking bronc, which he furthered with some shouts and a yee-haw or two. His grin made it all the more and he looked happy for once.

Just as the quiet intimacy had taken over my body, so did the fuck, and when I felt climax beckon, it was in the whole of me. Buttocks, thighs, calves, feet, arms, neck, you name it and it tensed, readying for what felt to be an explosion, and then it hit and I cried out as I couldn't be contained. My prick pumped long spurts into him and he called out he felt it go up his passage.

When I finally emptied, my muscles remained taut, and it took a minute for the effects to subside. I doubted I'd ever come in such a manner and I pulled Ben down on me, my spent cock sliding out, and I kissed him again. "You sure you have to leave?" I asked at which he kissed me.

I thought we'd settle in after this, bask in having done all we did, but Ben was not one to go easy. Something in him refused to give way, likely the part that drove his trigger finger, and I saw I'd not tamed him. Foolish of me to think my attention could get him past whatever held him captive. He never answered my question, and after a time of lying quietly, he got up and dressed. When I made no move toward cover, attempting to entice him by handling my dick, he gave just a glance before pulling on his boots.

"We've got a good thing going," I said. "Why not keep on?"

He had no answer and for a second I was sorry I'd pressed. He looked lost now, more boy than man, and I wanted to tell him we're not all shitheels, but I just lay, pulling my dick. He said not a word before he went out the door.

"Well, goddammit all to hell," I ranted when he'd gone. I got up, pissed, washed, and when I caught myself in the mirror I scolded. "You goddamn fool," I said to me. "Leave off him. Leave the hell off."

When I emerged from the hotel I considered Ben Wylie gone. He'd declared himself ready to leave and I pictured him rushing headlong down to the livery, mounting up, and riding north like he'd said. I went to the Oriental Saloon, figuring to get drunk. I was well along in this endeavor when shots were heard. Gunfire is common in Tombstone, yet I sprang to attention. Ben, I thought as I rushed outside.

A man staggered across the street, light from a store showing us the red blotch at his middle. He looked down, as if he couldn't believe himself struck, and he put a hand to the wound, trying to stop the flow of blood. Standing not ten feet away was Ben, pistol in hand. The shot fellow managed to speak and Ben replied, but, of course, it was too late for words. Ben was soon going to claim five lives instead of four. When the fellow dropped to a heap, Ben ran and I passed but a couple seconds before I did, too. My action was foolish, but a driven man cares little on judgments, even those issued by himself. I couldn't let Ben get away.

He ran toward the livery where his horse stood ready, and I followed, though my animal was standing about at leisure, unsaddled, the things he usually carried—bedroll and saddlebags—in my hotel room. I couldn't light out after Ben without fetching my possessions, yet still I ran, as if I'd go without. When I reached the livery, there came Ben flying by, horse at a gallop. I watched him ride off, then told the liveryman to saddle my horse and I hurried to the hotel to get my belongings. I did manage to slow myself to a brisk walk as I didn't want to be seen tearing after a fellow who'd just shot a man. Nor did I want to be seen chasing a nineteen year old and me thirty-two. Still, my blood rushed like I'd pulled the trigger.

The walk back to the livery, saddlebags slung over my shoulder, bedroll under my arm, took an eternity as all the while I considered Ben on the run. Knowing how such pursuit feels, I felt akin to him, but maybe this was anticipation as I'd soon be the one chasing him. The law would likely get up a posse, but I'd be ahead of them, having no idea what I was about. Catch him and then what?

My horse often proves himself smarter than me and did so on this occasion. He didn't balk at the saddle, gave no objection to the bridle or taking on my things. It was me he objected to, like he knew us on a fool's errand and meant, due to our six years together, to keep me from such pursuit. When my foot went into the stirrup, as it has hundreds of times, he pulled away which threw me off balance. "Easy, Red," I told him, but when I tried again he again acted like some stranger was attempting to steal him and ride off to nowhere. "Goddamn you,

Red, hold up."

Now he darted back without any attempt by me to mount him, acting skittish when he was too old for such nonsense. Yet he persisted. Though my temper continued to rise, I reined myself in and left off trying to get aboard. I stood silent a good minute before easing up to talk to my friend face to face. He looked at me with those endearing eyes and I've no idea what in hell he was saying in his silent horse way, but I felt his concern. "We'll be all right, boy," I assured him, wondering, as I said it, if he knew I was lying. He snorted and I chuckled and we passed another couple minutes before he let me climb up without giving so much as a twitch. We then set off at an easy canter because I refused to appear on the chase.

North was all I had from Ben. I'd get over to the road running along the San Pedro River and follow it to Contention and points beyond, if needed. Just had to hope Ben hadn't circled around and headed for Mexico. Thinking on this as Red and I went along, I decided Ben would indeed keep to his plan. I didn't see him wanting to disappear south of the border because a big part of him wanted notice. Claiming five kills to Mexicans who didn't know him was a waste, although claiming the same in Arizona Territory wasn't much better. Killing in Kansas remains there, unless the fellow is Doc Holliday or Wyatt Earp.

I rode until dusk, stopping twice at the river to drink alongside Red, to rest and piss such as was needed. I half expected to come upon Ben lying on his bedroll, dozing in the shade, hand in his pants. I'd done that often in younger years. Now I always waited until dark surrounded me to indulge.

I wasn't going to try and get Ben to go back to Tombstone and face justice as that would deprive me of his company. His business with the law was not my concern. Ours was a personal connection, I reasoned, and I could pursue that without breaking the law, though the law might see it different.

He'll stay in Contention, I decided. Or no, he'll camp outside town after taking a meal there. And a drink or two. I could see him strutting in a saloon, that fifth man weighing on him in the worst way, stirring him up instead of shutting him down.

I knew Contention well and thought ahead to places I'd look. Get myself a meal, get myself some drinks. Maybe stay over. Why run myself ragged for Ben Wylie? I had no occupation beyond earning enough to keep myself so there were no requirements on my person which is how I liked to live my life. Ben was actually an intruder, but I couldn't fault him as he was a welcome kind. But he had turned me sideways, if not upside down. My dick stirred to remind me how much I liked it.

I had supper in Contention after stabling Red and ordering him extra oats. I looked him in the eye and saw he'd forgiven me our possibly foolhardy direction. I wondered if that would continue. It was a good supper, but I scarcely tasted it as I had a window seat and kept looking out, hoping Ben would not only appear, he'd see me, come in, and say he wanted to fuck. This proved entertaining, but he never went by.

After supper I went around town in search, hitting every saloon and dance hall and getting drunk in the process. When I took a room at one in the morning, I didn't care on Ben Wylie, but when I woke next morning with a stiff prick, I cared a whole hell of a lot.

I left off addressing the foolishness of my pursuit until I'd worked myself to a good come, thinking on Ben doing the same. My spurts became his as he thought on me.

I took breakfast with about a gallon of coffee, again at a window seat, again without sight of Ben. I then fetched Red and rode on. By the time I rode into Benson, the pursuit was wearing on me, not so much in body as in mind. If he's not here, I told my foolish self, it's over. I'll ride back to Tombstone where I'd just gotten settled when he turned tables on me. This plan raised my spirits which, of course, meant something would stomp things all to hell.

I secured a room and again looked around town while trying to appear not looking at all. I played some poker as my money was getting low, but kept looking toward the front door. Whiskey was little help, but I did win.

I sought a smoke shop after this, buying a cigar and lighting up out front and there, as if sent by fate or maybe Satan, came Ben Wylie across the street, going along like he bore no concern at being wanted for killing a man. He strode with purpose when he likely had none, his gait meant to show his manliness. I was probably the only one taking note. I remained fixed as he went along and allowed him to get a good distance up the street before following. Of course, as I hurried along I tried to come up with something to do beyond fucking. On this I had no luck.

It was Ben who showed me the way. He suddenly turned up an alley and I rushed to catch up, fearful I'd lose what I'd finally gained. Going into the alley, I was grateful to be in daylight as this treated me to sight of Ben having a piss against a wall not twenty feet away. I stole close and took a pose leaning against the wall to watch his stream. "No need to put that away," I said once he'd finished.

Startled at first, he quickly warmed and began to pull his dick. As he worked, he turned to face me and I feasted on the sight, thinking I might, then and there, drop to my knees in manly worship. I was easing down when a voice spoke from farther down the alley. "Cain't get yourselves a woman?" came the taunt as a ragged and unshaven fellow stepped into view. He was bigger than us in both height and girth and I saw right off he used this to advantage. "Best you stick that purdy piece of meat in a cunt instead of this fellow's mouth. Or do you plan to put it up his ass?"

Ben shoved his cock into his pants, but I saw this wouldn't end the encounter. His hand hovered at his pistol so I said, as I rose, "Best move on, mister."

"Hell with that," he replied. "I'm fixing to watch you suck that little pink thing, seeing how that's what your kind does."

In the next second Ben drew and fired, but missed due to me again interfering. Once I'd knocked his aim all to hell, I lunged at the intruder and gut punched him low which I've found will usually drop a man. I was wrong on this occasion. He reeled back, swore, then lunged forward and hit me in the jaw while Ben flew at him, driving his knee up between the man's legs. This ended the encounter by sending the fellow blubbering into a heap. I turned to speak to Ben, but was caught by his fist which hit me near the eye and I lit into him with all I had. My need to fuck gave way to beating hell out of the little shit.

He was a scrapper, that I'll allow, but he was no match for me. I landed punches until he dropped to the ground, and I then pulled him to his feet and drove my fist hard to his middle. I heard the last of his heat escape on a desperate breath as he once again hit the ground.

I allowed a couple minutes to regain my own self as well as decide my next move which turned out to be getting him up and dragging him to my hotel room. He fell twice going up the stairs and each time I kicked his butt. He gave no fight, nor did he speak. Our brief journey was mostly grunts and my telling him to keep moving.

Once in my room I grabbed him by the shoulder, flipped him around, and slapped him so hard he flew back onto the bed. I didn't let him lie there as he likely hoped. I pulled him to his feet and this time slapped him twice, once with each hand, which sent him to the floor. Swearing accompanied all this and I doubt I missed any of the usual words in telling him what he was about. He gave no reply to any of it and, worked up as I was, I had no choice but to fuck him.

I did it rough, knocking him around, then tearing off his clothes. When I had him naked, I beat on him some more as my passion was a violent sort. Bruises were coming up on his face by the time I got out my dick, put him on the floor, and drove up him with all the force I possessed. I ached to come, fighting riling me, and I slapped his bottom as I pumped away, the rise coming on quickly. I said nothing as I emptied into him, riding to a standstill. And when I was done and pulled out, I flipped him over, shoved my filthy cock into his mouth, and made him lick me clean.

He made no move to work his dick and when he'd cleaned me he sat back, showing me he remained stiff. "You think I'm going to get you off?" I asked. "Think again. You're not worth shit. You're no more than a butthole for me to stick."

The fight may have gone out of him, but those eyes told that he saw through it all. He stood as he pulled his dick, and I couldn't help but look so there we were in silence, face to face, and him knowing he had me. He was right, of course. I'd proved that by chasing after him.

Soon he was pumping away, arching his back, and giving me a show. When he shot his load, a gasp escaped me as he was a sight to behold, young cock spurting an impressive distance. He kept on until he went soft, then let go and just stood, like his body alone was comment. "You came after me," he said.

"Only to keep you from more killing."

"Why are you so determined that way?"

I hadn't undressed to fuck. I'd done no more than free my cock, but now I began to strip.

"Why?" demanded Ben.

"You know why. I said it before."

"Tell me again."

I sat on the bed to pull off boots and socks, then stood to get out of pants and drawers. When I was bare I said what he wanted. "You've captured me, Ben. Hell of a thing, but I'm gone on you."

Saying such a thing is both good and bad: good in setting strong feelings free, bad if it's suspect by the other party, which it appeared to be with Ben Wylie. Why he insisted on hearing declarations from me I do not know since he obviously thought them untrue. "I'm not that other fellow, Ben. I don't say things lightly, nor do I mean to do you any wrong."

I patted the bed beside me, but he made no move. Even in

his naked state he bore the look of a man with a hand hovering at his pistol. "Why not come over here and allow yourself some pleasure?"

It was difficult to keep in mind the fact he was a killer, and not only that, the worst kind of killer, the kind looking for more. It was too easy to see him a boy not yet grown into his manhood, a boy saddled with that drive we all know when young, a drive that runs us, dick in the lead. Trouble was some found a gun barrel much the same as a dick and took to bragging on how many killed instead of how many fucked.

Ben came to the bed, but kept a distance so there we were, two naked and silent men. Finally I couldn't stand it and spoke. "I have some years on you, Ben, which means I've known more than you, lived hard at times, easy at others, mostly in between. There have been men of all sorts, mostly the passing through kind which I know you understand, but sometimes a fellow stuck and that's good. Something happens on occasion, I get that. And this is one of those occasions."

"I won't be roped," he said.

"That's not what I'm after. Caring about a fellow means looking out for him, helping him, enjoying his company, being a pard—and more. We've got the more down pretty good, so I'd like to get on with the rest. No rope involved. Free to go at any time. Right now if you choose."

When I stopped running my mouth, I was struck by fear he'd pull on his clothes, tell me he had no such feelings, and leave. I'd have to sit there and take it and worse, hold off chasing him further. I sat in agony until he scooted closer, put his head in my lap, and sucked my dick.

I petted him as he fed, knowing cocksucking was his way of saying he's with me. I stroked his hair, but after a bit eased him back and kissed him. "I want to fuck you," I said. And I laid him on his back, got his legs up on my shoulders, and got into him for a good long one. I took it slow and steady, twice having to pull out and add spit. He didn't pull his dick though it stood tall and I admired this as I know a young fellow wants to get off every minute. I took his restraint as homage to our bond.

As I pumped away, I allowed my heart its freedom, getting even more gone than before. I liked the hothead in him, running roughshod over all in his path, me included. He gazed up at me and I saw a swoon getting loose, like he couldn't keep the walls from tumbling down.

"Good, huh?" I said as I kept on.

He almost smiled. His eyelids fluttered, his head rolled on the pillow, and I shoved in harder which brought a moan. I've taken a dick or two in my time so I know the joy of penetration, know better the joy of doing the penetrating which started causing my nuts to boil.

"I'm going to come in you," I said as I started to thrust with some authority. "Holy God, I'm going to fill you." These were my last words before my cock set loose a come of great proportion. I pounded it into Ben, driving it deep, and I didn't leave off until I was beyond empty and going soft. I then collapsed beside him.

I was still trying to regain my breathing when Ben rose up over me, working his dick in a great show. He arched as his hand became a frenzy and then he shot big gobs of come onto my chest. I thrilled to the sight of his spew as I'd never had the stuff rain down on me in such a way.

When he was done he wagged his thing at me, grinned, then kneeled to lick me clean. If I hadn't just been done in, I'd have become aroused at the sight, but I was spent in that department. My mind, however, was fully erect and I petted Ben as he licked.

Once he'd had his fill, he crawled up and kissed me, offering a tongue full of his spunk which I welcomed. I swear kissing can be far more intimate than a fuck.

When Ben finally settled, lying curled into my arm, I told him he now had me for sure. "Gone and then some," I added.

"That's okay," he replied and I got how that was all he

could offer.

Later on, when we'd dozed a bit, I asked if he had a plan. "You're a wanted man," I reminded him. "The law will come looking sooner or later."

He took so long to answer that I saw he not only had no plan, he'd not given the matter any thought. The same thing that made him eager in sex, ruined him for practical matters, but I had to leave it lie, which was nearly impossible.

"I won't be roped," he said finally, much to my exasperation. I near bit my tongue holding back comment on possible hanging. To quiet myself, I sucked his dick.

Later on, when I was a sweaty mess and the room reeked of us, Ben lay sleeping like some innocent. I enjoyed the sight, deceptive as it was. If we never left the room all would be solved. Fuck away our lives. Outrun the law by staying put.

I was a fool to let a kid run me, but that was what it was. When we finally cleaned up and left the room, he went around town like he was free as a bird. I was the one watching for the law with one eye and Ben with the other, hoping to head off more killing. He might be more trouble than I'd thought.

When I saw a badge I seized up. My hand hovered at my pistol while Ben went along with a spring in his step, looking in store windows, not a care in the world. The lawman passed without notice of us and I about collapsed with relief because I wanted no trouble on my own behalf, not to mention Ben's. He, meanwhile, missed all this.

When we were finally settled in a restaurant, I almost told him of the lawman's passing by, then decided I'd best not as he'd take it as proof he need not exercise caution. And maybe he was right. Maybe nobody cared about a fool kid. Maybe the fellow he shot was of no consequence or maybe he didn't die. Ben would hate that, not getting his five.

Ben said little as we ate. I couldn't read him, wondering, after a time, if there was maybe nothing to read. Some fellows are simple that way, smart enough to get by, but not needing to figure things. Others of us are saddled with too much figuring. It surprised me when Ben said he meant to play some cards. I had no idea he had money and didn't want to speculate on where it came from. When he settled in at poker, I deferred to play some faro, then stand at the bar. Though I purposely didn't keep an eye on Ben, I did keep an ear, hoping voices wouldn't be raised. After a couple hours I went outside for a smoke, confident I need not worry. Once settled into a chair I had about two minutes peace before a posse rode in.

I wanted to jump up, rush inside, and take Ben out the back, but I knew better than to trust my present self. Feelings for him clouded my judgment so I just watched the men, five in number, two sporting badges. I recognized Marshal Dave Cox and Deputy Oren Goodwood from Tombstone and I also knew one of the other men as I'd gambled with him regular. They had no reason to take note of my presence so I gained just a glance as they walked their horses by, looking side to side in case their prey was standing there asking to get caught. Ben, inside playing cards, was surely not paying attention to his surroundings and that's something a gunman should never let fail. As I sat I thought on how to best take flight and decided the thing was to not do as expected. Ben must hide here in town, but I couldn't hide him in my room as we'd been seen together which meant I might be questioned. As I'd rather not have that happen, I'd have to hide with Ben. All this I pondered as the men dismounted a little ways up the street.

I meandered back into the saloon like a fellow with not a care in the world, which was my state until I took up with Ben Wylie. He was having a fine time with his cards, taking whiskey, joshing between hands, but that had to end. I sidled up beside him after a hand was played, I leaned down, and said a posse was in town and we'd best get scarce. He stiffened in his chair which I first thought was him digging in his heels, but I had that wrong. He stood, thanked the men for a good game, and followed me out the back.

"I believe we shouldn't run," I told him. "Hide somewhere until they've done their search and gone."

"We?" he said. "It's me they're after."

"True, but I've been seen with you so I'll get scarce, too."

"Where?"

"I figure the livery is best. I noted some storage above and I know the owner as we've gambled together in the past. He's not favorable toward the law and I believe for payment he'll hide us. But first we have to get our things, make like we've fled. We can go to the hotel the back way and come back same. Come on."

This plan went well and we acted without a care, got saddlebags and bedrolls, paid up, and left, doing all this separately. Ben went out the back while I went out the front, acting free as a breeze before going around to join him. We then skulked our way behind buildings until reaching the livery.

"We're in need of shelter from the law," I told John Riley, the proprietor. 'You look to have an attic space that I believe won't be noticed. I'll pay to get us up there and remain until the posse has gone. Ten dollars."

No man will turn down that sum to remain lawful. Riley took the money and got a ladder. "Not too comfortable," he said. "Just storage."

"Not looking for comfort," I replied. "If you're asked about us, Decker and Wylie, you say we lit out. Had you saddle us up and we took off, you've no idea where."

Ben held the bedrolls while I climbed up to see nothing but a rough floor with boxes of old implements, irons and such. A man couldn't stand, the slanting roof being so close. I shoved boxes to one side, then hauled up bedrolls and saddlebags. Ben followed, after which Riley removed the ladder. We then attempted to settle.

Since Riley was agreeable toward lying about us, we had only to wait. Ben laid out his bedroll as it worked well with us being prone. I bumped my head before I got mine in place and stretched out.

"How long you think we have to hide?" Ben asked.

"No idea. Depends on how fast and how thorough a search they conduct. A posse should ask every store, saloon, and hotel man if the suspect has been seen, but I've known posses to do far less. Marshal Cox is a persistent sort so I expect him to do a good search and possibly lay over as a result. Of course, once he gets down here and talks to Riley, they should ride on. For now, best to get comfortable, such as we can.

Ben surprised me by dozing right off. While I listened to every creak and snort, he breezed along in slumber which I almost resented as it felt like I was doing his time. Guess that's what a fellow will suffer when he gives his heart over to a questionable man.

I wanted to sleep, but couldn't. Every time I shut my eyes, they flew open at voices below and I listened to all manner of exchanges, some livery business, some just men jawing. When it was near dark, Riley put up the ladder and brought us food, whiskey, and a bucket "for the necessary," he said.

"Much obliged," I replied as I took up the offerings.

"The posse is still in town," said Riley, "going all around. I expect them here before long."

"You be sure and tell them we've gone, make a thing of getting the horses ready and such. They hear that, they should head out."

"Hope so."

It didn't go that way, of course. Ben and I stayed in that cramped and hot attic eating up the food, drinking up the whiskey, pissing in the bucket, and finally, because there was nothing else to do, having a fuck. This greatly improved the situation. I got him bare assed, lying on his side while I freed my dick and put it to him. We were quietly going at it when I heard Dave Cox announce himself Marshal of Tombstone, then say Ben's name.

"He was here," Riley said. "Rode out with Cal Decker couple hours ago. Didn't say where."

My prick was lodged in Ben's ass and I felt him suppress a giggle at the situation which, I had to admit, was amusing. I shoved in hard to let him know I got the joke, then resumed a quiet fuck right over the law's head.

"Goddamn," said Marshal Cox. "Goddamn son-of-a-bitch."

He offered no more, just left, and Riley went about his business. I also went about mine, getting up speed now and driving a load into Ben, who was working himself to a come. He issued a groan as he let go and I forgave him the noise since the law had gone. The posse would now ride on and we could remain in town.

We buttoned up and it wasn't long before Riley called, "You hear?"

"We did. Thanks for helping us out."

The ladder came up and we rolled and secured our bedding, threw them and saddlebags down, and quickly followed.

"You want me to saddle your horses?" asked Riley.

"We do," I said at which Ben bristled.

"Why take off now? We fooled the posse so we can stay on."

I blew out a sigh. "You're forgetting the local law. If they didn't take note of you before, they will now. No, we can't stay. Saddle us up, Riley."

Ben paced about in a stew and I left him to it. Time for him to grow up, get practical. When the horses were ready, our gear aboard, I climbed into the saddle and waited on Ben, who finally, with the look of a pouting child, followed. We then rode from town, but I stopped us a mile or so down the road.

"You realize we can't continue north," I offered. "The posse has gone that direction so we'd best make a turn. How about New Mexico? I hear Silver City has promise. We can play some cards, win enough to see us well kept, and have us a time."

As he pondered this, my gut seized something awful, fearing he'd say again how he wouldn't be roped. "Suppose," was what I got and in that one word all was set right. I cared not he was a killer, cared not he'd continue that way. What I cared on was indeed roping him and knowing, with time, he'd come to crave it.

TAMING BROOKS

BY R.W. CLINGER

MY ARRIVAL AT Ranch Brooks in Stockton County, Oklahoma is sweaty-sweet. My instructions are simply stated on the back of Dallas Brooks' business card: *Go to Cabin Longwood, unpack, rest, and meet up with the staff at eight P.M. in Custers' Hall for introductions.*

I'm early, I realize. After unpacking, I decide to meander around the ranch to become acquainted with my new surroundings instead of resting. Dallas Brooks' ranch is over three thousand acres, and tucked away in the northwestern part of Stockton County, next to the one-light town of Dunford. There are currently four ranch hands; I'm the newly hired fifth. The ranch is spacious and arid, a cowboy's dream. Everything is thick with the scent of hay and barbecue, and sweetly tainted with ragweed and Queen Anne's lace.

I find my way to the barn, kitchen, and other various sites of interest on the ranch. A charming and smiling dark-haired Sioux Indian boy tells me that the plumbing on the ranch has gone bad, and if I need to bathe, I'll have to use the nearby stream, Copperhead Creek. The guy takes me in with a heavy interest: five-eleven frame, one hundred and ninety-five pounds, scruff on my chin and cheeks, short black hair that's mussed, muscular chest and thighs, too-tight jeans. The bronco kid wants me, but can't have me. Oh well.

Of course I need a bath and end up on the southernmost side of the property where I find Copperhead Creek. I ease up on it slowly, listen to its rushing waters, and feel the sullen breeze lick at my bare neck and hands. Crickets chirp in the surrounding fields as I see a Mustang tied to the limb of an ancient oak tree. Keeping my view on the horse, I walk directly to a pile of clothes on the hard ground by the stream, stop dead, and stare down at the lump: tan-colored Stetson hat, jeans with a silver Dustin Stockyard belt, and Ariat Heritage Lacer boots.

NERVOUS AS HELL; this is how I feel about being at Ranch Brooks. Out of my head for getting the guts to come here. Money is needed, though. A life. My life. I need a change and a cowboy's world is what I want. Anyone will agree with me. Anyone at all.

Stinking hot here. Too hot when I arrive. Sticky and wet all over. Smell like a horse's ass. I like summertime, but there's a little price to pay for the nice weather, isn't there?

The heat always makes me horny, and it makes me want to come. Never fails. Horny as a bull. I'm the kind of man who needs to unload his dick and often. Pent energy swirls within my balls. A man has needs and I want to get laid. Maybe another ranch hand can help me out. They're handy, right? There's a lot of privacy on the ranch, though, and I can jerk off if I want to in one of the pastures, next to a set of birch trees. Brooks doesn't need to know about it. And neither does his hands. It'll be nice if Brooks will get the job done for me, though.

I want to stay calm, cool, and collected. I have to. Don't want my nerves to get the best of me. This will be failure. I swear to God in heaven I have to keep it together, but I'm not the type of ranch hand to take the Lord's name in vain, am I? A sinning man doesn't get to heaven, right? Nosiree.

Truth is I don't know if I can keep it together: mentally,

physically, and emotionally. I know how to be a ranch hand, but am I going to be good enough? Is a cowboy ever good enough? Don't know. Not sure. Another mystery that is somewhere in my near future, whether it has an answer or not.

Maybe, just maybe Brooks and I can share some cowboy talk together. He and I. Alone time. The two of us. He's not queer, though, is he? I'm dreaming, fantasizing—something. Cowboy talk with the man will never happen. Never. Who am I kidding?

I LOOK INTO the shimmering water and take in the sexiest, most handsome, and naked cowboy with soap in hand, bathing. The site of the cowboy catches me off guard, causes a flurry of embarrassment to skitter up and along my neck, and redden my pale, boyish cheeks. Out of curiosity, I stand behind a nearby oak and keep a steady gander on the prime, grade-A beef in Copperhead Creek, and discover a sexual longing for the cowboy.

Everything about the cowboy is chiseled and hot. As he sits in the clear stream, rolling an orange bar of soap over his dark-golden skin, I study his hazel eyes as they reflect brilliantly in the evening's light. The cowboy's muscles are lined with hard veins that cover his pumped limbs like the lines on a map. He has wet blond hair grazing his abs and pecs. As I lick my lips and feel something stir within my Wrangler's, my eyes gawk at the two hard nipples that are covered with white suds on the man's bulky chest. Slowly, the cowboy rinses in the clear water, stands up, spreads his legs, and begins to lather up his firm thighs.

With my heart triggering and pounding in my lean chest, I see the uncut cock between his legs. The man moves the bar of creamy soap from one thigh to the other; strong palms working skin and suds and muscles. He now stretches the bar up and over the blond triangle patch of pubic hair that looks like canyon brush. Next, the bar of soap slowly moves down the wide dick. He pulls on the end of his cockhead, stretching its rope-like length with ease and enjoyment.

The cowboy looks like glowing leather in the evening sun. Moistened just right with droplets of oil. Working leather that is smooth and soft, so perfect for my bare hands to manhandle. The stranger rinses again and causes his long dick to grow slightly hard, arched and pointing to the south. Our eyes meet in a questionable, blending action that usually doesn't take place between *assumed* straight men. "Who are you?" the cowboy squints his shimmering grass-green eyes and asks from the water. He stands with dripping liquid over his iron-crafted body, completely trim and perfect, already beginning to dry in the evening breeze.

"Randy. Randy Marke is the name. I'm the new ranch hand." I'm nervous and hard, and lick my dry lips. I can't come out from behind the strong oak because of the limb that's under my denim. With my head cocked to one side of the oak, I affix my solid gaze on the erection.

My history is rather simple: ranch hand since I was a young boy; born and raised in Houston; often visit my aunt and uncle in El Paso; anti-Facebook or any other modern social communication with the world; Louis L'Amour reader; interested in working with wood and building things; aggressive and butch mannerisms; have never really had a long-term relationship with another man.

"RANDY THE RANCH hand." A crisp smile is on the cowboy's rugged face as he begins to walk out of Copperhead Creek. He steps up and onto the dry bank with his arched dick swinging in the wind. He introduces himself, "Dallas Brooks. I believe we talked on the phone. I was the one who offered you the job."

I have to step out from behind the tree to shake his out-stretched hand because it will be considered rude and unmannerly not to. Almost immediately he notices my long cock hidden by Wrangler jeans, meets magnetic eyes with my denim, smiles, and rubs the blond bristles on the end of his chin with a free hand. As he shakes my nervous palm, still observing and concentrating on my handy goods, he says, "By your look, Randy, I think you're going to do just fine on my ranch."

"Thank you." I become crazy-hard. Crazy hard. My hand is strong in his grasp, steady and all power.

Brooks is beyond rock-sharp and stud-like. He is a rugged rancher of perfection in front of me: six-two, two hundred and ten pounds, muscular from head to toe, naked with a semi-hard and drooping cock. The cowboy smiles like a Hollywood actor and is candy-handsome...and looks like a legendary actor. I place him at thirty. No, thirty-two. He eyes up my bulky chest, Mexican-dark eyes and hair. Eventually, he ends our handshake and brushes a palm against my tight jaw, turns my head from left to right in a steady and stern action, and checks out my smooth and boylike features. He drops his hand and says, "I know I asked you this on the phone during your interview, but how old are you again?"

"Twenty-four." My eyes shift from his rugged-muscular chest to his long, uncut cock that hangs between wet thighs. It is a stunning thing in the light and causes my own cock to bounce within my jeans.

He instructs, "Turn around for me, Randy."

I listen to him, because he's my employer, because I don't mind at all, because if I don't he just...

He presses his tight hands into my shoulders, my biceps, stands directly behind me and continues to instruct, "Lift your arms." He finds the compact muscles on my sides, wraps arms around my crafted and pumped chest, and investigates my lower torso with delicate and probing fingers. "Feels great, cowboy. Enough muscle to get the job done in these parts." He spins my body around, stares directly down at my crotch, moves his right hand to my package, cups balls and stiffening dick, and asks in his cowboy drawl, "Showing off, aren't you?"

In a cocky action I respond with a country boy's smile, "Just proving a point that I'm the man for the job."

HE LIKES ME and finds me irresistible. I become a cookie cutter fit for his new personalized ranch hand role. I come off as being clever and smooth, which causes him to scrape up a hearty laugh as he massages my rod and hard balls. He catches my gaze with his and whispers in the evening breeze, "Of course you are the man for the job. Did you get all settled into your cabin?"

I nod and respond, "Yes, sir," and stand with my legs slightly parted as my Adam's apple nervously bobs up and down.

The cowboy slowly rubs his hand against the denim between my legs, hardening up my goods all the way, which causes me to feel dizzy and raw. "Are you going to be a gentleman and take a bath before this evening's introduction to the rest of the staff?"

"Sure." I smile, sound easy, naïve, and boy-like. As I begin to undo my buckle, buttons, and pull out my plaid shirt, I wonder which staff he is going to introduce me to…the group of employees back at the ranch that I will be working with for the next few months, or the piece of dick that is hardening between his thoroughbred thighs.

He catches me off guard, steps back a pace, and spreads his legs wide and wider. With bronzed hands, cowboy grasps his cock and begins to play with himself. He watches me slip out of my T-shirt, boots, and jeans. Within seconds, the only thing I'm wearing is a rawhide friendship bracelet that was given to me by a dude in Austin, a special someone who shared amazing rodeo blowjobs with me, he was into my juicy dick and lean body. Without any jerking, a smear of semen collects at the tippy-slit of its domed head.

Brooks licks his lips, ready for whatever can happen between us. He keeps his eyes focused on mine as he informs, "I think I'll break you in right now, Randy."

"Break me in?" I ask, challenged by his comment. If he plans on using his dick on my tamable ass then he'd better have some heavy duty lube.

"Come here, cowboy. Loosen up. I'm not going to hurt you. Everyone needs a little welcome." He's hot and gentle and all blond-perfection. He trains me with ease, gradually moves forward, and asks rather politely with Stockton County manners, "You have a boyfriend?"

"Not currently." I feel his cock press up against mine, both heads touch, ball-sacks dance a tango in the heated and sticky evening.

"There are real countryman things out here, huh?" I ask, eyeing the massive size of his hardening cock.

"Yes, siree." Brooks gently collides his chest with mine. Our erect nipples kiss as his tongue meets the elongated and tight shape of my neck. I feel the bristles of his chin-scruff against my flesh. He holds my hips in his large but steady hands, pulls his tongue off my skin, and whispers into my right ear, "Can a cowboy like me overcome the sight of a handsome, young stranger like you?"

It's like he's singing one of those sad country songs, or reciting windy poetry. I fall for it and chant, "It depends what's in it for me."

His left hand ropes my erection and his fingertips smear semen at its curved apex. Brooks pulls the appendage away, discovers my lips, and whispers, "A little chow, a hot cowboy, and a great big piece of Oklahoma can do a man good."

I taste my ejaculate, swallow the salty-sweet goodness down, lick my lips, kiss his rough fingertips, and feel his free hand draw one of my palms to his pulsating cock. He kisses me hard, pushing his tongue to the back of my throat as he gently bucks his dick into my hand with ease.

I'm dizzy and confused against him. Brooks is too steamy and massive to begin an escape from this tango. No escape occurs, though. Instead, I cling to his chest, working his dick with my right hand, kissing him hard and harder...unbroken.

He smells rustic and masculine, like strong mesquite beside me as I tug up and down on his erection. The cowboy moans, bites my neck, and my right nipple. As he falls to his knees, he touches every tight ab muscle, lapping at each with his extended tongue. With experienced fingers, he grazes the line of midnight colored hair beneath my navel to the triangular patch of pubes above my cock. Slowly his cowboy tongue moves the head of my dick in and out of his mouth, a stampeding motion that drives me wild. Eventually, he positions its hardness against his throat. He holds onto my hips with both hands, balances himself, and ropes me in his arms. With skill, he begins to work his tongue around my muscled rod again, slurping and moaning, totally into me; the idyllic cowboy at work.

I tour his mouth, hump, thrust forward, and buck his handsome face. Brooks squeezes my nipples, still on his knees. Because I haven't been with a guy in four months, I can't help popping off an immediate and spontaneous load of ejaculate. I yank my firm cock out of his mouth, feel a rapid vibration of pure lust shift through my core, and decorate my employer's left cheek, chin, and neck. I feel jitters of rhythmic pleasure flood throughout my entire body and begin to howl at the top of my lungs like a desert wolf.

My palms find the back of his head as I lean over the cowboy. With ease, I lap up every drop of my semen, locked in a state of hyper clean-up. The length of my tongue drags along his skin, removing every bubble and line of ejaculate that clings to his salty flesh.

Eventually he stands, spreads his legs wide again, and has his dick pointing at my sloped, rippled chest. As his muscled fists rotate up and down on his erection, Brooks grits his teeth and lets out a masculine sound that a coyote might make. Every part of his body is ripped and hard, glistening with sweat. And because I roll fingers up and down his chest, giving in to the muscles on his neck with my tongue and lips, pinching nipples, and grazing abs with fingertips, he sprays an endless amount of semen over my chest, hips, and still-hard cock.

Afterward, we head for Copperhead Creek together, ready to wash up.

Brooks says, "Welcome to Brooks Ranch, dude...I think I'm going to like having you around here."

I choose not to object; Dallas Brooks is more than a sweaty-sweet man...he's passed the test to be my new boyfriend.

LATER THIS WEEK, fireworks overhead in Custer Park fill the black night with an illumination of bright hues. Spirals of red-pink flowers pulverize the heavens. Green-blue-yellow zigzagging arcs of light explode above our heads. Bombs burst around our twosome and the violent sounds echo for miles. Fountains of floral colors paint the darkness, and mushroom-shaped clouds cover the festive night, visually intoxicating all of Stockton County in attendance. Boom after boom explodes above us to rock the earth beneath our jean-covered bottoms. The ricocheting sounds cause it to feel as if it is the beginning stages of Armageddon.

As more flashes of sizzling light decorate the onyx-colored sky, I snuggle against Brooks, place my head on his shoulder, and wrap an arm around his middle to comfort him.

Eventually one of his hands slips over one of mine and gives it a squeeze. He nuzzles his lips against the top of my head and kisses it, burying his mouth next to my scalp.

There are more than two dozen couples around our twosome. Some are straight and others are gay. All are nestled together with an arrangement of pillows and light blankets. Two picnic baskets are present and the scent of white zinfandel hangs in the elaborate night, which is consumed by semi-drunk onlookers.

We move even closer together and collapse lips. Our faces

meet and the kiss is overwhelming with a relentless amount of passion. The spectacle we concoct leaves heads spinning in our direction and mouths to open. Stockton County is liberal, though, and few are shocked by what they witness. Rather, the viewers of our connection—sparks flying between us, which are very similar to those fireworks in the night's festive sky—seem to enjoy our show of unquenchable lust and likings.

When the fireworks are over we gather up our blanket and two pillows, head back to his truck, toss the trio inside its cab, and meet at a traditional barbecue at Lloyd Mathew's residence, which sits across from the sprawling park. Lloyd, one of the county's congressmen, has an annual Independence Day party for all his family and friends. A bonfire is almost a story high and just as wide. Tables inside illuminated and screened-in tents are covered with an endless amount of food: every fruit pie known to man, a variety of salads, casseroles, a roasted pig, hamburgers, hot dogs, and everything under the moon to drink. There's music also: some country mixed with today's pop.

Brooks isn't shy about dancing with me: the two-step, a line dance, and what he calls a cowboy waltz. We celebrate the holiday chest to chest, swaying to and fro, kicking up our legs, and end up having the time of our lives, growing together as a couple, broaching something that we can label (although we don't, of course) love.

He drives us back to his ranch thereafter and the place is quiet and dark. We're a little drunk, I know, and we wobble into the main house, laugh like young men occasionally do, and he escorts me up to his bedroom, where I've been sleeping. But he doesn't want to sleep tonight, I realize. No siree. The cowboy has other things in mind that are quite sexual but not at all unrefined. He takes off my checkered shirt, then my cowboy hat, dropping them to the floor. I know exactly what he wants to do, agreeing with his unlimited hunger.

IT'S TWO DAYS later and I'm tucked into the third floor loft of the barn, feeding the Mustangs by forking hay down into their clean stalls. Sturdy rafters hang around stacks of golden hay in the sticky and sugary smelling loft. I'm shirtless and hot, ready to take a break. The afternoon sun shimmies its way through the open cracks of the barn. I breathe hard, sweaty and exhausted; the perfect skilled ranch hand. I decide to take a short break and lean into a loft doorway and study the view of Brooks Ranch...

The dry, vast fields seeming to go on forever. I see Brooks, taming a stallion in a smallish corral, straddling and riding the bucking and wild animal with all his might, hanging on for dear life. Brooks' lean and muscular body bounces up and down. Eventually, he gets bucked off the pissed stallion. The cowboy's tan Stetson flies down to the earth, and Brooks himself goes careening in mid-air, legs wide open, arms flailing, and lands on his tight ass. He stands up, brushes himself off with spread legs, bent knees, and an arched back. He is all masculine and rancher muscle, which totally drives a shiver of excitement up and down my spine. Growing hard in my jeans, I watch him collect his hat and act as if nothing has happened during his cowboy routine.

In the distance, Brooks decides to take a break of his own, slips his shirt and hat off, and places both on a fence post. Now, he pours water over his head. Chilled liquid decorates his pointed nipples and rounded abs on his firm stomach. The water dribbles down and over his silver longhorn belt buckle. It washes his blond chest, cooling him down.

I'm lost within the loft and can't help from pushing down a newly aroused erection. Everything about the moment is heated and erotic...just by watching him perform his everyday tasks. Fortunately, I'm alone and decide to unbuckle my belt and push my Wrangler's down to my ankles. As my view rests on Brooks with his created and soothing waterfall, I latch sweaty palms onto my extended and firm cock, start working the dick with ease, spread my legs as far as they will go, buck hips and ass forward, and turn myself on. Everything about my body is sweaty and stinging. Closing my eyes for the next few seconds, lost on my own range, I catch breaths of hay-filled air, groan, work my erection, ready to pop a load.

Loose boards squeak behind me. "Why don't you use that thing on me, Randy?"

Startled, I spin around and see Brooks in the loft with me; obviously he has had plenty of time to find me. He wears his hat, but is shirtless and sweaty, drop dead gorgeous and rippled. He has his arms stretched above his head, and practically hangs from a rafter, staring over at me and taking in my body. I see the blond curls in his pits and the pumped lines on his terrain-like chest above me. His jeans are unbuckled, which leaves me with a view of his drooping piece of cowboy-cock between his chiseled legs.

I hold onto my erection with both hands, feel a jolt of excitement that tells me to coexist with the man, and say, "You scared the shit out of me."

"Didn't mean to. I just came to see if you could tame me." His veined dick grows by the second, becomes harder, and rises to the sinful occasion of two hot and sexy men in a sun-bleached loft.

"Tame you?" I ask.

Brooks nods, reaches down between his legs with his right hand, and shares a delicious smile with me. "It's time for you to be handy, Randy."

SOME OF THE rafters are low in the loft and I hang from one by my hulking palms, looming over Brooks. I study the cowboy's spread legs and his open ass, which are both ready for my use.

Wearing nothing but his tan Stetson and his boots, he is splayed over a bale of hay on his back, perpendicular to me, and peers up at me with infiltrating desire in his hazel eyes; their allure telling me he can't wait to have his bottom lodged with my cock. The man begs, "Take a lick."

I listen to him, draw my tongue up the smooth length of his dick before positioning my lips over the head. I begin to suck him off like the good ranch hand that I am. My tongue ropes the head of his dick and plays with its excess skin, works it up and down, and drives the cowboy into a mad frenzy as he cries out like a delirious wildcat. I pinch his nipples and run fingers down and over each of his abs, suck his erection with skill and an almighty tongue that is quite...handy itself. I lasso his dick with a palm, cause him to hump and grind my mouth and throat until he is ready to burst his load.

Quickly, I cease my lapping and licking. Kneeling between his opened legs, the cowboy's clean-shaven ass glows at me, smiling. It's the hottest ass that I have ever seen, smirking at me for some oral satisfaction. With my cock burning hard between my legs, I spread his pink slit with my tongue, and probe his center like a good man, experienced. Here, I cause him to hum wildly on the bale of hay while he clenches palms over the lumber above his head, holding the beam for dear life.

He's no Oakie dipshit. No way. He's everything rough and tender. "You're driving me crazy, dude. Ride it now. Tame my ass like a bronco."

I fetch latex from his jeans and saddle it over my inches. I position myself between his legs, and rub my cock-tip against his needy, tight hole. I press...

He arches his neck back, spreads his legs wider, and demands, "Tame it, Randy...right now!"

Immediately, I push inside Brooks' asshole and cause him to call out my name. I pull out with ease, and rush inside him again, beginning to tame him. With skill, I hold onto his ankles, kick his ass like an angry horse, buck him with smooth hits, and open up his asshole with my dick.

Brooks thunders, "You're making me pre-cum, Randy."

I watch a line of pre-ejaculate wash against the cowboy's lower torso. He's so turned on by my bucking and riding that he can't keep part of his load in. The white bubbles of semen decorates his fine, golden hair on his tight abs and smooth naval. His pulsating dick bounces to my movements, ready to burst with very little touch, graze, lick, or…

My dick grows even harder and I grind, glide, bolt, race, and plow his asshole. My movements are careful and galvanized, rhythmical and pounding-hard.

Brooks can't help himself and whines up to me with wide eyes and stretched neck cords, "I'm broken, dude. Completely tamed." He latches one of his hands on his cock and begins to rotate palm and fingers over the uncut head.

As the sticky-hard cowboy beats his own dick, I quickly pull out of him, rip off the condom, and stand above him with my legs spread, and my cock directly pointed over his rising and falling chest. Together we form a rodeo of hands and cocks at work, eyes locked on each other's steamy bodies, teeth gritting and jaws locked. We thrust our hips in synchronized motion; continuous gyrations flooding through our bo dies; vibrations that cause endless jolts as pleasure persists.

Dual lines of semen fly out of our erections at the same time. We huff and blow in shared and exhausting actions.

Breathing heavily, spent in the barn's loft, I lean forward, slip under the rafter, climb overtop Brooks, and stick my chest to his chest, sealing us together. I place lips over his mouth, enjoy a long kiss with him, pull off, and ask, "Do I win a blue ribbon prize for riding you, bronco?"

He rolls me on my back, over the bale of hay, stands, and pushes my legs apart. He begins something else between us for the next half hour, grins down at me, hungry for his cock to meet my ass, and explains, "The biggest blue ribbon you can imagine, cowboy. That is, as soon as I'm done saddling you up for *my* ride, boyfriend."

IT'S EARLY MORNING, just before the sun rises and the roosters decide to annoy me. Brooks and I are inside his kitchen and I prepare coffee for us, which is always too strong. He looks tired this morning and I wonder what's on his mind. After pouring our coffees, I sit across from him at the small wooden table and ask, "What are you thinking about?"

"Us." His voice sounds deflated, lacking anything at all that resembles excitement.

"What about us?" I take a sip of the hot coffee, relish it, and go for a second sip.

"I'm a man who believes in marriage and can't accomplish that with you."

I become flattered by his comment, overjoyed that he wants to spend the rest of his life with me. "Someday," I say, reach across the table and pat his right hand with my left one. "Give it time. We'll have the right to marry soon."

"I don't think I can wait that long."

"So you're going to ditch me," I say, playing with him. "Uncle Sam fucks us over and you decide to become a cowboy player, right?"

He laughs.

I laugh.

"I'm not saying that at all, Randy, and you know it."

What I know is simple: we're combined by more than just sex, our hearts seem melded together, unbreakable.

LATER IN THE morning Brooks is bare-chested and working in the barn. He repairs one of the narrow long floorboards on the second loft, which is where a majority of the hay is stored for the horses. He's on his knees, pounding nails into a board, doing his repair. His tight ass is in my face, which I don't disapprove of at all. He's shirtless and his right biceps and back muscles stretch. A fine and decorative layer of sweat glazes his flesh.

He takes a break from his job, looks over his right shoulder at my arrival, and shares a glowing smile with me that exemplifies heartfelt tenderness mixed with a hint of man-lust.

"I brought you some water," I say, and extend to him a silver canteen with a narrow leather strap, which I have carried over my left shoulder, climbing the rungs, one after the next.

"Always thinking of me, aren't you?" He unscrews the canteen's lid and takes a long swig. The cords along his muscular neck flex as he consumes the liquid. Some of the water drips out of the corners of his mouth and glides down and over his chin. Once he is finished taking his drink, he wipes the back of his right hand over his mouth, shares a grin with me again, and adds, "I've been waiting for a guy like you to come around in my life. Glad you're here at my side, Randy. And I'm really glad that I like you the way I do."

I honestly don't know what to say. What slides between my lips is rather elementary, but to the point, "Flattery will get you everywhere."

We don't communicate in the loft in a sexual manner. Rather, he stands and we face each other. Then our chests collide , man positioned to man. Our mouths lock together and we share a heated embrace with our mouths and tongues.

Eventually I pull away, teasing, "You need help out here?"

"More than you know." It's not the truth, since I'm very much aware that he can accomplish the job by himself. Honestly, he prefers my company, having me at his side like the boyfriend or lover that I am. He nails a new board among other boards in the second floor loft.

"How can I help?" I ask, and kneel next to him, pass him a few nails from a thick cardboard container, and spend the remaining morning with him, and the afternoon, choosing to be in his company.

I'M BROOKS' BOYFRIEND now. He asks me and I accept. In his bed. Against his heart. It's exactly where he wants me to be. He spoils me. Lusts for me. Desires no one but me. And he says he's going to buy me a belt buckle like a wedding band. I believe him. This isn't a fantasy. It's more like a cowboy fairytale. Just the two of us united as one. Together. I can't ask for anything more: horses, a ranch, and a man I love. It's a cowboy dream come true. Never can I think of enjoying Stockton County so much, and everything that comes with it.

Best tell you that we do everything together (shower, shave, sleep, eat, chores, and all the cowboy things on the ranch) and that the four ranch hands know about our relationship, and respect it. Cowboys around here like to be with each other, and maybe this is the primary reason why I decided to come here in the first place, besides needing a job. Truth is I never meant to fall in love. Never. Not at all. This just happened on its own. It's sort of like how chickens lay brown eggs opposed to white; it just happens on its own and one isn't supposed to question the process or the end product.

"Ain't no reason to be afraid of what we have." This is what Brooks says, confident about his chatter. He also says that sometimes a man wants to be with another man, which is his given right. Some strange female rock star in New York City sings a song about it. Born a certain way. It's not a choice. Something like that. Not that we listen to much rock and roll in these parts. Brooks calls it companionship among or between men. Open-minded and things like that. Different than the rest of the world of cowboys. We're all strange, but we still love. All of us. I don't care who you are. Love is here. Honestly.

At nighttime we talk. Side by side in the bed we share. The two of us whisper. He says, "I don't know what I did with myself before I hired you."

"You probably had many ranch hands to choose from."

"Maybe. But you're the one I picked."

"I'm not complaining."

I turn on my side and face him. One of my index fingers discovers the scruff on his chin and brushes it. "Do you love me, Dallas Brooks?"

"I could."

I poke his chin and ask again, "Cowboy, are you head over boots for me?"

"You're my partner," he admits, and I take this for what it's worth; he does love me. Forever.

THE SPRING AT SLOAN POND

BY LEE CRITTENDEN

A BULLET SPANGED off the rock, and the roan mare spooked, tried to buck. Nick fought to keep his seat, hauled at the reins.

He fumbled his gun out then—but there was nothing the hell to do with it. He was surrounded by a wall of rock, an up thrust of basalt in the sere grass of the range, but the same outcrop kept him from anything to shoot at. He jerked around, identified a gap, and kicked his horse into position, but it was too late. Laughter and the whoops of cowboys were already retreating through the pines, accompanied by thudding hoof-beats.

Nick cursed at them, shaking with fury, but that was as useless as the gun, so finally he reined in the anger like he had the horse, and put the thing away. It was just as well. The blued steel Colt felt awkward and heavy in his hand. He'd never carried a gun in his life until the previous month, and it was still a clumsy weight on his hip. It left him off-balance in a lot of different ways.

Wet trickled down his face. The roan mare was in a lather, jerking at the reins and lashing her tail. The pack horse was rolling its eyes, sweating, too, and tangled in the lead. Nick got down from the mare and sorted them out. Then he wiped at his cheek with one sleeve and found the wet was blood. A chip from the rock must have cut him, though he didn't exactly remember it.

He cursed feelingly. It was a hell of a way to show up in town. Anybody who wasn't already gossiping like crazy about the trouble would start in when they saw him cut that way. He had recognized the crew that had taken off through the trees: Eisner's hired hands—or hired guns, maybe—he wasn't sure. The newest one, a dangerous kid named Raidy Hart, had only recently showed up. The misery had been going on for a while, but Hart was the devil that had started this harassment Eisner's crew found so hilarious. It seemed like they wanted to start a range war, but he couldn't reckon why.

Nick got his face cleaned up and the horses calmed down, but there wasn't a thing he could do about the brown stains on his shirt. Disgusted and still shaking with suppressed rage, he climbed back on the mare and rode on into the pines, headed for the river trail.

The Snow River was more like a creek. Every spring it flashed down out of the mountains like a real cascade, and then died down by mid-summer to only a trickle. Sometimes it was stagnant and yellowed in the heat, but it was always there—at least on the Bain homestead—like the way the sun rose in the mornings over the high peaks of the Sierra Nevadas. It was fed by a spring that nobody knew about until the previous year when the drought had lowered the level of Sloan Pond enough for it to show.

Now the water was at the yellow trickle stage and heat rose off the rocks like the waves of steam from a cook stove. The woods were usually full of the chatter of blackbirds, but now they perched in the shade with their beaks open and silent, and their flinty eyes dull, panting from the dryness. Further on toward Klammath, where the lodge pole pines and firs grew sparser, the creek formed a final scummy pool, its banks marked by the deep, muddy prints of cows, and then stopped running altogether.

After the shot Nick was more careful, skirting the edge of Eisner's land. Once he saw a cloud of dust and the specks of riders in the distance, but it looked like a freight wagon. Another time a deer crashed through the brush suddenly, making him start and grab for the handle of his gun. But there wasn't any sign of Eisner's crew where they were supposed to be, and so he rode on into town, leading the pack horse behind him.

Klammath Falls was different in the past year or so. The clapboard fronts of the stores were mostly white washed and clean looking, and a barber shop and a row of fine houses had joined the older, ramshackle cluster of hotels and saloons left from the gold rush days. Nick rode on up the dusty street and stopped in front of the sheriff's office.

The sheriff's name was Buckley. He was a virile, heavy-shouldered man with a thick mustache and a lustrous shock of graying hair. Bent over his desk, he was writing laboriously when the door swung open, but he looked up and leaned back when he saw Nick, ran a heavy hand through his hair.

"Well, Nick Bain," he said. "What are you doing here, boy?"

Nick took off his Stetson and sat on the edge of the extra chair, uncomfortable somehow just looking across at the man, at the weight of his shoulders, the heavy line of his jaw. Nick's eyes dropped to his hat, where his fingers were creasing the brim.

"Sheriff Buckley," he said. "I've come to report somebody's been butchering our beef. I've…found three or four dead steers in just the last week, over in our ravine."

"Well, have you now?" asked the sheriff, squinting. A sharp crevice appeared between his brows, and deep crows' feet cut into his sun-browned cheeks. He tapped the stub of his pencil on the desk. "How did you find them, Nick?"

"I found them same as the buzzards did—the ones circling over the carcasses, I mean. It's that Eisner crew," he went on. "Those skunks, they run over our range all the time."

"Who, Nick?" asked the sheriff. "What skunks?"

"Raidy Hart," said Nick, warming up, "and that Red Slocum and Tom..."

"Nick," Buckley said. "Now you know I can't arrest nobody on just your say so. It could be Injuns doin' it. Or have you got a witness?"

"Sheriff..."

"You got no proof," insisted Buckley, and then leaned forward like he meant to be personal. "Listen, Nick, I hear your brother got killed in a shoot-out over in Montana somewheres."

Nick flinched and shut up, feeling a slow burn set in around his heart. Nobody had mentioned Keith Bain for years, at least not in front of his dad, old Isaac Bain. Everybody knew Isaac and Keith'd had a set-to over something, and he had run the boy off. Keith had always been some wild, and people said he'd had gone from bad to worse after that, into outlawry. The past year word had gotten around he was finally dead, but Buckley had no call to bring it up now.

Nick got to his feet. "Sheriff," he said. "Thanks for nothing."

Outside he heaved out his breath and jammed his hat back on, headed across the street. To hell with the man. He'd been looking the other way from the beginning, and Nick should have known before coming in here what he would say.

Nick couldn't afford whiskey, but he liked a beer when he came to town. Now he wanted to cool off after the ride in through the heat, and to think about what Buckley had said, and about his own irritation.

The Briar Rose wasn't a fine saloon and it didn't have women, but it did have cheap drinks. After the glare outside it was dark beyond the swinging doors, and the rose print of the wallpaper made dim curlicues above the bar. The owner was Willard Holt. A solid, hairy chunk of a man, he had been a miner at one time, and he still had the hands for it. Outfitted in a white shirt and garters and a handlebar mustache, he was polishing glasses with a towel.

He cleared his throat as Nick leaned up against the bar.

"Uh," he said. "Howdy, Nick. What'll you have?"

"A beer, Willard."

Willard produced it, but his eyes slid away to the back corner of the room. Nick's eyes followed his gaze and found the reason Eisner's crew wasn't anywhere on the range. They were all sitting at tables in that corner, playing faro.

He straightened, ready to abandon his beer, but the warning had come too late. The men were already pocketing their winnings, headed Nick's way like a pack of hounds. They gathered around him at the bar, and he suppressed a thrill of panic, glanced over to find Raidy Hart leaning on one side and Red Slocum on the other.

They were so close he could feel the heat off them, the animal radiations of warmth and sweat and menace. Willard looked tense and uncertain, but for some reason, once Nick was caught this way, his nerves settled near to ice.

"Hey, Willard," said Raidy Hart. "Let's have whiskey all around." Then he turned and smiled slowly at Nick. "Well now," he said, "aren't you Nick Bain?"

"Yeah, reckon so," said Nick coolly. "Have we met?"

Hart appraised him with a derisive stare. The boy was no more than twenty, sun-dark and slim. His hair was black, long enough to curl across his shoulders, and he wore black chaps and a vest with silver concha trim. Something about his cheekbones said maybe he was a breed, but nobody dared say that to his face.

This close, his eyes had a dash of yellow, like a wolf—or maybe just a coyote.

"Name's Hart," the boy said, "from Idaho." He kept on smiling, like something amused him. "What the hell's happened to your face, Nick?"

"Little accident out on the range," said Nick. Their closeness teased him. He was surprised to find his own voice even.

"I guess you know how these things go."

"Yeah," said Hart. "There is some stray shit flyin' around these days."

One of the others laughed, but Nick ignored it, keeping his eyes on Hart. He lifted his beer to take a swallow and Red Slocum jogged his elbow, sloshed the beer down Nick's shirt and along the counter.

Nobody had a chance to react. Willard had his shotgun out from under the bar and had it leveled before the beer had fully spilled.

"Listen," he said. "There ain't going to be no trouble in here—this is a nice place. You boys finish your drinks and get out. Now!"

The cowboys shuffled their feet and muttered, but Willard was going red and white by turns, looking mean, and so they used good sense, drank up, and headed out. Hart slapped Nick on the shoulder as he went by, and his hand lingered as it slid along Nick's shoulder, too familiar.

"Nice meetin' you, Nick. Maybe we'll see you again out by that spring." He smiled again. The skin crinkled around his eyes, and his teeth seemed extra white against the dark brown of his face. He gave Willard one last yellow-eyed stare. "See you 'round," he said.

When the doors had swung behind them, Nick's tension eased. He brushed at his shirt.

"Thanks, Willard," he said. "I thought…"

"I meant you, too, Nick." Holt was still holding the double barrels even. "They wouldn't be no trouble weren't for you."

Nick started to ask for his money back, but he decided against it. Willard was still too white.

Maybe he should start back home. Nick couldn't think of a trip in that had ever gone worse than this—but disgusted as he was, still he had things to do. He started off down the street, watching out for the cowboys, but they seemed to be gone. People stared at him as he walked by in a pointed way he had to notice, like they could see he was unsettled by the encounter in the bar. He found himself thinking back on it.

Hart seemed nothing like Sheriff Buckley, but he had the

same quality, the same sharp, animal magnetism that Nick found so uncomfortable in a man. The boy affected him oddly.

He started back to reality suddenly, found he was about to pass the general store. He tipped his hat to the parson and his wife, then stepped up under the porch, glad to get off the open street. Inside, his boots sounded hollow on the wooden floor, but the sound was absorbed by the tumbled clutter on the shelves. He went right to the back and collected flour and sugar and coffee, a fifty pound sack of dried beans and a few cans of peaches, a handful of nails. It was enough to tide them over for a while. He added tobacco to the lot and carried it back up to the scarred, dark wood counter where the proprietor was waiting.

"How are you, Mr. Klemmer?"

"Fine, Nick," said Klemmer. "How's your old man?"

Joe had a creaky, old-man's voice. A wispy, dried up husk of a man, he looked like he'd blow away in a stiff wind—though he must have been wiry and strong as a kid.

"All right," Nick said, "and Joy, too. Just a mite dazed by the heat. Can I have credit again this month?" he asked. "I'll pay you back, but I don't have…"

Klemmer shifted his feet. "Nick," he said. "Listen. I'm sorry. I don't own the store no more. Lou Burke's bought it, that's partners now with Eisner. I can't give you no more credit."

Nick was floored. "But Mr. Klemmer…"

"Sorry, Nick. You'll have to have the cash up front from now on."

Nick felt a hot flush rise up his face, but there was nothing to do but leave the goods there on the counter. He left the store in a fog, wondering what he was going to say to Joy. What the hell were they going to eat for a month?

He stood on the porch for a while, aimless and desperate, but finally he realized people were staring at him. He was off balance again, thinking too slow. He still had to go to the bank—maybe he could keep a few dollars back from the payment.

The bank was the newest building in the town, faced with

white columns, and the floor was slick, varnished pine. Merle Lawton was the cashier that worked the window. His hair was always parted in the center, slicked down with oil, and his shirt was a spotless white, tight across his chest.

Nick waited through a short line, stepped up to the window.

"Mr. Lawton," he said. "I've come to pay on our debt, but I need to hold back some money for groceries. I can make it up like I did before…"

The cashier shoved back the bills. "Nick, I can't take your money," he said.

Nick was thunderstruck. "What do you mean?" he demanded. "Mr. Lawton, I been making the payments regular every month…"

"Somebody's bought out your mortgage, son."

"What?" said Nick. "Bought out what?"

He didn't know such a thing was possible. The land was all they had. Old Isaac Bain had never been rich. He'd started with that mortgage for a stake, and for thirty years he'd barely scraped a living out of his sparse homestead. His wife had died early on, and he ended up raising his two boys and a girl by himself off the few cows and whatever else he could scrape up to keep things going. And now…

"Who's bought it?" asked Nick tensely.

Lawton looked concerned. "Nick," he said, "I'm sorry. It was done through an agent, and whoever bought it didn't want you to know. Just wait…"

Nick didn't wait. He jerked away from the window and out the door, hearing the whispers start behind him, the sharp-tongued widow Hayes loud and clear. On the step outside he brought up short. It wasn't hard to figure this, and suddenly he felt wild and furious.

There was nothing handy for him to break, so he stalked back down the street like a thundercloud and thrust the bills at Klemmer with shaking hands. Then, loaded and mounted on the mare, he dragged the white-eyed pack horse out of town and onto the trail.

❖

BY DUSK HE was in sight of the broken-down shack and the barn and the rough corral that was home.

When Isaac ran off his oldest boy, that left Nick and his sister, Joy, to look after their dad when he got trampled by a wild steer and ended up a cripple. The old man couldn't afford to pay wages after that, and the cow hands he'd had on the ranch had all left. Nick was twenty-two, but he couldn't look after the whole place by himself, and so the homestead started to run down worse than ever—the barn losing shingles off the roof and the fences sagging. Then the drought set in, and the trouble had started with Eisner.

Joy had already lit the kitchen lamp, and she came to the door when she heard the horses.

"Nick?" she called.

"Yeah," he said. "It's me."

"You're back early."

"Yeah," he said again. "Let me get the horses up, Joy."

He unloaded the pack and carried the goods into the house, looked after the horses and let them loose in the barn corral. Joy had supper ready when he got into the house, and the good smell of sourdough biscuits and bacon filled all the nooks and crannies of the kitchen, as did the heat from the cooking. The three of them sweated through the meal.

Isaac Bain was a thin shell of what he'd been just five years before. He was humped and crooked, hardly able to walk, but usually his eyes were sharp and alive under his bushy brows, and his opinions were still full of fire and brimstone. That night he seemed exhausted, plagued by the heat, and he only asked about the cows.

"Yes," said Nick. "I told the sheriff," and left it at that.

The old man went right to bed, or at least into the back of the house where it was cooler. Joy started to clear the dishes.

"So," she said. "What happened in town?"

Nick tipped his chair back against the wall and told her, keeping his voice low enough that the old man wouldn't hear. "I don't like those hired hands of Eisner's," he said.

"Hired guns."

"We don't know that," he said.

"Don't we?" She snorted. "They're a bunch of low-life outlaws."

Nick frowned. "Some of them might be straight," he said.

Silence closed down on the kitchen. It was cooling off some now, the fire dying down. Joy's back was bowed as she washed up the dishes, and tendrils of her brown hair straggled out from the pins.

"Nick," she said. "I don't like the mood you've been in."

"What's that?"

"You know what I mean. You've got that same streak of wildness in you that…well, you know. You're just a lot like him."

"This whole thing's going to blow up soon," he said. "I know it's that spring."

"The spring?"

"Eisner, and that partner of his, Burke—they want our land. It's the cause of this trouble."

Raidy Hart, with his smart mouth and cutting tongue, had contributed the clue, and after it came to him, Nick had to wonder why he'd never figured it before. There were other springs on the range, but none of them so dependable. The insight didn't help him decide what to do about it. Instead it was Hart that stayed with him, the width of the boy's shoulders, the color of his eyes, and that curious magnetism…

The hound let out a growl just then. He was just under the window, and it wouldn't have carried far. Nick let down his chair from against the wall.

"I forgot to hang up the tack," he said.

Joy's eyes flicked around, but she didn't say anything. Nick got up and out the door, stood on the porch a minute like he was enjoying the night air, looking the place over. The dog was old, didn't stir much from the porch, but still he had a good nose. If he hadn't sounded off, it meant something was either cross or down wind, still a distance away. Maybe in the clump of pines off to the west, away from the trampled, bare yard of the house.

The night was dark, lighted by the spray of stars overhead, but a glow to the east meant the moon was rising. A slight wind tugged at his shirt. Nick headed for the barn, walking easy enough, but sweat prickled on him, cold and uncomfortable between his shoulder blades. He lit the lantern and left it in the hallway, stepped into the tack room. He slid out into the corral, light-footed around behind the barn.

It was darker within the trees, but open enough that he could see the glowing windows of the house, light coming through the chinks and knotholes of the barn. Fallen needles muffled his steps as he slid through the copse and the humped shapes of manzanita brush. It was quiet—only the wind. He shifted to get the light out of his eyes. The brush crackled behind him, and he crouched, grabbed for his gun. He caught the glow of green eyes close to the ground. It was only a weasel.

"Damn," he said.

He let his breath out, surprised at the way he'd reacted. Then he felt the cold muzzle of a six-gun slide up against his spine.

"Don't move."

It was a whisper. Nick eased up his hands, caught sideways motion, a reach for his gun. Just then the hound sounded off with a deep-chested bay.

It was enough of a chance. He swung his elbow hard, felt it connect in a solid slam. He had his hand on the gun then, swung his right leg, and heaved. They went down. Nick landed on top, but he lost the gun, heard it slide. He cursed, but then he needed all his breath.

The man under him was lighter than Nick was. Stunned by the fall, he'd felt limp and still for a second. But then, tight and muscular, he coiled like a spring, and Nick had lost the advantage. They thrashed and tumbled, grunting, came up against a tree. Then Nick was pinned, and the voice hissed in his ear.

"Hold still, dammit. I just want to talk."

Nick recognized the voice, the smell of tobacco and sweat, and he went lax with surprise. The weight was gone off him then, and he lay there panting, wondering what the hell.

In a minute he had his breath back and he heaved up.

"Hart?"

A shadow leaned against the tree. "Just keep the hell away from me."

"What?"

"I think you broke my ribs."

"Well, why the hell not?"

"Look, I'm trying to do a good deed," Hart said. "And this is what I get for it?"

Nick sat there, studying the shadows. A horse snorted in the brush now and stamped, unattended, disturbed by the fight.

"You want to talk?" he asked finally.

Hart moved. "Where did my gun go?" he asked. "I don't like sittin' here without it."

He lit a match, found it not far away.

"Eisner wants your land," he said, standing up and shaking out the flame.

"I know that," said Nick.

"Well, he's going to try for it tonight."

"What?" said Nick. "How?"

"He's going to drive stock with the brands doctored onto your range, and then in the mornin' he and the sheriff will come out and find them, sort of by accident."

Nick only sat there.

"It's not just Eisner," Hart went on. "That new partner of his, Burke, is the one behind it. The man's a swindler, got his hand in two or three other shady deals hereabouts. Are you listenin' to me?" he asked.

"Yeah," said Nick, and then catching up suddenly, he

shoved to his feet. "So what are you here for?" he asked flatly.

"Damned if I know," said Hart. "The sheriff's got you tried and hung already."

"So?"

Hart seemed to consider it, said something under his breath.

"What?"

"They'll be along after midnight," Hart said. "I guess I'll go out with you to stop 'em. Can the old man ride and shoot?"

"No," said Nick.

"Send him and your sister to town, then."

Nick spun on his heel, started for the house. When he realized Hart hadn't moved, he stopped and turned back. He didn't want the man behind him.

"Come in to the house," he said.

Joy made a move forward when Nick ducked back through the doorway, but then she stopped short, seeing the shadow of another man on the porch.

Nick said, "This is Raidy Hart." Then he turned himself, and had a hard look at Hart.

He hadn't been sure of much out in the dark, with only a voice to go on. Nick halfway expected the boy to look sullen and shifty, but he didn't. Instead, he looked wary, but generally civil. He even took off his hat.

"Joy," said Nick. "There's going to be trouble tonight." He believed that much, at least. Will you take Dad into town? Find some place to stay?"

Her face jerked back to him, suddenly dark. "Where?" she said. "The hotel? We haven't got any money."

They stood there for an awkward minute. Then Hart dug in his vest pocket and held out a gold piece, but Joy's face only darkened the more.

"I won't take it from you," she spat.

"Joy…" said Nick.

Hart's eyes had narrowed and his face flushed a little. He laid the coin on the table. "Take it, ma'am," he said. "I'm workin' off old debts."

Joy turned and went into the back to wake Isaac.

"I'll help you with the team," said Hart, and slid out the door.

They brought the buckboard up in front of the porch to get Isaac into it, and Nick handed Joy the old man's Colt.

"Will you be all right?" he asked, worried about this now.

"I'll wait 'till I hear," said Joy, and then they were gone.

The two men stood there, listening for the last creak of the wheels, and then Hart shifted, glanced into the kitchen.

"Is there anythin' to eat?" he asked.

Nick turned, thinking the boy was expecting too much. It was hard to drop the weeks of animosity, and it must have showed in his eyes. "I guess," he said finally.

"Where's the pump?"

"Over there," said Nick, and Hart went to wash up.

His hair was damp when he came back, and his eyes turned an amber color in the lamplight. Nick could see a shadowy bruise rising along Hart's jaw, where his own elbow must have hit. It didn't seem to affect Hart's appetite. He ate everything that was set out. Nick sat in the chair across the table and waited for Hart to finish.

"Tell me," said Nick, as Hart leaned back finally and started to roll a cigarette with brown, long-fingered hands, "what debts it is you're working off."

Hart's eyes flickered across to him, and then back to the makings. "You don't need to know," he said.

"Yes, I do," said Nick. "I want to hear it. Otherwise, I figure you're leading me into a trap."

It was what he was thinking. He'd expected some denial, or maybe a slick evasion, but instead it made the boy angry.

"You go to hell then," Hart said, and the ugly, dangerous expression came back to his eyes.

"You hate all of us," Nick guessed. "I can see it clear as day. You expect me to trust you?"

Hart's face seemed deadly.

"We might as well have it out now," said Nick, unusually angry and ready to fight. He leaned forward. "What are you doing this for?"

It was Hart that looked away first. "I knew your brother," he said. And then suddenly he shoved up from the table, stalked the length of the room.

"You're right," he said, standing there. A gust of wind bellied the curtains, guttered the lamp flame. "I came here to give you trouble," he said. "But I found out you were like to lose the land, and I couldn't stand that." He whirled and paced back, stopped too near. "Keith used to send money every month," he said. "You know it, don't you? He cared about the old man, regardless of what he did."

Isaac had sent the money back.

Hart braced one hand against the wall and leaned over Nick, too close, crowding him. Nick didn't move.

"You're a cool one," Hart said, seeing it, "like Keith always was." He stood there another second, and then he leaned over suddenly, and kissed Nick on the mouth.

Nick jerked up both hands to knock him away. But Hart had expected it, and his elbows were in the way. He leaped back then, out of reach, but in the last instant his teeth had drawn blood.

"You son of a bitch," said Nick, wiping his mouth.

"Damn you," Hart said. He took a breath. "I've got to see to my horse." He turned then, and went out the door.

Nick found he was shaking. Well, it all made sense. He'd always known there'd be someone like that. It was why the old man had run Keith off, after all. But Nick had always expected it would be an older man. It left him feeling strange, disoriented, like the world had dislocated somehow.

Hart was gone for a while, and when he came back his anger seemed burnt out. He only looked tired, and he fell into the chair by the table and leaned his head back against the wall.

"Sorry," he said. "I didn't mean to tell you anything, Nick. But listen. Nothing's going to happen until after midnight. I was up the last two nights prowlin' under peoples windows, and now I'm dead on my feet. Have you got a place I can sleep for an hour?"

"You can sleep in my bed," said Nick finally.

After that he sat in the kitchen alone, just thinking. Eventually he must have dozed off himself. He jerked up to find the wick had burnt low, and more like an hour and a half had passed.

Raidy Hart had taken off his clothes, and lay stretched on top of the blankets. The moon was well up now. Light spilled through the window, outlined the curved musculature of his shoulders, the rounded sweep of his back. His dark gun hung on a chair, well within reach.

"Raidy?" Nick said, at the door.

There was no response, so he went on in, laid his hand on the boy's shoulder. Hart moved then, but it wasn't a start, as Nick half expected. He sighed and rolled backward, caught the hand and pushed it further down.

Nick wasn't surprised this time, and he didn't struggle or jerk away. He only stood there, feeling something quiver up through him—something that belonged, like it had always been there. He straightened up, began to unbutton his shirt with trembling hands. Raidy Hart laughed softly and slid back on the blanket, giving him room.

Nick felt awkward and fumbling, but the kid knew what he was doing. He kissed Nick again, without biting this time, and his hands slid downward in a long caress. He pinched Nick's nipples and stroked the ridged muscles of Nick's belly. Nick was so hard that he hurt. He groaned when Hart took his cock and compressed the head, traced the line of the foreskin with one light finger, the tiny line of the slit. The boy began to work his hands up and down, generating a warm, sweet friction.

They kissed again and Nick reached for Hart, running his hands through the long, thick hair and across the lean shoulders, down the slender flanks. He moved more urgently after that, massaging the tight buttocks, the hard muscles of Hart's naked thighs. He found the tight ball sack, and the boy spread his legs wide for Nick to touch it. He followed the curve of scrotum and found Hart's cock was as big as his own, and just as hard. He held it, began to rub, but then the boy pushed his hands away and shifted directions on the bed. Hart leaned over Nick, a dark shadow against the window, and squeezed his balls, sucked the erection into his mouth, right down into his throat. Nick thought he would come right then, felt his balls get hard, but after a second the pressure eased off some, and he touched Hart's cock again, hanging above him now.

That only excited him more. Waves of lust rolled over him as he took Hart's cock into his own mouth, felt himself sliding deeper into the warm wetness of the boy's throat. He began to thrust hard with his hips then, going deeper still, and in minutes he had to come, gushing in a rush of pleasure like he'd never felt before. Hart kept up the pressure through it all, massaging his balls as he groaned and bucked.

"Do you want it?" Hart asked then, and Nick said, "Yes," without knowing what it was, really, that he wanted. He found out, though, gasping and hurting as the boy rolled him over and shoved that big erection into him.

"Wait," he said. "Stop," and Hart did.

"It only hurts for a minute," Hart said, trembling himself, stroking Nick's back with light, eager hands, urging Nick to relax. He was right. The pain turned to a kind of pleasure, and Nick wanted more of it as Hart thrust in harder. It ended finally as the boy came suddenly deep inside him, arching and shuddering at the peak of it, yelling, and then easing down slowly into peace and stillness.

Afterward, they lay a while in the darkness, resting side by side, and then Hart sighed and pushed up, looking for his tobacco pouch. His face lit briefly as he struck a match, and then he blew smoke into the moonlight.

"Believe me now?" he asked, cool and casual again.

"Yeah," said Nick.

"Well," Hart said, "it's time we got up." He didn't move.

"Where are they coming through?" asked Nick.

"Shit. I don't know," said Hart.

"You don't know?"

The cigarette glowed as he drew on it, dropped in an arc.

"Well. I've been thinkin'," Hart said. "The river road's too open, too many folks goin' by. They wouldn't come over the hills, either. Punchin' cows at night's no picnic; they'd never keep 'em together. They won't come by here, so they've got to come down the ravine."

Nick stirred. "That's rough driving even in the daytime."

"They don't have to come all the way, just get 'em past the fence. Your line's not the best up that way."

That stung. Nick sat up sharply and reached for his pants.

"I do the best I can," he said. "Get the hell out of my bed."

Hart only laughed, and reached to stub out his cigarette.

OUT NEAR THE ravine, there was a brisk wind blowing, sweeping thin clouds across the moon. It flowed across the rocks and down into the canyon like a river, gusted off through the shadows, rustling the sage. An hour before sunrise, it carried the trample and bawl of driven steers.

Nick stiffened, reached out to grip Hart's arm. The boy had been dozing, but now he snapped awake, reached for his Winchester.

"Wait a minute," said Nick. "What are we going to do?"

They were crouched behind a wall of rock on the lip of the ravine, a spot Hart had chosen for obvious cause. In fact, the reasons were so obvious Nick was some worried.

"I'm not going to murder those punchers," he said, and caught the glint of moonlight off Hart's cheekbone as the boy turned his head.

"Nick," he said. "You can't afford to let 'em get on your place!"

"Raidy..." Nick said, half afraid to argue now.

Hart groaned in aggravation, dropped his head against the rock. "All right," he said then. "Listen. You got a choice—the stock or the men."

Nick knew what he meant. They could shoot the steers before they pushed through the fence—or, they could shoot at the men. Once the punchers went down, the stock would scatter. He felt cold, thinking about it that way, but he had to decide what to do.

"The men," he said. They'd made a choice themselves, after all. "But no surprises!"

There were maybe ten steers and five cowboys, dark shapes on shadow horses that whistled and shouted at the cows, pushing them at the mouth of the ravine. The steers bawled and turned when they hit the sagging wire, but the men forced them back.

Hart stood up. "Stop!" he yelled sharply. "Get away from the fence."

He was answered by a flash of gunfire, and he dropped behind the rocks again, snapped off a shot of his own. Lead spanged off the rocks around them, hot and heavy. The rifle in Nick's hands kicked and bucked. The cows bawled and skidded, throwing up dust. A horse reared and screamed, crashed over. Then suddenly it was quiet.

The steers had made a break for open country, and most of the cowboys, too, it seemed. Only two of them lay in the dirt, Nick thought, with the dust settling slowly over them.

Hart muttered something under his breath.

"What?" said Nick.

"I said, 'Make you happy?'"

"You okay?" asked Nick.

"Yeah," said Hart. "Stay here and cover me. I'll go see who's down."

He slid down from the rocks and disappeared. Nick identified his shape in a minute, slipping through the shadows below, and after a while he was back.

"Red Slocum," he said. "And Tom Daw—both dead. We couldn't have done any better shootin', Nick."

He took off his hat, wiped a sleeve over his face. Then he took off his scarf and started to tie it around his arm.

Nick started. "Are you hurt?"

"Yeah. It comes of warnin' folks you're about to shoot."

Nick cursed, fumbled out a match.

"Leave it alone," Hart said. "It's all right."

"This isn't going to solve anything," said Nick.

"Yes, it is," the boy said. "Those two bein' down will cut the heart out of Eisner. And I'll fix it so they won't come at you again."

Something in the way he said it scared Nick.

"What are you going to do?"

"Don't worry about it," said Hart. He pushed up, headed for his horse. "We took care of things here, so go on into town and get your dad." He gathered the reins, swung up on the horse.

"Wait," Nick said, catching the bit, and then he had to decide what he wanted to say. "Are you coming back?"

"I hadn't planned on it."

Nick thought about it. To hell with old Isaac Bain—and Joy, too, if she wanted to side with him. "You're welcome any time," he said.

Hart sat there, staring at him through the dark. "Thanks," he said finally. "Maybe I will."

LATER IN TOWN, Nick heard Raidy had shot Lou Burke, and disappeared into the hills.

He picked up Joy and the old man at the hotel. Everything seemed quiet on the range, no sign of Buckley or Eisner, and he wondered if Hart was right—that everything was over now. That night when he went to bed, there was a brown envelope under the pillow. Inside was the mortgage, marked "paid in full."

ROGAYO

BY LANDON DIXON

THE TALL, LEAN man strode down the tunnel and into the tiny office located deep in the bowels of the Wyoming sports arena. He wore crotchless, cheekless cowhide chaps, a ten-gallon white Stetson, a pair of polished red cowboy boots, and nothing else. His hung cock swung along to his ambling gait, his big, shaven balls bouncing, taut, tanned, mounded butt cheeks clenching and unclenching.

"Well, lookee who's here!" Clint Adams, bossman of the Wyoming rogayo, exclaimed, looking up from the paperwork piled atop the small desk in the cramped room.

There were three other cowboys lounging around, getting their registrations in order. They were all displaying hanging cocks and dangling balls, hard, round, thrust-back butt cheeks, in various stages of partial western dress. They all turned their handsome, cowboy-hatted heads and looked at the new man who'd just strolled into their midst.

But he wasn't new at all, not to the rogayo circuit. "Hiya, Clint," Chad Crowder said, extending a large, strong hand to the seated promoter. "It's been awhile." His clear, brown eyes briefly surveyed the other competitors. He didn't recognize a one of them. He looked back at Clint.

"Awhile!? More like goin' on eight years, Chad," the big,

bluff, flamboyant man with the sunburned face and neon-red suit said, sizing up Chad's muscle-cleaved chest, tan nipples, and clean-cut cock with appraising, admiring eyes. "Looks like you kept in shape, though. What brings you back to the rogayo circuit? You already won it all."

Chad's full lips pouted a grimace. "And lost it all, too." He'd left his domestic partner of six years behind, their home broken and Chad dead-broke. Living and loving and working in one place just hadn't sat well with the free-range cowboy.

Wade Brubaker laughed. Chad and Clint stared at the man.

"This here is Chad Crowder, *boy*," Clint growled at the offending young cowboy. "The best ball-busting, bear-riding, man-roping, stud-wrestling gay cowboy there's ever been. Three-time champion."

Wade pushed off from the filing cabinet he'd been slouching against, stood tall in his black leather boots, his cock bobbing up. "Yeah, I've heard of you," he sneered at Chad. His bright blue eyes traveled over Chad's body, not with admiration, but with contempt. "A little past it, aren't you, pops?"

When Chad turned, his cock came a second behind with him—riding up fast and hard, obviously still willing to take on any challenge. "I guess we'll just see about that," he snarled back.

The two men's penises eyed one another, long and hard and heavy, pecs flexing, butt cheeks locking up in back.

"Boys, boys," Clint intervened. "Save the ridin' for the stampede ground. You, uh, know that Duff Blocker is here, too, don't you, Chad?"

Chad jerked his head back towards Clint, his sultry eyes gone wide. "Cowboy?"

"Stockman."

Chad grunted.

"I guess maybe he's even more down on his luck than you are, Chad," Clint observed. "Used to be one of the best toppers in the business—good as you, almost." He cleared his throat like a horse coughing. "So, uh, what events you goin' to enter, Chad?"

"All of 'em," the veteran cowboy replied.

Clint and the other two men blew out their cheeks. Wade grinned at Chad, hitching his hips and cock up even higher.

THE FOUR MAIN rogayo events were modeled after the four main rodeo events. Bronc-busting became ball-busting, the objective being to straddle a man's shoulders and ride the bucker for eight seconds, if possible, no hand-holding of any kind, points awarded both on the technique of the rider and the bucker. Bear-riding was similar to bull-riding, except the bull was replaced with a hairy man-bear, the cowboy's objective to ride atop the bear's bucking back for eight seconds, again no hands holding on, again with the same points system. While calf-roping became man-roping, a cowboy trying to lasso a running man with a velvet rope, truss him up as fast as possible, points awarded for bondage technique, also. And stud-wrestling was a variation on steer-wrestling, the animal replaced with a stockman again, the objective being to wrestle the stud down to the non-stick sand surface of the arena floor and pin him cock-to-cock, the quicker the better.

There were the cowboys and the stockmen. All participants in the events were almost totally naked, all boasting prodigious saddle horns and skill with their hands. Prize money was awarded on both sides, though the cowboys roped the lion's share of the haul.

THE ARENA STANDS were packed Saturday night, the fully-clothed crowd whooping and whistling and hollering, getting into the spirit of the thing. As the cowboys paraded out into the arena in their erotic nudity and rustic western finery, they waved to the crowd. There were twenty-five contestants, a mixture of circuit regulars and local yokels. A special cheer went up for

Chad Crowder when Clint belted his name out over the loud-speaker. Chad picked up his cock and waved it in acknowledgement, setting off another roar.

"Enjoy it while you can, old-timer!" Wade yelled in Chad's ear. "You'll be flat on your back before you know it!"

"You wish!" Chad entendred in return.

THE FIRST EVENT up was ball-busting. Chad watched some of the yokels get bounced off the bucking, shrugging, plunging shoulders of the professional stockmen. Then it was his turn. He straddled the smooth, padded railings that corralled the snorting, standing stockman. Chad had drawn Jesus, a short, stocky, dark-skinned man with broad shoulders and a surly expression.

"Buck off!" Jesus jeered at him over the anticipatory cheers of the crowd.

Chad looked down at the naked man between his legs, nodded, then dropped down onto Jesus' shoulders. The bell rang and the plastic gate swung open. They were off, Chad squeezing his thighs tight to the man's unshaven face, hooking his calves into the man's damp, unshaven armpits.

Jesus ran out onto the sanded stampede ground and leapt and jerked and shrugged and dipped and twisted. Chad hung on with his legs, his left arm straight out and wildly bucking, his right arm raised high and violently waving, his cock pressing hard into the back of Jesus' hairy, sweaty head. The crowd went wild. The horn sounded, signaling eight seconds. A standing ovation erupted, the fans stamping their feet on the make-shift metal bleachers to the tune of their smacking hands.

Chad slid off Jesus' shoulders and flopped down onto his back on the soft sand surface. Jesus dropped to his knees with Chad in between the cowboy's spread legs. The stockman grabbed onto Chad's cock and pumped it, stuck the cap into his open, gasping mouth, and sucked.

The crowd let loose again. Raw sex was one of the rewards for a good ride, if both cowboy and stockman were willing. That was one of the reasons rogayos had to be held indoors, in front of adult-only audiences.

Both men were more than willing, Chad's cock already rubbed erect against Jesus' head during the brief ride aboard the man's shoulders. Jesus pumped Chad's solid shaft and sucked on Chad's swollen cap, then dove his head down and ate up half of Chad's cock. He sealed his red lips tight and blew all he could, fisting the rest. Chad waved his right hand in mock-surrender, pumping his hips to Jesus' suctioning. The crowd swelled with more than excitement.

CHAD DREW TINY in the bear-riding competition. Tiny's name was the only thing small about him. He was a huge, barrel-chested, muscle-plated man with a coat like a brown bear, and a beard to match. Down on all-fours in the pen, he twisted his massive head up and glared at Chad. "Better enjoy riding me while you can," he growled, "'cause I'll be riding you soon enough."

"That's bull, bear," Chad responded calmly, legs spread and boots poised on either railing, cock hanging down sure and weighty.

He dropped onto Tiny's hairy back and hooked his legs tight around the burly man's chest, just as the bell rang and the plastic gates burst open.

It was pandemonium—eight seconds of bucking, leg-kicking, rearing, spinning, and whip-lashing. Chad was flung crazily backwards and forward, jerked to and fro, his arms akimbo and flailing, head and neck snapping, cowboy hat sailing. The horn went off and Chad jumped off over top of Tiny's bald head, the crowd screaming and applauding.

Now the hard-breathing, sweat and hair-bristled stockman was in for another kind of cowboy taming. Chad ambled in behind Tiny, his hard, bobbing cock leading the way. The bear compliantly knelt down on his hairy forearms and upraised his hairy ass.

Chad studied the bullseye, lubing his prong, a smile on his studly face. He waved his gleaming cock at Tiny like a matador waves a red cape at a bull, much to the crowd's delight. And then he hit the bear hole, filled it, ramming his cock balls-deep into Tiny's accommodating chute.

Chad groaned and Tiny snorted. The crowd cheered—everyone's eyes fixed on the old-time, sensuous riding rhythm now taking place on the arena floor—cowboy sawing his saddlehorn back and forth in stockman's anus. Chad gripped the hairy waist and churned the heated, tight chute. Tiny buried his burning, bearded face in the sand and bounced his enormous, hirsute butt back on Chad's penetrating prong.

THE SHOW WENT on.

After three events, Chad was tied with Wade Brubaker and a talented local yokel, Buck Skinner. The stud-wrestling event had separated the wheat from the chaff, the beef from the gristle. Chad and the other two cowboys had brought their stockmen down in near-record times, pinning them cock-to-cock, and then pumping; much to the pleasure of competitors and crowd alike.

It came down to the man-roping competition, where both speed and talent were required, points awarded subjectively and tellingly.

Chad watched Buck waste too much time chasing down and swinging the velvet lasso around his stockman's chest, then knotting the man up way too simply in his panic to make up for lost time. The small, wiry African-American was all-but eliminated.

But Chad, like the crowd, had to admire Wade's skill. The big, bronzed, blond-haired man lariated his stockman quickly, efficiently, and sexily, lacing a cock-ring knot onto the trussing. The cowboy's score was going to be tough to beat.

Chad was thrown—when he saw his stockman in the chute next to him. In all of the excitement he'd forgotten all about what Clint had told him earlier.

"Hey, Chad. How's it going?" Duff Blocker asked through the padded railings.

Chad stared into the familiar deep green eyes, now latticed with red veins. Duff was nude, his thin body pale, his brown hair wispy on top and his pretty face more drawn than Chad remembered. "Wh-What happened?" Chad croaked.

A decade back Chad and Duff had been fierce competitors on the circuit and fast lovers off of it. They'd been young, hung, and full of cum back then, neither one willing to back down, or bottom out. The match hadn't lasted, burning too hot, scorching the both of them. Chad had left the show soon after. He hadn't heard from Duff since.

Now, Duff looked earnestly into Chad's eyes. "I guess I went too fast, too hard, and too high," he admitted. "I lost my friends, my home, my money, and then I lost my nerve. I had to come back as...a stockman." He shrugged and smiled endearingly at his former foe, friend, and lover. "I guess I learned a bit about humility along the way, though. I get by."

Before Chad could digest it all, the bell suddenly went off. The chutes burst open, and Duff ran like hell.

Chad gave his head a shake, staring at those familiar twitching, taunting, tempting buttocks of his former buckle buddy— running away from him. He wanted them back, wanted Duff back. Chad slammed his cowboy hat down onto his head with his left hand and lifted the velvet rope with his right, and raced out of the chute, hot on Duff's trail.

The crowd stood and roared at the top of their lungs, knowing it all came down to this.

Back in the day, Chad had never been able to outrun Duff. The lithe, lanky man had moved too fast and erratically. But now time seemed to slow down, and maybe Duff, too. Chad felt himself flying, Duff's quivering, humping ass cheeks and rolling back and pumping arms coming closer and closer.

Chad swung the lasso, threw it, the brightly-lit lewd scene crystal-clear in his oft-jaded eyes. He couldn't miss. And he didn't. The velvet hoop dropped down over Duff's shoulders and noosed his chest. Chad dug his heels in and pulled back, rearing Duff to a halt in the sand as gently as he could.

It seemed to take all the fight out of Duff, if there was any. He turned and looked back at Chad racing up to him, his puffy lips broaching a smile. Chad grinned back, skidding to a stop. Then he lashed the lengthy velvet rope around Duff's chest, cock, and balls, and in between Duff's butt cheeks.

It was an awesome display of bondage mastery, in record time; the results even more lovely to behold. Duff's pale pecs and pink nipples stood out from the twin bands looping above and below. His balls bloated and his cock jutted, thanks to the roping. His buttocks were breathtakingly split and spread.

"Well, that's it, folks!" Clint bellowed over the loudspeaker. "Chad Crowder is champion of the Wyoming rogayo!"

Chad and Duff didn't hear the ear-splitting announcement nor the deafening cheers. It was just the two of them; older, wiser, less egotistical—and more in love.

Chad took Duff in his arms and brought the stockman down to the sand, their lips locked together in a tender kiss. Their hot, damp skin pressed together, their hard cocks squishing erotically. Chad pumped and Duff pumped back. Not cowboy and stockman, champion and also-ran; but equal lovers.

Chad broke his lips free of Duff's soft, wet mouth and dipped his head lower. In the shade of his cowboy hat, he swirled his tongue around one of Duff's engorgedly-raised nipples before moving to the other one, shining and swelling the rubbery pair still more. Duff moaned and shivered.

The crowd fell silent, no doubt sensing they were witnessing something more than the usual post-rogayo celebration.

Chad engulfed a nipple with his lips and sucked on it, gazing up into Duff's glistening eyes. He moved his head over, gently, urgently, and sensually sucking on Duff's other nipple, feeling it blossom even more in his mouth. Duff moaned and undulated his hips, pumping his hard, bound cock into Chad's ridged belly.

That's where Chad went next, down to Duff's cock. He trailed a wet line of fire along Duff's stomach with his tongue, then lifted his body away so he and the hushed crowd could see the huge erection Duff was sporting. The man's roped cock thrust rigidly into the air, vibrating.

Chad nuzzled Duff's tied balls, making the man shudder. Then he licked Duff's shaven sack, tongue-teasing the pair of nuts. And then he licked up from the balls, up along the underside of Duff's towering cock. The man and the crowd sighed.

Chad licked up from the velvet rope lashing the base of Duff's cock all along the straining, swollen shaft, around, up and down; stroking, painting, caressing Duff's prong with his moist, beaded, loving tongue. Duff spasmed and shot his cock up even higher. Chad jumped his head up and caught the bloated tip of the beefstick in his mouth.

A few in the crowd clapped. Others just held their breath, hands clasped to their mouths. Chad briefly sucked and chewed on Duff's hood, then began the long, stretching, sexy mouth-plunge down Duff's cock.

More raucous applause greeted the sight of Chad's lips kissing up against the ropes binding Duff's base and balls. Chad lifted his head high and brought it back down low, sucking on Duff's entire inflamed length, Chad's nostrils flaring, cheeks and throat bulging with the amazing erotic effort. Duff squirmed in the non-stick sand as his cock was consumed and suctioned over and over and over again.

Finally Chad lifted all the way up. He greased Duff's raging erection and his own rump, getting ready to mount.

The crowd chanted, "Ride 'im, cowboy! Ride 'im, cowboy!"

But Chad and Duff, gazing into one another's shining eyes, knew this sexual event was no contest, both men were winners.

Chad straddled Duff's waist and lowered his ass onto Duff's cap.

Duff's cock slid inside Chad's anus slick and quick, finding a familiar home. Both men groaned; Chad rearing his head up and revelling in the stuffed-full feeling of meat in his ass; Duff rolling his head in the sand. To the whoops of the crowd, Chad swept his cowboy hat off his head and rode Duff's cock, bucking up and down. Duff thrust his hips up to meet the rugged rogayo motion, tied arms, cock, and balls, but he was far from tamed.

It was a spectacular showstopper, well-worth the price of admission and more.

For Chad and Duff it was an open, unabashed renewal of their lust and love for one another, on a more mature basis than before. Chad grabbed onto his jumping cock and fisted, his anus getting searingly reamed. Duff bounced his gleaming body up and down, pounding his surging cock into Chad's chute. Their mutual orgasmic semen outburst was the sizzling brand to mark them officially as romantic lovers again, for a long time to come this time.

Chad's cock erupted and his body jerked and gyrated like he was going to be thrown, semen spouting and striping Duff's humping body. Duff spasmed and spurted, repeatedly shooting deep into the cowboy's convulsing anus that was riding his cock. Their lusty cries were echoed by the packed and packing house.

COWBOY THERAPY

BY HUNTER FROST

Many thanks and hugs to Vanessa, Anna, and Mia.

"OH, IT'S PERFECT, Jude."

Liz turned off the ignition of her Hyundai and I watched her take in the bustling ranch in front of us. My eyes followed hers—children, horses, and cowboys milled about in droves; the small clusters of kids and adults joking and smiling while they went about their tasks. Ranch hands cheered and hollered, patting the young ones heartily on their backs after the tikes had successfully completed a chore. Laughter and whinnies punctuated the rustling of leaves on the trees and...heaven help me, it was all so fucking quaint I could vomit.

I pulled myself from the car, grimacing, my ass bruised and my muscles sore. Liz and I had bumped and jostled our way down the uneven dirt road toward A Ride to Remember Ranch for what seemed like forever and a day, and I'd fought the urge to jump out and run the other way the closer we got. If Liz had mentioned we were headed to a ranch in the first place, I'd have told her to turn the damn car around and take me home. Horses, stables, or anything that goes along with that shit can eat me. The only thing you'll catch me riding is a skateboard, and I'd kill to be landing a sick roll-in deep in the bowl at Glenhaven right about now instead of kicking up gravel and dander in this hole. But my so-called best friend had kept our destination a secret until I saw the wooden sign overhead a mile back and by then it was too late.

"Did I do something to piss you off?" I asked, as the unmistakable smell of livestock and leather assaulted my nose, making my skin crawl.

Liz tore her gaze from the nauseating Remington meets Rockwell painting around us and got out of the car, her blue eyes looking more tired than usual. "Like you'd have come if I'd told you the truth."

"Damn right! You *know* how I feel about this crap. So why the torture tactic?" I followed her as she walked toward the building labeled Main Office, yanking her aside as she nearly stepped in a steaming pile of manure. Fantastic.

She gave me a weak smile in thanks. "Because Dom looks up to you. If you say this place is cool, he'll be more willing to try it."

For whatever reason, Liz's nine-year-old autistic son thought I was the bomb. I couldn't deny that I loved the kid as much as I did her. Hell, Liz and I'd known each other since high school, bonding after Captain Asshat of the football team got her pregnant and took off while my parents sent me to live with my uncle when they caught me kissing the boy next door. I'd do anything for Liz and Dom, but just being here brought back bad memories I'd hidden away for years.

"You didn't have to bring me all the way out here for me to tell him it's cool." I adjusted my shades, eyes darting around as I shoved my hands in my jean pockets.

She sighed, dragging her fingers through her blond curls. "Maybe I thought it could help you, too."

And there it was. I knew there had to be more to this. No one hauls their best friend to a place they despise for the fun of it. My knuckles ached from clenching my fists so tight. What did she really expect to happen? "I don't need or want your help, Liz." I didn't care if this was a ranch specializing in equine therapy for autistic kids; it still made me nervous to be so close to these animals—the four-legged ones and the ones in ten-gallon hats.

"Well if you're not going to give it a chance, then could you at least be civil while we're here?" She pursed her lips.

Man, I hated when she twisted something around to make it look like I was the one in the wrong. She lied to me! Yet, *I* had to be the polite one?

"For Dom's sake?" she added, and a twinge of guilt stung my heart. Bitch.

I growled. "Fine, but I deserve *something* out of this. How about you let me teach him how to skate finally?"

Liz furrowed her brow. "Too dangerous. He could break something."

I blinked, grasping at my slouched beanie as if my head would explode. "Are you kidding me? You'd rather let him loose near these half-ton animals, who could drag him around like a rag doll and stomp him into oblivion?"

"Stop it." She smacked my shoulder. "I know what happened to you ten years ago was traumatic, but these children aren't left to fend for themselves, and these cowboys are trained to work with kids with special needs. Everything is supervised and safe. They aren't ever without a professional nearby."

I knew she wouldn't listen to my reasoning after it seemed she'd already made up her mind. I huffed, but resigned myself to do this for Dom, no matter how much it killed me. I held the door open for her as I looked out at all those horses and cowboys. Suddenly, I was twelve years old again at Triple H Dude Ranch, wondering how the fuck I would get through another horrific summer. I shivered and went inside.

WE MET WITH the mental health specialist, Dr. Ackerman, who

Liz had talked to about getting Dom enrolled in the program. The doctor was pretty hot for a chick, in that hipster chic way—with long messy black hair and dark-rimmed glasses. She dressed in jeans and a flannel shirt, which seemed out of place with her title. I couldn't help but notice how Liz seemed flustered through the entire meeting, especially when the woman smiled at her. I filed that away for later.

I didn't dare open my mouth for most of the meeting considering I'd been told I had trouble hiding my true feelings. How about that? I kept a low profile, trailing along behind the ladies as the doc gave us the run-down of the program. I steeled myself as best I could as we toured the stables, the riding rings, and the other common areas, stopping to watch some of the children in action. *My* heart raced and my palms were sweating, but the kids seemed to love interacting with the animals despite my apprehensions about the size and heft of those beasts. They led the horses around, brushed them, and even fed them out of their own hands. I couldn't believe it. You wouldn't catch me with my hands anywhere near those big mouths.

The place appeared legit, but *I* didn't have to like it. I just had to tell Dom I did.

We rounded the barn and Dr. Ackerman told us to wait a moment while she went inside, and I got another disapproving glare from Liz. I stuck my tongue out at her, right as the doc returned…with a cowboy in tow.

A faded red Henley shirt covered an impressive chest and wide shoulders, tapering down to slim hips in worn Levi's. Even from behind my shades, his green eyes were dazzling, crinkling at the corners as his face lit up with a genuine smile. Shit, this dude was sexy. And oddly familiar.

I managed to pull my tongue back in my mouth and come back to my senses.

Ugh. I bristled. What was I doing lusting after a cowboy?

"Liz, this is Wyatt. He'll be working with Dominic if you decide to enroll," the doctor said, as Wyatt removed his light-colored cowboy hat to reveal a dampened mass of bronze and gold hair glistening in the sunlight.

"Nice to meet ya, Liz," Wyatt drawled, his accent not quite southern, but definitely not from the Pacific Northwest. He shook her hand and Liz cheerfully replied.

Then Dr. Ackerman turned to me. "And this is Jude."

He reached out to shake, but instead of taking his hand, I brought mine up and casually saluted him. I just couldn't bear to touch him. I couldn't let him notice how much I was quaking in my Vans.

He blinked and awkwardly withdrew his hand. "A pleasure," he said, looking confused. He slowly turned toward Liz. "I'm sure Dominic will love it here. We've seen amazin' results with our children and the horses. It makes my work incredibly rewarding."

Liz smiled, her eyes filled with that spark of excitement I hadn't seen in ages. I could tell she wanted this for Dom. She'd tried everything to help him live a more engaged life, but the older he got, the more withdrawn and less willing he was to communicate with anyone besides a limited few. She'd heard great things about equine therapy. Of course, she told me this in a mad rush on our way in, hoping I wouldn't bail from the moving vehicle. I couldn't help it if childhood trauma made the mere sight of a horse, cowboy, or stable virtually unbearable. I was already impressed with myself for remaining upright.

"That's wonderful to hear, Wyatt," Liz said, and I knew from the tone of her voice this was all but a done deal.

"I have a few more details to discuss with Liz for now," Dr. Ackerman said. "Thanks for taking a moment to meet us, Wyatt." She gestured for us to move along with her clipboard.

Wyatt put his hat back on. "Anytime," he said, and tipped the brim of his hat toward us. "Liz…Jude." The extended pause and emphasis on my name had my stomach clenching in fear. At least that's what I told myself as I quickly turned to avoid the cowboy's penetrating green eyes.

Once we were out of earshot of Wyatt, a sharp elbow in the

ribs nearly had me doubling over. I gasped. *Fuck!*

"You promised, Jude." Liz somehow managed to say between her clenched teeth. "That was anything but civil."

"And neither was *that*!" I said, rubbing my injured side. The doc wrote something on her clipboard as she walked beside us.

"I apologize for my *friend's* lack of tact." Liz narrowed her eyes at me.

The doctor nodded. "Liz mentioned you had problems on a ranch when you were a child, Jude. Did you want to talk about that?"

I looked at both of them like they were bat-shit crazy, then focused my glare at Liz. How could she already be blabbing to this chick about *my* problems? I stopped in my tracks. "You know what? You two go ahead and talk about what you should be concerned about—Dominic. I'm not interested in having my head shrunk right now. I'll be at that snack bar. Come find me when you're ready to leave, Liz."

"Jude!" Liz yelled as I turned to go.

I flipped her the bird without looking back and stormed off toward the little building we had visited earlier. A cold drink sounded awesome, but if the place was crawling with cowpokes forget it. I'd sit in the car if I had to. Liz could kiss my ass. I opened the door that jangled with spurs rather than a bell.

"Hi there!" A young woman behind the bar with a huge smile, red hair, and freckles—who looked exactly like Jessie from *Toy Story*—waved at me. I couldn't count how many times Dom made me watch that movie. I swear I could recite it by heart.

I waved back and removed my shades, slipping them into the neckline of my thermal. The small space was decorated like a saloon out of an old Western movie. Worn booths, a few wooden tables, and stools lining a bar shaped like the letter "L" gave the place an authentic flair, especially with the sepia photos and leather horse stuff on the walls. I decided to sit on the short side of the L. "Slow afternoon?" I asked, noticing I was the only customer. Thankfully.

The young woman nodded and looked at the kitschy grandfather clock on the far wall. "We don't get many folks in here until the afternoon session ends. Give it another fifteen minutes."

"I see." Perfect timing. Liz should be done by then, if she didn't decide to hash out more of my problems with hipster doc. I wanted to scream. And get back to my skateboard.

"Can I get you something?" The Jessie look-a-like asked, spreading her arms out on the lacquered bar.

I spied a soda fountain behind her. "You have Cherry Vanilla Coke?"

"I only have Cherry Coke, but I have some vanilla syrup and a cherry. Will that work?"

"That would be heavenly." Uncle Chet used to buy the stuff special just for me when I'd come over to escape the rough days at home with my parents.

"You got it, honey." She smiled, and quickly went about mixing in the vanilla and cherry. She handed it to me and I took one sip and clutched my heart. Cherry and vanilla burst in my mouth in a blissful blend. "Marry me."

She blushed as red as the maraschino cherry in my drink. "You're bad," she said, swatting at me with her dishtowel.

I took another drink and sighed as she giggled. Nothing like a cold pop to take my mind off of things.

Somewhere a phone rang.

"I'll be back in a minute," she said, untying her gingham apron and throwing it on a nearby chair. "I forgot about the late delivery today."

"Do you need some help?" I asked.

"You're sweet, but no thank you. I've got a load of guys out back hoping for a break from mucking out stalls." She smiled and walked out through a door behind the bar.

I took another pull from the straw, savoring the flavors as they calmed me. I was only alone for a minute before the spurs at the front jangled. I forced myself not to look, staring at the fizz of my drink. Like I cared who the fuck it was? Unfortunately, my racing heart called my bluff. *You have issues, Jude.* Issues that I had long hidden in the comfort of the urban sprawl of downtown Portland, now come to bite me in the ass on this god-forsaken ranch.

I could feel the eyes on me as the door bounced shut; the jingling spurs now silent. Boots echoed on the floor and I cursed under my breath. There was no doubt in my mind that it was a cowboy. Masculine heat poured into the whole place as sweat beaded on my forehead and upper lip.

I hoped the Jessie look-a-like would return and save me from the unknown, but if I knew my luck she'd never come back. I sighed, shaking more than any self-respecting man should. The quiet unnerved me, making me self-conscious of my breathing and the way my knee kept bumping the bar. I swore minutes passed. What was this guy's problem anyway? Couldn't get enough of the skater guy out of his element? We were still in the outskirts of Portland, thank you very much. Sure, it was a ranch, but it wasn't the sticks.

Out of my peripheral vision I caught jean-clad legs and fraying edges down near steel-toed boots. I gulped. Nothing good came of boots like that. Boots that could kick my ass around the entire barn.

Tired of this pathetic game, I hardened my voice and stared straight ahead. "Can I help you?"

A few nail-biting seconds passed.

"What're you drinkin'?" came the smooth drawl from earlier.

I turned to see Wyatt standing there with his thumbs hooked in his pockets. Up this close he was even more tan and rugged and...blazing hot.

"None of your business," I replied, before I let my imagination run away with me. I wouldn't let my guard down so easily. Men like this don't bother with guys like me. Unless he lost a bet with his cow punching buddies.

The man's blond eyebrow rose and a subtle smile crossed lips that were mighty tempting. He removed his hat. "Come on now, how am I supposed to buy you another if you don't tell me what you like?" He emphasized those last words in a low, husky timbre.

A shiver went down my spine. From fear for sure.

I folded my arms and leaned on them in front of me on the bar, trying not to show my nerves by adjusting the cuffs of my hoodie.

He ruffled his sweat-dampened hair as that sweet pair of green eyes studied me. This hunk of a guy should be out ropin' ponies or whatever these freaks do rather than standing here offering to buy me a drink.

"Vanilla Cherry Coke," I said, finally. "But I don't want another."

With a wider smile, Wyatt took a seat on the corner stool closest to me. I thought he'd smell like horse and tack, but instead his sweat reminded me of earth, trees, dew...and sex. The scent was delicious. What the fucking hell was wrong with me?

"I wonder where Betsy ran off to?" he asked, glancing at the back of the bar.

"Late delivery." I replied, assuming he meant the Jessie look-a-like.

"Ahh." The stool creaked as he shifted, and I could feel his gaze leveled at me.

Heat sparked my body as if his eyes touched everywhere they landed. I thought I'd feel violated, but it was like I craved the invasiveness. Why was he doing this to me? I needed this whole ruse to stop now.

"Listen—" I began.

"My mama always said it's not polite to refuse to shake someone's hand upon meeting 'em." Wyatt interrupted.

"Wyatt—"

"We could start over?"

"Fine, but—"

"Nice to meet you, Jude," he said, and offered his hand.

"You, too," I replied, wanting to scream with exasperation. Why wouldn't this guy let me get a word in? Was it some kind of cowboy power-play? But as his tan, calloused hand took mine I nearly gasped at the fiery sensation that crept up my arm. *Fuck me.* I reluctantly pulled away from his grasp. "I don't know what you're trying to do here. But you can just stop. I won't be the butt of your stupid joke. You and your cowhand friends can go fuck yourselves." I finished and chugged the last of my Coke, preparing to leave.

Wyatt caught my arm, much more gently than I expected. "Hold up," he said, and I rolled my eyes, trying to avoid thinking about the tingling where he touched me.

"I don't know what you're talkin' about. I'm not here with anyone but you, and I'm sure as hell not talking to you for any other reason than to get to know you."

I stared at him. *This* man wanted to get to know me? "Is that some cowboy euphemism for kicking my ass?"

"Pardon?"

"Why would you want to get to know me? You know as well as I do, I don't belong here." I narrowed my eyes and glanced around, anticipating the moment his buddies came rushing in to rough me up.

Wyatt gave me a funny look. "You want to know the honest to God truth?"

I nodded, waiting for the disappointing punch line.

Wyatt leaned in close to my ear. "Since I laid eyes on you out there, I can barely keep my cock in check." His breath caressed my face and I shuddered. I knew my eyes must be like saucers, and my face beet red, but my dick reacted most to Wyatt's confession. Jeans tight, I took a few calming breaths.

Wyatt watched me. "I don't make it a habit to hit on a man while I'm workin', but I'd kick myself if I let you get away before saying somethin'. You're stunning, Jude." Wyatt's husky voice was so thick it wrapped *itself* around my stiff cock.

"Quit it. My face is going to burst into flames," I said, wishing there was more ice in my drink. Where the heck did this Betsy go anyway? How could she leave her customers alone for so long? And with people that were clearly delusional. When had gay cowboys become so forward with strangers? What the fuck tipped him off that I swung his way?

"I know. It's cute," Wyatt said, grinning.

"It's not cute," I protested, but Wyatt kept on grinning. He had my heart going like I'd just nailed an Indy off a quarterpipe. "I'm not used to men who look like they've galloped in off the range where the deer and the antelope play finding me…appealing."

Wyatt eyed me intently and sighed. "Then, you're not attracted to me."

I may have been afraid of the guy, but damn if I could prevent my body from reacting to him. "Don't put words in my mouth."

Wyatt rolled his teeth over lips that I couldn't stop staring at. "That's a loaded statement." He chuckled.

My whole body caught fire. Shit, I wanted to hide.

Wyatt scratched his chin. "So why the snub earlier?"

I didn't want to tell him everything, but, fuck, his kind eyes enticed me. Something flickered in the back of my mind. Why did I feel like I'd met him before?

"Hey, Wyatt!" Betsy exclaimed as she came in from the back. She began filling a glass with ice.

"Hi, Bets," Wyatt turned his attention away from me. "Ya'll set back there?"

"Almost. The boys unloaded the truck, but I need to take inventory." She placed a glass of regular Coke on the bar in front of Wyatt and looked at me. "Can I get you anything else or would you like to settle now?"

"Pour another for Jude, please," Wyatt answered. "And put it on my tab."

"No way, I'll get it." I pulled a few bills from my front pocket as Betsy made another Cherry Vanilla Coke.

"My tab." Wyatt's tone was final.

I huffed. "Thank you." I couldn't be completely rude. Again.

"You're welcome," Wyatt replied and Betsy giggled.

She placed the drink in front of me and turned to go. "Behave, boys."

Wyatt grinned, and it was all I could do to keep breathing. Hell if I knew why this cowboy made me want to jump his bones rather than run as far away as possible. Which is probably what I should be doing.

"You didn't answer my question." Wyatt faced me, and I wanted to groan at the swell of his cut pecs underneath that shirt.

I took a sip of my drink to compose myself. "I haven't had the best experience with all of this." I gestured to him and the general space around us.

"What's 'all this'?" He asked, mimicking me with his brow furrowed.

"Horses, cowboys...and everything in between." I fiddled with my straw.

He looked at me sideways. It seemed like he was debating whether or not to push this line of questioning. "Is Liz still in with Dr. Ackerman?"

I nodded, thankful he'd moved on. "How long have you been here?"

His boot scuffed on the metal of the stool. "About a year. But I worked at an equine therapy facility in Montana before this." He took a drink and once again my eyes were drawn to his lips, this time as they wrapped around that straw.

Those lips almost distracted me from what he said. Montana. That's where Triple H had been.

He blinked up at me. "Is Liz related to you?"

"No." His fishing for information was mildly cute. *Gah!* No, what was I thinking? Not cute! Cowboys are *not* cute! I could tell he planned to ask more questions by the gleam in his eye, but I decided to save him the trouble. "She's my best friend and a single mom. I help her out when I can. Dom calls me Uncle Jude."

"That's great," Wyatt murmured. "You from Portland?"

I nodded.

"You skate?"

"Isn't it obvious?"

"You could be a poser, for all I know."

I choked. "You did *not* just call me a poser."

"I won't believe it until I see it." He smirked.

I shook my head. "If you had any decent pavement out here rather than dirt and gravel I'd make you eat those words, cowboy."

Wyatt's amused eyes went to my mouth and I licked my lips. Fuck. What was I talking about again? Skateboarding, yeah. That's right. "And I design custom boards."

"Wow, an artist…" he said, biting at his lip again. "Sexy."

God, I wanted to bite that lip for him and roll my tongue over it.

"Tell me why 'all this' bothers you so much?" He asked, leaning his elbow on the bar.

So we were back to this again. At least it put a stop to my fantasizing. I didn't really want to talk about this stuff, but I figured it wouldn't hurt to give him something. "I don't like horses."

"Why?" He lazily stirred his drink.

I sighed. "When I was twelve my family decided to go to this dude ranch. I thought horses would be cool and wanted to ride, but the douchebag wranglers gave me the meanest one. The fucker was evil incarnate. I couldn't get near it without getting bit or kicked. One day the beast finally got me good in the ribs. I came to face down in wet hay. Never wanted to get near horses since."

"Ouch." Wyatt grimaced. "That's horrible. Why did they give you that horse?"

Because the wranglers were dickheads. From day one they pegged me as the kid to pick on. If they weren't forcing me to work with the nastiest horse, they were cornering me in the stables, taking my stuff, pushing me around, and calling me names. They made my life miserable. The next two summers didn't get any better.

I shrugged, not ready to give over those details.

"This place must make you crazy."

I nodded. "Yeah, well, I'm only here to support Liz and Dom."

"You've got balls, that's for sure." Wyatt downed the rest of his Coke in four gulps.

Did he just call me brave? I never expected that. I stared down into my drink and finally popped the cherry in my mouth to suck on it. I glanced over at Wyatt to catch him wiping his brow with a bandana as he watched me. My nerves were on edge, but I was beginning to like his attention. What the fuck had gotten into me?

"Why don't you come with me?" He got up and tossed a ten-dollar bill in a jar behind the counter. "I've a friend I'd like you to meet."

A friend, huh? I debated whether or not it was a good idea to follow Wyatt anywhere. Sure, the dude was hot...and suspiciously attracted to me. This could have been some cruel joke, but for some reason I believed he wasn't yanking my chain. Even if he was a cowboy.

I got up hesitantly from the stool. *Why not?*

"You can trust me." Wyatt winked and turned toward the door, giving me an eyeful of tight ass. Jesus, the guy made me want to do things to him I shouldn't be thinking about; especially at a therapy ranch for children.

ONCE OUTSIDE OF the snack bar, Wyatt plunked his hat back on as I fell into stride next to him. The afternoon session had let out and families were leaving. Wyatt waved at a couple of children who called his name, their guardians waving back as they guided the kids toward the parking lot. He couldn't be all bad, right?

He led me into one of the smaller stables, his hand resting casually on my lower back, wreaking havoc on my guts as he nudged me forward. The smell of wood shavings and alfalfa surrounded me, and my heartbeat increased, the thumping loud enough in my ears that I thought Wyatt might hear it.

Horses popped their heads out of the stalls one by one like monsters in a Halloween maze, grunts and whinnies filling the emptiness like cackling witches and woken spooks.

They're only horses, Jude. Not demons…well…

Wyatt and I were alone except for the six beasts in their stalls. Definitely six too many if you ask me. I stood frozen in the center of the barn, avoiding the gauntlet of horse heads.

"Hey, guys, let the man breathe." Wyatt said, daring to pat their noses, as I followed in the safety of his wake.

They attempted to snatch pieces of flesh from our bodies as we walked by, and I shoved my hands in my pockets to protect them. I still felt the hot breath that gushed from their huge nostrils through my hoodie.

Wyatt stopped at the horse in the last stall—a horse with a dark cream-colored face and white hair. I couldn't remember the name of it. Paleo-something? The horse nuzzled him as Wyatt's hands held his long face and stroked it.

"I tell you I don't like horses and you bring me straight to one? My trust is failing fast."

"This isn't just any horse. This is *my* horse. Chief." Wyatt patted the horse's nose and looked at me. "You okay?" Wyatt removed one of his hands from the horse's muzzle and put it on my shoulder. "You're as stiff as a board."

Imagine that? The heat of his touch relaxed me a little, which was odd. Cowboys didn't calm me down. If anything they made me as nervous as the horses.

His hand dropped away from my shoulder and he removed his hat, hanging it on a nail near the stall. The horse glared at us with evil brown eyes.

"Give me your hand," he said.

I instantly backed away. "No fucking way. I didn't come with you to get my hand bitten off."

"Chief won't bite you. I promise." Wyatt looked sincere.

Either he was an amazing actor or he was genuinely kind.

I sighed and reluctantly slid my hand out of my pocket to give to Wyatt. I didn't need it. I could ride a skateboard and design them with just one, right? He pulled gently. "Come closer."

I tried to breathe as I moved in, Wyatt's warmth and the nearness of the horse fighting for my attention. He reached our hands up toward Chief's muzzle and I closed my eyes, muscles tensed. My jaw ached as I waited for our hands to be ripped off by big menacing teeth.

"Open your eyes, Jude." Wyatt said, as my hand touched a soft, whiskered nose.

I flinched and opened one eye. Noticing our hands still intact, I opened the other eye.

"It's a good idea to keep your hand flat whenever you touch a horse's muzzle. That way ya won't lose fingers with a nippy one."

I yanked my hand back at the mention of losing fingers and Chief jerked his head up.

"And try not to make any sudden movements." Wyatt found my hand again and put it back on the beast's muzzle.

"Thanks for the info," I said, as we stroked Chief together. It wasn't horrible. And the horse seemed to tolerate it. For now.

"Let's go in the stall with him."

I snorted. "Good one."

"I'm serious." He let go of me and began unlatching the door to the stall, Chief's head over his back. How did he know the horse wouldn't reach down and bite his ass? When he had the stall open he pushed at Chief's chest, moving him backward. "Back, Chief." Amazingly, the horse obeyed. Wyatt turned toward me once the horse had moved back enough for us to enter.

I froze—images of angry bites, stomping, and kicking all while being locked in a stall with nowhere to go flashing before my eyes. "I can't."

"Yes you can." Wyatt reached out to me, palm up.

I stared at him. "No, you'll pull me in there with you."

Wyatt nodded. "But you'll be right here next to me. I won't let anything happen to you."

I swallowed. I hated that I trusted him so quickly. However, it wasn't Wyatt I was really worried about. "Chief doesn't know me."

"No, but I know Chief. And he won't hurt you." He glanced at his open hand and smiled, his eyes sparkling. Fuck, he was persuasive. And hot. Criminally hot.

I closed my eyes and took his hand trying not to think about it. As he stated, Wyatt pulled me forward until I was inside the stall, but I didn't expect to be thrust up against his hard body at the same time. When I opened my eyes, I was inches from his sexy green ones. Shit.

"Hey there," he murmured, so close I could taste the pop he had earlier. He released my hand to drape an arm gently across my back. Somehow I didn't feel cornered or trapped, even as the click of the latch behind us told me he had closed the stall door with his free arm. My heartbeat skyrocketed, but not due to fear. I felt safe in Wyatt's arms, as if he was protecting me from every horse that had ever wronged me. How the hell did he do that?

Before I could make sense of it all, he brought his thumb to my lower lip, barely gliding over it. It tickled and drove me out of my mind with want.

"Please let me kiss you," he whispered, just as I was about to devour that finger.

I don't think I hesitated for more than a millisecond before leaning in to meet his parted lips first. I didn't anticipate the excruciating softness, the tremendous heat, and the throbbing ache deep in the root of my cock and balls. I groaned, instantly hard. My tongue swept into his mouth, hungry for more, and Wyatt moaned in return, pressing his hard-on against me. I melted into the kiss, lost in the slide of his tongue and the tight crush of our bodies.

I pulled away, stupefied. "What are we doing?" I whispered,

resting my forehead on his.

Wyatt's eyes were dark and dilated as he gazed at me under hooded lids, his breathing ragged. "Replacing old, useless memories of asshole ranch hands and unfortunate horses," he replied, his voice raw. He rested his hands on my waist.

Fuck, I'd completely forgotten about Chief behind us—and the constant fear that went along with everything about this place. Is that what this was to him? "Wait, so this is all just your idea of therapy?" I said, moving back. I knew it was too good to be true.

But he grabbed onto the belt loops of my jeans. "Jude, don't—"

"Fine." I yanked his wrists from my waist, and pushed them up over his head against the wall. It gave me the illusion that I had some control here. "I bet Liz and the doc put you up to this, didn't they?"

"What? Not at all. *This*—" Wyatt pressed his massive erection against mine—"*never* happens during regular therapy sessions."

We groaned together and I laughed despite my indignation. "I would hope not."

He smiled. "If I can get ya this close to *me*...and a horse...and have you enjoy it, why wouldn't I?"

Damn cowboy had a point.

"Regardless, I got what I really wanted," he drawled.

I shifted and licked my lips, wanting to believe this wasn't part of some plot. "And what is that?"

"You in my arms," he said, his eyes searching mine.

I'm no romantic, but shit if the guy didn't hit me right in the feels. Why'd those eyes have to be so kind?

Unable to stop myself, I pressed in close, kissing him deep and slow.

Because I wanted to.

I released his wrists and soon we were clawing at one another, grinding and squeezing. Wyatt's body could get as addicting as crushing multiple pivots on my board in a Monster Walk. But right now, all I wanted was to swallow him whole.

"I want you in my mouth." I said against his lips. "But not

here. You may have made some headway, but I'm not cured."

"Hell, Jude," Wyatt whispered, and I felt the grin on his mouth as he trembled under me.

It left me without any doubt of his true intentions and an even harder dick.

"Tack room next door," he growled, nipping my lip before turning to open the stall door.

I heard a low rumbling whinny behind me and whirled around to face Chief.

A horse. It's only a horse.

Balls to the wall, Jude. Balls to the wall.

To my surprise, I took a step forward and reached out to pet Chief's muzzle. With a *very* flat hand. Maybe these animals weren't all evil little shits.

"Should I be jealous?" Wyatt asked, as I stroked Chief's nose, my hand barely shaking.

I snorted and gave the horse one last pat before slowly backing into Wyatt. He slid his warm hand into mine and pulled me out of the stall after him.

We entered a room filled with an array of hay bales that looked like they were used as tables and chairs. Saddles and bridles were stacked on wooden pegs that lined three of the four walls. Large trunks took up the rest of the space.

Wyatt locked the door, the sound of the iron hinges clanking shut turning me on rather than instilling fear.

I wrapped my arms around him from behind, burying my face in his hair, inhaling him. "You're sure we're out of sight of any children, parents, or other innocent bystanders?" I asked as he rotated in my arms to face me.

"They've all gone home by now," he replied with a sexy grin, tugging my hoodie up and over my head. He tossed it onto one of the hay bales. "Besides, this stable is strictly off limits to anyone but ranch personnel."

I briefly thought that Liz might be looking for me as I untucked Wyatt's shirt and pulled it off, but one glimpse at his fine body had me tossing that thought out as easily as I tossed Wyatt's shirt to lie with my hoodie. Fuck, he was fine—all hot skin and smooth chest, together with those muscles tanned to golden perfection. He must live without a shirt. The image had me panting as I ran my hands over him, feeling his nipples harden under my touch.

His hands found their way under my shirt, and I gasped at the shock of his rough skin against mine. I ripped my shirt off and flung it over to the pile we were making. He growled and I pushed him back with both hands so that he landed on his back in the clothes. He grunted with a smile on his face as I climbed on top of him. He gripped my hips and I ground into him, our moans indistinguishable.

I leaned down to suck at his neck while his fingers found my hair, casting aside my beanie to scratch at my scalp. I purred, kissing across his delectable abs and then licking at the soft skin above his waistband. His muscles quivered under my lips, his sexy murmurs and breaths pushing me to get to that hard bulge below even faster. I tore at his jeans, unzipping them until the thick cock underneath strained to be freed.

"Well hello, cowboy," I whispered as he lifted his hips so I could work his jeans and boxers down.

He chuckled as his cock bobbed upward, dark pink and wet.

My mouth watered.

I inhaled the sweet musk at the base of his dick. He smelled like heaven as I sucked his balls.

"Damn, that's hot, Jude..." He had risen up on his elbows to watch as I wrapped my hand around his thick cock. I licked up the shaft, exploring each velvety contour, until I took him down my throat.

"Oh God..."

He filled my entire mouth, and I had to concentrate not to gag. It's not a horrible problem to have.

He grabbed at my hair and clutched at my head, squirming under me as I continued to suck him deep and slow. "You...

you gotta stop."

I pulled off of him. "Why?"

"'Cause I want a taste before we get off together."

I groaned. Like I was going to argue with that.

"Get those pants down," he said, sitting up and licking his lips.

I hustled to undo my jeans and push them to my ankles along with my boxer briefs. My cock sprang free, dripping. Wyatt moaned at the sight, and I about busted a nut right there at the ravenous look on his face.

I stood on the hay bale, and by some wonderful magic my cock was perfectly aligned with his mouth. He seized it, spreading my pre-come around the head with his fingers. I had to grab onto his shoulders for support as my legs nearly gave out. His touch made me want to jump out of my skin. How he could stroke with such tenderness and passion, with those rough, calloused hands was beyond comprehension. "Fuck, Wyatt, you better start tasting, or you're going to cause an explosion."

And suddenly his mouth was on me, taking my cock until his nose touched my belly. "Christ..."

He hollowed his cheeks, sucking like a pro. I wanted to keep watching, but I knew I'd blow in seconds if I did. I dropped my head back and let out a strangled cry, worried I'd bring the entire ranch to a screeching halt.

Dangerously close to coming, again, I pulled at his hair to stop.

He slid off my dick. "You taste incredible," he said huskily. He hauled me with him as we lay back on the hay bale, side by side.

I looked into Wyatt's eyes, flashes of familiarity still teasing the back of my mind, but I moved it aside as Wyatt's fist curled around my cock and stroked.

"So damn sexy," he said, his rough hand concentrating on my swollen head, working it to the point I could barely think.

"Me?" I said in between pants. "You're the one who belongs in a Western-themed Calvin Klein ad. Oh fuck..." My eyes fluttered closed as Wyatt's cock pressed against mine and he began stroking both of us together.

"Jude, I'm ridin' the edge already," his voice was raw and breathy and it made me squirm with need.

"Uh huh," I managed, then licked at his stubbled jawline. His head tilted back and he grunted.

I couldn't help thrusting my hips in time with his fist, bringing me closer and closer to a massive eruption.

"You ready, hon?" he asked, the term of endearment surprising me, but somehow making me even hotter.

I was a goner. My breathing sped out of control, my stomach rolling with each stroke, inside and out. "Yeah, yeah," I said quickly, as sparks ignited under my nuts and behind my eyes. "Fuck, I'm coming, Wyatt!" My orgasm detonated, cum shooting out of my cock as he continued to pump me.

"Oh, damn, Jude!" Wyatt came undone a millisecond after I did. He moaned loudly, startling some of the horses, considering the rustling and whinnies.

We jerked like crazy and I latched onto his chest, feeling the hot come land on our bellies. After my name tumbled from his mouth, he stilled, except for the rise and fall of his body clamoring for air. I caught the reflection of his skin glistening with sweat in the dim light of the tack room and smiled. I never thought I'd ever have this much fun with a cowboy, in a stable, on a ranch…next to a horse.

I crawled on top of Wyatt to avoid the sharp edges of hay poking at my body, not caring about the mixture of sweat and come between us. My head rested on his shoulder as he wrapped me in strong arms.

"I can't believe we just did that…" I sighed. "Here."

Wyatt chuckled and it vibrated through my chest and gut. "Me neither. Please don't think this is what I do. I've never—"

I put two fingers to his mouth and raised up to look at him. "I don't, cowboy." I searched his eyes, and they still gave me a sense I'd seen them before. I was beginning to think something beyond this world could be involved. What the heck was happening to me?

Wyatt kissed my fingers and I smiled, returning to lie on his shoulder.

"You sure are good at this therapy thing. Shit, I'll be forgetting everything that happened to me at Triple H Ranch before long."

He stiffened under me. "Did you say Triple H?"

I tensed, not used to the rigidity in his body. "Yeah, that's the ranch we'd go to in Montana."

"Oh hell," he said, squeezing me tight. "My older brother, Brett, worked there some time ago."

I instantly pushed off him and began pulling up my pants when I heard the name. "*Brett* is your brother?" But as I looked into Wyatt's eyes I knew the answer. No wonder he looked familiar. "He was the worst. He'd laugh when he'd kick the snot out of me!" I zipped up and reached around Wyatt for my shirt as he sat up.

"I'm not my brother," he said, and grabbed my arm. We both looked down at it as I started shaking. "Jude…" he whispered, sympathy in his voice.

I managed to pull out of his grasp and put my shirt on, attempting to do it without trembling, and failing miserably. The memories of Brett and his crew and every cruel thing he did made it impossible. I wanted to grab my hoodie and beanie and jet out of this place, but Wyatt still sat on our stuff. I could've left without them. yet something in Wyatt's kind eyes, kindness I never saw in his brother's eyes, kept me there.

"Brett's in prison. He got in a bar brawl and was convicted of aggravated assault after two of the guys suffered major injuries. He's servin' a ten year term." Wyatt stood to pull up his jeans and fasten them. "But he deserves a lot more for all the pain he's caused to scores of folks…and kids."

My mind whirled. How could this sweet, sexy man be related to such a jerk-off?

Wyatt sat back down and gazed at me. "My family tried to help him with his anger issues, but he didn't like anyone thinkin' he needed help, let alone offerin' it. Thankfully, I didn't get much of his wrath. I worried he'd go after my dad, then he left home at seventeen. Never heard from him again. We found out about the prison time from a friend. I'm so sorry for everythin' he put you through."

I stood there, mouth open, unable to find something to say. Wyatt had to live with that bastard? And he was apologizing to me...for that asshole's behavior?

He reached for me, and suddenly I was curled in his lap, sobbing like a fucking hormonal teenager. He rocked me, rubbing my back, letting my tears spill over his bare shoulders. I felt safe and protected—just like I had the first time he wrapped his arms around me.

Once I had sufficiently soaked the entirety of his neck and shoulder, I wiped at my eyes. I felt like an ass for many reasons. Mostly for *ever* allowing anyone to make me that afraid...of anything, especially the truly remarkable man holding me.

Buzzing came from the clothes behind Wyatt. I reached to grab my phone in my hoodie pocket. A text from Liz lit up the screen.

Where are you? We have to go. I only have the sitter for another hour.

"I have to get back to Liz. She's ready to leave." I moved off of Wyatt's lap and rubbed my hands over my face. I felt as if I'd run a marathon then cried for hours at the finish line. Pathetic.

"I could give ya a ride home," Wyatt offered, and my gut clenched at the possibility of spending the rest of the night with him.

"That is...tempting, but I really should smooth things over with Liz. And there's a certain little boy that needs to hear how awesome this place is. I want him excited to be here on Wednesday."

Wyatt smiled and twisted to grab our clothes. He handed me my hoodie and beanie. "Is it too soon to tell ya how much you've gotten under my skin?"

I chuckled and my face burned up. Damn cowboy.

We finished dressing and as I adjusted my beanie, I asked. "Is Dr. Ackerman gay?"

Wyatt laughed. "What brought that up?"

"I think Liz has a bit of a crush on her. Just want to know

that the good doctor won't take advantage."

Wyatt grinned wide and brought a hand up to stroke my cheek. "You're awfully sweet, ya know that? Lookin' out for your BFF."

"Shut up." I went to push his hand away, but grabbed it instead...and kissed it. Shit, I was going soft.

Wyatt found his hat and settled it on his head. "Yep, Simone's gay. It'd do her good to get out and have some fun—enjoy someone else's company. You won't have to worry. She's great."

That eased my mind. I didn't want to have to kick anyone's ass. I really wasn't very good at it.

He reached into his back pocket and pulled out a business card. "So, you gonna call me?" He put the card in my hand, his eyes sparkling.

I brought my phone out and tapped the number in as he watched. "As long as I can send you dirty pics, too."

"Like ya have to ask."

I smirked.

"I want to take you out, Jude. And I'd love to see ya skate." He said, snatching a piece of hay from my hair.

"Don't say such sexy things or you'll have me eating out of the palm of your hand as easily as Chief." I sighed and kissed him softly. "Anytime, cowboy," I whispered against his lips.

Wyatt hummed. "Ya better go before I decide I want more."

I quivered and adjusted my cock. Damn him for making me hard again.

"Get outta here," he said, turning me around and patting my ass.

I walked forward and looked back at him. "I'll call."

"Can't wait," Wyatt replied, and shoved his hands in his pockets as he watched me walk away.

Once I made it outside the stable, I texted Liz.

Me: OMW

Liz: Where were u?

Me: In with Wyatt and his horse, Chief.

Liz: Conscious?

Me: Yes. Wise-ass.

Liz: So u have the hots for a cowboy?

Me: Did you see him? Seriously...he's fucking amazing.

Liz: Must B. He got u in with a horse. I'm astounded, loverboy. :-P

Me: Shut-up. BTW Dom will <3 this place.

Liz: I know...but I'm glad you're on board. He'll be thrilled when u tell him. :D

Me: Yes. Yes.

Liz: I might also think about letting u teach him to skate.

Me: Don't tease.

I spotted the car and waved at her.

Liz: I'm not.

Me: XO

I pumped my fist in the air and opened a message to Wyatt.

Me: Too soon?

Within seconds a response came through.

Wyatt: Never.

I grinned.

Me: I could use more cowboy therapy.

Wyatt: Anything.

Me: Tomorrow @ 6pm—Glenhaven Skate Park. Dinner after.

Wyatt: Sounds perfect.

Me: Think about me?

Wyatt: Constantly. Now where's my dirty pic? :D

I laughed and shook my head. Cowboys.

A CHANGE OF PACE

BY DREW HUNT

"STOP IT! SOMEONE could come in!" Ian "Rusty" Redfern said, pushing at Bill's chest, forcing him to retreat.

Bill Webster stepped back from Rusty's hospital bed. "I just wanted to kiss you 'cause…" Bill wanted to show Rusty how much Bill cared for him, worried about him, loved him.

"Well don't," Rusty grumped, fussing with his blanket. "Fucking thing itches. And this gown…" He made a face and moved around in the bed.

Bill stuck his hands in the pockets of his Wranglers so he wouldn't be tempted to reach out and straighten the bedding.

Rusty let out a huff of air. "I'm sorry, Billy," he said, turning sad eyes Bill's way.

Bill's heart melted as it always did when Rusty called him "Billy" and gave him the sad-eyed look. His hands itched to touch Rusty again, but he remained resolute. When they were on the ranch, Rusty was much more open about their relationship. But in public, where folks he didn't know could see or hear, he locked himself in the closet.

Over the past few months, Bill had noticed Rusty slowing down. At first the older man denied it, but his symptoms eventually became too obvious to ignore. When Rusty admitted to periods of dizziness as well as passing out once or twice, Bill got worried and nagged Rusty to go see the doctor. Rusty steadfastly refused.

Bill would be lying if he said he didn't miss their marathon hard, sweaty fuck sessions—Rusty's idea of foreplay was to kick off his cowboy boots before launching himself on top of Bill—but the gentler, more romantic pace of late was wonderful, too. Evenings spent just sitting, cuddling, kissing, and falling asleep together reminded Bill of the earlier days of their relationship when they were first exploring the depths of their love.

The fifty-year-old foreman of the Lazy W was used to being in charge and leading by example. But Rusty's enforced slowing down meant he couldn't be the foreman he wanted—no, needed—to be, so Bill renewed his efforts to get Rusty to go to the doctor.

"Last time I saw the quack he put me on beta blockers. I bet that's why I feel like shit now. I'm gonna stop taking them," Rusty had declared.

"The hell you are!" Bill countered.

It took weeks of arguing before Rusty finally gave in and Bill drove him into town.

Two weeks after that doctor visit, there they were, in a hospital room, waiting for Rusty to have surgery. Yes, the beta blockers were partially to blame for what the doctor had called bradycardia something or other, but no, Rusty couldn't quit the pills and he needed a pacemaker.

"This is all your fault," Rusty snapped. "I don't need one of those fucking things stuck in my chest! I'm too young. If I just rest up a few days and stop taking those fucking—"

"Shut up!" Bill said louder than he'd intended. More quietly he continued, "You do need a pacemaker, and you have to keep taking the meds for your blood pressure. Doc Hathaway said so."

"What the fuck does he know?"

Bill ground his teeth.

"He hardly looks old enough to be out of short pants."

Dr. Hathaway did look young. Certainly younger than Bill's own thirty-two years. Attempting to lighten the mood, Bill said, "You like younger men."

Rusty grunted. "Yeah, right. Saddled with 'em."

If you looked up "sexy cowboy daddy" in the dictionary there'd be a picture of Rusty, stripped to the waist, his lightly-furred ripped chest glistening with…

"And the quack is just as bossy as you, too," Rusty said, breaking Bill's erotic mental musings.

"Yeah, yeah." The sudden tenting of Bill's jeans forced him to sit in the chair next to Rusty's bed rather than pace the small room with its three walls and one curtain. "We both know that you don't ever do anything you don't want to."

"You saying I'm stubborn?"

"As a mule."

"Prefer bull," Rusty said, failing to hide a smirk.

"And you're still as strong and as virile as one, too." Bill patted Rusty's left biceps but removed his hand before Rusty could object.

Rusty snorted.

"And even if you don't think so now, you will when they fit that device in your chest."

"Doubt it," Rusty said quietly, turning his head away.

It was pointless reminding him of what the doctor had said about his heart beating too slowly to get enough oxygen to his muscles and organs, and how, once the pacemaker was doing its thing, Rusty would be almost back to full strength. Rusty didn't trust doctors and so didn't believe what they told him, and that was that, end of story.

"I'm only doing this to shut you up, stop you worrying."

Speaking quietly, so no one passing outside in the hallway would hear, Bill said, "I worry because I love you. So fucking much."

Rusty turned to face Bill, his glower softening, and mouthed, "Love you, too."

That was it, Bill had to kiss his man. But no sooner had he got to his feet and leaned over the bed than the curtains parted and a nurse pushing a cart entered. Thinking quickly, Bill straightened Rusty's blanket before backing away and starting to sit. Then his southern manners kicked in and he straightened up again.

"Ma'am." Bill's right hand automatically reached up to touch the brim of his hat. Too late he realized he'd taken the hat off and put it on the foot of Rusty's bed.

Rusty snickered and Bill shot him a look. Rusty had often teased Bill about how unsettled he became around women.

The middle-aged nurse closed the curtain. "Good morning, gentleman. I just need to take a few measurements, Mr. Redfern."

"Rusty," Rusty corrected.

Despite the seriousness of their situation, Bill's mind instantly flashed the thought that he could tell the nurse Rusty's most important measurement.

The nurse unrolled the blood pressure cuff. "Rusty because of your last name?"

"No, 'cause of my red hair. Well, used to be red," Rusty mumbled.

Bill thought Rusty's curly hair was just as sexy as it had been the first day he met the older cowboy.

"Do you know how much longer it'll be before...?" Rusty asked, allowing the nurse to wrap the cuff around his left upper arm.

"First patient went down about an hour ago. You're next. So not too much longer." She popped something on Rusty's right pointer finger and stuck something else in his right ear. "Try not to worry. It's a routine procedure."

"Might be routine for you, nurse, but it's the first time I've been opened up."

"I'm sure Dr. Hathaway explained what will happen. The 'opening up' will be a small incision near your left armpit." She pointed.

She made a few notes on her tablet computer then disconnected Rusty from the equipment. "You'll be fine. We haven't lost a patient this year."

"It's only February," Rusty grumbled.

The nurse patted Rusty's arm and smiled reassuringly. "I'll see you later, Mr. Redfern."

"Rusty," he corrected again.

"Thanks, nurse," Bill said, finding the edge of the chair with the backs of his legs. When she left he sat down and let out a sigh.

BILL SAT IN the hospital cafeteria, silently staring down into his cup of black coffee. A plate of wheat toast lay untouched on the table in front of him. The room was fairly quiet, save for a low hum of voices and the gentle scrape of silverware on plates. This suited Bill's mood. Despite half the tables being occupied by a mixture of patients in robes and folks in regular street clothes, the place still had an uncomfortable, sterile atmosphere.

Bill took a sip of coffee and grimaced. Too late he remembered the warning the nurse on Rusty's ward had given. Bill should have gotten a bottle of soda or maybe just plain water from the water cooler, but he couldn't summon up the energy to get up from the table for some.

Bill and Rusty had had to get up early, even by their standards, and leave the Lazy W well before sunup in order to get to the city in time for Rusty to be admitted. Nance, the ranch cook, had offered to make Bill something, but Bill had politely refused. He couldn't eat, he was too nervous, and also with Rusty having to fast, he didn't think it right to eat in front of the guy.

Bill set down his coffee and picked up a slice of toast. He bit down. The toast was soggy and cold. It tasted like cardboard but he forced himself to chew, then swallow.

Mechanically, Bill ate the rest of the slice, but couldn't face the second. He picked up his coffee cup once again. Despite his outward confidence—especially in front of Rusty—Bill was scared that something would go wrong. Doctors discovered all kinds of unexpected things when they got someone on the operating table. Bill remembered Rusty's frightened look when the orderlies came to wheel him away. Despite his usual closed up nature in public, Rusty had stretched out his arm to Bill and grasped his hand tightly and quietly asked, "You'll be here when

I get back?"

For a second Bill thought about making a joke about how he would if he didn't find a better offer, but the idea died almost as soon as he thought of it. He just bit his lip and nodded a yes. Bill gave Rusty's hand a squeeze, then reluctantly let go of it. He then watched his lover being wheeled away, all the while keeping up his mask of confident support.

The memories caused Bill's hands to shake so much, he set down his cup. Mentally he told himself to cowboy the hell up. Rusty would be fine. He was a fighter.

In an effort to improve his mood, Bill pulled up one of his favorite and most erotic memories—the first time he and Rusty met.

TWENTY-TWO-YEAR-OLD BILL WEBSTER was out of work because the ranch owner's son had been kicked out of college and needed a job. As Bill had been last in, he was first out. Armed with a letter of recommendation and the advice to try at the Lazy W two counties over, Bill had climbed aboard his Harley and ridden west. He'd passed through the Lazy W's wooden archway and rode up the long driveway, impressed at the healthy look of the cattle grazing in the well-maintained pastures. He circled around the neat and tidy ranch yard and stopped next to a ranch hand unloading feed from the back of a pickup.

"Looking for the boss," Bill announced once he'd cut the engine and taken off his helmet.

"Uh huh?" the handsome cowboy disinterestedly asked as he leaned against the side of the pickup, regarding Bill with a bored expression.

Bill, showing confidence he didn't quite feel, introduced himself and explained what he wanted.

"You'd have to talk to Rusty. He's the foreman. But I know we don't got no need for more hands."

Bill's spirits dimmed. "Well, I'm here now, so...the foreman you say?"

The tall, lean cowboy shrugged his narrow shoulders and jerked his head toward a set of open barn doors. "Rusty's in there."

Bill dismounted his motorcycle and engaged the kickstand. He walked into the barn's dark interior, the familiar smells of shavings, hay, and horses washing over him. As with the rest of the ranch, Bill was impressed by how well-maintained everything seemed. Clearly lots of money and man-hours had gone into keeping the place looking so good.

Bill walked down the swept-clean aisle, noting how tidy each stall was. He heard a soft baritone quietly singing and walked toward the sound. Turning to look into the final stall on his right, Bill froze in place. A perfectly formed ass hugged by faded Wranglers swayed in rhythm to its owner's movements. The cowboy—presumably the Rusty he was looking for—was naked from the waist up, a folded green T-shirt tucked into his belt. Rusty straightened to dump a manure scoop of dirty shavings into a wheelbarrow. A solid black colt in a neighboring stall nickered, no doubt disturbed at the presence of a stranger. Rusty stopped singing and offered a few words of comfort to the horse through the stall's bars. The colt moved closer to the partition and Rusty reached through the bars to pet the horse. "You're a good boy, Ranger."

The horse let out a long huff of air and pressed harder against the wooden wall. Bill's dick, which had been half-hard at the sight of the sexy older man, now was at full bone. Bill swallowed, but resisted the urge to adjust himself.

Rusty turned, evidently feeling Bill's eyes on him. If his rear view was fine, it was nothing to the perfection that was Rusty's front. Solid full chest, strong ranch-honed muscles softened by a light carpet of red chest hair, thick arms, granite chin with maybe a day or two's growth of beard, firm cheekbones, piercing green eyes, and a dusting of freckles across the bridge of a wide nose. More red hair peeked out from under a battered black cowboy hat.

If Rusty was surprised to see a stranger checking him out, he showed no sign. "You must be Bill Webster." The man's speech was a slow drawl, low and deep.

Bill's balls ached. He opened his mouth, found it dry, closed it, swallowed, and tried again. "Yes, sir."

Rusty ambled out of the stall, his walk one of the sexiest things Bill had ever seen. He pulled off his right work glove and held his hand out for Bill to shake. "Names Ian Redfern. Though most folks just call me Rusty."

Bill accepted the proffered hand—warm, dry—strong, firm—and instantly shot a load in his jockeys. "Oh, God."

"Like I said, most folks just call me Rusty," the man said, the corners of his eyes crinkling.

For the first time in his life, Bill was flustered. "Yes, uh, sorry, sir, uh, Rusty. I...oh, hell."

His expression and tone not changing, Rusty asked, "Can I have my hand back?"

Bill instantly let go Rusty's hand. "Sorry." Thanks to a miracle he managed to ask something sensible. "You were expecting me?"

"Foreman at the Triple G called this morning, said you'd probably be by."

"Uh, right." Bill was surprised but pleased his old boss had gone to the trouble. But then Bill had been a good worker. "But, uh, I guess you don't have any work."

Rusty took off his hat and wiped his sweaty face with his T-shirt.

The man's pale skin and red hair made Bill think of strawberries and cream. He licked his lips, so wanting to taste Rusty's skin to see if the fantasy matched with reality. Bill became aware that Rusty had said something that he hadn't caught. "I'm sorry, what did you say?"

"What makes you think we don't have any work?" Rusty repeated.

Bill recounted his conversation with the cowboy in the ranch yard.

"I do the hiring and firing around here, not Slim Walker," Rusty said, putting his hat back on his head and puffing out his impressive chest.

Bill fought hard to keep his gaze on Rusty's handsome face and not drop to the man's impressive set of chest muscles.

"The boss has just bought another thousand acres, so we need another hand." Without missing a beat, he continued with, "Heard you're good with horses."

"Uh, yes. I pretty much ran the barn at the Triple G."

Rusty nodded and scratched his chest. Bill lost the battle and found himself staring at the man's pecs.

"Well, I'm in charge of the barn here."

Bill forced himself to meet Rusty's eyes.

"So long as you don't forget that, you'll get on okay."

"Yes, sir. Uh, Rusty."

"You can change in the tack room and help me muck the last couple stalls."

"Thank you," Bill said, realizing the interview was over and he'd got the job.

If only it had been as easy to get the man as it had the job. Rusty was gay, Bill was sure about that, but no matter how hard Bill tried to get close to the older man, Rusty kept things on a professional if friendly footing, treating Bill like he did every other ranch hand.

BILL'S CHANCE TO get closer to the older stud came a couple of months later. Bella, Rusty's mare, had been showing signs she would foal that night and Rusty had asked Bill if he'd watch her with him. So there he was, in a birthing stall with his idol, watching Bella pick at the contents of her hay rack.

"This will be her second," the proud if anxious cowboy said, pacing the large stall like a nervous expectant father. "The first went off okay, but..."

Bill smiled to himself. He'd never seen Rusty in anything other than complete control. He guessed it was different when the horse was your own. "Want some more coffee? I think she'll be a while yet."

"Uh, yeah." Rusty came to sit on the stacked square bales of straw next to Bill.

As he poured from the Thermos, trying to keep his hand steady, Bill could feel Rusty's body heat through the layers of clothing that separated them.

"Thanks for doing this," Rusty said, accepting the cup, their fingers touching briefly.

"Pouring you coffee?" Bill asked.

"No." Rusty shook his head. "Staying up like this. I wouldn't trust anyone else."

Bill swallowed, knowing Rusty had just paid him a huge compliment. "'S okay."

He wanted to say more, wanted to tell Rusty that ever since their first meeting, he'd known Rusty was the man for him. Wanted to say that he'd pictured the two of them living in cowboy domestic harmony in Rusty's cottage—white picket fence, couple of dogs and…but he knew he couldn't tell Rusty any of that.

Rusty set down his cup, took his hat off his head, and began to run the brim through his fingers. "Hope she'll be okay."

"She'll be fine," Bill assured, putting a steadying hand on Rusty's forearm. Okay, so what if his motives for touching the older cowboy weren't totally pure.

"Yeah." Rusty let out a long breath. "I know. Just being stupid."

"Not stupid at all." Bill didn't know where he got the courage, but he slid his hand down Rusty's arm to take the man's hand. "Bella means a lot to you. It's natural you'd be concerned."

"She's all I got, after…"

Bill waited for Rusty to go on, but when the man didn't, he prompted, "After?"

"Bella was Freddie's horse. She wouldn't let anyone else ride her so the boss gave her to him. But when Freddie died

Bella chose me as her human. Weird, but…" Rusty shrugged his wide shoulders.

Bill had heard some of the older hands talk about Freddie, he'd picked up that the man had died, but he didn't know how.

"But enough about my boring past," Rusty said in an obvious effort to change the subject. "Tell me about Bill Webster. You're kinda young to know as much about ranching as you do."

Bill shrugged and started to tell Rusty the carefully edited version of his life story. However, the cozy intimacy of their lit corner of an otherwise darkened barn, the late hour, the warm solid presence next to him, all combined to encourage Bill to tell Rusty the whole truth, beginning with being kicked out of the house when his bigoted father found him in bed with the second baseman on the high school's baseball team.

When Rusty didn't react to learning Bill was gay, Bill went on with, "Wouldn't care, but Sam, the baseball player, wasn't my type."

Rusty turned so he was almost facing Bill. "And what is your type?"

Bill swallowed, gathered up his courage, and looked Rusty square in the face. "Someone older, more mature, wiser, stronger, dependable, genuine."

"And do you think you see those things in me?" Rusty asked quietly.

Bill nodded, unable to believe the sudden turn of events. Was he dreaming? Had he fallen asleep on duty? Heart pounding and mouth dry, Bill leaned forward, intent on kissing Rusty's full, pink lips.

Rusty turned his head to the side and stood. "Shit!"

It took Bill a second to realize what had happened. Rusty was standing over Bella, who had laid down. The not-yet-born foal's nose was poking out of Bella's vulva, along with its front hooves. No, Bill took another look. There was just one hoof. "Fuck!"

"Call Dr. Russell!" Rusty demanded, sinking to his knees behind Bella. "Fuck, I was afraid something like this would happen."

Gathering himself, Bill stood and approached Bella to get a

closer look. "I've seen this before. If—"

"Call the fucking vet already!" Rusty snapped, causing Bella and some of the other horses nearby to become unsettled.

"Okay, boss. Doing it now." Bill pulled his cell out of his jeans pocket and brought up his contacts.

Unfortunately, the vet was on another call some distance away and wouldn't be able to get to them for a couple of hours at least. The news caused Rusty to start swearing. Bill did his best to keep both cowboy and mare calm. He assured both vet and cowboy that he'd seen this before and ran through what he'd done the previous time.

"That's it, son, you got it," the vet said. "Just make sure you slick up your arms thoroughly, all the way to your armpits."

"I know," Bill said before telling Rusty the plan.

Rusty didn't look happy, but Bill knew there was no alternative. Bella couldn't wait for the vet to arrive. Rusty was somewhat reassured when he was told the vet would stay on the line and Bill put the phone on speaker.

Within a few moments, Rusty and Bill were stripped to the waist and had slicked up. The vet directed Rusty to lay on his side on the stall floor and gently push on the foal's nose, pushing it back up the birth canal. Bill then lay chest to chest with Rusty—determinedly focusing on Bella and the foal and not on being so close and intimate with the object of his affections.

As Rusty held the foal back, Bill searched for and found the errant hoof. Lining it up, they both withdrew their arms and stood up.

Within minutes the foal emerged.

"Congratulations," Bill told Rusty. "You're the proud father of a healthy filly."

They watched Bella get to her feet and lick the birth sac and continue to clean up her baby.

Rusty's smile lit up the already bright birthing stall.

"What you gonna call her?" Bill asked. "Rustina?"

The vet laughed down the phone.

"I was thinking Billamina," Rusty countered.

Despite the vet still being on the line and their arms covered with birthing fluid, Rusty and Bill shared a hug and a kiss.

Later, as the men sat watching Bella and her unnamed filly sniff each other, Rusty cleared his throat.

Sensing his boss was about to say something important, Bill turned to face the man.

"Before all this," Rusty waved in the direction of the mare and foal, "I asked if you thought I was the kind of guy you were looking for."

"Yes?" Bill's heart rate picked up.

"You're a great guy, Billy. Any man would be proud to have you as a partner."

Bill's heart sank. He could tell a "but" was coming.

"But I can't." More quietly he added, "Not again."

"Again?" Bill didn't understand. Was Rusty talking about Freddie? Had they been more than foreman and ranch hand?

Rusty sighed and tugged at his red curls.

Taking Rusty's hand, Bill said, "Stop it. You'll give yourself a headache."

Rusty calmed but made no move to let go of Bill's hand. Bill was happy to just sit there and wait, passing the time by watching Bella bond with her new foal.

"We'd had an argument. Me and Freddie," Rusty eventually said. "Can't remember what it was about now. For the last few months of his life we fought a lot. He was a stubborn son of a bitch." A ghost of a smile appeared on Rusty's lips. "I know, just like me."

Bill returned the smile but stayed quiet.

"We fought, he stormed out of the cottage, I heard his murdercycle start up and go down the driveway. Couple hours later the cops were at the door to the big house." Rusty swallowed and Bill squeezed his hand. "Seems a semi didn't stop at a light and…Freddie was dead on arrival at the hospital."

"Oh, no."

"So I can't…won't go through that again."

Bill slipped off the bales of straw and knelt between Rusty's legs. "I'm not Freddie. Please, Rusty. Give me a chance. Hell, I'll even sell the fucking bike. You're way more important to me than a hunk of metal."

Rusty looked down at him, but remained silent.

Bill tried for humor. "And I thought you thought I looked hot in my leathers. I saw you checking me out the other day."

"I did. You are hot, whatever you wear. But you'd be cold lying dead on a mortuary slab."

"CODE BLUE!" THE hospital's public address system blared out. "Room five-sixteen!"

Rusty was in that room! Bill's stomach lurched and he feared he'd throw up. He leapt to his feet, knocking his chair over in the process. He snatched up his hat and ran out of the cafeteria and down the hallway. There was a knot of people in front of the bank of elevators. Through the pounding in his ears he could hear the code blue message playing on an endless loop in his head.

Bill charged through a door marked "Stairs" and took the steps two at a time. Despite being physically fit, he was finding it hard to breathe, and his vision was graying at the edges. Dimly he found it odd that he could hardly feel his feet as his boots pounded the stairs. Rusty was his…everything. He had to be okay, he just had to.

Turning a corner, Bill almost collided with an older lady coming down, holding a pair of crutches.

"Sorry, ma'am."

"You okay, young man?"

Bill didn't stop. He would never be okay again if anything happened to Rusty. He made it to Rusty's floor, ran down the hallway, and burst into the ward.

"Hey, where's the fire?" the nurse who'd checked Rusty's blood pressure earlier asked.

"Rusty," Bill gasped, out of breath.

"He's still in the OR."

"Code blue. I heard a code blue for his room."

The woman looked momentarily confused then understanding dawned. "That was for the fifth floor. This is the third floor. And, like I said, he isn't here, he's in the OR."

"Oh." Bill felt weak and sagged against the wall.

"Come on, sit down before you fall down." The nurse gestured to a chair next to the nurses' station. She then calmly explained that even if Rusty's heart had stopped in the OR, they wouldn't call a code blue because they had all the equipment to get it going again right there.

Bill felt doubly stupid, but a tiny part of him still worried that something was wrong.

"Tell you what. Do you want me to call down and see if anyone knows anything about how Mr. Redfern is doing?"

"No, that's okay. I was just..."

"You love him. I understand."

Bill was about to ask how she knew, but he guessed his over-the-top reaction had clued her in. Rusty would be pissed at their secret getting out.

"I'll make the call." She picked up a phone, dialed a number, and waited. "Gladys, it's Mary Simpson from CCU. Yeah, I know, long time." They exchanged pleasantries for a few moments, Bill trying not to fidget at the delay in getting any news. Eventually the nurse got to the point of the call. Then she lowered the receiver from her mouth and said, "She's just checking."

"Thanks." Bill fought the urge to bring his hands together in prayer. He was being stupid.

"He is...uh-huh...? Right. Thanks, Gladys." There was a slight pause, then the nurse continued, "Yes, next time she hosts one, ask her to send me an invite." The nurse replaced the receiver and turned to Bill. "Mr. Redfern is still in surgery but everything is going to plan."

"He's okay?"

She smiled. "Yes, he's okay."

Bill let out a breath.

"If you don't mind me saying so, you look...tired."

"Didn't sleep last night, what with the worry and having to get here early."

The nurse nodded. "If you go to Mr. Redfern's room, you could maybe rest on his bed? Though if anyone asks, I didn't tell you to do it."

Bill nodded, offered his thanks, and shuffled off to Rusty's room. Now the adrenalin had left his system, he felt totally wrung out. Another emotion washed over him—guilt. It was because of his pushing Rusty to have the surgery that they were here. Had he made Rusty have the pacemaker out of a need to keep the older man alive for his own selfish reasons? If Bill had left it up to Rusty then they'd both still be at the ranch. Even though they weren't married, hadn't had a ceremony, hadn't promised to be with each other in sickness and in health, Bill would gladly nurse Rusty because he loved the man so much.

Then Bill had another thought. Was some of Rusty's fear of hospitals because one had failed to save Freddie? The older man rarely mentioned his dead lover, and Bill was always reluctant to bring him up. Part of that was envy. How stupid was that? How could he be jealous of the time Freddie had had with Rusty?

Another idea sneaked, unwelcome, into Bill's brain. Did part of Rusty not want the pacemaker because he wanted to die and be with Freddie?

Bill blinked back tears. Thank God he was in Rusty's room with the curtain closed where no one could see him fall apart. He knew he was overtired, and that was why his brain was coming up with all these stupid ideas that didn't make any sense.

"Pull yourself together!" Bill told himself.

Bill eased off his boots and swung his legs onto the mattress. Even though Rusty had only been in the bed an hour or so, Bill could smell his man's scent on the pillow. That, more than anything, gave him comfort.

Maybe he'd just close his eyes for a minute. There was no chance he'd actually be able to sleep, not with the worry of Rusty still being in surgery.

BILL HAD FANTASIZED that now the truth was revealed, the older stud would throw Bill over his shoulder and haul Bill off to his cottage where they'd fuck, sleep, fuck, kiss, fuck, snuggle, and fuck. But Bill hadn't figured on the glacial pace Rusty took to make any important decisions.

Rusty's first reaction after Bill's confession was to be more affectionate when they were alone. Within a few days the tender looks and touches also occurred in front of the other hands. If anyone had a problem with their foreman being touchy-feely with another guy, they didn't show it. But then most of them probably remembered Rusty and Freddie being an item.

After a couple of weeks, Rusty told Bill that rather than eat at the big house with everyone else, he would cook supper in his cottage. Thinking this was it, Bill pressed his best shirt and newest pair of Wranglers. He nixed the idea of a bolo tie, but spritzed some cologne he'd been given for his twenty-first birthday.

As he stood in front of the sink shaving, he realized he didn't have anything to give Rusty as a gift. He thought of chocolates, flowers, bottle of wine. What did you give a guy on your first date? Bill had little experience. He didn't think, however, Rusty was the type of guy who'd appreciate chocolates or flowers, and he doubted the man was a wine drinker. Maybe a six pack of his favorite beer? Bill glanced at his wristwatch. He had to be at Rusty's in a quarter hour, and that wasn't long enough to get into town and back. And since he'd sold his motorcycle, or murdercycle as Rusty had called it, Bill would have had to borrow one of the ranch's vehicles. Anyway, Bill didn't know what Rusty's favorite beer was.

"Shit!" he said, noticing blood on his chin. He looked down and saw he'd got it on his shirt, too.

The evening had ended up being nice, very nice, but by the end of it Bill was no closer to his goal. Rusty was an excellent cook and they'd spent forever at the table, eating and talking. Then Rusty had looked up at the clock and declared they both had an early start in the morning so after a too-short hug and even briefer kiss on the lips, Bill found himself standing alone on the front porch. At least he'd found out what brand of beer Rusty liked.

OVER THE NEXT few weeks Bill found himself drawing ever closer to Rusty on an emotional level. He now could admit, if only to himself, that he was in love with the older stud.

Their courtship, for that was how Bill saw how Rusty was treating him, had progressed to walking hand-in-hand along the riverbank, having picnics in a meadow, and kissing under the stars, watching fireflies zip around them.

On one such evening, their heavy petting had led to Bill feeling Rusty's aroused manhood through his jeans, but when Bill had gone for the zipper, Rusty had stopped him.

"Rusty, please, I'm dying here"

Rusty smiled. "You ready? Don't just mean for sex, I'm talking about a relationship, commitment, monogamy. You're only twenty-two. You should be sewing your wild oats, not hitching up with—"

Bill rolled on top of Rusty and silenced him with a kiss. "If you were about to say something like 'not hitching yourself to an old man,' you can stop right there." Punctuating his words with frequent kisses, Bill went on, "Going slow these past few weeks has shown me that you're the man for me, the man I want to live with, settle down with, have sex with, make love with."

Rusty put his hands on the sides of Bill's face and lifted the younger man's head so they could properly see each other. Rusty was smiling. "So you saw why I was holding back."

Bill nodded.

"Cause I wanted nothing more than to pull down your pants that first day when I saw you in the barn and bend you over and fuck the snot out of you."

Bill was shocked at Rusty's language. He was also very turned on. He ground his hardness into Rusty's.

"But I didn't because I knew you were someone special. I hoped and prayed that, despite the age difference, you'd think I was special, too. And I also needed time to come to terms with me needing someone again, you know, after...Freddie."

"I know." Bill caressed Rusty's cheek. "And you are special." Bill broke Rusty's hold on his head and dipped down to kiss the man soundly on the lips.

"But I needed to be sure."

"And are you now?"

Rusty rolled them over so he was on top. They spent several minutes kissing, rubbing, and exploring, before Rusty got to his feet, offered Bill a hand up, and led his young lover to his cottage and his bed.

THE NEXT MORNING, Bill sat at the breakfast table with the other hands. The Lazy W being the small, tight-knit community that it was, people had a pretty good idea what had happened the night before and were ragging Bill about it. Oddly, no one said anything to Rusty, who was distant with everyone, including Bill. Did Rusty regret what they'd done? Had he changed his mind? Had Bill disappointed him in some way, done something that he didn't like? Bill didn't know. His stomach rebelled and he pushed his breakfast around his plate, not eating much of it.

Then Rusty began to give out the day's work assignments.

"…And, Bill, I want you and Slim to check the water tanks over on the eastern border. Take the Ford truck and load it with plumbing supplies, just in case."

Bill dropped his fork. He couldn't believe it. Why was Rusty sending him off to the farthest part of the ranch with the cowboy he got on least well with? Slim had been cold with him ever since Bill had rode onto the ranch his first day. "But what about Billhamina? The vet's coming this morning to check her bindings." Because the foal had had a difficult birth, her right foreleg was still unstable, although Bill was pretty pleased with the progress she was making.

"Gary will see to that," Rusty dismissed. "I've spoken to Nance, she's making up some bag lunches for you because you won't be back here until this afternoon." Rusty didn't look up from his page of notes and continued to rattle off chores for the rest of the hands.

BILL SPENT ONE of the most boring days he could remember, checking water tanks for leaks and seeing that they were pumping correctly. All were in good order, as he'd expected. Slim hardly said a word to him all day.

By mid-afternoon, the two cowboys were headed back to the ranch, Bill still no nearer figuring out what had crawled up Rusty's ass. Part of him wanted to get back there and have it out with Rusty, while another part craved to stay away longer, not wanting to know the reason for Rusty's odd treatment of him.

But arrive back they did, and after stowing the unused plumbing equipment, Bill rounded the corner of the ranch yard and stopped dead in his tracks when he saw what was going on outside Rusty's cottage.

Rusty, along with a couple of the hands, were about three quarters done putting up a white picket fence around the cottage's yard.

Spotting him just standing there, mouth open, Rusty set down his tools and jogged over. "Like it?"

Bill closed his mouth, swallowed, then asked, "What? Why?"

Rusty smiled and pulled Bill into a hug. "Did you know you talk in your sleep?"

"What?" Bill didn't understand.

"Well, lover, you do. What I heard last night was pretty interesting and darned hot. Though I gotta say, some of the things you said you wanted to do to me sounded like they'd be anatomically impossible."

"What?" Bill repeated. What had he blabbed in his sleep? "Oh, God."

"Yeah, you called me that." Rusty chuckled. "Reminds me of the first time we shook hands."

Bill felt his face heat as he recalled coming in his shorts like a lovesick idiot.

Rusty slapped him on the back. "Go wash up. We're expected at the Davidson's spread in a couple hours."

"Huh? Why?" Bill still wasn't capable of forming complete sentences.

"They have a litter of border collies that they're looking for good homes for."

Hell, he must have told Rusty everything.

"Now that we have a fenced in yard, we have a good home, wouldn't you say?"

Bill squeezed Rusty tightly. "You're perfect. Do you know that?"

"I KNOW. BUT you need to wake up 'cause you're in my bed."

"Huh?" Bill opened his eyes and sat up. He was in Rusty's hospital room and Rusty was lying on a gurney next to him. Bill yawned. "Did I fall asleep?"

"Sure did." Rusty and the two orderlies chuckled.

Bill felt a blush wash over the top half of his body. "Was I, uh, talking in my sleep?"

The orderly at the head of the gurney laughed. "Just a little, yeah."

"Crap!" Bill sprang off the bed and stood at the other side of the room, mortified.

Rusty started to lever himself up, but was told to take it easy by one of the orderlies. Rusty waited for the side of the gurney to be lowered and then was lifted into his bed, grumbling about how he wasn't helpless.

Bill, recovering from his embarrassment, reminded his lover what the doctor had said about what he could and couldn't do after his procedure.

"Doctors, what do they know?"

"A lot," Bill said, looking at the healthy pink of Rusty's skin. "You look good."

Rusty smiled. "Feel good." He turned to the orderlies. "Thanks, guys. Any idea when I can get out of here?"

"I expect the doc will be by later. He'll tell you when you can go," the orderly farthest from them said, opening the curtain.

"But I want to go now. I feel great!" Rusty protested.

"Good luck," the second orderly said, winking at Bill.

Did the man know about them? What had he said in his sleep? "Thanks," Bill said, nodding at the man. Once the orderlies and gurney had left and the curtain closed, Bill turned to his still smiling lover and opened his mouth to apologize for forcing Rusty into having the surgery.

But Before Bill could speak, Rusty took Bill's hand, gave it a squeeze, and said, "Thanks for pushing my stubborn ass into having this thing fitted. I feel great."

Bill smiled. No way would he crow. He was just glad to get his lover back in one piece, and seemingly as good as new. "What was it like?"

Rusty squeezed Bill's hand. "No problem. Weird though." At Bill's look of surprise, Rusty continued, "I was sure I saw Roy and Duke lying at my feet on the operating table."

"Huh?"

Much to Rusty's consternation in the early days, their dogs slept at the foot of their bed at home. But Bill didn't understand why Rusty thought he saw them in the operating room.

"The doc said that sort of thing ain't unusual," Rusty told him. "It's the drugs they pump you full of."

"Oh." Bill smiled and withdrew his hand from Rusty's. He didn't want his man to get upset with their public display of affection.

Rusty took Bill's hand again. "Been thinking," he said, raising Bill's hand to his lips.

"Don't raise your left hand above your head," Bill told him. "Remember what the doctor said."

"I'm trying to be romantic here," Rusty grumped, but remained smiling. "Life's too short to hide what I feel for you. This past few months have shown me that. I love you, Billy." More loudly he added, "And I don't care who knows it. Now come here so I can kiss you properly."

Rusty's right arm shot up and pulled Bill down toward him.

They shared a brief kiss, Rusty's lips feeling warm and soft and alive.

Bill started to rise but Rusty pulled him back down again. Bill resisted. "Stop it! Someone could come in!"

"Let 'em!" Rusty said, kissing Bill again.

FIREFLY RANCH
BY REBECCA JAMES

To Dad. Love you.

"I'VE BEEN HERE a month, Mary-Jim." Carver West looked out the window of the ranch business office at the long expanse of fields and men working with the Hereford cattle. "How am I supposed to do my job when one of my most competent hands is so antagonistic towards me? Did Sutter get along with Guy when he ran the place?"

"Sutter's the owner—everyone has to get along with him." Mary-Jim Landover, long-time bookkeeper at Firefly Ranch, sat at a desk piled with papers, a pen stuck behind her ear, ash-blond hair falling in tendrils from a half-hazard bun.

"Don't worry yourself about it, Boss Man. Bishop will come around."

"Please stop calling me Boss Man; it makes me uncomfortable." Carver turned from the window. He swung a chair around, straddled it, and rested his chin on folded arms.

"Well, get used to it; that's what we've always called the foreman around here. Come on, you can tell me…is Bishop the only one giving you a hard time? Just because you're pretty don't mean you can't run a ranch, and I'll have their balls for a necklace if they don't straighten up."

Carver ducked his head to hide the flush blossoming over his cheeks. Not only did he dislike being called "pretty," but Mary-Jim sounded as though she thought he needed protecting. Damn his sorry tendency to blush! He raised hardened eyes to her with no effect.

"Sorry, Boss Man. I know you're tough…but with that blond hair, those baby blue eyes, and legs that go on for miles…you're one cool drink of water, honey." Mary-Jim ended this assessment with a flirtatious wink, then laughed when Carver blushed again.

"Tell me what you know about Bishop Guy," Carver said. "I mean, more than I've learned working with the man for the past month—which is next to zero since he says as little as possible in my presence."

Leaning back in her chair, Mary-Jim took the pen from behind her ear and tapped it on her palm while she thought. She wore jeans, as pretty much everyone did on the ranch, and a Dallas Cowboys t-shirt under a blue sweater. Carver knew that not only did Mary-Jim keep Firefly Ranch in the black with her unerring instinct on how to cut costs without giving up quality, but she also managed to know everyone who worked there and much of what went on with them.

"I know he's worked here eight years and has a sick mother in Austin." Mary-Jim studied Carver's face, which had thankfully lost the warmth of its flush from a moment before.

"The man's got passive-aggression down to a fine art," Carver said. "He does what I tell him, but with an attitude that could freeze beer. I can't figure out what he's got against me—I haven't done anything to him."

"Oh, but you have."

"What?" Carver ran the past month through his mind on fast-forward. He was certain he had never said or done anything that warranted the kind of animosity Bishop Guy showed him. Carver had worked hard to prove himself to the work hands, and after a week on the job, every one of them had come to respect him and realize that, despite his surfer-boy looks, Carver could get down and dirty with the rest of them. Everyone except Bishop Guy.

"You took his job."

"I what?" Carver sat up straight, and Mary-Jim put up a hand to quiet him.

"I know, I know. Sutter hired you when he retired." She folded her hands on her desk. "The thing is, Bishop's put up with Sutter for a long time, obviously hoping to take over when he retired—something Sutter was always talking about." She leaned back again and sighed. "I think Bishop really could have used the raise in pay; I hear his mother has a lot of medical expenses."

"And Sutter decided Bishop wasn't up to par? That's not my fault!"

"Bishop would have made a good foreman," Mary-Jim said. "And Sutter knew it."

"Then why didn't Sutter give him the job?" Carver ran a hand through his hair. He was confused and wished Mary-Jim would just get to the point.

"Bishop's good at what he does, and he towed the line for Sutter," Mary-Jim said. "That wasn't the problem. Rumor has it that Bishop wouldn't give Sutter the one thing he really wanted from him, even when it came down to him not getting the job as foreman."

"And what's that?"

"Everyone around here couldn't help but notice that Sutter spent a good amount of time staring at Bishop's ass—not that it isn't worth staring at. But Bishop wouldn't give Sutter the time of day when it didn't have to do with the ranch, and he wasn't willing to change his mind in order to get the job as foreman."

"Are you saying what I think you're saying?"

"I'm just telling you what I heard, and judging by Sutter's lengthy infatuation with Bishop's physical assets, it makes sense. Anyway, what other reason would Sutter ignore the most obvious choice for the job and hire some stranger from California instead? No offense."

Seeing Carver's consternation, Mary-Jim shook her head. "Don't let it trouble you, Boss Man. You had nothing to do with it, and Bishop will come around, you'll see. He made his choice, after all."

"Some choice—either he gives in to unwanted sexual advances, or he loses the promotion he deserves. Is Bishop even gay?"

"Any particular reason you're asking?" Mary-Jim raised a brow, lips forming a smirk. When Carver just met her gaze with a sharp stare, she sighed and shrugged. "I don't think it's my place to say whether he is or he isn't."

Funny, you've said just about everything else, Carver thought but didn't say out loud. Mary-Jim may be a gossip, but the information would help him out; if it was true, that is. It could just be gossip, and Bishop might only be one of those men who resented working under someone who didn't meet the expectations of what he thought a ranch foreman should look like.

Bishop should talk—he wasn't exactly hard to look at himself. But his attractiveness lay in a rough and tumble appearance that was perfectly at home on a ranch.

"If you want something to worry about, Boss Man, worry about the snow headed our way." Mary-Jim returned her attention to the spreadsheets on her computer screen.

Mary-Jim was right. As Carver exited the main building and looked up at the gray, heavy-laden sky, he figured he had more important things to think about than Bishop Guy.

CARVER TRUDGED TO the barn in a flurry of snow. He'd spent the past twenty-four hours, other than the scant five he'd taken to sleep, making sure all of the three-sided sheds and fences were sound, and that there were plenty of hay bales and water in the corrals for the cattle. Satisfied, he headed to the barn where they housed the animals that required more nutrients and care in bad weather.

It irked Carver to think he might not have been first choice as foreman. Carver prided himself on his work experience as well as his work ethic, and being a pawn in Sutter's revenge against Bishop for not giving in to him made Carver angry. He reminded himself that the whole thing might not be true, but his irritation remained.

As Carver opened the barn door, a great gust of wind blew through, almost knocking him off his feet. He quickly shut it out and blinked into the dimness of the interior, waiting for his eyes to adjust. The sweet smell of hay met his nostrils, overlaid by the singular scent of the cows. A lantern glowed in a back stall, alerting Carver to another human presence.

"Hello?" In spite of the frigid weather, the barn was over-warm, and Carver peeled off his coat and hung it on one of the steel hooks on the wall.

He walked forward, eyes drawn to the man in the shadows systematically bending and straightening as he forked hay into the cow feeders. Carver immediately recognized Bishop Guy by his ass—high, curved, and what looked to be a perfect handful. It was no wonder that Tim Sutter ogled it. Realizing he was being no better than Sutter, Carver dragged his gaze upward.

"Shouldn't you be in your bunk for the night? It's getting nasty out." Carver stopped a few feet away and tried not to notice the play of muscles in Bishop's back as he continued to pitch the hay.

"I'm going to weather the storm in here." Bishop didn't turn to look at Carver. "A couple of the cows haven't been eating enough, and I want to make sure they do."

Several pairs of soft, bovine eyes regarded Carver from the surrounding stalls as though waiting for his reply.

"That's why I'm here." Carver rested his arms on the steel bars of the stall door. A long sweat stain caused the back of Bishop's shirt to cling to him, as did the curls of dark hair on his neck.

"I'm staying, so no need." Bishop straightened and stretched his back, muscles working beneath the denim shirt. "It's my job; I'm in charge." Carver's patience was wearing thin. "Yes, you are." Bishop stuck his pitchfork into the hay with a little more violence than necessary and finally turned. "You don't have to remind me."

"You resent me for it." Carver studied the man before him. He had a square jaw covered in dark stubble that leant a rough quality to an otherwise elegant face for a ranch hand; his nose was long and his forehead high without the promise of a receding hairline. But Bishop's eyes were what really drew Carver, the eyebrows dark and arched like a raven's wings over forest-green irises ringed in black, surrounded by the lushest lashes Carver had ever seen on a man. Carver lost track of his thoughts until he realized Bishop was staring at him, waiting for a reply.

"Sorry, what?"

"I said," Bishop spoke slowly, as though to a small and particularly stupid child, "why do you say that I resent you?"

"It's been obvious since day one in everything you do and say where I'm concerned." Carver fought to control his anger at Bishop's attitude and insubordination but found it a losing battle. He needed to know if what Mary-Jim had told him was true, or if Bishop was like every other man under Carver's charge who couldn't handle taking orders from a "pretty boy."

"I don't hate you." Bishop pushed past Carver and closed the stall gate. "I don't think about you at all."

"You're lying." The brief physical contact as Bishop's arm brushed against Carver's sent a ripple of awareness over Carver's skin that was difficult to hide.

Bishop swung around, and despite his belligerent look, Carver took a step toward him, the ghosts of dozens of others who had underestimated him in the past egging him on.

"You probably think someone who looks like I do has no business running a ranch. Go on, admit it. Wouldn't be the first time I've heard it."

The subsequent slow journey of Bishop's eyes over Carver's body made Carver's blood boil in his veins, and not only because he was angry.

"Too much of a coward to admit it?" Carver was determined to get a reaction out of the stoic man.

"Your looks have nothing to do with it, so get over yourself. You shouldn't be here at all." Bishop took a step closer until they were standing only inches apart. "I should have gotten the job!"

So Mary-Jim was right—Bishop resented Carver because he got the job. But did Bishop lose his chance at it because of sexual harassment?

"I've worked here for almost a decade," Bishop continued, voice growing louder in the quiet barn, "doing everything for that sonofabitch Sutter, helping him build this ranch into what it is today, and you come waltzing in here from God knows where and take over...it isn't fair!"

"California."

"What?"

"I came here from California." Carver crossed his arms over his chest. Didn't Bishop know anything about him after a month?

"Well, that figures."

"What's that supposed to mean?"

"Just look at you." Bishop gestured at Carver with his hand. "All blond and California-boy."

"Oh, say something I haven't heard a million times before, why don't you? I've proven myself here, and you damn well know it. It's not my fault you got passed over for this job; Sutter's the one who hired me, so why don't you take it up with him?"

"It wouldn't do me any good to talk to that snake. He made his decision."

"So, you take it out on me?" Carver shook his head. "Look, I know you've been dealt a raw deal, but I'm not the cause of it. Maybe you should file a lawsuit on Sutter for sexual harassment."

Bishop grew very still, a wary look settling over his face.

Suddenly, the sounds of cows shifting in the straw and rhythmically chewing their cud seemed incredibly loud around them.

"What are you talking about?" Bishop's gaze bored into Carver, and Carver wondered if it had been a mistake to bring it up. But he had to know.

"Word is that Sutter made a pass at you, and you turned him down. That's why he didn't give you the job."

"Where did you hear that?"

"It doesn't matter where I heard it. All I really care about is that you get over yourself and get rid of the attitude before I have to take action."

"Is that a threat?" Bishop narrowed his eyes.

"What?" Carver frowned.

"Are you threatening me? Because I'm gay. Like maybe you don't want a fag working under you, so if I don't bend and scrape to you, you'll have me fired."

"No!" Carver couldn't help it, the laugh bubbled up of its own accord; because if Bishop only knew him, he'd realize how ridiculous that accusation was. Turns out that laughing was the wrong thing to do; before Carver could blink, Bishop pulled back his fist and slammed it into Carver's jaw, knocking him to the ground.

The easiest and probably smartest thing to do at that point would be to explain from where he was sprawled in the straw, but Carver had never been known to go with the easiest and smartest thing. Surging forward, he tackled Bishop by the legs, sending him toppling backward. Before he could right himself, Carver was on him.

"Get off!" Bishop struggled, but Carver not only had the advantage of being slightly larger than Bishop, but also of having grown up on a ranch defending himself against bullies while trying to prove himself. Still, Bishop was no weakling, and there was a tussle before Carver finally pinned him. What he hadn't expected was the way his body would react to being pressed against Bishop's. His erection could cut steel.

Carver watched Bishop's eyes dilate, the green almost disappearing altogether. He smelled of sweat and spice, and suddenly Carver just wanted to bury his face in the man's neck. Bishop Guy might be an ass, but he was also sexy as hell, and there seemed to be a fine line between annoyance and sexual frustration for Carver where he was concerned. Eyes on the wide mouth with lush lips, Carver pushed his hips forward, grinding against Bishop's groin, delighting in an answering hardness there; but when Carver shifted his gaze from Bishop's mouth to his eyes, the cold venom he saw there was enough to make him ease up his hold and sit back. The cock might be saying 'yes', but the eyes were definitely saying 'no.'

"I was not laughing at you," Carver said. "I was laughing...with you."

"What the hell?" Bishop tried to buck Carver off him, but Carver held firm, thighs tightening on narrow hips.

"Would you just listen? I'm not about to laugh at you for preferring men when I feel the same way. Understand?"

"Tell me something I can't already feel through your jeans." Bishop glared up at Carver, lips pink and slightly open, breath coming in audible huffs. Carver couldn't stop himself; he leaned in and kissed those lips.

Bishop stiffened, and Carver drew back.

"I could say something similar about your jeans." Carver rocked on Bishop's hard cock where it pushed against the crack of Carver's ass through both their denims.

"And that gives you the right to attack me?" Bishop breathed heavily, and although Carver would have liked to think it was because Carver had that effect on him, he was pretty sure it was from having a hundred and seventy-five pound man pinning him to the floor. He let go and moved off, half-expecting Bishop to punch him again.

Bishop surged up, but rather than knock Carver into next week, he pushed him over into the straw and crushed their mouths together. Carver's heart tripped, loving the heat and the feel of Bishop taking charge. Muddled by lust, he lifted his hands to encircle Bishop's waist but quickly let go when Bishop clamped sharp teeth onto Carver's lip.

"Ow!" Carver shoved Bishop away and brought his tongue out to taste blood. "What was that for?"

"For thinking the same thing Sutter did—that I'm ripe for the taking."

Bishop got to his feet and brushed off his jeans before looking down at Carver.

"You were right—no need for both of us to stay here. You're the Boss Man—you handle it." Grabbing his jacket off the side of the stall, Bishop strode out of the barn.

Carver lay in the straw, both aroused and ashamed. Bishop had a right to be mad; Carver had acted just like Sutter. He was undeniably attracted to Bishop, but he'd had no right to do what he did.

With a sigh, he took a handkerchief out of the pocket of his jeans and wiped the little remaining blood from his lip before getting to his feet and checking on the cattle.

CARVER'S INAPPROPRIATE BEHAVIOR in the barn persisted in popping up whenever his mind wasn't on work. He wanted to apologize, but he needed privacy for that and wasn't about to corner Bishop somewhere and make the man think he was looking for round two. Carver waited over a week until he spotted Bishop alone fixing one of the fences in the south field. The open area made it less likely that Carver would be seen as a threat, so Carver strode toward Bishop where he crouched in front of the fence, stopping a few feet away.

"Need any help with that?"

"Nope." As usual, Bishop didn't look up from his task.

"Bishop." Carver squatted down, hands dangling between his legs, "I'm sorry about that day in the barn. I acted like an asshole."

"Okay." Bishop kept hammering at the fence. Carver wanted to jerk the hammer out of the man's hands and make him listen—at least get a glimpse of those emerald eyes—but he'd said what he came to say, and there wasn't much else he could do.

Carver straightened and stood but lingered, scratching the back of his neck.

"It was bad form. I just…" He took a breath, "…really find you attractive, that's all. I swear I don't usually try to force myself on people like that. After you punched me and I tackled you, well, I couldn't help myself. I'm sorry; that's no excuse."

Bishop stopped hammering and stared at the fence a moment before raising his eyes to meet Carver's.

"Apology accepted. And I'm sorry for hitting you."

Taken off guard, Carver stared for a moment. Not wanting to press his luck, he gave a small smile and nod before turning and striding toward the bull pen. He got the feeling that Bishop watched him go.

After that, Bishop seemed to thaw towards Carver, although he still remained guarded in his presence. The animosity gradually disappeared, and their working relationship improved. The fact that Carver wanted more from Bishop would have to remain buried.

February melted into March, and many of the cows got ready to calve. Word had it that Sutter would make an appearance sometime that month, and when he did, Carver wanted to be ready for him. The impending visit put him on edge, and if he was truthful with himself, he had to admit that a good deal of his apprehension had nothing to do with the ranch and everything to do with Bishop Guy.

On a brisk spring day, Carver and Bishop finished putting out hay, as dark clouds moved over the sun. A roll of thunder shook the ground, and Carver realized he would have to push back lunch in order to get his morning tasks done.

"John, Burke!" Carver yelled across the field to the two men on horseback. "Start cutting the heavies so we can get them penned before the storm hits."

Bringing the cows that were closest to calving to the field by the calving shed would allow Carver to anticipate any problems. The last thing Carver needed the owner to see was the loss of a calf, or worse, its mother. Carver felt Bishop's eyes on him as he watched the two men bring in the heaviest cows. Their task wasn't easy, as most of the animals would rather remain with the herd. Carver and Bishop helped by yelling at the animals and smacking their rumps to help maneuver them through the gate.

Cows could be obstinate, and by the time the two men on foot were finished, both breathed hard and dripped with sweat.

The sky had darkened considerably in the time it took to herd the cows, and a flash of lightning was followed by a loud crack of thunder. The wind suddenly picked up, almost blowing Carver's Stetson off his head. Carver stood in the pen and surveyed the group of cattle with a discerning eye, patting one heifer on her crop.

"This one's been restless all day." Burke pointed out a particularly uncomfortable-looking heifer. The large man leaned over the fence, a piece of straw hanging from his mouth, lifting his face to the cooling wind. "I noticed her before. I wouldn't be surprised if she doesn't drop it tonight." Another flash and roll, closer this time, again brought Carver's eyes to the threatening sky.

"You're right; we'll get her in the shed. They quickly surveyed the other heifers and chose a few more to go in as well.

All the while, Carver felt Bishop's eyes on him like a touch, and it made him hard. Carver noticed Bishop watching more and more of late, but after what happened in the barn, Carver had promised himself he wouldn't act on his attraction again; Bishop would have to make the first move.

"Lunch in an hour," Carver said before resolutely turning and striding out of the holding pen, through the corral, and toward the main house. He made it to the screen door, slipping inside just as the clouds let loose with a torrent of rain. He turned and saw Bishop make a dash for the calving shed until the worst of the storm blew over. Carver wished he could be in there with him, minus Burke. His cock throbbed, and Carver had to take several deep breaths and will it into submission before turning and heading for the business office and his meeting with Mary-Jim.

WHEN NIGHT FELL, Carver left the small foreman's house at the edge of the ranch with his umbrella open against the steady downfall of rain. When he got inside the shed, he looked over the heifers and noticed that the one Burke had pointed out earlier in the day walked with her tail straight out, a sure sign she was getting ready to drop her calf. He fashioned his bed in the straw just outside her stall where he could see her between the bars of the gate and sat back to wait, ready to help if needed.

Rain pattered steadily against the roof, the sound lending a cozy feel to the small building and lulling Carver into a half-doze. When the door to the shed suddenly opened, Carver looked over his shoulder in surprise.

"Thought I'd find you here." Bishop closed the door and slipped off his raincoat before walking over and taking a seat beside Carver in the straw.

"What are you doing here?" Carver regarded Bishop as he removed his hat and tried to smooth out his wild hair.

"Thought you might need some help or at least enjoy the company."

Carver wasn't sure what to say about that, so he remained silent. Bishop made him hard by just being in the same room. He attempted to adjust himself without Bishop noticing.

The rain continued to drum against the roof. Carver could smell the clean scent of Bishop's soap and feel the warmth of his body close by. He swallowed, mouth dry.

"Sutter's taking his sweet time in coming, isn't he?" Bishop turned from where he'd been watching the cow and looked at Carver.

"Yep. Wish he'd give me the day. Hell, the *week* would be nice."

"It's like him to leave you to stew like this, the bastard." Bishop glanced at Carver's profile. "Don't be nervous; you're doing a good job."

"I'm not nervous."

Bishop laughed and tossed his Stetson over to where Carver's lay in the straw.

"What?" Carver turned to look at him.

"You're lying; I can tell you are."

Carver frowned. He was nervous, of course, but he liked to think he hid it well.

"Don't worry; I'm sure nobody else realizes it, but I've worked close enough to you the last couple months to learn your tells," Bishop said.

"I just want to do my job well." Carver wondered that the man could read him so well. Bishop seemed to have gone from ignoring Carver completely to paying strict attention to him.

"I know that." Bishop leaned back in the straw and propped his head on his hands.

"What are they?" Carver turned, his eyes immediately drawn to the sliver of skin between Bishop's bunched up shirt and his jeans.

"What?"

"My *tells*."

"Oh. You get this twitch by your left eye."

"I do not!"

"Yeah, you do." Bishop smiled. "And sometimes you stutter a little." When Carver was silent, Bishop looked over at him and laughed. "Stop sulking!"

"I'm not sulking!" Carver sat up, back straight. He didn't know what the hell Bishop was talking about. He did not have any tells, and he certainly didn't sulk.

"You are so—you look like a little kid." Bishop's voice softened, but Carver didn't notice—all he heard was the word *kid*. He started to get up, but Bishop wrapped a hand around Carver's wrist, holding him there.

"Don't. Come on, Carver—I didn't mean anything by it."

"You're implying I'm acting immature, which I'm not. You know, just because I look young doesn't mean—"

"You don't look young," Bishop said, his hand slipping down from Carver's wrist to grip his palm. "You look...innocent. I like that about you; it's damned sexy to find out you're not so innocent underneath."

It took a moment for the words to sink into Carver's brain. When they did, his mouth dropped open, and Bishop leaned in and captured it with his own.

Carver forgot all about where they were and what they were arguing about. His cock throbbed as Bishop's arms came up and wrapped around him, pressing their chests together so Carver could feel Bishop's heart pumping as fast as his own. As their tongues tangled, Bishop's erection pressed against Carver's thigh, a hard promise of what was to come.

"You aren't going to bite me again, are you?" Carver asked, and Bishop laughed softly.

"Not unless you ask me to, Cowboy."

Bishop turned Carver in the straw so he was on his back with Bishop covering him, continuing to kiss Carver while one hand slipped down to unzip Carver's jeans.

Carver groaned when Bishop took Carver's cock from his briefs and enclosed his fingers around it. Carver turned his head to catch his breath, and Bishop's mouth fell to lick and suck at Carver's neck while warm fingers danced over his cock.

Carver's balls ached with need. He lifted his hands and unbuttoned Bishop's shirt with trembling fingers.

Bishop leaned back and undid his own fly before shoving his jeans down to his knees. The delectable feeling of a hot cock brushing against his own almost made Carver come right then and there, but he steeled himself, not wanting things to end too soon. He sat up and peeled off his t-shirt, tossing it away. Bishop's gaze burned into Carver's skin as it traveled over the vast expanse of muscled chest and toned belly, and Carver was suddenly thankful for every bit of hard work he'd ever done.

"You're no little kid." Bishop ran his fingers lightly over Carver's pectorals, stopping to tweak a nipple. "You're gorgeous." He leaned down and kissed the bud before sucking it into his mouth, causing a throb that made Carver wonder if it was somehow internally attached to his cock. Carver writhed under Bishop's attentions, moving his hands to get a good grip on the luscious globes of Bishop's ass.

"Hair like sun-bleached wheat, eyes as blue as the sky." Bishop bent and flicked his tongue over the nipple again. "A face like an angel's and a body like the Devil's."

Carver only half processed what Bishop said as his eyes devoured his tormentor's body. Broad shoulders, firm pecs, washboard stomach with a tantalizing trail of dark hair leading to a long, blushing cock that Carver *really* wanted to suck. With his grip on Bishop's ass, Carver brought him closer and pushed against him, desperately needing some friction.

Getting the message, Bishop straddled Carver and thrust his hips, the delectable slide of cock against cock short-circuiting all of Carver's brain function until he couldn't think any more at all, only feel. The faster Bishop moved, the more Carver cried out, until the barn filled with his moans and Bishop's grunts of pleasure.

Toes curling in his boots, Carver tried to spread his legs, but his jeans restricted the movement. He could feel his fly pressing against his ball sac, cold teeth of the zipper scraping him with every thrust, the small discomfort only adding to the glorious sensations running through him. He was so close.

As Bishop undulated against him, he kissed Carver deeply before once more trailing his lips to Carver's sensitive neck. Carver turned his head to give Bishop better access, the sucking and biting ballooning his pleasure to the breaking point. As his body strained with oncoming release, his eyes focused on the cow, barely registering the red strings of a broken water bag hanging from her tail and the two down-turned hooves that followed.

Carver's balls tightened, and he dug his fingers into Bishop's ass, yanking him forward so their groins pressed even more tightly together. Bright, all-consuming light filled Carver's vision, bursting in iridescent fragments as his body jerked through climax, warm spunk shooting onto his chest. He felt Bishop tense and reached lower so the index finger of his right hand brushed down Bishop's crack. Bishop gasped, arching his back, and Carver watched as white ropes of cum shot from Bishop's cock before Bishop fell forward in exhaustion.

Carver floated through the pleasant aftermath, limbs weak, Bishop's face buried in the crook of his shoulder.

Carver blinked, details around him gradually delineating, to find two sets of brown bovine eyes gazing back at him. Carver smiled.

Bishop let out a breath, warm against Carver's neck, and Carver nudged him.

"Look." Carver gestured to the calf standing on wobbly legs. Bishop raised his head and chuckled breathlessly.

"Well, that was the most fun I've had during a calving."

Carver had to agree.

TWO DAYS LATER, after a hearty breakfast, during which Carver tried rather unsuccessfully not to stare at Bishop where he sat several seats down the table talking to a couple of other ranch hands, Carver made his way across the pasture to a fence that had been recently damaged by an ornery bull. His mind kept wandering to the calving shed and Bishop—the way Bishop had felt beneath Carver's hands and against his cock. Frequently, Carver would catch himself mid-hammer, staring into the distance and seeing a muscular chest and simmering green eyes rather than the bull corral. Carver hadn't had an opportunity to say anything to Bishop since that night other than in passing, and he wondered if it might be possible to get Bishop alone any time soon.

No more than an hour had passed when Carver got word that another heifer was ready to give birth, this one having a hard time of it. Putting away his tools, Carver hurried toward the corral and calving shed, arriving a little out of breath to find one of his hands waiting for him at the door.

"We have company," Kendall told Carver in a low voice.

"Tell me it isn't Sutter arriving just in time to witness a problem." Carver's heart sank.

"Of course. That's the way things always go, right?" She stood back and gave Carver an encouraging pat on the back. "I've already washed her for you."

Carver thanked Kendall and walked to the stall, where Tim Sutter stood watching the struggling heifer, which was on its side in the straw. Sutter was a large man in his late fifties with salt and pepper hair, a barrel chest, bowed legs, and steely blue eyes that showed little to no emotion. Carver had trouble keeping a neutral face as he nodded to the man, glad he could turn his attention to the cow. Carver knelt and ran a hand over her white head and smooth brown back as Kendall walked into the stall carrying hot water, soap, antiseptic, and towels. She arranged the supplies on a crate and stood back.

Raised on a ranch, Carver had learned at an early age how to help a cow through a difficult labor as long as things weren't too dire. The first thing he needed to do was determine what the problem was. Since Kendall had already prepped the cow, Carver stood and pulled his shirt over his head before walking to the tub of water and thoroughly washing his right arm all the way up to his shoulder. He turned back to the laboring animal and knelt behind her.

"I think she's far enough gone to be cooperative," he said, getting down on his side. Carefully he pushed his hand all the way into the cow's vagina, until his cheek pressed against her rump.

"I feel its legs," Carver said, voice tight.

"Front or back?" Sutter shifted forward where he leaned on the gate.

Carver felt up along one of the calf's legs until he came to a wet nose, feeling a bit like Sutter was testing him.

"Front," he said with relief. He could do this himself. Carver winced as the cow's next contraction squeezed his arm with her strong inner muscles. Carver glanced up in time to see Bishop join them. Carver immediately flicked his eyes to Sutter, whose expression was nothing short of lecherous.

"What do you think the problem is?" Bishop walked into the stall to stand next to Carver. He hadn't acknowledged Sutter's presence at all.

"Seems to be in the correct position and posture." Carver looked at Kendall. "Chains?"

"Already sterilized, Boss Man." She bent to pull them from a clean towel.

"Feel like helping?" Carver turned his eyes to Bishop.

"That's what I came for." Bishop gamely walked to the crate to wash.

They secured chains on the calf's front fetlocks as well as below the knee, and with both Carver and Bishop tugging on them, they were able to ease the baby animal's shoulders through the pelvis one at a time as the heifer pushed through each contraction. After that, the cow gave another great heave and expelled the calf on her own.

"The calf's a bit larger than normal." Carver cleaned the amniotic fluid from the calf's nostrils and watched it take its first breath. "She just needed a little help getting it out." He wiped the sweat off his brow and smiled at Bishop, who grinned back.

"Nice job," Sutter said. Carver had almost forgotten the man was there. He gave a short nod at the praise and watched Kendall take the calf to another stall with fresh straw. Carver led the mother cow there so she could nurse in peace.

"Meet me at the main house in half an hour, West," Sutter called to Carver, who turned and saw the ranch owner heading toward the door. "Guy, I'd like to speak with you now."

Bishop paused in his washing up and glanced at Carver, who wondered what Sutter had to say to Bishop and if Bishop would try to get out of talking with him. But Bishop only nodded, drying off his arms and rolling down his sleeves before following Sutter out of the calving shed.

"Wonder what that was about?" Kendall gathered the supplies for sterilizing.

"Don't know." Carver washed and dried his arms before pulling his shirt back on. "Thanks for the help, Kendall."

The sun was high in the sky when Carver exited the shed, and a sharp, clean wind blew from the west. An array of wildflowers dotted the fields with blues, pinks, and purples, but Carver barely noticed any of this as he made his way to the main house. What could Sutter need to talk to Bishop about without Carver present? Nothing Carver could think of, and that sent a ripple of disquiet through him.

When he pushed open the screen door to the kitchen, he met Masie coming around the corner with a pile of clean dishrags.

"Did you see Sutter and Bishop come through here?"

"Your office." Masie jerked her head toward the back hall, and Carver started that way. He heard them before he even got near the closed door.

"What the fuck makes you think I'd change my mind?" Bishop's voice was loud.

"I just thought maybe you've had time to consider your poor mother and her tremendous medical bills."

"You're an evil sonofabitch, you know that?"

"You could have had the job, Bishop. It was within your reach. It still is." Carver leaned closer to the door, fists clenching as he barely caught Sutter's next words. "I still want you."

"Are you saying you would take the job away from Carver after you've already given it to him?"

148   *Cowboy Roundup*

"Positions can be taken away as easily as they're given. If you decide your mother's health means more to you than your pride..."

"So what this boils down to is, I let you fuck me, and you'll take Carver's job away from him and give it to me."

"And you can better pay your mother's bills. How is your mother, by the way? I've heard she needs expensive treatment."

"Like fuck I'll tell you anything about her. You can take your disgusting offer and shove it up your ass."

Bishop almost toppled Carver on his way out of the office. When Carver reached the partially open door, Sutter turned, the look on his face telling Carver he obviously thought Bishop had come back.

"If you think I didn't hear any of that, you're wrong." Carver fought hard to tamp down his raging anger.

For a moment, Sutter looked stunned and was obviously mentally running through everything he'd said to Bishop.

"Perhaps you aren't right for this job, West." Sutter sat down at Carver's desk as though he'd never retired as foreman.

"Something you probably don't know about me," Carver said, attempting a casual lean against the doorframe while his heart pumped double-time in his chest. "My sister's an attorney in Houston. A damned good one. She'd like nothing more than to take on a sexual harassment case." He waited a beat, watching Sutter try to hide his concern before he added, "I did a little investigating about you recently and found out something interesting. You married a rich widow last month. Wonder how she would feel about what you've been trying to do to Bishop?"

Carver was gratified to see Sutter's face blanch.

"Bet she doesn't know about your penchant for cock." It seemed Sutter had a few tells himself, as his right eye started to twitch.

"Obviously, you're under the impression you heard something damning about me." Sutter visibly tried to gather his wits. "You're mistaken."

"Really?" Carver straightened and fully stepped into the

room. Down the hall he could hear Mary-Jim's voice as she entered the hall and spoke to Masie. Sutter's eyes flicked to the open door. "I could have sworn I heard you say—"

"I don't have much time, West. Why don't we get down to business?" Sutter opened his leather briefcase. Carver walked to the desk and planted his hands on it.

"Before we do that, let's get a few things straight. You're going to leave Bishop Guy alone. In fact, you're going to leave all my workers alone. You hired me to run this ranch, and I'm going to do it right."

"Of course." Sutter nodded, eyes not meeting Carver's. "Wouldn't have it any other way."

Carver decided to press for one more thing before letting the matter drop.

"I think my top ranch hand deserves a raise in pay. How about you?"

Finally, Sutter's brown eyes lifted to stare into Carver's. They were hard and angry, but Sutter merely nodded and indicated that Carver should take a seat across from him.

THE EVENING SUN had dipped beneath the horizon by the time Carver saw Sutter off in his newly acquired silver Jaguar. Carver was hungry, but he'd already missed supper with the hands, and he itched to talk to Bishop. Sequestered as he'd been in his office all day, he hadn't seen Bishop since the man had stormed out after speaking with Sutter.

The bunkhouse was a one-level rectangular building located at the far end of the large corral with individual rooms and a shared porch. Carver knocked on Bishop's door, and a muffled voice told him to come in. Carver stepped through the door into the dim interior to find Bishop sitting on his bed.

Carver glanced about the room. It was furnished the same as all the others, with a double bed, nightstand with lamp, a curtained front window, and a dresser and closet. A suitcase sat by the door.

"Not planning on leaving, I hope," Carver said, shutting the door and taking a seat at the end of the bed.

"I can't stay here. I was waiting to say goodbye to you."

Carver looked at the man he'd become much too fond of in a short amount of time and hoped he could convince the guy to stay.

"Where will you go?"

"Don't know." Bishop shrugged. "Jade Ranch, maybe. It's nothing to do with you, Carver. Don't go getting that into your head."

"I know it's because of Sutter. I was standing outside the door listening, remember?"

"Right." Bishop's face loosened a little. "Then you know why I can't stay here. It's never going to change, and every time I turn him down, the bastard will find a way to take it out on me." He shifted. "Besides, I need more money than I'm earning here."

"Your mother's pretty sick, huh?"

Bishop looked away, and Carver reached out to place a hand on his leg.

"Listen, if I could guarantee you more money and that Sutter will leave you alone, would you stay?"

"You can't give me that guarantee, Carver." Bishop swallowed and stood up. "Look, I like you. Please don't make this harder by being such a nice guy."

"I'm serious, Bishop. Sutter isn't going to fool with you anymore. If he tries, just tell me and I'll make him stop, but I don't think he'll try. And I've secured you a raise. I just came from an all-day meeting with the asshole."

"What are you talking about?" Bishop looked down at Carver with disbelieving eyes. "You can't possibly keep Sutter from doing whatever the hell he wants. He's the owner of the ranch, for fuck's sake!"

"There's where you're wrong. I mean, yeah, he's the owner, but I've got Sutter right where I want him. I told him straight out that my sister's a lawyer and will pin his ass to the wall for sexual harassment." Carver grinned.

"And that got him? He wasn't very concerned when I mentioned that the first time."

"Maybe not, but he certainly listened when I told him I knew he'd just gotten married to a very rich lady. Did you see the Jaguar he drove here? Compliments of the missus. I simply reminded Sutter that a sexual harassment suit wouldn't go down well with his new wife, particularly one dealing with him and another man, and he immediately wanted to forget the whole thing happened. Then I pointed out that my top ranch hand needed a raise, and he agreed."

"Sutter got married?"

"I've been doing some snooping. He tried to keep it hush-hush, but Mary-Jim brought the Jaguar to my attention, and I got suspicious. They married at the courthouse two weeks ago." Carver watched a slide show of emotions run over Bishop's face, ending in wondering disbelief.

"You did that for me?"

"Yeah." Carver stood, putting his hands on Bishop's shoulders. "And I don't want you getting the wrong idea that now *I* expect something from you. You're a good worker, and I don't want to lose you, and besides that—Sutter's a dirty motherfucker who needed to be taken down a peg."

Bishop stared into Carver's eyes, his own slightly moist. Raising his hands, he planted them on each side of Carver's face.

"You really are an angel."

Carver felt the blood seeping into his cheeks and shook his head.

"Don't you start."

"No, really. I can't believe you stood up for me like that; you didn't have to."

"I don't want to lose you."

"Only because I'm a good worker?" The corners of Bishop's mouth twitched, and Carver let his hands run down Bishop's arms before wrapping them around the cowboy's waist, pulling the muscular body toward him.

"I would have done it for anybody, but I'll admit I have a little more of a reason for wanting you to stay."

"And what's that?" Bishop leaned closer until their mouths were only an inch apart.

"I hear you can cook," Carver said,.

Bishop's eyes widened before he leaned his head on Carver's shoulder and laughed. "With a cook like Masie in residence, I'm supposed to believe it matters to you that I can cook?"

"Well," Carver curled a finger into one of Bishop's belt loops and tugged him closer again, "I'd like to hit the trail this summer for a bit, and I thought you might like to come with me." He pressed a kiss to Bishop's temple and spoke against it. "Millions of stars overhead and only a fire to keep us warm."

"*Only* a fire?" Bishop pressed his body closer to Carver's, both hands firmly planted on Carver's ass. Their mouths met, immediately opening for one another in a delicious slide of tongues.

Carver brought one hand up Bishop's back to grasp his shoulder and the other one around his waist. Carver's mouth opened wider as Bishop swept his tongue so far inside, it threatened to brush Carver's tonsils. Carver's cock pulsed in his jeans, and he felt an answering twitch in Bishop's as they moved to topple onto the bed.

"Want to fuck you so bad," Bishop said into Carver's ear before breathing into it. Carver bucked his hips impatiently and let out a moan. Bishop pulled back, sultry green eyes sending Carver the clear message that he was about to be hammered into the mattress. Bishop turned to the nightstand and slid open the drawer while Carver tried hard not to cream his jeans then and there.

"I just want you to know," Bishop said as he opened the tube of lubricating gel and stripped a condom from its package, "I'm doing this because you're the sexiest man I've ever met and I've wanted to jump your bones since day one, not because you just saved my job."

"Of course," Carver grinned up at him from the bed.

"Strip," Bishop said, and Carver didn't waste any time obeying. By the time he was nude and lying flat on his back again, Bishop stood watching him, cock at full attention. Carver swallowed in anticipation as Bishop knelt on the bed and crawled toward him.

"How do you want me?" Carver asked, surprised at how husky his voice sounded.

"On your knees, hands on the headboard." Bishop's words went straight to Carver's cock, and he readily complied.

When Carver was in position, Bishop planted tiny kisses over his neck and shoulders while easing a lubricated finger inside him. Carver was already so turned on, he barely registered the intrusion. Bishop's lips and tongue set Carver aflame, and he had no doubt at that moment that the man could easily keep him warm on a chilly night on the trail, even without a camp fire.

The entrance of a second finger beside the first brought a prolonged moan from Carver's lips, and he pushed back onto the invading digits. Bishop swore and curled his fingers, sliding against Carver's prostate, bringing an array of goosebumps over Carver's back and arms.

"Beautiful man," Bishop said into Carver's neck, free hand gliding from Carver's hip bone across his belly, fingers dancing along ribs until they reached a taut nipple to give a gentle squeeze. Carver found he didn't mind being called beautiful when it was Bishop saying it.

Bishop withdrew his fingers. Lifting his other hand, he turned Carver's face toward him and kissed the man once, twice on the lips before concentrating on rolling the condom onto his engorged cock. When the head touched Carver's entrance, Carver held his breath.

"Ready?" Bishop asked.

Carver nodded fervently, anticipation making him tremble.

Bishop took Carver in one smooth slide, the pain and pressure of it secondary to the glorious feeling of being filled so completely. Carver clutched at the curved headboard, bracing himself with his arms as Bishop began to fuck him.

"Oh, God," Carver said on a breath, and Bishop nibbled on the soft skin of his shoulder, switching to shallow thrusts that drove Carver out of his mind with need. He reached down and grabbed his cock, stroking it, head falling back onto Bishop's shoulder.

"You're so hot," Bishop said in Carver's ear. "All smooth and blond and…" he cried out, rhythm staggering and hand's gripping Carver's waist. Carver's groin tightened, and a rush of pure pleasure shot through him, white spunk spilling over his fingers.

"There's so many things I want to do to you. With you," Bishop said when they'd collapsed beside one another on the bed. It was dark outside, and every so often a coyote howled.

"I'm completely on board with that." Carver ran his hand up Bishop's arm. "Can't wait to hit the trail this summer." He winked.

Bishop placed his hand on Carver's cheek in a way that was fast becoming familiar as well as endearing.

"Me, too, Boss Man."

"Don't call me that." Carver shook his head.

"You know," Bishop ignored him and ran a finger down Carver's sternum, "what Sutter did was lousy. But if you ever want to sit in that leather chair in your office and demand a little something from me, you just go right ahead. *Boss Man*."

"Fuck." Carver kissed along Bishop's neck until he reached the man's ear and nibbled at the lobe, Bishop's heart beating strong and fast under the palm of Carver's hand.

"So, you'll do it?"

"Whatever you want, my gorgeous man, whatever you want." Carver sighed contentedly.

"I'll hold you to that."

ON A HOT night in June, Carver and Bishop lay on a blanket behind the barn, an expanse of night sky laid out above them, and dozens of tiny flickering lights all around.

"Fireflies," Carver said, as though they were something new to him. They weren't, of course, but the sheer abundance of them in one place certainly was.

"I think they like how dark it is at night here and that there aren't a lot of trees around." Bishop ran his hand through Carver's hair. Everyone at the ranch had staggered to bed after an exhausting day of branding, and Carver and Bishop were taking advantage of it. They lay on a blanket, Carver's head resting in the crook of Bishop's arm.

"So that's how the ranch got its name. I'd wondered."

Bishop nodded, eyes still trained on the sky where Carver recognized the Big and Little Dippers.

Carver sighed happily and took Bishop's hand, entwining their fingers. When he accepted the job as foreman at Firefly Ranch, he never thought he was going to fall in love; but he had, and he was happier than he'd ever been in his life.

"I think Tim Sutter did one good thing," Bishop said. "He brought us together."

Carver squeezed Bishop's hand, never taking his eyes off the fireflies as they twinkled far into the distance, blending in with hundreds of stars shining in the inky blackness of Texas sky.

Bishop squeezed back, and Carver smiled.

WILD RIDE
BY KASSANDRA LEA

THE SUN SAT low in the sky, a cool breeze making the long grass sway, the leaves on nearby trees whispering. It carried to Mica Daly—*no, it's not Daly anymore*—strains of an upbeat country song and the chatter of voices. There was a right good shindig going on behind the big ranch house, partly in his honor, but feeling overwhelmed, Mica slipped away, hopefully unnoticed. He ducked into the barn, assaulted by the smell of hay and pine shavings, leather, and horses; the sorts of smells he hadn't been familiar with eight months earlier.

Eight months...

Feeling light headed he sank down onto a nearby bale of hay, head hanging down. He closed his eyes and tried to focus on just breathing in and out. Panic threatened to seize hold of his heart, to make him choke on the air passing through his lungs. Mica pressed his hands against the side of his head, elbows digging into his thighs as he fought back the sudden urge to cry. Unshed tears burned behind his eyelids.

You're supposed to be happy. Not having a complete meltdown in the barn. But eight months...

Mica rubbed his hands over his face and let his gaze wander

over the stalls, most of them empty since the horses were out in the pastures. The only two current residents were a big bay gelding and a little buckskin mare. There used to be a time in his life when he wouldn't have known the difference, they'd have been brown and golden, nothing more. There weren't a lot of horses in the city where he was born and raised, where he spent twenty-seven-years of his life.

Right up until February of the current year when the company he worked for suddenly saw fit to transfer him. It might not have seemed like a big deal for some people, but he'd gone from car clogged streets and an apartment with paper thin walls to a city where cattle outnumbered humans. No more black tie galas or rubbing elbows with famous people. He had ditched his Italian suits, the fine threads hanging in the back of his closet with the obscenely overpriced loafers he used to sport. He still refused to wear cowboy boots finding them uncomfortable, picking out a pair of good hiking boots instead.

And the hat...

You have absolutely no problem with Forrest when he wears one.

Mica sighed, running a hand through his hair.

The barn door scraped against the ground. Opal Singleton, blond hair done up in curls, stepped inside. Decked out in a western style cream cut dress and cowboy boots she looked like she belonged on the ranch when in reality she preferred to strut around in heels and designer duds. She had been his best friend since they literally ran into each other in the school hallway during second grade. There was no one else he could think of from his big city life to invite out for the big day, aside from his parents and considering the way his dad reacted when he discovered Mica had given his heart to a guy...well, he wasn't surprised to see they hadn't shown up, though it did hurt.

"I thought I might find you in here." Smoothing the flowing fabric of her dress she sank down on the bale at his side. "Hiding?"

"I needed to catch my breath."

She reached over, taking his hand in hers, giving it a squeeze. "It certainly has been a whirlwind adventure, hasn't it?"

"Yeah," the word came out strangled.

Opal rested her head on his shoulder, her hair smelling of strawberries and sunshine. "Right now you're scared, but tomorrow I know you'll be over the moon."

Mica bit down on his bottom lip, something akin to a whimper escaping him.

She gave his hand a reassuring squeeze, sitting up and prompting him to look at her, brilliant green eyes gazing into his lackluster brown. "I've known you a very long time, buster, and I have seen you fall head over heels before, though never for a guy," a smile turned up the corners of her mouth. "And that's how I know this, what you have with Forrest, no matter how quickly all the pieces fell into place, that's how I know it's the real deal."

He could do nothing more than look at her with eyes wide, brow furrowed.

For some reason this prompted Opal to chuckle, patting the back of his hand. "The way you feel about Forrest, it's all over your face every time you look at the man. Hell, even if you're talking about him or someone else brings him up, you get all…" She gestured with her hand. "Smitten, lovey dovey, you know, that lovesick look young girls get."

"Did…did you just compare me to a young girl?"

She quirked an eyebrow. "Yeah, actually, I did and what are you going to do about it? You know I'm right, always am, especially when it comes to your love life."

And that was one of the things that endlessly baffled him. Within one meeting Opal could tell whether or not a girl was right for him, though all things considered he'd been going out with the wrong gender. Unfortunately, she seemed unable to find a man of her own. Successful, fun loving, bright, and beautiful, she should have been rolling in dating offers, and yet her last relationship ended two weeks before his transfer.

Maybe you can help her find someone out here and then she'll stay and you'll have your best friend. Everything will be okay. Everything will be like it was eight months ago....except you're married. To a man.

"Ah, there you are," a deep baritone interrupted, cutting off Opal's next no doubt optimistic remark. Mica glanced—*you're staring and maybe drooling a little*—over his best friend's shoulder at the cowboy standing a few feet away. *Your husband.* His mouth went dry. *Husband...oh my...how long until I get used to that term? Or the ring?* Mica absently fingered the gold band. "I was wondering where you'd gotten off to." There was a mischievous twinkle in his bluer than blue eyes. "Do I need to be worried about you two?"

Planting a quick kiss on his cheek, Opal sprang from the hay bale and stopped in front of Forrest. For the umpteenth time she gave him an appraising look, sighed, and shook her head. "I have got to find me a cowboy." She squeezed Forrest Kettrick's right bicep. "Especially one as fine as you." Her comment brought forth a pleasant chuckle from Forrest, one that sent a tingle racing down Mica's spine where it settled in the pit of his stomach and began to stir up all sorts of desires. If possible he paled even further. *It's not like he hasn't already seen every square inch of Mica Daly, damn it, Kettrick, it's Mica Kettrick now.* "I am so jealous, Mica." She stepped quickly over to the barn door, stopping with a dreamy expression on her face. "You two are so adorable. Congratulations, guys."

"Thanks," Forrest said, never once taking his eyes off Mica, who was acutely aware of it.

The unrelenting stare began to make him uncomfortable and he squirmed on the bale. An image from a few days ago popped into the forefront of his mind, heat rising in his cheeks. He'd come to the barn, something he now realized was becoming habit, to escape the hustle and bustle of the upcoming wedding. He just wanted a little peace and quiet. Instead what he got was a hard cowboy backing him up against a stall door, hands doing such pleasant things to his body and then...Mica shuddered with pleasure at the memory of Forrest getting down on his knees and though Mica had feared getting caught he certainly didn't try to put a stop to their little tryst.

The man touches me and sets me on fire. The mere brush of fingertips on my bare flesh burns.

"What's going on in that mind of yours, Mr. Mica Kettrick, husband of mine?"

Mica blinked, the image fading away. Despite the fact he wore cowboy boots, the tips a bit scuffed, Forrest had managed to close the distance between them without making much noise. Heat radiated off of him and the ache in Mica's stomach sank a little lower. Forrest Kettrick, the blue eyed, black haired cowboy with the body that told of years of labor working the land looked befitting of a romance novel cover.

They'd met by chance at a bar, of all places, though it paled in comparison to the joints he used to visit back in the city. The music was strictly country pumped out of a jukebox—*who even knew those still existed?*—and clearly audible, not the eardrum rupturing beats blared from hidden speakers, words unintelligible. There were no flashy lights or overly priced, oddly named drinks. Just lots of wood, the typical country bar fair, and of all things, a mechanical bull in the corner. The very same bull on which Forrest had been riding when Mica first entered the joint. There had been only a cursory glance in that direction, Forrest whooping for joy, and then Mica walked up to the bar, feeling multiple sets of eyes on the stranger in town.

The majority of the night had been uneventful. Mica enjoyed a decent burger and managed to keep to himself right up until the moment he stood to leave and bumped into Forrest. Their eyes met and all the oxygen from his lungs vanished. When Forrest smiled, Mica went weak in the knees. The rest, as they say, was history. In eight months he went from the new guy in town to dating Forrest to living with the cowboy and now...

Forrest held out his hand, a matching gold band around one finger. Forrest lightly tugged Mica to his feet, pulling him close, one arm wrapped around Mica's waste, a hand resting on the small of his back. How quickly the ache morphed into a near desperate yearning to feel the caress of Forrest's lips on his bare skin. The cowboy was solid, radiating heat. And he knew all the ways Mica liked to be touched.

Like fire...how I love to melt.

As though reading his mind, Forrest traced the outlines of Mica's lips with his own, the kiss starting off soft. But how quickly it grew into a toe curling promise of pleasures to come. Mica moaned, hands sinking into the back pockets of Forrest's jeans. He cupped firm cheeks, wishing there wasn't a single stitch between them. Back in the city with a handful of failed girlfriends, he had been Mister Boring, Mister No Frills in bed. Sex with Forrest, though, was different every single time they joined. A morning romp might be slow and sensual while an afternoon quickie was hot and heavy.

And every place was fair game; the bedroom, the kitchen, barn, pool, the bed of Forrest's pickup truck...

Forrest broke the kiss, remaining close enough that when he spoke, his breath tickled Mica's swollen lips. "How about we ditch the rest of the party and slip out early? I have a little surprise for you, husband of mine."

"What?"

"Now, now," Forrest chuckled, his hand moving in a tight circle over the small of Mica's back. "Telling you that would ruin the surprise. But trust me," he briefly nibbled Mica's earlobe, "you'll enjoy every moment of it."

His heart skipped a beat, a wave of heat rushing over him. "Okay," the word popping out, his voice husky.

When Forrest drew away, he left a temporary void the likes of which Mica had never experienced before. It was like losing a piece of his heart, a chip of his soul, which only slipped back into place when he curled close to his...husband. *I really do like the sound of that. Forrest Kettrick, my husband.* And though it hurt that his parents weren't accepting of their relationship, the love he felt for Forrest was enough to drown it out.

"Do you want to get Solo ready to go?"

Forrest stood in the stall of the large bay gelding, Ransom, the horse his usual mount around the ranch. One stall down stood Solo, the slightly shorter, somewhat thicker mare that Mica had learned to ride on. He was still far from considering himself a cowboy but he'd gained enough confidence over the past few months that he joined Forrest on occasional rides across the acres of ranch land. Of course, despite the offers to try new mounts, the ranch rife with good horseflesh, Mica stayed with Solo. She made him feel safe.

The mare, her coat a soft creamy shade Forrest referred to as buttermilk, nickered as Mica entered the stall. He gave her a loving scratch on the forehead. From the boy who didn't care for dogs or cats or any pet for that matter, to the man who found solace in the steady unbridled spirit of a horse. Solo nosed him gently in the shoulder and some of the last of the nervousness he'd been feeling melted away.

Without sharing another word the two of them worked to get the horses ready, leather saddles creaking as both of them mounted up a few minutes later. Mica shifted slightly, Solo twitching her ears, tail swishing to chase away the pesky late afternoon bugs. On the far side of the barn, he could still hear strains of music from the party, even without them it would carry on well into the night, and that fact either hadn't occurred to Forrest or he simply didn't care.

They stood in the swaying grass, the sun having sunk lower toward the horizon. The breeze was cool, refreshing. Forrest, readjusting the set of his tan cowboy hat, considered Mica with those envious blue eyes. "Ready to head out and see what I have planned?"

What could Forrest have possibly come up with that required them to ride off into the sunset? *That was a cliché thought. I think you can safely say your city street cred has gone completely out the window. Do you care?* Mica scanned the horizon, hoping to catch even so much as an inkling to what awaited, but aside from clusters of trees and rolling grass covered hills he saw nothing.

"Well?"

In response Mica urged Solo ahead until he drew up next to Forrest. "You aren't going to give me even the slightest hint, are you?"

That twinkle returned to Forrest's eyes. "And spoil the fun? Of course not." Ransom side stepped and their knees bumped. Forrest leaned over to steal a quick kiss. "Come on, darling, the sooner we leave, the quicker you can satisfy your curiosity."

Darling? I don't know where the hell he pulled that one from but...

Mica hoped wherever they were headed it wouldn't take long. After all, there was a marriage to consummate.

THE SUN HAD disappeared from the sky, replaced with a sliver of moon and a blanket of stars Mica was still getting used to. The sights and sounds of the city had completely faded away. if tasked with having to get back home on his own, Mica would be hopelessly lost, wandering the planes. The thought was enough to send his heart racing. Solo tensed underneath him, picking up on the subtle changes in his body. *Relax. Just relax. Unless something terrible happens to Forrest you'll be just fine.* To help ease his racing mind he took a deep breath and attempted to lose himself to the night.

The whisper of the grass as the horses moved through it. The creak of the leather saddles. The usual choir of crickets and toads and other nightly creatures, including the occasional forlorn owl and, much to Mica's dismay, the howl of a coyote.

Not for the first time he wondered where exactly they were headed, and judging by the low grade pain in his back they'd been riding for quite a few hours. What he wouldn't have given at that moment to have a hot tub to relax in, one of the jets positioned to hit him in the lower back. Maybe a glass of wine, some candles, a good looking man to keep him company...

At least I've got the man.

Forrest rode just to the front and side of him, the gelding plodding along in the dark, much like Solo. It gave Mica a great view of Forrest's backside, the way his hips moved with the motion of the horse, back and forth, fluid and hypnotic. Mica had learned quickly that years spent in the saddle had given the man amazing control over his hips, every thrust powerful and hungry, yet somehow always gentle.

If I keep letting my mind wander like this I'll find myself in a very uncomfortable position.

He cleared his throat. "Are we almost there?"

"Just about."

"How can you be so sure in the dark?"

Forrest chuckled. "Because I know the lay of my land, hon. And the ride will have been worth it, trust me."

He tried to work the kinks out of his back by shifting around, earning a displeased snort from Solo. At least he no longer felt like a sack of potatoes when he climbed on her back, though he definitely wouldn't be entering any rodeos any time soon. Or ever. "The truck would have been faster," he grumbled, thinking of Forrest's blue pickup.

Forrest may have snorted; it could have been Ransom, hard to tell.

When they rounded the next hill Mica brought Solo to a stop, instantly feeling like a jerk for his whining, including the thoughts he kept to himself. Something inside of him shifted and though he could not quite explain why, tears welled in his eyes. He blinked fiercely to keep them back. Apparently, not only had he married one good looking cowboy who certainly knew how to please his man, but there was a hidden well of romance within the cowboy.

Out there in what was basically the equivalent of nowhere someone, most likely Forrest, had set up a canopy, its frame outlined with twinkling strands of white lights. How they were being powered Mica didn't care. Sheer fabric had been wrapped about them, more flowing like curtains, dancing in the gentle touch of the cool night breeze. He could make out shapes within the canopy, one of them looking to be an inflatable bed; an interesting sight given he knew how much Forrest liked to camp out under the stars. Roughing it, he called it.

This certainly doesn't seem like roughing it, at least now as I thought of it.

So transfixed with the beautiful, private place he was jostled back into reality when Forrest rode toward it, Solo following along behind Ransom like some lovesick puppy. Forrest swung down out of the saddle and moved to catch Mica as he half dismounted, half fell, his legs a touch numb from the hours of riding. Now that he was married to a true cowboy he'd have to see about spending even more time on the back of a horse.

As soon as Forrest's arms were around him, Mica tore his gaze from the bedroom-canopy and in the soft glow of the lights he gazed into a pair of enchanting blue eyes. His heart may have skipped a beat, the yearning desire to be touched in so many delicately delicious ways growing as Forrest slipped strong arms around Mica's waist. They were as close as two people could be with the unwelcome presence of clothing, a minor issue, of course.

"So is the trek worth it? Surprised?"

"Very." Mica sort of sank into the hard form of his husband, and oh how he was learning to enjoy that word. Arms resting lightly on Forrest's shoulders he went in search of a kiss, his lips ghosting over those of his lover. As the kiss deepened, he buried a hand in Forrest's hair, for a moment indulging in the desire to never part. Strong hands worked their way down to cup his ass, then slowly moved up snaking under the hem of his shirt to brush lightly against bare skin. It sent a shiver up his spine, a moan easing from him.

It was Forrest who broke their kiss, though he stayed close enough that his breath tickled Mica's cheek when he spoke. "If we keep this up we'll never make it over to enjoying our little honeymoon spot."

"I'd be okay with that," Mica said, more than willing to pick up the promising path the kiss had laid before them.

Instead, Forrest granted Mica a quick peck and a pat on the butt before turning his attention to the horses. "How about I make sure these two are good for the night and you go get comfortable?"

Every time Forrest pulled away, Mica was chilled, the temperature around him dropping by a few degrees. He couldn't recall it ever having been that way with anyone else. Being around Forrest gave him a buzz, one he had grown addicted to. Mica always wanted to be around the man, to talk with him, touch him; he was even fine being with Forrest in silence. *Is this what it means to be in love? Of course, you buffoon. From hardly knowing the man to being his husband in less than a year...*Mica's heart swelled as he observed the man who stole his heart, the gentle caring way he tended to the horses.

"I'm a lucky man," he said under his breath, making his way over to the canopy.

Ducking inside, he was transported to a little slice of heaven. Though treated to the offerings of the surrounding wilderness, it was like the outside world disappeared; someone could have stuck one of those nature CDs in a radio. There was, as he suspected, an inflatable bed complete with pillows and a soft blanket. A cooler with a picnic basket sitting on top of it pointed to the fact that someone else had been around not too long before them, otherwise a number of critters would have happily partaken of the food. To either side of the bed, a safe distance off, were hip high shepherd's hooks with encaged candles dangling from them.

It was simple, beautiful, and purely romantic.

Mica settled on the foot of the bed, then flopped back to test it out. Through the gauze-like fabric he could still see the stars.

"I hope you aren't getting comfortable without me," quipped Forrest.

Propped up on his elbows, Mica flashed a coy smile. "Maybe I am..."

"Trust me," Forrest countered, ditching his hat by the picnic basket, "it'll be more fun if you wait for me, you know that."

"Maybe I'm tired of waiting."

Forrest sauntered over, sliding effortlessly between Mica's legs. Desperate to be touched, teased, to be set ablaze, Mica wiggled his way back on the bed. With anticipation, Mica watched as Forrest slowly undid the buttons of his shirt, carelessly discarding it in the grass, revealing hard-earned muscles and evenly tanned skin. Quickly he kicked off his boots, then started on his jeans. In a flash Mica sat up, wrapping his fingers around Forrest's wrist, stopping him.

"Let me," his voice husky.

Deftly he undid the snap and pulled down the zipper. On his knees he kissed his way up Forrest's stomach and chest, taking a moment to flick his tongue over each nipple a few times, Forrest gasping. His lips danced along Forrest's collarbone, he paused to suck gently on the nape of Forrest's neck before finally moving on to claim his lover's lips in a hungry kiss. All the while, he kept his hands busy rubbing at Forrest's growing erection, slipping a hand beyond cotton fabric to wrap his fingers around the treasure waiting there.

I want him. I want him in every imaginable way. I am his and I will never belong to another.

"I love you," he practically whispered.

A hand cupping Mica's cheek, Forrest replied, "Never more than I love you."

With those words bouncing around in his head, Mica lowered himself back down, pushing both the jeans and boxers from Forrest's hips, letting them fall to the ground. Mica licked the tip of Forrest's erection, every flick of his tongue earning him breathy gasps from Forrest, who worked capable fingers in Mica's hair. Until Forrest, he'd never been with a man—*you sure didn't waste any time in figuring out the best way to get him off*—and now he couldn't think of being with anyone else.

From licking Forrest like an ice cream cone to parting his

168 *Cowboy Roundup*

lips and drawing Forrest into his mouth, sucking him like he was a lollipop.

"Mica," he groaned.

When he says my name that way....

He worked his mouth and hand up and down, teasing Forrest to the brink.

"Please," Forrest pleaded.

Instead Mica stopped. "No....I want you."

"Well, in that case." He pursued Mica back across the bed, naked and buff, fire burning in his eyes. "I want to devour you, Mister Kettrick, tonight and every night from now until the end of time."

"Oh, don't go making promises."

"I will never have enough of you to satisfy my hunger," Forrest whispered in his ear.

Mica shivered, his jeans growing increasingly uncomfortable, butterflies fluttering in his stomach. Normally he enjoyed the long drawn out foreplay Forrest liked to put him through, but all he wanted that night was to have his man, to be with his husband, and to get his point across he bucked his hips up, denim rubbing against Forrest's erection.

"Feisty. Is there something you want?"

"You."

He was quick to wiggle out of his shirt, desperate for the sensual touch of skin on skin. Forrest mimicked his earlier moves, leaving a trail of kisses down his body until the cut of denim brought him up short. The article of clothing joined the others on the bed of grass, but his briefs remained, Forrest nipping at him through the fabric. Lips touched his inner thighs, the backs of his knees, and every place but the one where he wanted them most. At about the point he felt he might have to beg, Forrest slowly tugged down his briefs, tossing them aside, and then in one swift move, not one ounce more of teasing, Forrest swallowed the entire length of Mica's erection. The warmth, the swirling touch of Forrest's tongue, it made Mica groan, his back arching, his toes curling.

He grabbed fistfuls of the blanket, eyes closing as he lost himself to the sensations sweeping through his body. It was a bliss he never wanted to come to an end. He ached, but in an entirely different way from before, this one born of the promise of pleasures waiting right around the corner, the heavenly high that always sent him tumbling. And just when he thought he might topple over the side of the cliff, Forrest stopped, rising up to give him a kiss, the heat between them almost too much for Mica to bear.

Now in the perfect position Forrest began to move his hips, their erections trapped between them, rubbing against each other. Lips parted and tongues met, performing a delicate tango. Mica ran questing hands up and down Forrest's back, his sides, once or twice cupping his ass in an attempt to somehow pull the cowboy in closer. And then he was there, soaring into that sweet spot, finding release, a momentary thought straying across his mind—*it was never this good with any of them, not a single one. It was meant to be him, always.*

Forrest groaned, going still as he joined Mica in the after-shocks of their lovemaking. They lay that way, Forrest propped up on an elbow, their chests together, Mica holding onto his man, shuddering as they both slowly came down. The cool night breeze created quite the pleasant sensation on sweat glistened skin. Mica gave Forrest a kiss, never wanting the moment to end. But eventually Forrest rolled off to his side and after a moment, something unspoken passing between them, both men wiggled underneath the warmth of the blanket. It wasn't exactly chilly out, but laying there naked under the glow of the stars, the dancing flames of candles, Mica knew he felt exposed, never mind the fact they were miles away from the nearest house.

"I love you," Forrest said, pulling Mica close. "I have from the very moment you walked into the bar. You know," he smiled, light dancing in his eyes, "it was the sight of you that caused me to lose focus and get tossed from that stupid mechanical bull. My reputation took a little bruising that night."

"I'm sorry," Mica said. *Why does he always smell so good, like sunshine and cotton and all those good things in life?*

"Why?" Forrest looked him straight in the eye. "I'm not. That was the day, Mica Kettrick—and may I just say how much I love the sound of that?—that I realized you were the man for me."

"A fish out of water."

"Maybe, but you were my fish and I was more than willingly, completely eager, to drag you into my pond." Forrest began leaving feathery kisses along Mica's jawline, the curve of his neck. Mica could already feel the familiar stirring in his groin. As long as the day had been, something told him neither of them would be getting much sleep, at least not that night. "Tell me something, my splendid city fish, how are you enjoying the pond?"

Mica turned, rolling onto his back so he could look at Forrest, always more than willing to get lost in those magnificent blue eyes—*they really should be considered criminal.* Before he answered, Mica ghosted his fingers down the length of Forrest's body, finding that his man was already growing hard, ready for another round.

"I wouldn't exactly say I'm swimming around," he stated, kissing Forrest. "Haven't you heard, I've been hooked?"

GUY WALKS INTO A BAR

BY GEORGINA LI

VIC WATCHED THE kid wind his way through Max's Bar, one of a handful of watering holes in town, wearing too-tight jeans and a tee shirt so thin Vic wasn't sure the threads would hold together through the night. Vic recognized him from previous years, though he'd never taken the time to learn his name. He'd been too young. He was young still, but clearly, the kid was grown now. Vic could tell by the way he carried himself as much as anything: the kid knew what he wanted.

At least he thought he did.

Vic figured he wanted more than he knew how to ask for, figured he'd been like that once himself, was sure as shit relieved those days were behind him.

Vic was too busy on his family's ranch to spend much time in town, which looking at the kid he was kicking himself for now, but ranching was long days and long nights, not enough sleep in between more often than he'd like. So it had been a while since he'd been to Max's. He and Max had come up together, had always been tight and always would be, both of them cut from the same cloth—two sides of the same coin, his Aunt Junie always said. Max had done well for himself with this place, but he still worked as hard as he always had, poured for his customers every night, talked to everyone who sat down, and never hesitated to step in when shit went south. Bar fights were less common at Max's Bar than most, but even Max couldn't keep a lid on cowboy tempers forever, no matter how much practice Vic had given him back in the day. Sometimes, shit was still gonna go south.

But shit was an inevitable consequence of ranching, and Vic knew that as well as anyone. Half the county had gone tits up or damn close, ranchers selling off to big buyers, young folks leaving, old folks dying. Crofford Ranch was holding its own for now, but tough times had hit them hard back when his uncle died, and it was all his Aunt Junie could do to hold on until Vic got out of school. He'd turned things around slow and steady, got the ranch running in the black again. He raised up the finest small-herd cattle in the county, was actively expanding the ranch's business, and had opened part of their land for the Bighorn migration, just like Uncle Joe had always wanted. Aunt Junie said he ought to have his own dreams now, didn't need to be following hers and Joe's like he was, but Junie and Joe Crofford had given him a home when his good-for-nothing father couldn't be bothered, and loved him when he was unlovable, and Vic was pretty sure there was no better dream than the one he was already living.

"Grew up good, right?" Max said quietly, drawing Vic's attention back to the here and now. "Not you, asshole. The kid. And don't even try pretendin' to me you didn't notice, Vic Crofford. I'll toss your lyin' ass right off that stool."

Vic tensed. He didn't talk about this shit, not with Max, not with anyone. He finished his drink, watched Max refill it, said, finally, "Yeah. I noticed."

Max just rolled his eyes. "He's hired at Old Wickers' ranch again. Been in a few times with the guys, leaves with 'em, too." Max nodded like he'd said what he had to say and moved on down the bar, pouring drinks, talking to his customers. Vic watched him work, smiled to himself. He was damn lucky to have a friend like Max.

Max made it look easy, shooting the shit, refilling drinks, working his way back to Vic again. He poured Vic a fresh Stagg, smirked, said, "You remember that shithole down in San Angelo?"

Vic laughed. "I remember the blonde started that fight gave you killer crabs." Vic had come to the next morning with a black eye and half-busted ribs, his boots gone all together, never to be seen again, but at least he wasn't clawing at junk for a week after.

"She was stacked, though," Max smiled, wistfully, of all damn things. Christ, the gal gave him crabs, and he remembers her fondly. "You can at least admit she was hot, man. C'mon."

"Sure," Vic said. Her boyfriend hadn't been bad, either, but this was Max's trip down memory lane, not his. "Sweet rack, right?"

"She had a sweet ass on her, too, boy," Max said, grinning, shaking his head at the memory. He could always pick 'em. "Hell of a night, hell of a fight. You were a damn brawler back then. Don't know how you ever had the hands for ridin' and ropin' like you did."

"The hell you mean, did? My hands are sweet as—"

"Oh, hey, save it for the kid." Max kept grinning, and Vic let the comment wash over him, let Max's easy way make him easy, too. There was a reason Max's Bar had stood the test of time. He had a way with people, even assholes like Vic. "Those were good days."

"They were," Vic agreed. Vic's fighting days were pretty much over now, but he'd grown up fighting, started with his daddy and went on even after the old man got himself shot in a shitty Vegas motel, leaving Vic behind for good. Thank God for Joe and Junie, Vic thought for the millionth time, toasting them, and Max, too, with a tilt of his glass. "Good days ahead, too."

Max smiled, clasped Vic's arm quick and firm. "Don't run off my customers," he said as he got back to work, and Vic nodded, smirked into his drink.

Vic wouldn't dare.

Folks came and went on the stool beside Vic, grabbing a fresh beer, a whiskey, and Vic made small talk, caught up with the folks he hadn't seen in a while. Vic knew all he had to do was wait for the kid to find him, so he sipped his drink, kept his counsel, and caught up with the goings on all over the county. Still, his eyes wandered. Belt buckles and big hats, beer bottles and shot glasses and the kid smiling and flirting his way through the bar. He had a sweetness about him still, like he knew he could be choosy, but just couldn't quite believe it.

The kid wound up beside him eventually, leaning on the bar, smiling at Max and ordering himself another beer. He turned to Vic, smile gone shy, said, "You're Vic Crofford."

"I know," Vic said, leaning closer. "And you are?"

"Tennyson," the kid said, laughing, his hand covering his mouth for a moment, then landing on Vic's bicep. "Tennyson Ayers. I been working up the nerve to come over here and introduce myself to you forever. I can't believe I forgot to do it!"

Vic couldn't help laughing with him, couldn't help the grin when the kid inched his stool closer to Vic's. "Good to meet you, Tennyson."

"I go by Tenn, mostly." Again with the easy smile, Vic noted, as Tennyson explained, "I'm hired on at the Wickers again. Seasonal for now, since this is the first year I don't have to go back at end of the summer. I finished up my Masters in December. Couldn't wait to get back here this spring."

Vic nodded. "Heard the lambs started early at Wickers', and just kept on comin'," he said, and Tennyson beamed, and the conversation flew on from there. Tennyson's calloused hand found its way back to Vic's arm, and Vic's boot landed on the lowest rung of Tenn's barstool, the most natural thing in the world.

Vic walked Tennyson back to his truck, the parking lot beside the bar nearly empty, the night quiet. "Have dinner with me next week," Vic said, and Tenn nodded, licked his lips. Vic slid his hand up from Tenn's shoulder, around to the nape of his neck. "I'm gonna kiss you now," Vic said, and pulled him close.

Vic's thigh pushed between his legs, and Tennyson gasped into the kiss, giving as good as he got. Vic had no idea at all how much time had passed when he forced himself to put a little distance between them. A very little, but still. Tennyson was hard and panting, his plush lips kissed red, skin pink from Vic's stubble, and the last thing Vic wanted to do was stop, but he did it anyway. He wanted more than a quick rut against the kid's dusty old Chevy, no matter how good it would be, and Christ Almighty, he knew it would be good.

"Fuck, Vic, c'mon," the kid breathed, and Vic kissed him again, had to, then had to make himself take a step back.

"Saturday," he said, and opened the door to Tenn's truck, closed it again as soon as Tenn slid inside. Vic didn't want to wait a week to see him again, to taste him, but that was life this time of year, and they both knew it. Tenn wasn't in the truck but sixty seconds before regret hit deep in Vic's gut. He wished he'd jerked Tenn off when he had the chance, wrapped his hand around Tenn's hard cock, fast and dirty right here in the parking lot, wished he'd be driving home with Tenn's scent on his fingers, Tenn's taste on his lips. He regretted the fuck out of it, and one look at the kid, sitting in his truck, lips parted, jeans half undone, he was pretty sure he wasn't the only one.

"Saturday," Vic said again, gruffly.

Tenn nodded, watched Vic walk to his own truck before he finally started his engine, and pulled away.

PEOPLE TALKED, VIC knew that better than anyone. He'd been fodder for the rumor mill most of his life. Couldn't be helped, his daddy being who he was, and Vic's own wild days being what they were. But Vic had long since settled down, learned the difference between giving a damn and taking everything personally, and pretty much kept himself to himself. There was no telling what Tennyson had heard about him, but the fact of Vic's solitary nature was certainly old news by now. It also wasn't actually a fact, but that never mattered when tongues were wagging.

Truth was, Vic loved the Crofford Ranch almost as much as he loved the Croffords, and the only fights he had these days were with himself, late nights out grazing with the herd, the sea of stars overhead his only witness. On the one hand, he was happier than he'd ever been. On the other, he was lonely. He'd always wanted a partner to share the ranch with, he'd just never met the right man. He realized he didn't have many meetin' opportunities out here, but he didn't have it in him to look anywhere else, either. His one serious relationship had been at University, but that hadn't lasted after Vic took over the ranch. He'd been with men since then, of course, but not seriously. He played when he travelled, lovers in different cities he'd known for years, but he'd never brought any of them out to the ranch, never even wanted to.

Even if a guy chanced to catch his eye here at home, Vic hadn't ever looked twice until Tennyson.. He knew he should take Tennyson out to the Chop House in town, buy him a decent steak, and let him see for himself Vic wasn't closeted, wasn't whatever it was he'd heard, but Vic wasn't going to do it.

He was going to invite Tennyson over instead, show him the ranch he loved, grill up the steaks he'd raised and butchered himself, watch Tenn enjoy every bite. Vic was going to spread Tenn out and touch him all over, run his hands over every inch of Tenn's beautiful body, blow him until he couldn't remember his own name. Because that's the kind of man Vic was, and he wasn't about to start pretending otherwise now.

He had a feeling Tennyson wouldn't mind.

When Tennyson's truck pulled up to Vic's the following Saturday evening, Vic met him outside, the fading light golden on his skin, in his hair. "Hey, Vic," he said, smiling, and Vic knew he'd figured right. He couldn't help kissing Tenn as soon as he stepped out of his truck, jeans and boots and a button down shirt, crisp white tee showing where he'd left a few buttons open at the collar. Vic's hand slid around the curve of Tenn's neck and up through his hair, holding him close, breathing him in.

"Hey yourself," Vic said, finally. Tenn's smile must have been contagious, because Vic couldn't seem to stop smiling, either. "Come on in for a minute, let's grab a couple beers. Was thinkin' I'd show you the ranch while there's still light, eat after?"

"Sounds great," Tennyson said, as Vic led him inside. Vic didn't give much thought to his house anymore, but Tenn said, "Vic, this place is gorgeous. You build it yourself?" and Vic remembered what it was like when he was first building, how he was awestruck by it nearly every day, exhausted and thrilled.

"Mostly," Vic said, grinning. "I had a lot of help. Friend of mine from school turned my ideas into real plans, blueprints, and my guys here helped with the construction. We built their cabins first, got the basics figured out. Hoping to start building out again, soon."

"Wow," Tennyson said, and Vic knew he was thinking about the Wickers' Ranch, the old trailers where the ranch hands stayed, the shabby conditions. "That's awesome."

"The Crofford's have always done things a little different," Vic explained as he grabbed two bottles from the fridge, opened them both, handed one to Tenn. "My Uncle Joe had a lot of ideas."

"Yeah?" Tenn asked, taking a swig as he followed Vic out the kitchen door. "What about you? You got ideas, too?"

Best idea Vic ever had was going to Max's Bar last week, second best would be fucking Tenn right here, his land stretched out around them and glowing in the setting sun, but he didn't think that was what Tenn meant. Then again…Vic stole a quick look at Tenn, caught the sparkle in his eyes. "Oh, I got ideas," Vic growled, kissed him again, headed toward the stables. "What about you?"

Tenn laughed. "So many ideas!"

Vic couldn't believe how right it felt, walking the ranch with Tenn, talking about the land, the mountains, the bighorn project, the bison coming back. Vic took a long pull from his beer, stole another kiss as they approached the barn. "Thanks for this," Vic said. "When I invited you out to dinner, coming here probably isn't what you were thinking."

"Can't say I was thinking at all," Tenn said, and the way he looked, the way he sounded, was driving Vic crazy. "You're kinda mind-blowing, Vic Crofford."

It was all Vic could do not to press him up against the sun-warm wood and make him beg. But he had a plan, and fucking Tenn tonight wasn't part of it. "Back at ya," Vic said instead, adjusting himself, watching Tenn watch him.

They saddled up a couple horses, Tenn moving around the stable like he'd been born to it, comfortable with the animals, clearly an experienced rider. Vic pointed out the cabins, the area he was planning to build next, answered Tenn's questions without going into too much detail. He didn't get the impression Tenn would've minded, though. His questions were thoughtful, intuitive. So far he'd avoided saying a whole lot about himself, but Vic was a patient man. In the meantime, riding with Tenn was easy. Vic wished they had time for more than a quick look around. "You guys take the horses off-ranch much?"

"I wish," Tenn said, wistfully, as they turned the horses back. "Too busy, anyway."

"Yeah," Vic said. Lord knew days off on a ranch were a rare thing, even for a hired hand. But Uncle Joe had always said, if you wanted the time, you had to make it. Vic had never really wanted it before, but with Tenn riding beside him, he sure as hell wanted it now. "You get a chance, I'd love to take you. Do some fishin', spend the day.

Tennyson nodded, Vic watched him swallow, duck his head.

While Vic fired up the grill, Tenn talked about school, the work he'd done as a field tech as an undergrad, restoring an artificially diverted stream to its natural course, finishing his Masters in Wildlife Biology, the paper he and two of his fellows published last fall in the Journal of Wildlife Management. He spoke less about his mom and dad than he did about his older brothers—one lawyer, one investment banker, both married—and less about his family as a whole than his friends, his work, his education.

Vic noticed. He didn't like it, but he left it alone.

"This is amazing, Vic," Tenn said when they sat down to eat. It was just a simple meal, steaks and sweet potatoes, cold beer, Junie's sourdough bread, but it was one of Vic's favorites.

"Thanks," Vic replied. They talked as they ate, Vic telling Tennyson about the hunting trips he'd started the previous fall, how he took the first group on a four day ride, provided the gear and the water and did all the cooking. It was a blast, but a whole lot more work than he'd expected, even though this group of guys were all experienced trail-riders.

"How come this is the first I'm hearing about these trips? Is it some kinda family secret?"

Vic flushed. "Not exactly," he said, forcing himself to meet Tenn's eyes. "But I'm a private person, and I do my best not to give folks much to talk about in town. Plus, I wanted to try it out first. If it didn't fly, I didn't see any reason to set it out there."

"Cool," Tenn said. "So, did it fly?"

"Yeah, it did." Vic grinned, "I got a few trips on the schedule for this year already, might add more if I can hire on. I'm thinking it could be a good thing for us. This has always been a family ranch, you know? I ain't ever gonna sell, but...."

He trailed off, concerned he'd said too much already.

Tennyson had no reason to care about Vic's plans for the future of his family's ranch. Except Tennyson said, "I'd love to hear more sometime, if you feel like talking about it," and he sounded like he meant it. Looked like it, too, big gorgeous eyes meeting Vic's, smiling, sincere.

Christ.

Vic was in so much trouble here. He nodded, cleared his throat. "So, Wildlife Biology. I'm impressed. That's a serious science degree."

"I love it," Tenn said, simply. "I love being out here."

Vic nodded. He loved it, too. "I thought about doing something else for about a minute, when I first started school," Vic admitted. "But I could never really see it, sitting in an office or something, wearing a suit every day."

"Sounds awful," Tenn laughed. "On the plus side, I bet you look amazing in a suit."

Vic shook his head. "Not worth the trade."

Tennyson looked away, smile fading. Vic asked him gently, "Your family doesn't agree?"

"They're pretty comfortable with the suits," he said, trying for nonchalance and missing it by a mile. Tenn looked young and sad for a moment, alone, and Vic wished he could wipe that look off Tennyson's face, make sure it stayed gone for good. "They don't really get me. I guess I'm the black sheep of the family."

Vic knew there was more to that story, knew whatever it was would piss him off, but he did his best not to let it show. Instead he reached across the table, stroked Tenn's hand, the inside of his wrist, the rough scrape on his forearm. "That sucks, Tenn. I'm sorry."

"It's cool," Tennyson lied, though he sounded more resigned than anything. "I'm happy with where I am."

That part, at least, was true. "I'm happy with where you are, too," Vic said, meeting Tenn's eyes. "Let's leave the dishes," he suggested, standing up and pulling Tenn up beside him. "We can start a fire, make out, save dessert for later."

"You made dessert?"

"Nah," Vic said, laughing, steering Tenn through the wide-open archway to the couches by the fireplace. "It is homemade, though. My aunt."

"Sweet," Tenn said, letting Vic press him to the couch, grinning as Vic stared down at him. Christ, the way this kid looked, half rent boy, half ranch hand, legs splayed, lips parted like he wasn't seven kinds of hurt inside.

Vic knew better, had known better when he brought Tenn's family up, wished he could take the words back as soon as he said them. He couldn't, but he could do this, build a fire, kiss Tenn until his lips were numb and swollen and cherry red, kiss him and touch him and let him know this wasn't a casual thing for Vic, wasn't something he did easily. *Or ever*, supplied the little voice inside his head that sounded suspiciously like his Aunt Junie, though he figured he'd leave that part out for now.

Tenn's lips were soft against Vic's, firm and plush, his tongue tangling with Vic's, hands roaming over his chest and shoulders. Vic let him touch, let him feel the heat of his skin and the strength of his muscles, the steady beat of Vic's heart when he pressed his calloused palm to Vic's chest. Vic ran his own rough hands under the layers of Tennyson's shirts, pushing them up, exposing Tenn's lean abs, hard and smooth, drinking in the golden skin beneath his fingers.

Tenn gasped when Vic's fingers found a still-tender bruise on his side, mumbled, *ornery ram, it's nothing*, against Vic's lips, and Vic covered the bruise with his palm and pressed with intent this time, Tenn's hips bucking up, drawing Vic in close.

Vic drew Tenn's arm up, dragging his shirts over Tenn's head until they tangled around his biceps. He pulled back a moment just to admire the view, Tenn's hard dick straining in his jeans, his bare belly, the soft skin under his arms, the thatch of hair Vic had to bury his face in and breathe deep, kissing and sucking right there until Tenn laughed and squirmed against him. Vic moved on to his nipples, biting and licking and promising them more, later, before taking Tenn's sweet mouth again, slow and easy.

"Vic," Tenn breathed, licking at Vic's mouth, shifting his legs so they lined up better, making himself groan. "Vic, c'mon, tell me what you like."

"I like this," Vic said, "Kissing you, touching you. I like seeing you stretched out for me, strong and gorgeous. I like that you like this, that you're letting me touch you as much as I want, that you're going to let me get you off just like this, send you home sticky with your own seed."

Tenn moaned, and Vic pressed their hips together, rubbed his cock against the length of Tenn's, ducked his head to bite at Tenn's lips.

Vic kissed and sucked and licked and kept his hands out of Tenn's pants, though he was so tempted by the damp patch of denim it nearly killed him. He bent to taste it just once, covering it with his mouth, running his chin along Tenn's hard dick before he surged up again, kissing his throat, the skin under his ear, murmuring about what else he liked, what he wanted to do next time, what he wanted Tenn to do, too. Tenn moaned and panted and flushed so pretty, and Vic took mercy on him finally and flipped their positions.

Tenn tossed his shirts away and begged Vic to keep talking, fingers digging into Vic's chest, grinding his dick against Vic's. Vic kissed him hard, murmured against his lips until Tenn groaned, said, "I'm gonna come just like you said, shoot in my jeans like a kid."

"You're so fuckin' gorgeous like this," Vic told him, palming Tenn's ass and thrusting up. He wasn't going to come, but Tenn was, and Vic wanted to see it. "C'mon," he said, "come for me," and Tenn did, shaking so hard Vic couldn't help wrapping his arms around him, holding him close.

"God, Vic," Tenn said after a while, Vic stroking up and down Tenn's back, his arms, rubbing his scalp. Tenn was boneless, a warm heavy weight on top of him, and Vic loved it, was almost sorry Tenn was coming back to himself so soon. "You didn't, hey, let me—"

"Not tonight," Vic said, kissing him softly. "This is what I wanted tonight."

"Okay," Tenn said, but he sounded uncertain. Vic was still hard, still pressed against Tenn's hip. Vic could understand his confusion. "Are you sure?"

"What about me, about anything I said or did, anything that happened tonight, makes you think I wouldn't tell you exactly what I wanted?"

Tenn flushed all over again, obviously remembering that Vic had done exactly that. "Well, when you put it that way," he said with a grin. "So you were serious? About next time?"

"Yes," Vic said simply. "Do you want that, too?"

Tenn leaned up and pressed a kiss to Vic's mouth. "Maybe," he said. "I definitely want a next time."

"Me, too," Vic said, leaving the rest up to Tenn. He would do as Vic asked or he wouldn't, and Vic wanted to see him again either way.

He was still sending Tenn home with come in his jeans, though.

WHEN TENN LEFT last Saturday, Vic knew he hadn't made up his mind yet and Vic hadn't pushed. Had kissed him for another hour or so, talking and laughing, and had put him into his truck with a promise to talk soon. Once Tenn's taillights disappeared in the night, Vic jerked himself off furiously, coming with two fingers as deep in his ass as he could get them, his cock in a death grip, unable to make it last without Tenn to hold his focus.

Now, though, Vic had other plans. He would go with whatever Tenn decided, but fuck, he *wanted*. He was wound up like a wildcat with wanting, had been terse with his crew all day, last few days, probably, if Vic knew himself at all. When finally he heard Tenn's truck outside, he took a deep breath for what felt like the first time in days.

He stalked the length of his house, bare feet silent on the wood floors, chime of the porch bells fading as he approached. On the other side of the thick door Vic knew Tennyson was waiting, six feet of lean muscle and golden skin and big brown eyes that looked at Vic like he was the only thing that mattered.

Vic opened the door and there he was with his big open smile, hat in hand, every bit as beautiful as Vic remembered. It had only been a week, but the time had passed slowly for Vic, and it was all he could do not to fuck Tenn right there.

Vic looked him up and down, hand snaking out to wrap around Tenn's wrist, pulling him inside in one swift move. He pressed Tenn back until the door closed behind him, and let himself just breathe for a minute. He focused on Tenn's sweet scent, soap and fresh air and clean sweat underneath, and reined himself in. It shouldn't be this good, just standing here like this, Vic's thighs spreading Tenn's legs, Vic's hips pinning him against the door.

"You're here," Vic said, needlessly, lips barely moving against Tenn's. Tenn started to reply, "Yeah," or "Vic," or something else, it didn't matter, because Vic was already kissing him, one hand behind his head, fingers carding into his hair, swallowing whatever Tennyson was going to say. Vic was irritated with himself for whispering those words in the first place, but now, with Tennyson arching against him so sweet, Vic's equilibrium was reestablishing itself in a hurry.

One quick move and Tenn's legs were spread, his wrists held together in Vic's right hand and stretched along the cool wood of the door. Vic's other hand was still cradled behind Tennyson's head, protective. He twisted his fingers in Tenn's hair, dark blond curls catching on his calluses, Tenn's breath catching in his throat.

Vic mouthed the skin just there, right where Tenn's breath caught, worked his way to Tenn's lips, soft and plush, sweeter than Vic had any right to, but he sure the hell wasn't about to pass it up. Who would? Fuck, he was gorgeous, so new there was still a shine on him, desire spilling off him in waves.

"Did you get yourself ready for me?" Vic asked, and Tenn's pulse raced, skin flushing true.

"Yeah," he breathed. "It was kinda hot."

Vic wished he hadn't asked Tenn to shave bare and clean

himself out before he arrived, not because Vic had changed his mind about wanting it, but because now he wanted that pleasure for himself, wanted to watch the bare pink skin emerge from beneath the golden thatch of pubes, feel Tenn's cock stiffen, his balls pull up. "Yeah? You come?"

Tenn's blush turned fierce. "Twice."

Vic hmmmed, nipped at Tenn's skin, pressed a hand against his tight abs. Tenn moaned, and Vic knew he'd fill Tenn himself next time, imagined the sounds he'd would make, the way he'd squirm, helpless, cared for, safe. Vic didn't like the idea of Tennyson getting himself ready in one of the old trailers at Wicker's Ranch, didn't want him to be alone like that next time.

Tenn's hips were fighting a losing battle to hold still, Vic's body pressed against his too hard to resist, the friction too good. Tenn's cock was hard, flat against his belly, head of it poking out of his low slung jeans, wet and ready. Vic could smell him already, Christ, so fucking sweet.

Vic pushed Tenn's shirt up, pulled away enough to watch his skin pebble, watch his own thumb swipe against the dark head of Tenn's dick, smear the pre-come against the sensitive crown. Vic pressed his thumb to the slit, tapped it, and another bead of pre-come welled up, as if on command.

"Nice," Vic said softly, pressing the fat swell of his own cock against the hard line of Tennyson's, getting another moan, another sweet spurt of fluid against his thumb. "I'm gonna fuck you now," Vic told him, and Tennyson swore, pressed his hips hard against Vic's, his shoulders still against the door, his hands still right where Vic put them.

Vic nodded, almost to himself, and gently brought Tennyson's arms down from the wall, kissed his mouth again, ripe and perfect, held one hand as he led the way through the house, into his bedroom with its wall of one-way glass overlooking his family's ranch. There were no sight lines from the main house, where Vic's Aunt Junie lived, to the plot Vic had chosen for his own home, Vic just liked his privacy. He liked to see the wide open country stretched out before him every morning, liked the way the land seemed to glow at dusk, night falling over the ranch until it was black as pitch, held close by the mountains to the west, the moon and stars overhead.

Vic thought their reflections in the glass looked good together, Vic broad and thickly muscled, close-cropped hair glinting with silver, dulled by the blue light, and Tennyson, all lean lines and sharp angles, their faces blurred, softened. Vic was torn between uncovering Tennyson's body inch by tortuous inch, making him beg, making him crazy with need, or simply watching Tenn strip as fast as he could manage so they'd be naked all the quicker. Vic avoided the decision and kissed Tenn instead, unbuttoning his own shirt with one hand and moving Tenn inexorably toward his bed.

Vic shrugged off his shirt, tossed it onto the chair by his dressing table. Tennyson's hands were immediately on Vic's bare skin, covering the thick muscles of his arms, his shoulders, his chest. His hands roamed over Vic's back, up his sides, down his abs, hesitated at Vic's zipper. "Vic, I," Tenn breathed, warm rush of air, lips ghosting the stubble along Vic's jawline, his throat. "I want to suck you, okay?"

Well, since he asked so nicely. Vic grinned, stepped out of his pants, and draped them over the chair with his shirt. He wrapped a hand around his own thick meat, jacked himself slow while Tenn popped the buttons on his straining jeans—carefully, Vic noticed, like he didn't want to touch himself too much. Tenn's dick was dark against his abs, wet, leaving slick trails on his skin as he quickly shed his clothes, barely taking his eyes off Vic's big cock.

Vic pulled him close again, let their dicks slide together, his hands full of Tenn's sweet ass, almost too good to let go. But let go he did, Tenn sitting on the edge of the bed, looking up at him, lips just slightly parted. Vic stood between his legs, rubbed the fat head of his cock over those gorgeous lips, slow, so slow. Tenn's tongue flicked out, wet and soft. Vic watched the taste register on his face just before his eyes closed, lips wrapping around Vic's thick cock. Perfect, Vic thought, the heat of his mouth, the bump of his soft palate, his cheeks hollowed, lips stretched so pretty.

Vic's hand wrapped into Tennyson's hair again, easy, like it belonged there, as he pushed in deeper, just enough to feel the first clutch of Tenn's gag reflex before he pulled back again. Vic loved the way that felt, the way it looked, Tenn's face flushed, strong hands gripping Vic's quads, digging into solid muscle, thumbs edging up close to Vic's balls, wanting more but unable to take it.

Tennyson whined as Vic pulled out, tongue tracing the thick vein, sucking where Vic's fingers were wrapped around the base of his cock. Vic bent to kiss him, grinning as Tenn's eyes blinked open. He couldn't resist chasing the trace of his own skin on Tenn's lips, in his mouth, running his hands over Tenn's body as he eased Tenn onto his bed. Vic wanted to do everything—eat Tenn out, fuck him slow and then again, hard and wet, eat him out again after. He wanted to watch Tenn's face when he came, wanted to be buried balls deep while he watched Tenn blow his load. He wanted to fuck Tenn face down, arms spread wide, ass in the air, and Vic wanted to suck him after, finger the come back into his ass, make him shoot again.

For now Vic tweaked a nipple and kissed a trail through the sticky smears on Tenn's belly and down to his bare balls, ignored his cock, pressed a thumb against his hole. "Vic," Tenn moaned, "C'mon, Vic, fuck," and Vic slicked up his fingers, pressed two inside. Tenn was breathing heavy, moaning, his fingers gripping Vic's broad shoulders, pulling at the sheets, scrabbling at the headboard. Vic sucked at Tenn's balls, at the tender skin hidden between his heavy thighs, three fingers buried deep before he licked around Tenn's rim, pushed his tongue in to taste.

"Fuck," Tenn swore, and Vic couldn't make himself wait any longer.

Vic lubed his cock, rubbed the rest around Tenn's hole, and pushed into the tight heat of Tenn's body, kissed him through the initial resistance, Tenn gasping and moaning sweet. Vic pushed himself up, wrapped a hand around Tenn's still-hard dick, stroked him slow and easy as he fucked his way in deep.

Tenn pushed Vic's hand away from his cock, desperate, and Vic stilled, let Tenn catch his breath, hips just barely moving, slow, easy pulses. Tenn leaned up for a kiss, gasping into Vic's mouth, wanting more, wanting less, Vic wasn't sure if Tenn even knew. But when Vic nipped Tenn's bottom lip and eased him down again, pressing his knees toward his shoulders, Tenn grinned up at him and slid his own hands around his thighs, so Vic figured he'd gotten what he wanted. Vic leaned back for a better view, Tenn's hole gripping him so sweet, rim dragging along his cock as he pulled almost all the way out.

"Vic," Tenn begged, "Vic," and Vic growled, pushed in deep and started fucking Tenn for real.

Christ, he was sweet. Vic couldn't get enough of him. So gorgeous like this, knees pulled up, skin flushed, lips kiss-swollen. "You're fuckin' gorgeous," Vic told him. "Fuck, Tenn, I wanna fuck you all night, keep you here tomorrow, fuck you till you can't move."

"Oh God," Tennyson breathed, shaky. "God, Vic, stop talkin', I'm gonna blow."

Vic grinned, fucked in deep. "Yeah? You like that?"

"Fuck, seriously," Tenn's hands grabbed his ass, held him right where he was, fingers digging in. Vic kept himself as still as he could, his cock buried balls deep, Tenn's muscles clenching around him. "It's too late," Tenn sounded sad for a moment, lost, and then, "Vic, fuck, I'm gonna come."

Vic stared down at Tenn's dick, blood dark and twitching on his belly, untouched. Tenn's breath was ragged, like a colt run too long. Vic soothed a hand over his cheek, his throat, his chest, hoping to ease him down. But Tenn's breath caught way up high anyhow, the sound so beautiful Vic couldn't stop his hips from twisting just a little. He had to, fuck, Tenn's ass so tight on his cock, the feel of him, the sound, and then Tenn was shooting, thick white spurts striping his chest, his belly, just from Vic's dick in his ass, from the sound of Vic's voice.

Vic kissed him hard, wrapped a hand around Tennyson's dick, and stroked him through the last of it, so gorgeous, the way Tenn panted against Vic's mouth, thrashing so sweet beneath him, Vic's hips rocking slow, cock hard as fuck inside him. "God, Vic, feels like I'm gonna come forever."

Wouldn't that be a treat? Vic thought. "Tell me more," he growled, pinching one of Tenn's tight little titties, hips picking up their rhythm again. Tenn's hands slid up his back, down his shoulders, getting some leverage of his own. Vic nuzzled at his throat, pushed up, said, "Want to hear you, Tenn."

Tenn's voice was breathy when he spoke, the rasp in it making Vic crazy, "Your cock, fuck, Vic, right there, you keep doin' that, feels like I'm gonna fly apart. Never, ahh, never come like this before."

Vic figured that was probably true. He was going to make Tenn come again, no question, though didn't know how long he could keep hitting Tenn just right, not with the scent of sweat and spunk already so thick between them. "I'm gonna come inside you, eat you out again," Vic told him, and Tenn groaned, muscles clenching down hard. "You want that?"

"God, Vic." Tenn's dick was already hard in Vic's hand again, balls tight, his body aching for more. "That's so fuckin' hot. Gonna shoot again you keep it up."

"Yeah?"

"Yeah, Vic, fuck me harder, love the way your cock stretches me. You feel so huge in me, wish I could see it, your cock in me. Can you see it, Vic?"

Vic flipped him over then, and Tenn got his knees under himself quick, head down, ass in the air. They did look amazing together, Tenn's bare pink hole stretched wide, clinging to his dark cock with every stroke, tender skin dragging over Vic's meat. Fuck, it was beautiful. Vic licked his finger, rubbed it around Tenn's rim, soft at first, harder when Tenn keened. Vic couldn't wait to get his tongue in there, lick him clean.

Tenn was moaning with every breath, jacking himself, and Vic was so fucking close, pounding into Tenn's tight ass. He wrapped his hand over Tenn's, let his hips take over the pace, bringing Tenn off with a shout just a few seconds before he lost the rhythm himself, coming so hard he couldn't move, couldn't see, couldn't do anything but hold Tenn close and load out.

Vic had hauled Tenn against his chest even before his brain was back online, mouth pressed to Tenn's throat, their legs twined together. Tenn shifted comfortably in his arms and exhaled a long breath, and Vic smiled against Tenn's sweaty skin. It still surprised him, sometimes, how good his instincts were while coming his brains out.

"Hey," Vic murmured, rubbing his stubbled cheek over the messy scar on the back of Tenn's shoulder. Got caught by a mean-ass bull, he guessed, then realized he didn't have to do that. Guess. "You ever get your eight seconds?"

"Nah," Tenn said easily. "Thought I might, but I just kept growin'. Center of gravity ain't right for bull-riding."

"Don't know about that," Vic teased, thrusting his hips a little.

Tenn snorted. "Well, you are hung like a bronco," he said, rolling his eyes and laughing.

Vic laughed, too. It felt good. He hadn't fucked and laughed in a long time, longer still since he wanted to fuck again after, but he damn sure wasn't done with Tenn now. Vic's dick made an effort to get hard again, but he knew his limits. He knew a lot of things.

"Hey," Tenn said, gentle-like, "You good?"

Vic nipped the soft skin just beneath his ear. Good? Vic was a hell of a lot better than good.

Tenn laughed again, squirmed in Vic's lap. "Not like that, Vic. God, you were amazing."

"Ain't done yet," Vic said, easing them down to the bed

again, using his knees to spread Tenn's thighs. Tenn whined when Vic's cock finally slipped out, moaned when Vic slid two fingers back in, his come slick and hot inside. Vic wanted to plug Tenn just like this, keep him dirty, keep his seed right where it was. Tenn stifled a yawn in Vic's pillows, and Vic smiled to himself, thought about adding another finger, bit at Tenn's hipbone instead.

"Think you can sleep like this?" Vic asked.

Tenn shifted, drew one knee up a little, gasping at the change in angle. "Maybe. Lemme clean up a minute?"

"Not a chance," Vic said, twisting his fingers deep. He pulled a quilt over them with his free hand, made himself comfortable. When they were both settled, Tennyson snugged up close, Vic kissed the skin he could reach. "Get some rest," Vic's voice was sleep buzzed, and Tenn shivered against him, breathed out slow. Vic said, "Gonna eat you out again soon as you start dripping."

"Fuck, that's dirty," Tennyson murmured. "You keep this up, I won't wanna leave."

Vic just pulled Tenn closer, ran his thumb around Tenn's swollen hole. Right then he couldn't think of a single reason he'd ever want Tennyson to go.

When Vic woke up a few hours later, Tenn was still pressed up close, sweat-slick everywhere they touched, their scents hanging heavily in the air. Vic repositioned Tenn easily as he licked his come from Tennyson's leaking hole, ate him out until he was writhing, face down in Vic's bed, fingers twisted in the sheets, pillows scattered across the floor.

"Vic," Tenn moaned, his voice raspy with sleep and sex, "Vic, Vic, please."

Vic slid two fingers inside him easily, licked over the bare skin of his balls, the crease of his thigh, back up between his own fingers. "Gonna fill you up again," Vic growled, and Tenn pushed himself to his knees, his ass in the air, begging. Vic wrapped his free hand around Tennyson's straining dick, stroked him slow, fucked his cock in deep.

Tenn made the most delicious sounds. They filled Vic's bedroom, his whole house, probably, the sounds of their fucking echoing all around them, into the night if he'd've left the windows open, spreading over the whole ranch. Just the thought of it made Vic crazy, his hips losing the rhythm already. Tenn made him want, made him wild. He tried to rein it in, slow down and make the it last, but Tenn was pushing back against him, winding his fingers with Vic's and picking up the pace, so Vic let himself go, rammed in hard and fast, let the fuck take him over.

Vic came so hard he missed Tenn's orgasm, gently rolled Tenn to his back after, and licked the jizz from his fingers, his belly, kissed over his throat, his jaw, his mouth.

"You're amazing," Vic said softly, and Tennyson smiled, curled onto his side, and pulled Vic with him, holding Vic's fuzzy arm to his chest as he drifted into sleep again.

Vic didn't think he'd be able to follow, was surprised to wake up with the sun streaming through his windows already, alone in his bed, burrowed under the quilt he'd last seen on the floor. Life on the ranch was never really quiet, but there was a certain stillness to it that Vic had come to love, a stillness that was very clearly missing this morning, though Vic couldn't rustle up the brain cells to put two and two together quite yet.

"Fuck," he grunted, dragging himself upright, feet slung over the edge of the bed, still rubbing the sleep from his eyes. When he blinked them open again he spotted Tenn's boots up against the wall, one falling over the other, and realized he could hear the kid in the kitchen, talking softly, voice pitched low.

Vic jolted upright. There was only one person Tenn could be talking to in his kitchen on a Sunday morning, one person whose warm laughter could shake the last of the sleep from his foggy brain and have him jumping in and out of the shower too fast for the water to heat through. Vic had barely toweled off, muttering, "Fuck, fuck, fuuuuck," as he tugged his jeans over his still-damp legs, leaving them hanging off his hips as he pulled a tee shirt over his head. He was halfway to the kitchen before he forced himself to slow down, zip up, take a deep breath.

"Morning, Junie," Vic said on a long exhale, bending to kiss his aunt's cheek where she sat at his table with a big basket of her homemade blueberry muffins, drinking coffee, sweet as you please. Tennyson sat across from her, beaming happily, a big cup of creamy coffee half-empty in his hand, a buttery muffin more than half-decimated on his plate. The shirt Vic had been wearing last night was hanging off his shoulders, and something in Vic's chest opened up seeing him here like this.

"Morning, Tenn," Vic said easily, dropping a kiss on his cheek, too. "I see you've met Aunt Junie. She's the light of my life and I worship the ground she walks on, but Tennyson, this ol' gal lies like a damn rug. You can't believe a word she says."

"Oh, hush, you," Junie said, swatting at him as he refilled her coffee, and Tenn's, too, before filling one of the big white mugs for himself. "That's what you get for keeping this young man to yourself instead of bringing him 'round the house to meet me proper. You were raised better, Victor Wayne," she said sternly, though he could tell from the laughter in her voice she was mostly teasing him.

Tennyson murmured, "Victor Wayne, I like it," and Vic winced internally, tried not to let it show. Only his aunt called him that now. These days he was just plain Vic to everyone else, but then Tenn said it again, and Vic looked up, couldn't keep himself from smiling. He thought he could get used to hearing his given name from Tennyson, too.

"I haven't been here all that long," Junie continued, tucking her hair behind her ear where it'd come loose from her customary bun, same as he'd seen her do a million times. "But I'm afraid I about startled Tennyson out of his boots, coming in through the back while he was busy starting the coffee."

"He's not wearing boots," Vic commented, remembering how pleased he'd been to find them in his bedroom, pushed to the wall right where Tenn shucked them the night before.

"Well, he wasn't wearing any pants at the time, either," Junie said with a smirk and, good lord, was that a giggle? "But who am I to fuss? Such a pleasant surprise!"

Tennyson laughed, and Vic couldn't help but join in, though he didn't find it quite as funny as they did. It warmed him how easily Tenn seemed to take it all in stride, how quickly he caught on to Junie's sense of humor, how they both seemed mutually charmed.

Still, he knew his aunt, and Junie wasn't one to waste words. She may have been teasing him, but she also had a point. She knew Tennyson wouldn't be in Vic's kitchen, with or without pants, if Vic wasn't serious about him. He'd never so much as brought a 'friend', as she called his distant lovers, to see the ranch, never mind leave one of them to roam about while Vic slept soundly in his bed. It wasn't the sort of thing they spoke of often, but his aunt had made her position clear—she loved Vic dearly, and she couldn't care less who he loved in return. Junie always said she'd spent enough years on the ranch by herself to know it wasn't the sort of life a person was meant to live alone.

"Victor Wayne," Junie said when she'd gathered herself again, "Are you just going to stand there, or are you going to join us at the table?"

Vic did the only thing he could.

He opened the refrigerator, breathing a sigh of relief. After verifying he had plenty to work with, he looked his aunt in the eye, then turned to Tennyson, then back to Junie again. "I was hoping you'd let me make up for not introducing you and Tenn sooner by staying for breakfast?"

"Omelets?" Junie asked, as Vic started pulling various ingredients from the fridge.

"Anything you want," Vic agreed, and Junie nodded, settling back in her chair as was her due.

"You got bacon in there?" Tennyson asked, hip-checking Vic on his way to start another pot of coffee.

"Of course I've got bacon," Vic answered, stealing a kiss while Tenn was standing right beside him. "What kind of man do you take me for?"

"Ha!" Junie barked. Both men turned to her, grinning. "Don't mind me," she said. "I'm just a little old lady, eating a blueberry muffin and minding my own business."

Vic rolled his eyes, but he was smiling, too. "I think we all know that's not true."

"Hey, Vic," Tenn said, derailing them before their back and forth really got going. "You mind if I grab a quick shower while you cook?"

Hell, yeah, Vic minded. He liked Tenn just like this, fucked out and dirty still; he liked knowing that underneath his clothes, Tenn was sticky with lube and covered in dried come, but he wasn't about to say any of that in front of Junie. If the color rising on Tennyson's cheeks was anything to go by, though, Vic's eyes said enough to get his point across.

Vic wanted to join him in the shower, wanted to soap him up, press him against the tiled shower walls and get him dirty again, but instead he just spread his own arms and gestured one hand back toward the master bedroom.

"*Mi casa es su casa,*" Vic said, feeling his heart hammer at his ribs before it up and skipped a beat.

"Sweet," Tenn answered, smiling that big open smile Vic already couldn't resist and trailing a hand across Vic's shoulders, promising he'd be back in a flash.

Vic hadn't given the words a moment's thought before he'd said them, but now that they were out there, he knew they were true. Vic turned back to the sink and washed his hands, pulled out a couple of bowls and started on the prep work for the big Ranch-style breakfast he'd promised.

"I like him," Junie said, as soon as they heard water start up in Vic's shower. "He suits you. And he really brightens the place up, too."

Vic looked around his kitchen. Like the rest of his house, it was all windows and sunshine and panoramic views, but he knew damn well Junie was talking more about the sad aloe plant that usually served as Vic's only cooking companion than about the relative brightness of the space. "Really, Junie?"

"Don't be an idiot," she said, fondness in her voice despite the words. Vic shrugged, started cracking the eggs. "I like him a lot," she said again, giving him one of her pointed looks.

Christ. When Vic was a kid, he dreamed of a day she wouldn't be able to look at him like that and make him confess.

He knew better now.

"What?" he said finally, breaking under the weight of her stare. "Yes, okay, I like him, Junie. I like him a lot."

"I know you do," she said happily, as if she hadn't just used the glare of doom on him. Again. "And I know Tennyson likes you, too."

Vic heard the shower turn off, and breathed a sigh of relief.

Mi casa es su casa.

It was crazy, and it was way too soon, and Vic meant every word.

NEPHI TAKES A HUSBAND

BY BOB MASTERS

NEPHI SORENSON LOOKED up into the late summer sunshine pouring down over the hilly plains of San Rafael Swell, admiring the beauty of the wide open space and rough terrain. He adjusted his wide-brimmed cowboy hat to shield himself from the relentless rays. Planting his plain brown high-top boots firmly in the dusty soil, he raised his hammer and pounded a small nail into a cracked wooden fence post, firmly fastening the new line of barbed wire. It was necessary to keep the fence line mended at all times, so here he was, planted in the middle of Utah country all alone for the next day or two, mending the interminable fence that kept the cows inside the Whitmore cattle ranch.

He stopped to ponder how wealthy his employers were. Mr. Whitmore had brought five hundred longhorns up from Texas some five years earlier and now he was one of the wealthiest Mormon cattle ranchers in the entire territory of Utah. A far cry from his own situation Nephi thought. He was lucky just to earn a dollar a day, plus maybe a supply of vittles to subsist on. But when Nephi thought about it, no way would he give up the life of a cattle drover and move back to some cramped town like Salt Lake City. Maybe drovers like him were looked down on by the sophisticated folks in town; maybe they weren't worth a plugged nickel in their eyes. But those sophisticated folk never felt the thrill of a cattle drive in springtime, when the dust was so thick from thousands of pounding hooves that you had to cover your mouth and nose with your trusty bandanna, when the horse you were riding felt like a part of you, and Then, when you finally did your bidding with the buyers, after it was all said and done, the moon sailed on up over the camp come nightfall and a million stars filled the sky.

He suddenly heard the steady pounding of hooves coming up the Old Spanish Trail from the west. That was strange. No one used that trail anymore. The Spaniards in Santa Fe had used it to trade Indian-woven blankets and such with other Spaniards in Los Angeles back in the old days. They brought hundreds of horses back with them as payment. But they had also liked to round up Indians, mostly Paiute women and children, along the way. They then sold them into slavery at both ends of the long, hardscrabble trail. The Mexican-American war had changed that situation by 1846, when California and New Mexico became U.S. Territory. Now it was 1855, and Nephi's people had been here for some eight years. They frowned on taking Indians as slaves. Indians were their allies against the U.S. government that had allowed them to be chased here from Illinois.

Nephi walked over to his pack and pulled out his rifle. He checked to see it was loaded properly and waited for the now visible figure to come into focus. Gradually, he could make out what the stranger looked like. He was a young man like himself, probably a few years beyond his own age of eighteen. He had a bright red shirt in the Spanish style, with a beautiful blue bandanna around his neck. His boots were shiny brown and tan leather, and looked new. His denim pants fit tightly around his legs. Topping it all was a big, ten-gallon sombrero.

"Halt!" he cried out as loud as he could, trying to sound authoritative.

The colorful dude pulled the reins in on his handsome

white steed and brought it to an abrupt halt.

"Name your purpose and where you come from, stranger! This is the Whitmore cattle ranch. We don't like strangers sneaking up the Old Spanish Trail. Too many rustlers these days..."

"Name's Johnny Holden," offered the well-dressed buckaroo. That was the term for California cowhands. Nephi knew they had their own culture, still strongly influenced by the Spanish. "Just passing through on the way to Santa Fe. I am on my father's business and mean no harm."

"What business can you have on the Old Spanish Trail? No one uses it these days. There are lots of wagon freight trails that can ship goods a lot more easily. It's 1855, mind you, not 1842," Nephi countered, still wary, but relaxing just a little.

"I know. My father thinks he can drum up business again, if the traders in Santa Fe promise not to grab any more Paiutes, that is," offered the fancy dressed cowhand.

"What's he want to trade?" asked Nephi, now taking in the deep green eyes and dark skin of the stranger's face.

"He's got lots of horses he wants to sell. He figures he can re-awaken the horse trade that was so well-established in the old days. He is kind of a dreamer, I know. But the trail is not too horrible, even now."

"But nobody uses it!" objected Nephi.

"Cause they might get scalped! Those Paiutes have got a long memory! I had to explain myself probably twenty times," said Johnny, palpably letting some tension loose.

Nephi could see why. Johnny's dark skin and hair combined with his sombrero and bright red shirt made him look almost Spanish. The Indians probably wanted to kill him. Lucky for him, his features were clearly Anglo.

"Well, I don't envy you. I don't think modern traders are going to want to revisit the traditions of their forefathers anytime soon."

"I don't mind. I like to see the country anyway. California is nice, but sometimes I just want to get out and go."

Now the conversation was turning friendly, reckoned Nephi. What the heck, he was too well-dressed to be a rustler. And he was traveling all alone. Just like himself, he thought. All alone on the great big Utah plain—it could get lonely out here.

"Well, I see no reason to detain you. But if you would like to pause and rest here for a spell, I reckon that would be fine."

Nephi watched as the young Californian buckaroo thought over his suggestion. His own thoughts pondered how nice it would be to own such fancy duds like this Californian. But his Mormon brothers would never allow that! One was expected to be modest, right down to the uncomfortable garments he had to wear underneath his plain white shirt and work pants. They were supposed to provide spiritual protection, but Nephi sometimes thought all they did was make him sweat more in the Utah desert heat.

"Don't mind if I do, brother. Say, I don't recall hearing your name," he said as he gracefully dismounted the beautiful white steed.

"Nephi. Nephi Sorenson. I work for the Whitmore cattle ranch. It is one of the biggest ranches in the Utah territory."

"You don't say," said Johnny as he tethered his horse to the fence post that Nephi had just been working on. "What kind of name is…Nee-fi?"

"It's from the Book of Mormon. He was a righteous man," explained Nephi, a little embarrassed but also proud, all at the same time.

"I see. I should have guessed. This being Utah and everything," he said, winking at Nephi.

"You know much about our gospel?" asked Nephi.

"No, I am afraid I am not very religious. Sometimes I go to the Catholic Church back home, more often when I was just a kid. Learned a lot of Spanish that way. Well, then, are you also righteous?"

"I try to be. I can tell you about doctrine later, if you are interested. I guess I better get back to work now, though. I have to mend this whole five-mile southern fence of the ranch."

"I would be glad to help out. Nothing much else to do, seeing as how the day is getting short. Thought I might like to camp out here tonight—near civilization—for a change, if you don't mind. But I like to earn my keep."

"That would be fine. Can't pay you, but you are welcome to share my grub when I finish off this evening."

"Sounds fine."

So they began inspecting the string of fence line that seemed to stretch off into infinity. Together they unspooled and replaced barbed wire, re-planted broken or damaged posts, and dug up roots that stretched the wire open too far. Nephi Sorenson and Johnny Holden talked and chatted like two young men are apt to do. Nephi found himself stealing glances at the tight-fitting denim pants that Johnny wore so unselfconsciously. He wondered if he would ever be confident enough to wear something so, well…immodest. That was the word that first formed in his mind, but that wasn't really what he felt when he stopped to think about it. Attractive was closer. He never thought of himself that way, but now that he was eighteen, it was natural that he would begin to have such thoughts, even comparing himself to other men, he told himself. Even so, it made him feel uncomfortable, as if some inchoate tension inside him was beginning to well up.

The two young cowpokes stood in their pointed high-top boots, one in shiny and fine leather, the other in plain tanned cowhide, for several hours. Nephi's feet became sore and his leg muscles ached. When the sun finally began to sink towards the horizon, bathing them in glorious gold, reds, and yellows as they looked on with wonder, they decided it was time to mount their horses and make it back to Nephi's little camp.

Nephi commenced to build a fire and set a frying pan over it. The Whitmore Ranch provided pretty good food for their drovers. He added a well-salted piece of venison meat into the pan with some carrots and even an onion. He added some water from his canteen to slow down the cooking and sat down against his bedroll to relax. This was one of the best times of a cowhand's day, when the work was done and a few hours of relaxed companionship could commence.

"Sure smells good. Can't tell you how much I done been missing a hot cooked meal, partner," offered Johnny.

"Glad to have someone to share it with. A man can get mighty lonesome out here at night."

"It ain't right for a man to be alone all the time. I swear I go crazy if I didn't have my four-legged companion with me on this trip," said Johnny.

"I expect to be pressured into marriage soon, myself. Can't get to heaven, otherwise."

"What do you mean, you can't get to heaven?"

"Doctrine of the church. To get to highest heaven, the elders say it is necessary to have a lot of wives."

"You going to do that?" asked Johnny, obviously taken aback at the notion.

"I ain't no rich Salt Lake City boy, Johnny! I am just a cattle boy! I wonder how I am going to finance a first wife."

"Well, I don't aim on getting hitched to no woman anytime soon, myself. Life is too short to get tied down with kids and bills and all that."

"I feel the same way sometimes, Johnny. Don't tell anyone in these parts I said so, will you? Looks like the grub is ready!"

Nephi lowered his head and uttered a prayer before he began to eat. Johnny did not join in, but refrained from taking his first bite, Nephi thought out of respect. The two young men did not take long to wolf down the meal once they began, however. In less than five minutes, they were both finished eating and trying to convince themselves their rather small meal was completely satisfying. It was something a cowhand, or a drover, or a buckaroo—there was even a new kind of slang word being used here and there these days—"cowboy"—got used to.

"Where did you learn to cook? That was one of the best meals I have had since leaving Los Angeles!" exclaimed Johnny.

He was clearly happy. He explained this had been the first good meal he had had for a very long time.

"I help with the cooking for the company of men when we go on long drives in the springtime. It is a good way to gain respect, let me tell you."

"Yes, I can see that. Nothing makes a man more popular in a group of hungry men than being the one to feed them. Oh, that reminds me, I better feed my horse. He hasn't had his daily ration of rolled oats yet."

Nephi looked longingly at the handsome white horse, silently watching them from a few feet away. "That is a pretty animal. What breed is it?"

"White Mustang. One of the best of the breed, Samson is. I had my choice from over three hundred. My father's horse ranch has two hundred acres of grazing land for them. I have been riding them since I was six years old. Want to see how good a horse Samson is? I can give you a small demonstration."

"Sure, I love to see a good horse perform."

"Wait till you see this!"

Johnny quickly moved over to his horse and patted the animal on the head a few times. Then Nephi watched as he carefully removed the bridle from his horse. He then jumped up on the saddle and uncoiled the rope wrapped around the pommel that kept the horse tethered to the fence post. Johnny leaned forward and whispered something into his horse's ears while he gently tapped his fancy boots against the horse's lower body. The beautiful animal rushed forward suddenly, filling the young evening with the sound of rhythmic hooves, setting up a cadence of powerful strides. Nephi sat in astonishment that Johnny was able to ride with only neck reins, simply using his feet and reins along the horse's neck to control him. They seemed to be a single unit as the horse performed elegant and graceful moves.

Nephi became engrossed with Johnny as he expertly guided his ride through its paces, his tight-fitting jeans wrapped closely to the sides of the animal as he lowered his slender body forward so his head was almost against the horse's neck. Nephi could tell there was closeness between them. The colorful sight of the athletic young man in his brightly hued clothes maneuvering the graceful horse with so little effort filled Nephi with unexpected happiness. He watched with unabashed admiration as Johnny gathered both reins into his left hand and then uncoiled the tethering rope he had hanging from the saddle. Johnny expertly guided the beautiful white steed with his left hand while he made a lasso with his right, twirling it over his head as he rode. It was a sight to behold, and it made Nephi's heart skip a beat as the utterly handsome figure of the young cowhand showed off his consummate skill and prowess in everything to do with being an expert cowpoke. A sense of solidarity began to form inside Nephi's mind. He had heretofore retained a kind of reserve inside of himself towards Johnny. The elders had constantly harped on how the Gentiles were not to be trusted. But Johnny was a poor cowboy, just like him. He smiled inside at that thought.

Johnny brought the horse to a trot, gently saying, "Whoa, Samson, whoa," as he led the horse back to the fence post where he had tied the animal up before. He dismounted and then unfastened a bag of feed from the saddle and tied it so that the horse could stick his long snout into it. Nephi jumped up to greet Johnny as he sauntered back to the small encampment with its quietly glowing embers, providing a beacon of light in the vast expanse now rapidly growing dark.

"That was fantastic, Johnny! I never seen anyone ride so good without even a bridle on their horse!" expounded Nephi, overcome with excitement.

"Aw, shucks, anyone can do ride a horse with neck reins, if the horse is good as Samson is, that is," said Johnny, a little bashful now, even though he had obviously done his best to show-off for Nephi.

"You are some buckaroo! I can tell you love your horse, too."

"Yes, I don't know what I would do without my Samson.

He has kept me company for the past month now," said Johnny, turning to look back at the big steed contentedly nibbling at his feed bag.

"Well, uh, it is getting pretty dark. We best should get some shut-eye, don't you think?" suggested Nephi.

"I can't think of a better thing to do, after mending fences with you! I thought riding the trail was hard, but you reminded me what simple labor is like, Nephi."

With that, Johnny turned back to retrieve his bedroll from the back of the horse while Nephi stripped down to his white garments emblazoned with sacred symbols meant to protect him from Satan. He unrolled his own bedroll close to the dying embers so as to help ward off the night's oncoming chill. Johnny trudged up before Nephi had a chance to slip into the bedroll.

"Those are some fancy underwear!" Johnny said with a little laugh.

"We are supposed to wear these at all times. Supposed to keep you safe."

"Well, I am all for keeping safe," said Johnny.

Nephi was happy that Johnny had not asked more questions or made fun of him. He guessed not all Gentiles were as bad as his elders had made out. He crawled into his bedroll and tried to relax.

"All I got to wear are these stinky long johns I been wearing for the past few days," added Johnny as he stripped his shirt off and peeled his tight-fitting blue jeans from his legs.

Nephi could not help but look at Johnny's body as he undressed, taking in the young dude's well-shaped muscles and tan skin. He had a nice, youthful appearance that became more apparent as he undressed. He made Nephi think about how he looked like without clothes on himself. He wondered if he was at all as good-looking a fellow as Johnny.

"I swear I can't stand to wear these dirty long johns one more night," Johnny suddenly announced. He then pulled his arms out and then pushed the red underwear down his body so his entire naked self was exposed in the desert air.

Nephi was astounded. He realized he had never seen a completely naked man before. All of his Mormon buddies insisted on never taking off their undergarments, even when they bathed. He felt both excited and guilty as he let his eyes settle on Johnny's flesh, his naked chest, his slender waist, and the muscular thighs that had just a little black hair covering them. But he could only glance at what sat so glaringly between those thighs. Johnny's private parts were right there out in the open and he didn't seem to pay any mind. In fact, Johnny stopped to yawn and then absentmindedly reached down to scratch...his private parts!

"Feels so good to get out of those stinky things! Say, you mind if I lay out my roll close to you? Helps to keep warm if we are close together," Johnny said without embarrassment or guile, as far as Nephi could tell.

"Uh, suh-suh-suh-sure," mumbled Nephi, almost without meaning to, so confused was he.

"Sure appreciate it," said Johnny as he unrolled his bedroll so that only an inch or two separated it from Nephi's. He brought his naked body close enough to Nephi so the young man could even smell Johnny's masculine scent as he lowered himself into the folds of his bedroll.

"Good night, Nephi. Thanks for letting me stay"

"Good night, Johnny. I hope you reach Santa Fe in one piece."

"Thanks. You are a nice fellow."

Nephi looked up into the desert night and let the beauty of the stars fill his senses. It was nights like these that kept the low pay and danger of the trail and desert worthwhile. There was nothing quite like it in the entire world.

"Nephi?"

"Yes?"

"Don't let those elders talk you into getting married too soon."

"Why, Johnny?"

"Cause I been noticing the way you been looking at me. I

have been putting on a show for you all night, so don't get all riled up over what I have to say. I am convinced you don't want at all to get hitched to some woman."

"But I won't get to heaven if I don't have wives…"

"God don't care if you need to love someone others don't approve of. It ain't right to pretend you is something you ain't. I been watching the look in your eyes and I can tell you feel the same way about me that I feel about you. Now look, there ain't anyone around for at least a hundred miles and the only two souls who have to give a damn about what is between us is us," said Johnny, somewhat breathless.

"I never even seen a naked man before," offered Nephi. It was dangerous and forbidden and he couldn't believe the wanton nature of what he had just said. But the hardness between his legs threatened to make him not care anymore, if he could only manage to get over his fear.

"How's about we put our sleeping rolls together, and see what touching each other might feel like?" asked Johnny.

"The Lord won't mind if we just touch each other" said Nephi, his voice trembling with apprehension.

"The Lord don't mind at all. He created you and me just the way we are."

Nephi sat motionless as Johnny scooted his bedroll closer. Johnny then opened the side of Nephi's bedroll, moving his naked body over right next to Nephi. Nephi could feel the warmth of Johnny's skin as it made contact with his body, sending waves of excitement through him. He could barely breathe as he felt Johnny move his head closer and begin to nuzzle against Nephi's neck. He could not believe this handsome dude from California had decided that he was handsome and desirable. He hadn't realized that he needed just this kind of touching to make him feel good inside.

"Can I kiss you, Nephi?" asked Johnny, whispering into his ear.

"Yes, I think that would be nice."

Johnny turned Nephi's face towards his own and then

pressed his lips against Nephi's mouth. He gingerly kissed Nephi for a few seconds, then pressed his tongue deep into Nephi's mouth and began to passionately kiss the young virgin. Nephi felt the ground beneath him give way as Johnny's lusty tongue penetrated his mouth. It sent sensations of erotic abandon deep into his bones and made his toes curl with desire. He began pressing his body against Johnny's and was very surprised by the utter pleasure he felt after pressing his hard cock against Johnny's naked flesh.

"Whoa, partner, that is some hard cock you have down there!" Johnny said, breaking from the kiss.

"This is the first time I ever felt it press against something!" Nephi exclaimed.

"You mean you ain't never even given yourself pleasure?" Johnny asked, sounding surprised.

"It is against the word of God to spill your seed. Almost a sin against the Holy Spirit!"

"Almost a sin...Lord!" said Johnny. He immediately reached down and undid the buttons holding the crotch together in the garment Nephi was wearing. Johnny gasped.

"You have a beautiful dick. I want to be the first to ever give you pleasure down there." He then lowered himself so his face was close to Nephi's eight-inch long cock. Johnny began to kiss it all over, from the tip down to the root, and then paused to lick his tongue against the delicious balls that lay nested beneath it. Nephi moaned and trembled with sexual pleasure. He fumbled and finally managed to undo the ties around his undergarment, pulling it up over his chest and then pulling his arms out. Johnny paused to help him lift his legs from it. He began to kiss Nephi's feet, taking time now and then to suck on the naked cowpoke's toes, making Nephi moan and laugh at the same time.

Johnny began to use his mouth to travel up Nephi's calves, kissing and caressing them tenderly, making the inexperienced boy appreciate the virtues of unabashed carnal lovemaking. When Johnny progressed to Nephi's thighs, he ran his tongue up the insides, and Nephi practically screamed with erotic anguish. All eighteen years of it.

"Nephi, I figured out a way for you not to spill your seed," said Johnny.

"How?"

"I want you to put your big cock inside my ass and fuck me hard, like I know you can," said Johnny.

"Show me how." By now the sexual pressure inside Nephi had built up from Johnny's loving so much he had lost his trepidation. He needed to find release.

Johnny lowered his head and took Nephi's cock into his mouth. He began to suck it, bobbing his head up and down. Nephi felt himself grow wet and stiff as a piece of granite. Johnny spit into his palm and moistened his butthole. Lying down on his back, Johnny spread his legs wide open and guided Nephi so that his cock pressed against Johnny's quivering ass opening.

Nephi slid his hard cock into Johnny's ass and on up until he felt Johhny's inner muscles resisting.

Nephi did not have to be instructed on what to do next. His sexual instinct took over and he began to pulse his eight inches back and forth inside Johnny's ass. Johnny started to meet Nephi's thrusts by squeezing his ass muscles tightly around Nephi's shaft.

"Oh, Nephi, you are so good!" Johnny almost shouted.

"This is the best night of my life so far," replied Nephi, panting.

Johnny wrapped his legs around Nephi's back and pulled the young man harder and harder into himself with each thrust. Johnny put his arms around Nephi's shoulders, gently pulling him down so his face was only inches above Johnny's own. He then pressed Nephi's mouth against his lips and repeated his deep tongue penetration of the cowpoke's mouth. Nephi responded by coiling his tongue around Johnny's, now a willing participant, wanting to give Johnny pleasure, too. But Nephi had to break off from the kiss as his fucking motions began to take on a life of their own. He could not control himself as his entire pelvis began to shake and shiver. He began bucking like a wild bronco right on top of Johnny.

Johnny's dick spurted a thick load of hot cum between them, splash after sticky splash arcing up between their bellies as Nephi continued to lose control. The warmth and messiness of Johnny's cum was enough to make the youthful stud surrender however. Spurt after spurt of hot cum shot out of the tip of his red hot cock and right into the depths of Johnny's insides.

"I love you!" cried Nephi as he lost himself in the ecstasy of orgasm, his first ever.

Nephi collapsed on top of Johnny and allowed his cock to continue its jerky tremoring deep inside his lover's beautiful ass while relishing the warm stickiness of Johnny's sperm that seemed to fasten their bodies together like glue. Slowly his throes of orgasmic ecstasy subsided and he lay quietly atop his handsome partner.

"I hope you enjoyed that as much as I did," Johnny said after several seconds of silence.

"That was the most wonderful thing I ever felt," answered Nephi.

They fell asleep like that for almost an hour. When they woke up, Nephi washed off his dick with Johnny's canteen and they sat embracing for several minutes. The half-moon hung in the desert sky and a million stars surrounded it. They could hear the howl of a coyote off in the distance and its call seemed to celebrate their togetherness. The two young men found their cocks growing hard once again and Johnny showed Nephi how to lie together so that each other's crotches were facing the other. They took each other's cocks into their mouths and passionately sucked and licked each other for close to an hour before they could no longer resist and let their cocks explode simultaneously in each other's mouths. Nephi was afraid to spill Johnny's seed so he swallowed it down. It tasted salty and sweet and filled him up with joy and satisfaction.

Finally they fell asleep in each other's arms.

WHEN THEY AWOKE early the next morning, Nephi was kind of lost in thought. He didn't say a lot while he fried cured bacon in the revived embers of the previous night's fire. When the bacon was finished and they sat enjoying their breakfast, Nephi finally spoke.

"Johnny, I want to thank you very much for last night. I don't know if you will have me, but I feel I owe it to you to offer my hand, seeing as I had marital relations with you last night."

"Marital relations?" said Johnny, visibly taken aback.

"Yes, I had intimate contact and now I feel I should show you respect."

"Well, Nephi, I am honored that you feel that way. I was wondering how I was gonna ask you to take off from these here parts with me."

"I been thinking. I can remember when some of the elders came to my pa's and began to pressure him to take more wives when I was just about eight. After they left, my ma absolutely forbid it. She pulled out an old copy of King Follett's Discourse she had taken with her from her days in Nauvoo."

"What did it say?"

"Well, my mama said once the Prophet died, two of the leaders—Parley Pratt and Brigham Young—had to justify their polygamy. There was a passage in the Discourse where Joseph said little children would be resurrected just as they are and remain children forever on thrones ruling with God. That paragraph has been struck out now and the polygamists say little children have to wait to grow up in the spirit world and get celestially married before they can sit with God and become like him."

"That's crazy!"

"I know. I have ponderin' over it all night. I think my ma is right. I don't need to get married to some woman just so I can produce spirit children in the hereafter. I can be like a little child and inherit the kingdom anyway, just like Jesus said."

"Does that mean you would be willing to saddle up and go live by my side until one of us dies?"

"I am used to the government frowning on unusual marriages. I don't see why we can't be sealed to each other. I am going to have to do it, though. I can! I am a Melchizedek priest."

"You is only eighteen!" said Johnny, astounded.

"I know—we all get the priesthood when we turn eighteen."

"Well, then, I accept your proposal. I will be honored to be your partner, Nephi."

And so they performed a simple ceremony, with Nephi doing most of the talking. Then Nephi left a letter thanking his folks for everything, especially his ma for showing him how to be free. He didn't elaborate, but was confident she was smart enough to figure it out for herself. Johnny said he admired Nephi's thoughtfulness and wondered how he would break the news to his pa back home, if ever.

BY MID-MORNING THEY were saddled up and ready to move. It was decided they would continue on to Santa Fe and see if they could drum up some business for Johnny's father. If it worked out, they would set off for California. They didn't plan any further. Nephi and Johnny were confident they could face the future without fear, as long as they were together.

FLYBOYS AND COWBOYS

BY MICHAEL MCCLELLAND

DEPENDING ON WHO was asking, Guy Harris called himself an aviator, a pilot, or a soldier of fortune. He used *aviator* when he was looking for work. *Pilot* he'd say if he didn't care much about the conversation, usually if he got cornered by a woman in a bar. If he ran into a man like himself, a man who was *that way*, that's when Guy was a *soldier of fortune*.

It was July of 1930, and Guy was in Panama City, en route to Venezuela, where the American Museum of Natural History was paying top dollar for pilots to fly over Venezuela's Gran Sábana, a massive, unexplored grassland. The museum said their goal was to map the region for "scientific evaluation," but the five thousand dollars they were offering said they were looking for oil. It didn't matter to Guy; they'd be paying him for his flying, not his opinion.

Guy had no intention of testing the limits of Duke, his Metal Aircraft Corp G-2-W Flamingo, so he was taking a leisurely route south from Oklahoma down to Ciudad Bolivar, which would be his base in Venezuela. He'd bought the snazzy aircraft right off the field at the National Air Races in Cleveland. It had been piloted by Elinor Smith herself and Guy had reveled in her shock when he'd handed over the biggest bag of sugar she'd ever seen, twenty-five thousand dollars, every penny his daddy had left him. She shouldn't have been too surprised; flying was not a poor man's business. Guy wasn't rich, but he'd needed to spend his dead daddy's money on something the man had loved. And flying was the *only* thing his daddy had ever loved.

Guy had already stopped in Brownsville, Mexico City, Guatemala City, and San José and would be making further stops in Barranquilla and Caracas before reaching his destination. He'd chosen his locations based on Pan Am stops and Air Force bases, which had mostly worked out well for him. Between the tequila and the prostitutes, the competition had been too much in Mexico City, but he'd knocked knees with a stout, foulmouthed Pan Am pilot in Guatemala and sweet-talked a blue jay out of a wide-eyed second lieutenant in Costa Rica.

Panama City was the place Guy had been looking forward to most, however. First off, being *that way* wasn't illegal, and Guy found it much easier to get a hard-on without the prospect of jail hanging over his head. Also, even though it had been over fifteen years since the *SS Ancon* had first passed through the Canal's locks, the US of A sent a steady stream of impressionable young men down to guard the Canal Zone, Prohibition leaving their dry lips thirsty and unprepared for a man with more than enough coin to buy them some leg-spreading libations.

After fueling up and negotiating a place to stow Duke for the night, Guy decided to head into the city to find a bar. He ran into a Pan Am stewardess waiting for a taxi outside of the airport. She had perfectly curled amber hair and, according to her shiny metal lapel pin, her name was Helen.

"You headed into town, mister?" Helen asked. She smelled of floral perfume and cigarette smoke.

"Planning on it. Do you know anywhere I can get a drink?"

"Depends," Helen replied, giving him a full scan with her heavily made-up green eyes. Her gaze lingered on his arms and again on his mouth. He knew to be careful around stewardesses.

They had a tricky way of getting you to buy them drinks even if you weren't interested. "Are you just looking for a quick drink-avous or a full toot?"

She spoke like a flapper, though she looked quite the opposite in her crisp blue uniform.

"Just a quick belt. I'm flying again in the morning."

"You're a flyboy?" Helen licked her lips. This dame was not subtle, which Guy could appreciate, even if he wasn't interested. He'd tried being with women many times and it just wasn't for him.

"I'm a pilot."

Helen had turned out to be quite a gas, and they'd ended up laughing the whole way into the city in a shared taxi. A sawbuck seemed an absurd amount for a ride in what was obviously an illegally obtained motorcar, but five each hadn't seemed too bad. There were a few horse-drawn taxis around, but Guy didn't think smelling like a horse would help him seduce anyone.

Helen was heading to a dance with some girlfriends and had invited Guy to come along. He'd told her dancing wasn't his thing and it wasn't—with women at least. He didn't really know what dancing with a man was like; there weren't a lot of joints where you could do that out in the open and when he got a man in private Guy was too focused on more carnal pleasures.

Helen recommended a place called Pete's, which in her opinion had just the right mixture of locals and foreigners. She'd winked at Guy and said Pete even rented out the rooms upstairs. Helen and her friends would be headed there after some dancing and she'd said she would be sure to look out for him.

Guy found Pete's without a lot of searching. It was an open-air bar jutting off the side of a chalky white two-story stone building on a dirt road called Canal Boulevard, nowhere near the canal. The bar itself was set up against the side of the building in a stone courtyard with several tables placed around it. The bar and the tables had gas lanterns on them for lighting, but none were yet lit as the afternoon sun was still doing a good job of illuminating everything.

The tables were all empty and only one man sat at the bar; a broad-shouldered fellow with a tawny cowboy hat perched atop his head. Underneath, Guy saw his hair was blond as an Oklahoma wheat field. The closer Guy got, the more he liked what he saw. The blond wore a dark blue collared shirt with a leather yoke, which stretched beautifully tight across his back. He had the body of a decathlete, broad at the top, tapering into a slim waist. Then he tapered out again, his pants stretching remarkably across his rear and pressing against the barstool so naturally that Guy imagined him an apple waiting to be plucked off the stem.

This was exactly how Guy liked to meet men. Foreign location, temporary stop, no chance of any awkward talk of *making this a thing*. Tomorrow morning he would be back in the sky, free as a bird, but hopefully with some good memories of Panama.

Guy leaned against the bar next to the blond, who was no less spectacular in profile than he had been from behind. He tried to engage the man in conversation, but when the blond turned towards him, Guy was muted by the other man's eyes, blue like Oklahoma sky.

He felt suddenly stupid, fawning over the eyes of a man like some cow-eyed Victorian heroine, and said the first thing he could think of.

"Now what beer is the least likely to make me vomit?"

Inwardly, Guy cringed, but he made sure to give the blond, who head-on looked to be a few years younger than his own age of thirty-five, his most roguish smile.

"I'm afraid even the least likely is still very likely to cause you some trouble," the blond replied, his voice principled, New England. He smiled and his dazzling, square teeth reminded Guy of the tiles of that Mahjong game from the East his stepmother was so fond of. They were framed by full lips the color of red earth, and Guy quickly found his own mouth cotton dry.

"I'll take my chances, then. What are you having?" The blond's glass was still half full but Guy wanted him to stick around for a while.

The blond held Guy's forward stare and Guy felt his pulse quickening. "Atlas, best of a conspicuous bunch. What's your name, friend?"

"Guy Harris. And yours?"

"It's McCracken. Call me Mac," the blond replied, tipping his hat.

Guy signaled the bartender, who was doing an excellent job of avoiding them. Guy then feared he was being too forward, standing out. It might not be illegal to be *that way* in Panama, but it wasn't something any barkeep would let happen in his bar.

When he managed to garner a look from the bartender—a short, round-faced, mustachioed man—Guy made sure to use his most gravely voice to say, "Two Atlas beers, please."

The man stood still, keeping his eyes on Guy but not moving. Stress crawled into Guy's belly.

"*Dos*," Mac said, and Guy turned to see he was smiling even more broadly. "Forget where you are?"

"Surely the man knows what *two* means," Guy responded.

"It's a matter of respect." A statement that could have a rebuke. Mac's warm eyes told him it wasn't, though.

The bartender got to work, and Guy said to Mac, "I just flew in. That's my excuse." He maintained eye contact, looking for interest, the sign he was *that way,* too, or at least willing to try.

Mac arched an eyebrow. "Are you a pilot?"

"You could say that. I prefer *soldier of fortune*."

Mac smiled. "Well, Guy, it just so happens I'm looking to hire a pilot. A *soldier of fortune*, I mean."

Guy had two rules: never make a business decision while drinking and never bed a man he was in business with.

He was ready to break both rules.

Mac's eyes were intense, pinning Guy to his seat. "What do you say, Guy?"

"I could be your man," Guy said, and let the words sit. This time, both eyebrows went up, and that big, wide, Mahjong smile spread across his face.

Mac wanted more than a pilot.

"I need a pilot for six weeks. I'll pay five thousand—American, not Balboas—plus fuel."

That was a massive amount of kale, the kind folks offered for a pilot who wouldn't ask any questions. Which was fine with Guy, but six weeks was quite the commitment. Hadn't he just been thinking about his freedom? Surely they could just get this fuck out of their systems and then go about business. In his current state, his hard-on told him he would fly Mac for free, anywhere, to get a look at what was in those tight trousers. Guy decided to bed him and then he'd be able to make a level-headed decision.

The bartender deposited their beers in front of them sloppily, warm foam spilling over the rims of the glasses.

"You've got yourself a deal," Guy said.

Mac raised his glass. "Tell you what, Guy. I'm renting a room here. Why don't we finish our beers and then discuss the details of our arrangement upstairs?"

Guy raised his glass and clinked it against Mac's, sealing the deal. He couldn't help but think, *What the hell are you getting yourself into, Harris?*

MAC WAS TERRIFIED. It had been years since he'd had sex with a man and the prospect made him dizzy with lust and nerves. He'd fumbled around in dark alleys and barroom stalls, but it hadn't been since university that he'd had another man in his bed.

Then Mac wondered if he was paying Guy and he slept with him, would he be paying Guy to sleep with him?

His mother would be horrified.

He was horrified.

The first thing Mac had noticed about Guy Harris had been his bicep as he leaned against the bar next to him. It was almost obscene, the bulbous muscle gently pushed against the tightening skin, hardening as Guy held himself up. Every part of him, every visible part, was thick and strong. He was wearing white linen trousers, a thin undershirt, and suspenders. He looked half-dressed and entirely inappropriate, but they were in a bar in Panama, not one of Mac's mother's garden parties.

Then the dark-haired, dark-eyed man had said he was a pilot, a *soldier of fortune*, and it was like Fate Herself had delivered Guy right to his barstool. Mac had *déjà vu* back to ten years before, when he'd met a pilot in this very bar. He'd ended up screwed out of two-thousand cattle at fifty dollars a head and abandoned in the middle of the *sábana*. There had been no romance that time, just old-fashioned backstabbing. This time he was going to be more careful. And if he were going to be screwed by a pilot, it would be the happy kind of screwing.

Mac, as a rule, refused to show any carnal interest towards men, even men who ran their eyes over him with obvious lust like Guy had. It was just too dangerous.

Making cattle drives in Central and South America had been Mac's career, on and off, for ten years. He knew that, just like anywhere else, even the *enlightened* US of A, these weren't places to be aggressively pursuing men. He had gotten a reminder just weeks before.

He'd been friendly, just friendly, with a lieutenant named Barry who could come by Pete's every few days. One evening, Barry had a few too many and while practicing his elementary Spanish skills on a group of locals, had rested his hand on the thick thigh of a young man in the group. Observing, Mac had winced, but had figured Barry would be okay. He'd been sure Barry would be able to play it off as a simple mistake.

No sooner had he thought that, they had attacked Barry with a startling, hateful force. By the time Mac had reached Barry to try and help, he'd been beaten so badly he couldn't even open his swollen eyes. Behind the bar, Pete hadn't said a word, just shook his head and checked the kegs.

And that story was tame compared to the reports Mac had

heard about men who had been notoriously *that way* found dead in the canal, people laughing about it like it was what they deserved. He was not going to be one of those men.

Guy, however, on some deep level, had made Mac feel safe from the second they started talking. The thought made Mac feel a little disgusted with himself. He didn't need any man to make him feel safe. He was strong and worked hard at it.

Still, something about Guy made Mac want to take a risk, told him he would be okay if he did.

They finished their drinks and Mac looked Guy in the eye. He tried to sound smooth but his throat was tight. "Let's head upstairs, shall we?"

Pete eyed them from the bar, and Mac worried, even though plenty of men retired to their rooms with other men to smoke cigars and talk bull.

Plus, when he'd rented his room from Pete six months before, he'd given the barman a chunk of gold the size of his fist, and Mac assumed that would buy him a bit of discretion even if basic humanity did not. Mac also had the sneaking suspicion old Pete had more in common with them than he would ever admit.

They went around the building to which the bar was attached and reached an enclosed courtyard framed around the back wall of the building. It mirrored the one in front, except in place of a bar this one had a row of johns and a trio of bathing stalls within it. Mac led Guy to a large wooden door on the back wall of the building. He pulled his heavy iron room key from his pocket and unlocked the door, which led directly to a stone staircase. They reached the top of the staircase and down the short corridor, passing three doors on the left and several framed pictures of orchids on the right, before reaching a fourth door, Mac's room. He used the same iron key in the lock.

Guy chuffed. "The same key opens the back door and this room? Can you open the other three rooms with this key?"

Funny he didn't ask if the tenants of the other rooms could get in here, Mac thought. Was Guy a vagrant?

"I was worried about that, but the other rooms are all long-term, all three very old ladies."

"I was just thinking that, if they weren't occupied, you could have yourself a parlor, a dressing room, a smoking room, and bedroom all for the price of one," Guy smiled.

Not a vagrant, Mac thought, *just a man who appreciates a deal.* That he could understand.

Mac led Guy into his small quarters. Quite different from the comforts he'd enjoyed growing up, but it did the job. It was dark, even in the afternoon. There was one window on the wall to the right of the entrance, and while there was a thick curtain covering it, the room would have been impossibly hot without the breeze. Mac hung his hat on a small rack to the left of the door before moving into the room, careful to step over his suitcase as he moved to turn on the gas lantern in the back left corner.

The light from the small lantern was enough to fill the tiny room, which was about twelve feet wide and ten feet deep. It had a twin bed, its headboard bolted to the back wall. Small tables sat either side, serving, for Mac at least, as a nightstand on the left and a bar on the right.

Directly over the bed's headboard was a map of Central America, the Caribbean, and the northern countries of South America. Mac had picked up the map ten years before, when he'd taken his shiny Harvard biology degree and headed as far south as he could go, eager to find some way to give his mother the fortune she had always wanted, the one his father had always held just out of their reach. He had never worked with his hands before, but he knew animals and he knew the real money to be made from them was down in South America, driving cattle up into the Panama Canal Zone. On his trips back and forth over the past decade, he had gotten her just enough to stay in the expensive apartment his father had set her up in when she'd been his mistress, but this time would be different. He was going to make them a fortune.

Now that he could see, Mac turned to Guy, who was leaning in the frame of the door. The man was built like a baby grand. His muscles looked taut under his shirt, ready to pounce. His gaze rolled slowly up and down Mac's body. Mac could see Guy had one thing on his mind and it wasn't discussing their business arrangement.

Mac became even more nervous. He wasn't ready for this. What was *this*, anyways? Mac had never been good at separating sex from feelings, and here he was trying to seduce a flyboy. Flyboys didn't really have a reputation for sticking around. Impulsively, he asked Guy, "Do you want a drink?" He continued, "I've got a jug of water Pete boiled and bottled up for me, or I could pour you something stronger."

Mac hoped Guy didn't think he was slowing things down because he wasn't interested. He was just worried he would faint or throw up—or both—if Guy did so much as touch him.

Guy smiled. "Stronger would be great."

Maybe I just need some liquid courage, Mac thought. If Guy's forward approach was anything to go by, the pilot was experienced in matters like this. Mac was not.

He went over to the other bedside table, which had three large bottles on it, two green and one brown. The green ones were filled with water. He pulled two glasses out from the shelf below and poured two fingers from the brown bottle into each glass. He held a glass out to Guy, who finally left the doorframe and met him halfway, at the foot of the bed.

"Here's your cocktail, flyboy," Mac said.

"What's on the menu?" Guy asked, holding the glass out to survey it in the dim light.

"Cane spirits. Bootleg back at home but less than a clam for a whole case here."

Guy gave it a sniff and winced. "How about a toast? I've got a good one.

"If wishing damns us, you and I
Are damned to all our hearts content;
Come then, at least we may enjoy

Some pleasure for our punishment."

Mac was enthralled by the soft movement of Guy's lips, which were light pink, the only light thing on his tan face. Those lips hugged every word, taking Mac's imagination to dark places.

Mac raised his glass to meet Guy's, and with both their gazes and glasses touching Mac was sure Guy was going to kiss him. Then Guy took a sip of his drink and coughed and spat the drink out in a mist, coating Mac's face with cane spirit.

"Holy Hell, man, that stuff is dangerous!"

Mac wiped his face with his rolled up sleeve and put his arm over Guy's shoulder, slapping him on the back as he coughed. "Here, sit down, old boy." Mac eased Guy down until they were both seated at the foot of the bed, where Guy's coughing turned to laughter.

Mac felt comfort in touching Guy, which surprised him, as he had never felt comfortable touching any man. He was always afraid his hand would move too far, that it would reveal some interest he wouldn't be able to hide.

Guy said, "Okay, Mac, you'd better explain this job to me before I get distracted." The word *distracted* set McCracken's heart to a hammering pace.

"Sure," he croaked. "How about I show you on the map." He pointed to the head of the bed.

"After you."

Mac removed his shoes and crawled to the top of the bed, took a gulp of his drink before setting it on the table, and raised himself up onto his knees so he could point to the map. He leaned one hand on the wall and used the other to point, his back to Guy.

He pointed to Panama City. "We're here, you see?"

"I see."

Mac looked over his shoulder and saw Guy was certainly not looking at the map.

Emboldened, Mac said, "Come closer so you can see what I'm talking about."

Mac turned back to the map and heard two thunks as Guy's shoes hit the floor. He felt Guy crawl onto the bed, stopping directly behind him, also on his knees. He placed his hands on the wall, on either side of the map, caging Mac in. Guy had the smell of a man who worked with machines, that light scent of gasoline and oil, but beneath those baser scents were notes of cinnamon, sandalwood, and sweat.

"Okay," Guy said. "Show me."

Mac struggled to remember what he'd been speaking about. He was so overwhelmed his lust was turning towards nausea. He wondered if he had bit off more than he could chew. He returned his focus to the map.

"So, we head east. First we need to get here." Mac pointed to the bottom part of Venezuela, which stuck out like the foot of a clam. "San Carlos de Rio Negro."

"Mmmhmm. Keep going," Guy whispered, his hot breath on McCracken's neck.

"From there we need to fly north over the Amazon Jungle, toward Angostura. Though this map is outdated; it's called Ciudad Bolivar now. We'll stop here, at the Gran Sábana," he said, pointing to a big empty stretch in the southeast corner of Venezuela.

"I was headed that way anyways," Guy said, and moved his hands from the wall to Mac's hips. Mac felt Guy's knees move in between his, pushing them gently wider. Mac felt pinned and exposed, but, once again, Guy made him feel safe.

Safe and incredibly aroused.

On the other hand, Mac didn't want to be Guy's girl. He was roughly the same size as Guy, just a bit more slender, but in this position he felt like he had relinquished power.

As if he'd read Mac's thoughts, Guy moved his hands up, pressing his index fingers into Mac's hard abdomen. "So strong," he said into Mac's neck.

Guy worked his hands up to Mac's chest and started undoing the buttons on his shirt, slowly and precisely.

Mac didn't know if he should continue discussing the trip

or just completely submit to the seduction, but he figured outlining the journey would distract Guy from his inexperience. "I don't need to travel all the way up there. What we're looking for is northeast of the rainforest but south of Ciudad Bolivar."

Guy moved to the second button. "And what is it we're looking for?"

"Cattle. I'm a cowboy. They're paying a pretty penny for outsiders to come down and drive cattle back up to the Canal Zone."

It wasn't a lie, but it wasn't the whole truth. Mac wouldn't make the mistake of trusting a pilot with a secret again.

Guy pushed his erection against Mac's backside while starting on the third button. It felt huge and McCracken felt more nervous and even *more* aroused, which he hadn't known was possible.

"You don't have to go all the way to Venezuela to find a bull."

Mac snorted.

Guy buried his head in Mac's shoulder and Mac felt him smile. "Okay, that was bad. Let me try again. How about, why are you willing to pay so much to get to this bull?" He pushed his erection against Mac again.

Mac went silent, suddenly worried Guy really was doing this for money, that he wasn't interested in him, just the payment.

Guy stopped his movements and said, serious, "Not funny?"

Surely honesty had to be best in this situation, Mac thought.

"I don't want to pay for *this* bull," pushing his ass back against Guy, drawing a moan. "I'm *paying* you to be my pilot. I *want* you, for free." The joking had gone on too long and Mac felt like getting down to business.

Guy finished on the third button. Mac's chest was now exposed. Guy flicked Mac's nipples.

"Holy shit!" Mac shuddered, his mind blanking. Who knew *that* felt like *that*?

"I'm not doing this because you're paying me. I'm doing this because you're gorgeous," Guy said firmly in his ear.

Mac couldn't think of any sweet talk to reciprocate with, so pushed back again. He wanted to show appreciation and he also, experience be damned, wanted to be an active participant in this encounter.

After several moments of that delightful, mysterious chest stroking, which left Mac frenzied, Guy moved his hands down to Mac's trousers. Unlike his languid pace with the shirt buttons, he undid these clips lightning fast.

He began to pull down McCracken's trousers. "Lift up," Guy said and when Mac did he swiftly pulled them down past his ankles and tossed them to the floor. Mac thought he must look absurd, kneeling there in his Jockeys, ass in the air, chest bursting out of his shirt, garters and socks still on.

Guy brought his right hand up and grabbed Mac's chin, pulling it firmly to the right. He aligned their faces and planted a kiss on Mac's lips, and the kiss told him, sure as a map, exactly what Guy planned on doing with him.

GUY STARED AT the stunning man bent in front of him. Mac's thick ass was in the air, white underpants stretched absurdly tight across it. The blond's whole body, strong and corded with lithe muscle, was trembling slightly, waiting for Guy to make the next move.

Guy grabbed Mac by the chin and gently pulled him up, placing a soft kiss on his gorgeous lips. Mac opened for him and their tongues met. It was electric and he opened his eyes to see if Mac felt the same. He did. His blue eyes were wide open, direct, and aroused.

Guy was fascinated by Mac's odd mix of innocence and fire. The way he'd summoned Guy to his room so directly and then bent over on the bed in what looked to be an explicit invitation to fuck him senseless contrasted with how his nervous hands had shook as he'd poured them white lightning and his shocked rapture upon having his chest touched.

He wanted to know more about this cowboy. Guy hadn't

been able to help himself from smiling as Mac had breathlessly tried to discuss their itinerary while Guy had been disrobing him. There was a sweetness about him Guy had not picked up on at first, a goodness that mixed enticingly with his blatant sexiness.

Stop it, Harris, he told himself.

He could feel himself getting curious. *Getting curious* could lead to *getting involved,* which was not in the cards. This is about fucking and, maybe, business. Not getting to know each other.

He softly pushed Mac back towards the bed, once again staring at his strong back and beautiful ass. Guy was so hard that he was shocked he hadn't split his pants open. He pulled Mac's white underpants down slowly, relishing the show. Guy spread Mac's cheeks apart, exposing smooth, pink hole. The firm ass cheeks in his hands were covered in very light blond hair, nearly invisible, so the entirety of Mac's ass appeared smooth. Leaving the underwear around Mac's thighs, Guy spit on his index finger and rubbed the tight rim of Mac's hole.

Mac turned around and met Guy's eyes, his desire blatant on his beautiful face. Guy kept their eyes locked as he inserted his finger into Mac. He nearly stopped when he saw the brief flash of pain cross the other man's face, but Mac's expression turned so quickly into one of satisfaction that Guy continued. He pushed his finger in and hooked it, finding the spot. Mac's eyes went wide. "More. Please."

Guy didn't know if he had ever been so turned on. He inserted a second finger, keeping his eyes locked with Mac's the whole while. Mac was beautiful, strong and supple, his muscles straining as he held himself on all fours, his glorious ass pointed at Guy, begging to be fucked. Guy realized he was still clothed, and something about that made him even more aroused. He spit and pushed a third finger into Mac's ass. Mac was so tight it barely fit, and Guy knew he would have to work the man a bit more if he was going to get his cock in.

Mac was moaning loudly. He pushed back into Guy's fingers. He was a beautiful sight with his underwear still framing the bottom of his ass, Guy's fingers expertly sliding in and out of his pink hole. Guy memorized the image, knowing it would bring him great pleasure even if he were alone. Their eyes remained locked, Guy smiling as he worked Mac's ass. Mac's expression was one of shock. He seemed almost overwhelmed with pleasure, and that thought made Guy breathless.

Mac started to move his mouth but seemed to be struggling to form words. "I want you to do it on my back. I mean I want to be on my back while you do it. I mean, I want to look at your face while you do it."

Guy's initial reaction was another one of arousal. Then the voice in his head reminded him he was getting dangerously close to making this more than just a fuck. A frantic hump in this guy's room was one thing. Staring him in the eyes, *pleasuring* him, was entirely another. Still, Mac had asked, and Guy was finding it hard to say no to him.

"Roll over," Guy told Mac, his voice heavy. Guy's fingers were withdrawn and the blond rolled himself over onto his back. Guy barely held in a gasp.

Mac was even more stunning, or equally stunning, from the front. Despite what had seemed like modesty earlier, Mac lay on his back, his legs spread as wide as his underwear, still wrapped around his lower thighs, would allow. The entire view was breathtaking. The rippling muscles in his stomach, the strong pectoral muscles, and perfect pink nipples, his thick thighs. Most attractive to Guy at this current moment was Mac's impressive dick. It was under a dusting of more light blond hair, and was sticking straight out, long and thick above a pair of heavy balls. Mac was hard as a rock. A pearl of moisture glistened at the end, indicating his excitement.

Guy bent down and licked it up, swirling his tongue around the head of Mac's cock while he was there.

"Holy shit!" Mac yelped.

Guy sat back and then pulled Mac's underwear down and flung it away, letting him spread his legs even wider. Guy unclipped his own suspenders and pulled his shirt over his head.

Normally he would do it slowly in order to show off his muscles, which he knew to be pretty impressive. Growing up on an Oklahoma farm had served him well in that department, and he loved the way men *like him* fawned over them. But right now, all he could think about was being inside Mac.

"You're beautiful," Mac said, and it stopped Guy in his tracks for a second. Something about the way Mac had said it made him melt.

"You're pretty amazing yourself," Guy responded.

Stop it, he told himself again. *This is just a fuck.*

He unzipped his pants and pulled out his dick. He couldn't believe he hadn't burst while he'd been fingering Mac.

He looked to Mac, who still lay there, legs splayed. His eyes were firmly fixed on Guy's cock. He was *definitely* still turned on but he now also appeared to be nervous.

"It's been a little while," he said. "And I don't think I've ever had one that big."

Guy had seen enough cocks to know his was well above average size, and he'd be lying if he said he wasn't proud of that.

"Are you sure you're ready? There are plenty of other things we can do," he said, concerned.

Again he had surprised himself. Normally if a man had himself laid out for Guy like Mac was, Guy would have been several thrusts in already. With Mac, he found himself concerned about the other man's experience, his pleasure. And he wanted it to last.

Mac looked determined. And his own dick was pointing straight out, clearly anticipating the experience as well.

"Aren't you going to take off your pants?" Mac asked.

Guy hadn't even thought about it. Normally, he kept his pants on so he could be out of there quickly once he was done.

He pulled his linen trousers down and then got back to the job at hand.

He pulled a small bottle of oil from his pocket and poured

some on his hand before working his cock with it. He hoped Mac was too horny to think about this; a man with a bottle of oil in his pocket was obviously looking for sex and Guy didn't want Mac thinking he was willing to fuck anyone.

But aren't I willing to fuck pretty much anyone? Guy thought. He was getting further into dangerous territory.

Guy curled himself out over Mac, meeting his eyes and engaging in a deep kiss. He inhaled Mac's scent, which was fresh, like lemon and saltwater. Guy broke the kiss; he wanted to be looking into Mac's eyes as he entered the cowboy. Mac was breathing heavily. Guy lined his cock up with Mac's hole and slowly pushed in while staring into those blue eyes.

Mac's eyes widened. Again, a brief look of pain clouded his eyes. Guy stilled. "Are you okay?"

Mac smiled and held Guy's gaze. "Yes, keep going."

Guy pushed in all the way and Mac's eyes went even wider, this time filled with pure pleasure.

"You like that?" Guy asked. He couldn't believe how much Mac's arousal was arousing him.

Mac stared up into his eyes, and Guy felt the stare in his chest, in his belly. He had that mix of shock and lust in his eyes.

"I love it. Don't stop."

Guy began to slowly work his cock in and out of Mac's tight hole. It felt amazing, and it was heightened by Mac's beautifully expressive face, which was telling Guy exactly how every thrust was making him feel.

"I love how you look while I'm fucking you," Guy breathed out. He didn't know how he was holding on so long, but he was giving Mac such obvious pleasure he didn't want it to end.

Guy bent down over Mac, pinning the cowboy in with his arms, kissing Mac passionately as he thrust. Guy opened his eyes and stared directly into Mac's as he fucked the man. It was electric.

Guy pushed himself back up and began to thrust harder, loving the methodic slapping his balls made against Mac's meaty ass. He reached down and gripped Mac's erection as he thrust.

"No, I won't last long," Mac said.

"Yes," Guy said, thrilled to be in control of another element of Mac's satisfaction.

He worked Mac's dick and soon desperation entered the blond's eyes.

"Oh my God. Oh my God. Oh my God," he was repeating it over and over.

"Yes. Come for me, baby," Guy said.

Baby? He shocked himself again, but no sooner had the alarm risen in his mind than Mac's thick release was spilling out between them, onto his hand and onto Mac's chiseled stomach. That was enough to send Guy over the edge, and with a couple more quick thrusts he was coming as well, shooting deep inside Mac before collapsing on top of him.

After a moment, he pushed himself up. He was still inside Mac. Mac was looking up at Guy, his eyes warm and sleepy with satisfaction. Guy wanted to kiss him, hold him until they fell asleep.

Another surprising thought. Normally, his first thought after coming was about where he'd thrown his shirt or how quickly he could get away. Feeling like this was too dangerous. If he were smart, he'd get up and say goodbye, embrace his freedom and let Mac find another pilot. He'd mixed business and pleasure before and he'd nearly died.

But he couldn't fight himself. He knew there was no way he was going to be able to say no to Mac.

"So, when do we leave, cowboy?" he asked.

WILD WEST SHOW

BY ROB ROSEN

For Kenny, always and forever.

JOBS BEING SCARCE in those parts, I tore the sign off the hitching post and stuffed it in my britches right quick. I waited until I got home to read it, figuring that once word got out there'd be a stampede to the hiring wagon—and I wasn't about to go tipping nobody off.

Buffalo Bill's Wild West it read, in big, fat, bold letters. *Hiring rope riders, wranglers, sharpshooters, cowboys, and cooks. Be a part of the biggest tour of 1890.* My heart thumped beneath my vest as I looked the poster up and down, hardly believing my sore eyes. Seeing as I ain't never been more than a day's ride from where I was born, and pretty much believing I never would be, this thing here was a gift from God himself, my ticket out of that one horse town of mine.

Now then, truth be told, I wasn't any of them things they was looking for, no siree, but I figured that, give me some meat and some potatoes, plus a pot full of hot water, and, by golly, I could rustle me up some grub if I set my mind to it. Guess they believed me, too, because I was the first cook they hired. Didn't hurt none neither that I could read and write and fill out an application. Yep, left them other applying fellers in the dust and didn't never look back.

A week later, they packed us tighter than a can of sardines in that long, long train of theirs and shipped us out to the middle of nowhere. Training grounds, they called them. Chock full of cowboys and injuns of every size, shape, and color. Not to mention a whole bunch of folks I ain't never heard of before: Turks, Arabs, Mongols, and Cossacks—all from places I couldn't find on a map even if I tried.

All in all, there were hundreds upon hundreds of us, mostly entertainers of some sort or another—all except me and a bunch of others, of course. We was there to feed them, wash them, fix their gear, darn their clothes, and keep them fit and healthy. In other words, do whatever it took to keep the outfit moving and making money for that crazy, old Buffalo Bill Cody, who we didn't ever see hide nor hair of, except maybe during show days, out in front of the huge crowds that gathered to see the spectacles he had waiting for them.

Don't get me wrong, though. Them there shows were a sight to behold, bigger than life and louder than thunder. Cowboys were only something most of them paying people had ever read about. And injuns, well, they were frightening to see, whooping and hollering, shaking their tomahawks over their devil-painted faces. Sakes alive, first time I seen the show, up close and personal like, I done nearly shit my drawers.

Of course it was just an act. Those injuns were tamer than a pack of lambs, the way I heard it told. And you couldn't talk to them other foreigners, what with them not knowing a word of English. And the cowboys, well, they done kept to themselves, mostly. Quiet bunch, they were. That is until you got them liquored up some, which was more often then not, I reckon. Then the real show would start.

Oh, sure, I'd met cowboys before. Back home, you couldn't throw a stick without hitting one. And, trust me, I threw my fair share of sticks hoping for just that: to hit one, land one, get one in bed, if you know what I mean. Again, the liquor didn't hurt none in that regard, a hole being a hole when all is said and done. Still, might've been nice to have one of them fellers stay longer than a night, but, heck, I wasn't complaining.

Anyway, the west was shrinking from what it once was, but in that camp of ours, well now, it was just as wild as it ever was. Especially since what few women there were, not counting Annie Oakley and them Sioux squaws, were all huddled off in a corner of the camp somewhere, far away from the menfolk. And without women to keep men in their place, well, that just leads to a whole heap of trouble.

Not to mention, it made them cowboys randy as all hell— present company *not* excepted.

Lots of men wandered the camp, eager for a fight, a way to release some steam, work off the booze they done drunk. Of course, there are other ways to work off steam, mind you.

One night that first week, after a good fifth of Kentucky bourbon, I staggered back to my tent, drunker than a skunk. Only I couldn't rightly find said tent of mine. Heck, they all looked alike, especially in the dark: hundreds of them lined up in neat, little rows. Anyhow, I ended up falling into someone else's. Someone already inside. Someone abusing himself, nekid on his cot.

"Oh, sorry," I said, sputtering as I tried to look away. Or at least tried to look like I was trying to.

The guy just grinned and kept on pulling on his tool—and damn if he didn't have one mighty fine tool at that. "No problem, partner. Something we all do, right?"

I paused, suddenly hearing the edge to his voice. I'd heard that edge before, and my own cock began to get stiff upon hearing it again. "Yep, that's mighty true, friend," I replied. "Mighty true indeed."

He sat up, the grin growing even wider on his stubbled face. I squinted into the darkness. Feller was nice looking, about my age, give or take. "Fact is, though, it's more fun with two than just one," he said, the words coming out all syrupy sweet.

"Meanin'?"

"Well now, I suppose if'n you help me out, I could help you out." He pointed to the obvious strain in my britches. Truth was, I was surprised the material was even holding by that point.

Working all those years on the ranch, doing odds and ends, I had me some experience with lonely men, so I said, "Okay," and then, quick as wink, peeled off my shirt, kicked off my boots, and slid out of my britches and drawers before tying the tent flaps behind me.

"Goodness," the man then said, with a whistle. "That sure is a big'n you got there."

I looked down at my stiff cock, jutting out like it was, and proudly swayed it back and forth. Staring down at his, I said, "Same for you, partner." I reached down and took his slab of meat in my hand. He spread his legs apart and groaned, then reached out and took my own hardness in his calloused grip, giving it an eager tug. It felt good, it did. Flesh on flesh. It'd been a mighty long time. Too long, in fact.

Then he looked up at me with a curious grin. "Um, you ever ride a man like a bull rides a cow?" he asked, that edge to his voice growing even sharper.

Matter of fact, I had. Truth be told, I'd even been the cow once or twice. I snickered at the thought. "You want me to poke you up the ass, partner?"

He snickered back. "Well, now, seems like a shame to let a fine specimen such as that go to waste." He gently slapped the specimen in question, sending it shaking and bobbing in place.

"Fine by me," I told him, hopping onto his small cot. "On your knees, cowboy."

He did as I asked, his solid, hairy rump staring up at me. I spit into my hand and wet his puckered hole, while he spit down into his hand and slicked up his willie. Knowing how big my cock was and how tight a man's hole could be, I stretched him out a bit first, sliding two of my fingers up and in and back. His ring tightened at first, but then he exhaled and relaxed, allowing for them fingers of mine to work their magic.

"Yeah, partner," he moaned, softly. "Break that hole in."

Well now, that's just what I did, joining a third finger with the first two. He bucked his ass into my fist, getting himself ready for the bull ride.

Pretty soon, I got on my knees and popped my fingers out of his ass. I placed the head of my spit-slicked cock up against his pink, crinkled hole and gave it a good old shove. It went in like a shot and made its way to the far side of his asshole, until my balls were pressed up tight against his ass. The stranger moaned again, deep and low, which rumbled through me like a locomotive. That's when I let him have it with both guns, ramming my cock in and out of him while he pulled on his meat, until we both got the same rhythm going.

"Close, partner. Close," he eventually rasped.

I grabbed a hold of his cheeks and gave one final hard, deep thrust, sending a big, old bucketful of hot, white cream up his ass. He sighed and spewed a load down onto the cot below. Both of us were panting and moaning by then, sending that tent of his rattling back and forth something fierce. Then I popped my cock out, hopped up off of that cot of his, and got dressed. He flipped over onto his back and watched.

"Thanks, partner," I said, when I was ready to leave.

"Yep. Anytime," he replied. "Gets plumb lonely out here, you know."

"Yep," I agreed. "Sure does." I smiled down at him. "And maybe next time you can do the bull riding."

The smile returned to his face. "Next time, huh? Well now, I think I might like that. Matter of fact, if you're up for it, I know of another bull in the pen you might like to meet, alongside me."

I paused, my mind racing. I'd never given what he said any thought before. Truth was, while I preferred men to women, I'd never met anyone else who did, not really, let alone someone who wanted to have relations with two men at the same time. My cock was already rock hard at the idea of it. "Well now, partner, I ain't never been too good with numbers, but the way I reckon it, three is always better'n two."

"That's the spirit," he said. "Name's Wayne Smithson, by the way."

"Shem Lockheart," I told him, reaching down to shake his big, strong hand. And that's when I recognized his name. "You the same Wayne that tends to Buffalo Bill's horses?" I let go with an appreciative whistle. "That would make you a real, honest to goodness cowboy then."

"Honest, yes, but goodness ain't got nothing to do with it." He laughed. "Why, ain't you never took a cowboy up the ass before?"

"Well, sure," I replied, almost out of breath as the image splashed around inside my head. "Though I ain't never had one make me an offer like that one."

The grin grew wider on his handsome face. "Well then, I'll get to workin' on it. Once we make camp again, count on that offer bein' more than just some words."

Trust me, I was already counting.

And, fortunately, it didn't seem like I had to go above three.

WE WERE HEADED southwest by train by the next morning. I was in the meal car serving up some grub for a bunch of the sure-shooters, when in he walked. His eyes landed on mine and he smiled, knowingly.

"Shem," he said, with a wink and a nod. In the light of day, he really was a handsome sonofabitch, even more so than I first thought in the dim light of his tent. He was rugged and lean, with a glint of wickedness in his twinling blue eyes. Yep, a feller could get lost in them peepers of his.

"Wayne," I said, with a nod of my own. "You hungry for somethin'?"

"Awful hungry, partner," he replied, the meaning lost on everyone present but the two of us. When he was done eating, he handed me a note and left. I waited until I was back in the kitchen to read it. It said that he'd be picking me up when my shift was up. My heart began to beat hard, imagining what he had in store for us.

Little did I know how off my thoughts actually were.

Hours later, and as promised, he walked back in, the sound of his boot heels echoing throughout the car. He nodded when he saw me and bade me to follow him. And so follow I did, down the train, through one car after the next, all the way to the very end.

I stopped him before the last car. "Um, Wayne, that there is Buffalo Bill's private quarters, ain't it?" He nodded. "No one's allowed in there."

He shrugged. "Well now, not no one. I mean, Mister Cody's allowed in there." His smile returned. He looked around. We were alone. His lips met mine as an explosion of white burst behind my fluttering eyes. No man had ever had that effect on me before. Was a scary thing, it was. Scary and exciting. "And," he soon added, "Mister Cody's in a meetin' right about now. Way back in the dining cabin."

"Way back?" I whispered, my cock already twitching inside my britches.

"Way," he said, the kiss repeated, then repeated again, a spark suddenly travelling down my spine before it went *BOOM!* inside my balls. Like I said, scary and exciting, especially once we walked through to Buffalo Bills car, the cook and the cowboy in the most famous man alive's sleeping quarters.

I gave an appreciative whistle as I had myself a look around. I'd never seen furniture like this before, all carved in some sort of expensive wood—and on a train no less. There were trinkets everywhere, obviously souvenirs from our boss's travels, plus pictures of men and women, most likely every last one of them famous for something or another. There were rifles and pistols hanging from the walls, trophies too, and hats and boots strewn all over the place, all of it fancy, obviously expensive.

And then I turned around, and everything was put to shame by what I saw next.

"You don't waste no time, cowboy," I said, staring down at Wayne, who was already buck nekid and spread eagle on the brass bed.

He gave me a thoughtful look. "Seems to me, I wasted plenty already."

Was he being romantic? I gulped. This wasn't how things went. Never before anyway. Cowboys, I'd found, weren't exactly the romantic types. I mean, all men fucked the same, sure, but they didn't all act the same before and after that fucking part, not like he was acting, at any rate.

"Damn, you're beautiful, Wayne Smithson." Which was about all I could think to say, all things considered.

He laughed, tight belly rumbling, fifth limb of a cock swaying. "Ain't something anyone's ever said to me before, but thank you kindly. You ain't half bad yourself, Shem, though I figure you'd look twice as good without them clothes on."

I nodded, the gulp repeating. He was asking me to get nekid. In Buffalo Bill's sleeping car. Was I dreaming? If so, it sure as shooting was one mighty fine dream. In any case, I was indeed nekid in no time flat, boots and britches flinging this way and that, never taking my eyes off of him, just in case I blinked and he disappeared like one of them desert mirages.

I started to hop in bed with him when he held his hand up for me to stop. I froze on the spot. He smiled, his eyes moving up and down. "Yep, beautiful," he said.

"Nuh uh," I said in return.

He nodded. "Trust me, I've seen beautiful before, and you, well now, when you can't take your eyes off of something, that's beautiful."

I blushed. Me, a grown man. "You talk like this to lots of folks, Wayne?"

"Nope," he said. "You're the first."

My smile rose skyward. I got in bed with him, our lips meeting before the rest of my body could make it even with his. His hands roamed my back. Mine worked their way across his broad expanse of hairy chest. When at last the kiss was broken, I opened my eyes and stared into his. The sky above was never so vast, so blue.

"You been lots of places, Wayne?" I asked. "With Mister Cody, I mean?"

Again he nodded. "Lots, why?"

I chose my words carefully. "This, what we're doing here, calling each other beautiful and all, does that, you know, happen often?"

He sighed. "Only needs to happen once, far as I'm concerned."

Damn, I thought, where had this man been hiding while I'd been fucking nameless dirty strangers? I kissed him and fell down on him, our sweaty bodies slipping and sliding over one another, the brass bed creaking as the train squealed around a sharp curve.

He rolled us over, me on the bottom now. His mouth moved from my lips down my neck, goose bumps rising up my arms as he bit down on a nipple. I writhed as he chomped, his hand stroking my cock now, mine running through his thick mane of hair.

Down further he went, tongue slithering and sliding over my belly. I giggled. His mouth found my aching prick. The giggle turned to a groan. He sucked on it as I stared at his work, my tool appearing and disappearing all the while. His eyes caught mine. It was like we were tied together, like that cock of mine was some sort of hitching post.

Lower still he went, licking and lapping at my balls, taking each one into his mouth, yanking on my nut sac as he did so. My back arched off the bed, cock dripping with spit as it aimed for the ceiling. He stopped licking and straightened his back as he stared down at me. "Ready?" he just about purred.

I smiled. He had that effect on me. It was a nice effect. "For?"

"Some bronco busting," he giddily replied.

I looked around. "Lots of shit in this place, but, uh, no cattle. Not as far as I can see."

He pointed down at my prick, which stood like a cactus, tall and sturdy. "Different kind of bull."

My cock throbbed, a bead of spunk dripping out of the piss slit. "Bust away then."

He crawled up, one meaty thigh on either side of my waist, his muscle-dense body glistening with well-earned sweat. Beautiful, so fucking beautiful. I wished I'd had more words for it, but one seemed plenty. He then aimed my prick for his hole and sank down. It vanished inside of him as he sucked in his breath, eyes rolling back inside his head.

Me, I began to pant, my insides feeling like they were suddenly lit on fire. I bucked into him as he pressed down on me. There was that tether again, though I had a feeling it would be there long after my cock extracted itself from his mighty fine rump.

Up, down he went. Up, in, out I went. He swirled one hand over his head, the other stroking his prick. "Ride 'em, cowboy," I said, barely able to catch my breath now as the train lurched one way and he lurched the other.

One final shove down on top of me, and he shot like a geyser, hot come raining up before splattering down. His asshole clenched around my prick. I shot a second later, filling his insides with a heavy load of my hot seed, which soon dripped out and coated my balls and bush.

He laughed as he drained out every last drop. I laughed watching him laugh. If we got caught right there and then, got fired, thrown off the train, I would still have been the happiest man that side of the mighty Mississippi.

He slid off of me and collapsed across my body, his mouth finding mine like a divining rod finding water. I kissed him like I'd die if I didn't. All in all, that might not have been too far from the truth.

"We make camp tomorrow," he told me, that devilish smile

of his returning, many minutes later, once we were dressed and after we cleaned up any traces of our little adventure. "You ready to cash in on that offer of mine?"

My cock twitched at the words, at the sound of his deep, rumbling voice. "I do so like my cash, Wayne."

He laughed. "Then get ready, because you're in for one hell of a payday."

THE NEXT NIGHT, we made our way off the train and over to a nearby hill. The moon hung high overhead, bathing the countryside in a silver glow and shining off the tepees strewed out before us.

I froze in place. "This is where the injuns sleep, Wayne."

"Yep, Shem, sure is. Though sleepin' ain't what we'll be doing." He grabbed my hand and led me forward.

I whispered in his ear, "But the injuns are kept separate from the rest of us."

He didn't respond, just kept pulling us between the odd looking leather homes before he stopped in front of one. Bending down, he split open the entrance and walked us inside. I'd never met an injun before, let alone stood in one's tepee. This one was sitting cross-legged, dressed in tanned leggings and a fringed vest. "This here is Eagle Feather," Wayne told me. I gulped. I was standing before the son of Sitting Bull. I introduced myself. He remained stone-faced. Wayne explained, "His English ain't so good. Don't worry none, we won't be needin' it."

I watched as the barest hint of a smile spread across the injun's dark face. The tepee was lit by a small fire in the center, so I could see him clearly enough. I watched in awe as he removed his vest, revealing a thick chest and a belly littered with muscles. His skin was dark all over and hairless as a baby's. He stood up and kicked his moccasins off, then removed his britches. Right quick, he stood before us, nekid as a jaybird and hard as a tree stump.

"I ain't never seen one so big before," I whispered into my

friend's ear.

"Bet you're in for a lot of firsts tonight, partner," he whispered back, shucking off his clothes and motioning for me to follow. Pretty soon, all three of us were standing there nekid, stroking our pricks by the glow of the warm fire.

Eagle Feather walked over and stood before us. Wayne reached out and stroked the injun's chest, taking a thick-nubbed, brown nipple in between his thumb and index finger. I in turn ran my hand across the man's chest, which was as solid and smooth as polished marble. When my fingers found his other nipple, the injun moaned and shut his eyes tight. Soon enough, though, he sunk to his knees and took my cock in his mouth, something I never imagined an injun would do, let alone a warrior like Eagle Feather.

I looked over at Wayne, who smiled over at me. "He's pretty good at that, huh?"

"Yep," I replied, coaxing my willie further into the injun's warm mouth.

Wayne walked behind me, his fat cock pressed snuggly between my cheeks, and ran his hands across my chest before pinching at my nipples. A shot of lightning bolted through my belly and circled around my crotch. I moaned and pumped my cock with a mighty force into the mouth below. The injun swallowed me whole, stroking his giant limb while he did so.

Then he surprised me for a second time by standing up before wrapping his arms around my waist, so that his body was pressed hard against my front and Wayne was up tight against my back. He then leaned his head across my shoulder and kissed my friend hard and full on the lips. Now then, I'd kissed men before, clearly, but had never seen two of them going at it—and boy howdy was it a hot sight to see.

When they broke free, the injun looked me deep in the eyes and brushed his lips against my own. He smelled of roots and earth, his lips soft as a down pillow. When he kissed me, I eagerly kissed him back. He snaked his tongue over mine and groaned at our contact. Wayne whispered into my ear, "Can three play at this game, partner?" Before I could answer, he sidled around me and joined his mouth with ours, three tongues now sliding around in three wet mouths, three hands stroking three rock-solid cocks.

That tepee was mighty hot by that point—and it was about to get a hell of a lot hotter.

Eagle Feather pulled away first, getting on all fours with his brown rump facing our way. Like the rest of him, it was hairless and shot through with muscle. Wayne got on his knees and I followed suit, both of us running our hands across the injun's back and ass and hole and legs, all smooth as silk and hard as stone.

"I ain't ever felt anything like him before," I managed to squeak out.

Wayne laughed. "He tastes pretty different, too," he told me, reaching between the man's ass cheeks and pulling his cock between his legs. "Here, try this out."

The fat head was already shiny slick. I bent down and took it in my mouth, tasting the saltiness of it as it throbbed across my tongue. Wayne coaxed my head further down around it, gagging me at first, but I finally managed about half of it—no mean feat, mind you.

"How's it taste?" Wayne asked, rubbing my back with his hand.

I popped the injun's hooded cock out of my mouth and replied, "Like jerky, I s'pose. Only better, softer."

Wayne laughed. "Now try this," he said, letting go of Eagle Feather's prick before spreading his cheeks apart for me.

"Nuh uh. You want me to lick his hole?"

"You already done sucked his cock. Why not his ass? Thing is sweet as apple pie."

I doubted that was true, but figured that Wayne hadn't led me wrong yet, so I got on all fours and stuck my face in between the injun's cheeks. He smelled like sweat and musk, an odor that drew me in even deeper, until my tongue took a good lick around his brown, puckered hole. Eagle Feather groaned as I slid my way inside of him, bucking his rump into my face all the while.

"Wanna see what that feels like?" Wayne whispered into my ear.

I continued sucking and slurping, and mumbled, "Uh huh."

Wayne got behind me. I could feel his hands spread me apart and then his tongue tickling its way around my hole. Eagle Feather began to stroke his cock while I ate his ass, and I stroked my own as my friend ate mine. We were like three cars on a train now, connected by our mouths. When I was good and wet, Wayne got up on his knees and placed his fat cock head up against my ring. I felt the familiar burn and strain as he eased it inside of me, slowly, gently, working his way in. My back arched as he filled me up with his thick slab of meat. Eagle Feather crawled in reverse and rubbed his fine ass against my hardness. "Fuck him," Wayne panted, biting down on my earlobe.

I reached for my cock and slapped it against the injun's hole before shoving it in deep. Eagle Feather exhaled and pushed farther back, until the three of us were again pressed snug together, Wayne's hands roaming across my shoulders and down my arms while mine pulled and tugged on the injun's thick, sensitive nipples.

My entire body felt alive now, getting fucked from the back while I fucked from the front. It wasn't like any feeling I'd ever felt before. Got to a point where I didn't know where one of us ended and the other began; we just felt like one great whole, all sweating and grinding and filling that tepee with the sounds of our snorts and grunts. Growing up, playing cowboys and injuns wasn't anything like this. For one, we always killed the injuns, not fucked them silly.

When Eagle Feather began a quick, steady stoke on his long, thick cock, I knew he was close. Good thing, too, because so was I. Wayne was pounding on my ass something fierce by that point, coaxing the come up from deep within my swaying balls, which started a slow rise up.

I looked over the injun's smooth shoulder and watched as his giant cock exploded, all that hot, white cream gushing out onto the dirt floor below, which caused his already tight hole to grow even tighter around my cock. And then I came as well, filling Eagle Feather's insides with a thick coating of juice. Then, of course, it was Wayne's turn. Seconds after me and the injun shot our heavy loads, my cowboy friend bucked his cock one final time up my ass and then filled it up but good, shooting and shooting and shooting deep inside of me.

When the three of us were spent, we collapsed on top of one another in a big, sweaty pile of flesh, each of us trying our best to catch our breaths. I pulled out of Eagle Feather and Wayne pulled out of me, but we held on good and tight, not wanting to let the feeling end.

But end it did, soon enough, without so much as a word spoken by our injun friend. Heck, he probably didn't know but a few words of English to begin with, just like Wayne had said. Then again, for what we just did, he didn't need any.

Oh, and, yes, what we just did, we did again and again, from one town to the next to the next one after that.

Like I said, the west was shrinking, but it was still as wild as ever. Especially in that camp of ours, which was chock full of randy cowboys and injuns. And if Wayne and I had any say in the matter, which we seemed to do, it was sure as shooting gonna stay that way.

RIDING FOR THE BRAND

BY J.D. RYAN

HANK COLLINS TOPPED the rise and reined in the buckskin. For a long moment, he just sat there enjoying the view. There was just nothing like the satisfaction a man felt at the end of a job. The fence ran back along the property line, every rail in place, just like the boss wanted. It crossed the rolling hills beneath the Sandias and headed for the ranch house. Hank was well aware the fence was an oddity—who ran a fence along the open range, anyway? But if the boss wanted a fence, then a fence was what he got. And it was a fine fence, even if the T-Lazy-A riders said so themselves. It would certainly keep those M-L Connected skunks from running their scrawny cattle across T-Lazy-A land.

The stocky redhead swiped at the back of his neck with his already damp bandana. He was happy to be done with the unaccustomed chore. The only thing better than finishing a job well done was relaxing after that job. He'd headed this way with only one thing in mind: the waterhole at the end of the draw. A cold natural spring fed the pond, keeping it full even in the dry season. The ranch hands were all in the habit of sluicing off a day's sweat in the deep hole. He was lucky the rest of the crew was working at the other end of the fence, or he'd have had to fight to find a place in the water.

Hank's gaze shifted downslope, to the pond below. Damn it all! Looked like he wasn't the only one who'd thought the waterhole was the perfect end to a long, hot day's work. He didn't recognize the pinto cropping the grass beneath the cottonwoods, at the water's edge. Then, the animal turned a shoulder his way and he spotted the brand. M-L Connected. What were those low-down coyotes up to now?

The buckskin pricked up his ears as he caught sight of the pinto, and snuffled at the breeze blowing from that direction. Hank clapped heels to the animal's side and they started down the hillside. Not much grew on the hills but sagebrush and the tough grass their cattle thrived on, but the cottonwoods had grown up in the moist soil to shade the waterhole from the still-blistering afternoon sun. Hank had been looking forward to that cool water since lunch, but now it looked like he'd have to clean out the pond before taking a dip.

Hank reached down to loosen the Henry in the scabbard, and slipped the thong off his Colt Navy revolver. The big galoot floating in the middle of the pond didn't look to have any weapons on him, but he might just have some friends who needed to be reminded of the property line.

The galoot wasn't as dumb as he looked: he honed in on Hank's progress as soon as the buckskin started down the trail from the top of the hill. He could swim, too. Before Hank was halfway to the waterhole, the M-L rider had reached the bank and made a dash for the pinto's side. Hank prodded the buckskin into a trot, and they reached the waterhole just as the man pulled his old Henry out of the scabbard and whirled.

The tall rider froze when he spotted Hank's Colt, already aimed at his middle. Hank had to chuckle at the sight of the cowboy, naked as the day he was born.. His height and muscle might have been intimidating if he'd been dressed in the usual workingman's gear. As it was, he looked more like a half-drowned bull calf than a dangerous foe. His black hair was plastered to his head, and he kept blinking at the water dripping into his brown eyes.

"Go ahead and shoot," the cowboy called, lowering his rifle. "Be just like you T-Lazy-A coyotes. You want I should turn around so you can shoot me in the back?"

"You're the coyotes," Hank retorted, nudging the buckskin closer. He kept the Colt on the man's midsection. "I ain't the one trespassing on private property."

The cowboy snorted. "That waterhole's smack dab on the property line, and you know it. I got as much right to be here as you do."

Hank plucked the rifle from the man's hand and waved him away from his pinto. "You was over the line. Why, you was nearly across to our pasture."

The man's big hands fisted at his side. His brows lowered. He looked like he might try to rush Hank, even if there was a pistol pointed at his belly. "So what if I was? Ain't no harm in a man taking a swim."

"Maybe I don't want my waterhole polluted by no filthy M-L skunk. Might have to drain the pond anyhow, just so the cows ain't poisoned."

"Why you..." The big man started forward, and Hank had to shove the pistol in his face to remind him who was boss.

"Big talk from behind a gun," the cowboy said, crossing his arms and glaring up at Hank. "Let's see you back up them words in a fair fight."

Hank considered the proposition. Nobody could say Hank Collins ever backed off from a fight—and he'd had a right frustrating day with those fence rails. Now, to find a blamed M-L rider poaching on his waterhole. Well, it just naturally raised a man's hackles. Hank gestured with his pistol, backing the other man away from the pinto, where he'd stashed his clothes and weapons.

"I reckon you need a lesson," Hank said. "Maybe after I beat some sense into you, you'll stay away from our waterhole."

The big galoot's foot came down on a rock, and he flinched. "M-L's got just as much right to that waterhole as you T-Lazy-A coyotes."

Hank swung to the ground, keeping his pistol pointed at the cowboy's middle. "Like you think you got a right to our cattle, too, huh? Reckon that's why the boss put up that fence."

"You lot are the ones rustling from us, you low-bellied snake. Everybody knows they called it the Lazy-A for a good reason."

That did it. Hank slid his gun back into the holster, then shucked his gun belt, and hung it over the saddle horn. He took three strides toward the M-L rider, and the other man met him at the edge of the water. He probably thought Hank would be all riled up at his prodding, ready to jump right in with both fists. Hank had been in a few fights, though. He knew better than to start flailing away without sizing up your opponent. He circled the big man, both of his fists held at chest height to block anything the other might throw his way. It wasn't that the M-L rider was that much taller than Hank. In fact, without his boots on, he barely topped Hank's six-foot-one. It was more a matter of bulk. The other's shoulders were massive, bulky with muscle and sinew. He looked like he could throw a steer single-handed, without even a cowpony to back him up. A barrel chest tapered down to a trim waist. Say what he would about the cowboy, Hank couldn't deny that the man was in fighting shape.

And fighting mad he was, too. As Hank circled, watching his opponent, the M-L rider threw the first punch—a quick jab with a lot of power behind it. Hank twisted sideways and managed to avoid the blow, then countered with a jab of his own toward the man's midsection. The cowboy blocked that and snapped out a return blow that made it past Hank's defense and smashed against his ribs. Hank sucked in a breath—the man had a mean right. The two of them settled in for a long battle, feinting and ducking, landing the occasional blow.

"Have to admit," Hank panted, "you're a pretty fair fighter."

The cowboy flashed him a quick grin, wincing as the

movement pulled at his split lip. "You ain't so bad yourself—for a Lazy-A rider."

Hank threw a quick uppercut that connected with the man's ribcage and knocked the grin off his face. His own face throbbed, courtesy of a jab to his right cheekbone that had his eye nearly swelled shut. He ignored the discomfort and blocked another attempt at his belly.

"Too bad you M-L boys can't work as hard as you fight. You might have an outfit instead of a rawhide ranch."

"I'll show you work!" The naked cowboy launched himself in a low tackle. He connected solidly with Hank's midsection, bringing them both to the ground. Hank hit hard, and struggled to catch his breath. The M-L rider wrapped his legs around Hank's waist and used his larger size to try to pin Hank's shoulders down.

Hank shook his head, trying to get past the feeling that he was smothering, trying to clear his thoughts and win this fight. He twisted his hips and managed to get one knee underneath himself. With a great heave that nearly burst his lungs, he bucked the cowboy loose. Before the other could regain his hold, Hank rolled onto his belly and shoved with both hands, trying to get to his feet.

He managed to suck in a deep breath, and coughed hard enough to see spots. The M-L rider grabbed at Hank's ankle, and Hank kicked out, felt the blow connect, heard the grunt. He pulled his knees beneath him and pushed to a shaky stand. The cowboy crouched nearby, both arms wrapped around his middle. Hank spotted a big, muddy boot print in the middle of the man's chest.

"Ready to give up?" he asked, leaning forward to rest his own hands on his thighs, still trying to pull in enough air.

The M-L rider grunted again, more loudly, and shook his head. He struggled to his feet as well, looking as shaky as Hank felt. "Not giving up to no Lazy-A coyote."

He threw another haymaker at Hank, but his aim was wild and Hank just took a step back and avoided the blow. His breathing had gotten easier, and he shoved the hair out of his eyes and put up his dukes again.

"Let's get this over with," he said.

"Fine talk against a naked man," the other muttered. He held up a hand, palm out, and Hank grudgingly gave him a minute to catch his breath.

"Might have known you Lazy-A skunks would figure this'd be a fair fight," the cowboy said with a sneer. "You and them big clod-hoppers kicking a fellow when he's down."

"Ain't my fault you shucked out of your clothes and jumped in our waterhole."

"Ain't your waterhole, dammit." The M-L rider straightened to his full height and raised his fists.

Hank stepped back once more, looking up at the big man with frustration. How in hell was he going to take this bull down and corral him? His eye throbbed, and his ribs ached. He could only assume the other felt nearly as bad: his lip was swollen and bleeding, and that blow to the chest had to hurt. Yet he stood there, ready to keep fighting. Hank was more than ready to finish this.

Maybe there was a way he could end the fight and still get his swim. He had to grin as he lowered his head and charged the M-L rider. The man was caught flat-footed. Hank wrapped both arms around his middle and shoved him backwards into the waterhole. Both men sucked in a breath as they hit the cool water. If Hank hadn't had his arms full of bull-headed cowboy, he'd have been right comfortable. As it was, he was going to have to end this fight quickly, so he'd have time for a relaxing swim before supper.He found bottom with his boots and bore down with all his weight on the cowboy's chest, forcing the man under the water. The M-L rider flailed with arms and legs, and Hank lost his grip on the slippery skunk. The big man quickly got his feet underneath him. He aimed a haymaker at Hank's head. Hank just ducked and reached out with one leg, sweeping the cowboy's feet away from the bottom again.

The other man sputtered and coughed as he came to the surface. "Is this a fist fight or a wrestling match?" he asked with narrowed eyes. "Coz I can whoop a Lazy-A dog either way."

"I can whoop an M-L skunk without even trying."

"Then you'd best get to whooping before I tie you in a knot." The big man leaped forward, colliding with Hank.

The two men grappled frantically, feet slipping on the muddy bottom of the pond. Hank might be shorter than the M-L rider, but his stocky build was bulky with muscle. The riders stood chest to chest in the muddy water. Their biceps bulged as each one struggled to shove the other off his feet. They glared into one another's eyes, teeth bared in predatory snarls.

Hank shoved against the hard chest, his fingers slipping as he sought a hold on the M-L rider's brawny arms. Despite his anger, he quickly became aware that his opponent was quite an armful: brawny and fit, his muscles toned by hard days of work. The man's big cock pressed up against Hank's thigh as they wrestled. It was a good thing Hank's trousers suppressed the evidence of his sudden interest. The other man countered with a grab at Hank's belt. He hauled hard and threw Hank sideways. As the water closed over Hank's head, the cowboy lunged after him. Hank backpedaled wildly, flailing both arms to keep away from the big hands.

The M-L cowboy missed his hold and splashed down only inches away from Hank's chest. Hank twisted and pushed off with one foot, sliding over the top of the big man before he could get back to the surface. The cowboy bucked, but Hank wrapped both arms around the man's chest. Both of them went under again. Hank pulled the rider close and maneuvered his hands into position behind the taller man's thick neck.

The cowboy probably would have fought the hold harder, but both men were running low on air, so when Hank found bottom with his boots and stood back up, the M-L rider went along for the ride.

"Ready to say uncle, yet?" Hank asked in the man's ear.

Hank thought briefly of nibbling on that ear, maybe slipping one hand down to see if the man's ass was as muscular as the rest of his body.

The rider reached over his head, trying for a hold on Hank's hair, but Hank jerked his head back out of the way. He put a bit of pressure on the back of the man's neck, the muscles he'd built up from years of wrangling cattle bulging as he struggled to hold the larger man.

"Don't make me hold your head under until you give in," Hank told the man. Hank hauled backward and the cowboy's feet slipped in the mud and flew out from underneath him. It was all Hank could do to keep his grasp on the slippery body, but he dragged the M-L rider along with him to the bank of the waterhole. "I'm willing to let you ride off if you holler calf-rope," he said. He thought it was big of him not to ask the man to suck his cock first.

"I ain't giving in to you." The cowboy got his feet under him and shoved hard. The two men flew backwards, hitting the water hard enough to loosen Hank's grip.

The M-L rider twisted as he freed himself. He trapped one of Hank's wrists and hauled the arm behind Hank's back, pulling upwards until Hank was forced onto tiptoe to ease the strain.

"Now who's gonna holler calf-rope?" the cowboy taunted. He slid his other hand around to Hank's belt buckle. "Let's get things a little more even, how about?"

Hank struggled, but the harder he pulled away, the worse the strain on his elbow. He was forced to let the cowboy unbutton his trousers and yank them down to his knees. He'd wanted the man's attention on his cock, but this wasn't how he'd envisioned the scene. His face flushed, and he ducked his head to hide the fact.

"Now you ain't such a big man," the M-L rider sneered. "Let's see you kick a fellow with your pants down."

"I reckon you just wanted to see me naked."

"I reckon I'd rather kiss my pinto than look at your bare ass. I'm just tired of being the only man with his balls hanging in the breeze. Ain't a fair fight if you ask me."

Hank threw his head back and grunted as his skull collided with the cowboy's forehead. They'd both have a headache in the morning. The big hands let go of his wrist and Hank jerked free. He whirled and aimed a haymaker at the cowboy. The M-L rider flung up his arm and blocked the blow. He ducked underneath Hank's next swing and grabbed at Hank's trousers, hauling them further down. Hank's feet slid on the muddy bottom of the waterhole and he fell backwards. He kicked out with both feet, feeling intense satisfaction when his boots collided with the cowboy's belly, flinging the larger man away with a giant splash.

By the time the big man's head popped back to the surface, Hank had regained his feet. He yanked at his trousers, but it was going to take a determined effort to wrestle the wet wool back up over his legs.

"Damn your hide," he yelled, hauling one boot off instead. "Back off a minute and give a fellow a chance to even the playing field."

"Didn't bother you none when it was you against a naked man," the cowboy retorted, crossing his arms with a sneer.

Hank dragged off his boots, tossed them onto the grassy bank, and shucked out of the trousers. As he threw those out of the water, he glared at his opponent. "Satisfied?"

Without waiting for an answer, he shoved toward the cowboy, fighting through the waist-deep water. The wave Hank pushed forward collided with the wave in front of the other man as he rushed toward Hank. They met in a great fountain of water. Neither could find purchase on the slippery body of his opponent, and neither could brace his feet in the muddy bottom of the pond. They found themselves instead in a rough embrace, arms wrapped about each other, legs entwined, faces only inches apart.

"Give in, you overgrown ox," Hank growled through gritted teeth.

"Back down, you big galoot," came the reply.

Hank shoved hard at the big man's chest, all too aware of the hard body shoving back against him. He wondered what the cowboy would do if he slid a hand down between their bellies and fisted that pig pistol the man was packing. He glared into the brown eyes and tried once more to grab a wrist and throw the rider off balance. The big cowboy lunged forward at the same time, and they butted heads. Hank's sore cheekbone collided with the other's mouth, and he winced and jerked his head back.

"Damn your stinking hide," the cowboy muttered. He reached out a brawny arm and fastened his fingers in Hank's hair. Hank twisted, but the rider hauled his face forward, glaring with narrowed eyes. Hank froze as the man suddenly leaned in to close his mouth over Hank's.

This was no lover's kiss. The M-L rider punished Hank's mouth, grinding hard against Hank's lips and sucking them deep within his own mouth. Hank squirmed for only a moment, then slid one hand up and fisted the cowboy's long, black hair, holding his face close. He opened his mouth, letting the man's tongue inside to grapple with his own. Their teeth grated together, and Hank's cock throbbed. He groaned into the cowboy's mouth.

The man responded by increasing the intensity of the kiss. He plumbed the depths of Hank's mouth, his teeth mercilessly scraping the already tender lips. His fingers hauled hard on Hank's hair. A big hand slid down and closed over Hank's throbbing cock. Hank groaned again as the cowboy fisted him hard, pumping his rod like the man was jacking a cartridge into his rifle chamber. He forced his own hand between their bellies and found the man's cock, as hard as his own.

The M-L rider pulled his mouth away long enough to growl. "Get me off good, cowboy. Maybe I'll forget about pounding you to leather scraps."

Hank jerked hard at the thick cock. "You get me off," he countered, "and maybe I'll forget about thrashing you."

The cowboy lunged forward again. His hard mouth found the tender skin beneath Hank's jaw, and he bit hard at Hank's neck. Hank tightened his grip on the man's hair and bucked his hips against the big hand on his cock. He pumped the other's cock just as fast as the big man pumped his, and the two of them soon found a rough rhythm. Their fists moved in unison. Their hips ground together. They panted and grunted like a couple of bulls in rut.

Hank threw back his head to allow the cowboy full access to his throat. The other sucked and bit, bringing as much pain as pleasure as he ran his teeth along the muscles and down to Hank's collarbone. Hank's balls jerked upwards as he shot a thick wad over the big hands around his rod. His hips quivered as he shoved against the cowboy's hips and forced the last of his juice out. The water between them turned white as the cowboy released his own load. Hank pumped the thick rod hard, and the M-L rider clamped his teeth down on Hank's shoulder and bucked his hips like a green horse.

When it was over, the two just stood there for a moment, their legs wobbly.

"I won," said the M-L rider. "Got you off faster than you got me off."

"Didn't know it was a damn contest." Hank muttered, raising his hand to shove at the broad, hairy chest. He let go of the cowboy's hair and pushed his own bangs out of his eyes.

"Yep," came the reply. The other man shoved back, hard enough to make Hank take a step to balance himself. "Winner gets to poke the loser. Got some grease in the saddlebag that ought to do the trick."

Hank drew back. "Anybody gets poked, it ought to be the one caught on the wrong side of the line."

"Fair's fair." The cowboy turned toward the bank, where his pinto was contentedly cropping grass beside Hank's buckskin. "I'm better at it than you are, so I get to do the poking."

"You ain't better'n me, you coyote. You just started before

I did." Hank sloshed after the man, his ire returning. By thunder, he was going to get his pistol off the saddle horn and show this galoot what was what.

"Bigger, better, faster." The M-L rider reached the bank and started for the horses. "And hornier."

Hank picked up the pace, sloshing water chest high as he trotted after the annoying cowboy. "Ain't *nobody* better'n me. Nor hornier. And I ain't going along with this crazy idea of yours, neither."

The man rummaged about in his saddlebag. "You lost, you get to bend over. Only fair."

"I'll show you fair, you M-L skunk." Hank grabbed one wrist and whirled the man around to face him. "You want a contest? Then let's just finish that wrestling match you started. For real, this time."

The cowboy's brows furrowed. His other hand reached out for Hank's arm, but Hank pulled back and yanked him off balance.

"Winner gets to poke the loser," Hank said. "That's what you want, right?"

The M-L rider swung his arm back in the other direction, hauling Hank's arm along with it and making him take a step back to keep his balance. "Get ready to bend over, you coyote."

The two shoved against one another, chest to chest once more. Hank kept hold of the other's wrist, but the cowboy fastened his free hand in Hank's lapel. Neither could throw the other, no matter how they pushed and twisted. Hank jerked the rider's arm sideways and thrust one foot behind the man's leg, but his opponent turned with him and they both ended up on the ground.

The horses snorted and trotted away from the men as they rolled one way and then another, each trying to pin the other's shoulders to the grass. However he might despise the M-L Connected riders, Hank had to admit that this one was a crafty fighter. Every time Hank thought he had the man safely subdued, his opponent would wriggle free of the hold and turn the tables.

After a few minutes, both men were covered with dirt and

grass. Hank's cheekbone was throbbing again. If his shirt wasn't already wet from the waterhole, it'd be wet from exertion. The M-L rider shook his head as his sweat dripped into one eye.

"Damn it," the cowboy muttered, twisting out of Hank's grasp and rolling into the top position again. "I'm gonna need another swim if you don't give in quick."

"You're the one giving in." Hank bucked the man off and regained his position.

The cowboy snorted. He scissor-kicked his legs and Hank found himself on the bottom again. They continued switching places until Hank was about tuckered out.

"You ready to holler calf-rope?" he asked, panting. He twisted around to the top once more.

The cowboy didn't seem to have enough air to answer. He merely shook his head grimly, his teeth bared in a snarl. He yanked on Hank's shirt so hard that the lapel ripped free. He took a new grip on the front of the shirt and bucked his way around to the top. He gave a mighty heave and hauled his wrist free of Hank's grip. That hand fisted in Hank's shirt alongside of the other. He lifted his torso and bore down with all his strength on Hank's chest.

Hank struggled fiercely. He kicked both legs. He grabbed the cowboy's wrists and heaved. It was no use. He was pinned. The M-L rider saw the truth in Hank's eyes, and his snarl changed to a sneer.

"Gonna admit the truth now?" he asked. "The better man won twice."

Hank could do little more than squirm. He let out a frustrated bellow. "You ain't better'n me, damn it. You had to grab my shirt to win. I ought to cry foul since you ain't got one for me to grab."

"Not my fault," the cowboy said with a smirk. He shifted his position, trapping Hank's legs between his powerful thighs. His elbows straightened and he shoved down on Hank's chest like a steam piston.

Hank's breath escaped in a whoosh. He struggled to breathe, feeling his face flushing. The cowboy kept up the pressure until Hank thought his lungs would pop. He pounded both fists on the rider's chest.

"Give in?" the man asked with a grin.

Hank could only nod. The M-L rider let off the pressure, and Hank sucked in a deep breath. He lay there, panting, as the cowboy shoved to his feet and caught up the pinto.

"Here's what I was looking for," the man said, holding up a tin of salve. "Good for what ails you."

Hank gave the man a sour look as he levered himself to his elbows. "Let's just get this over with. I want a swim before I get back to the bunkhouse."

The sun had already started down toward the horizon, and deep shadows lay underneath the trees. The cowboy—

"What the hell do I call you, anyhow?" Hank asked. He gave his own handle.

"I'm Tom Plant, but they call me Tex because I'm from Dallas." Tex pried open the lid of the tin and dug out a handful of salve. "Roll over so's I can get at your hole."

Tex greased up one hand. Hank rolled onto his belly. The idea was starting to interest him—or his cock, at least. The idea of taking the other man's big rod up his ass stirred the root of his own rod. He spread his legs and let Tex slide a finger inside his hole. Felt weird at first, but he quickly grew used to the sensation as Tex slid the finger in and out a few times. The second finger was unexpected.

"Got to get you loosened up," Tex explained as Hank glanced around. "I like a good poke as much as the next man, but I like the other fellow to enjoy it, too."

He slipped both fingers deep within Hank's ass, and something inside there liked the feeling. A buzz started in his balls, and his cock thickened. Hank rose onto his knees and shoved back against Tex's hand.

"Not half bad," he muttered. "Let's get 'er done."

"Hang on, cowboy. You ain't as ready as you think you are." Tex slid a third finger beside the other two. It was a tight fit, but Hank tried to relax and stretch his hole for the man.

"Push down," Tex suggested. "You got to open up."

Hank pushed, and Tex had three fingers inside him within no time. Hank sucked in a deep breath at the sensation of his ass stretching open. He shoved backwards as Tex shoved forward, letting his ass get used to the feeling. Tex slid his other hand around Hank's waist and fisted his cock. That sure helped him relax. Within a few minutes, Hank was taking all three fingers without a thought, sliding back and forth like a bucking cowpony. And, like a pony, he was ready to be ridden.

"Let's get the show on the road," he said, grinding his ass against Tex's hand. "I'm as ready as I'll ever be."

Tex's big hand left Hank's cock and moved to his ass cheeks, spreading them apart. Hank felt the hard knob of the man's cock at his puckered opening. He swallowed hard, wondering if this was going to work or not. Tex pressed forward slowly.

"Get a deep breath," Tex said. "Imagine your hole opening up when you let it out. I'll go in quick so's it'll hurt less."

Hank took in a lung full of air, trying to relax his asshole. He wasn't exactly certain he was doing this right, but Tex seemed to know the ropes, so he'd follow along and hope for the best. He pushed down as he exhaled, thinking about his backside opening for that big cock.

Tex gave a shove, and Hank sucked in another deep breath as the thick knob went past his sphincter. That was one fat cock. He let out a soft groan and Tex gave him a moment to get used to the intrusion. Hank focused his attention on his throbbing asshole, willing the muscles to relax and accept the other man inside.

It took a while. His ass was convinced it was split open like one of the rails on that fence. Tex started a gentle rocking motion, pulling his cock back just a bit, then pushing further inside. Hank took deep breaths and pushed down as hard as he could.

Damn it, if other fellows could do this, he sure as hell could.

Tex was inching his way inside Hank's hole. His big hands roamed over Hank's ass, digging hard into the muscles, spreading Hank's legs further apart. Just about the time Hank started to get used to the feeling of that big rod up his hole, he felt the wiry hair of the cowboy's pubes against his ass. He glanced back once more, to see Tex pressed up against his backside.

Tex slipped a hand around to fist Hank's cock again. "Ready to be ridden, cowboy?"

Hank nodded firmly and pushed back against Tex's crotch. Tex slowly pulled back, easing his cock back out of Hank's tight hole. He withdrew until only the head of his cock was inside, and then slowly pushed forward again. Hank's ass wasn't complaining any longer. In fact, when that big rod eased up inside, it hit that spot that the fingers had brushed—hit it dead center and rang the bell.

"Harder," Hank growled, shoving backwards. "Let's do this."

Tex grunted and slapped Hank's ass hard. "You asked for it."

He set up a punishing rhythm, pounding his cock inside Hank's ass, slapping his hips against Hank's cheeks. Hank's balls swung like a pendulum as the cowboy slammed into him over and over again. Tex's big fist pumped Hank's cock in time with his thrusts. It felt good, really good, but Hank's cock just wasn't getting hard again. Must be because most of Hank's attention was focused on that tree trunk shoving up his asshole.

Hank lowered his head and braced his hands and knees against the grassy bank of the waterhole. He pushed backwards in time with Tex's rhythm, trying to give as good a ride as he was getting. Just because he'd never done this before didn't mean he was going to be a greenhorn about it. He knew what made a man's cock hard, what made his balls shoot their wad. And he was going to do his damnest to do those things and bring Tex to a rousing finish. He tensed his ass muscles, and Tex groaned.

"That's good, cowboy. Take me for a good hard ride."

Hank bucked back against the man, wanting that thick rod deep inside. He dimly felt Tex slap his ass cheek again, felt him digging his fingers into the muscles there. He was concentrating on the sensations coming from his hole. It felt like he had a fence post up inside him, like he was splitting apart—and he wanted every inch of that thing. He wanted his hole to spread wide open and take whatever that cowboy had.

Tex thrust hard and fast, and every movement sent waves of pleasure straight to Hank's balls. He couldn't believe he actually had that big cock inside of him, and the thought of what it must look like moving in and out of his hole made his belly quiver with excitement. His cock leaked pre-come even though it was only half hard. Tex continued to pump his rod, milking the clear fluid and adding to the sensations coming from Hank's groin.

Hank was past coherent speech. He could only grunt and moan, spreading his legs as wide as he could and shoving backwards to take as much of the cowboy's cock as he could. All too soon, he felt Tex give a great shove. The man's belly quivered against Hank's ass cheeks, and he felt hot wetness spurting inside his ass. Tex grabbed Hank's hips with both hands and hauled him close as he shot his load deep within Hank's insides.

"Damn," he groaned, giving a couple more hard shoves. "You sure are a good ride, cowboy."

Hank moaned softly as Tex withdrew his wilting cock. His come dripped down Hank's leg. Hank's asshole sagged open, protesting the sudden lack of that big rod. "Ain't had no idea it'd be that much fun," he muttered.

Tex shoved to his feet, his legs shaky, and extended a hand. "Let's get that swim and finish you off."

Hank allowed the man to help him up—his legs wouldn't work right at first, anyhow—and staggered to the water. He waded in and just flopped onto his back, gasping as the cool water hit his steaming body.

Tex came up next to him and closed a meaty fist over his cock. "Ain't right to ride off without finishing things."

Tex pumped Hank's rod, bringing him to full hardness within seconds. Hank's balls were ready to go, full of juice and throbbing. He braced himself against Tex's shoulder and shoved his hips forward against the man's fist. Tex grinned as the hot wad shot upward and splashed against his belly. He pulled every drop out of Hank's cock, then let go and floated away. Hank let his quivering legs fold under him and floated beside the man.

"Still don't like you much," he muttered. "And you're over the property line again."

"You was on our property the whole time I was poking you."

"You need a good lesson in manners."

"Right back at you."

Hank glanced over. Tex's big brown eyes looked back. His cheek dimpled. "Same time next week?" the man asked.

Hank grinned back. "I reckon I could mosey past the pond around this time Saturday. But I don't reckon I'll lose another wrestling match to you. You're going to end up getting poked next time."

"Bet I won't." Tex swung one muscular arm, sending a wave of water over Hank's face. "Besides, you liked getting your chute plowed."

He had at that. Hank's face flushed. Just because he'd enjoyed himself didn't mean he'd lost the damn contest. Then, he thought about the next week. About how that rod might look pistoning in and out of his hole. There had to be some sort of position that would let him watch that sight. He'd have to do some thinking on the subject. He watched Tex float beside him, watched the cowboy's thick cock and heavy balls bobbing gently in the ripples from their movements.

He might just lose that wrestling match at that.

DANIEL IN DISTRESS

BY FERAL SEPHRIAN

THE COUNTRY ROAD was rougher than Daniel had imagined. Recent rains had washed away some of the soil cover, exposing many of the larger rocks. He was grateful that this day was only overcast with little to no chance of rain. The bed of his new used pick-up contained his few belongings and the back of the cab had several bags of groceries strapped to the seats. Daniel had bought the food from the nearest grocery store to the Seyda Ranch, named for Jake Seyda and his fathers before him who had owned the land. Daniel would be renting a small cabin on Jake's property, if he ever reached it.

Daniel made a right at the first fork in the road past the welcome sign. He sighed in relief, knowing his journey was almost over. It had been a long way from Chicago. Now Daniel was getting the new start he had needed for a while. Packed carefully in the boxes beside him on the passenger seat were his various cameras and their accessories. After years of being an urban photographer, selling his work to various galleries, Daniel decided to return to his country roots and go full-freelance. Wyoming had exactly the landscape he was looking for, and he couldn't wait to get out there and see it.

The truck shook violently and Daniel heard two successive bangs before everything shifted to the left. He panicked for a moment and slammed his brakes. Cursing his life and the universe itself, Daniel opened his door to confirm the worst; both his front and back left tires had blown out. The road behind him was almost nothing but jagged rocks jutting up from the ground like bristling scales. Daniel had hoped the truck was tough enough to make it over safely, but he supposed he should have checked the tires more thoroughly at the used car lot.

When kicking the hubcaps yielded nothing more than a dull pain in his toes, Daniel retrieved his phone from the cup-holder and called Jake.

"Hey there, Danny-boy!" Jake answered. "Made it there safely, I take it?"

"Not quite," Daniel sighed. "I'm still about a half-mile away and I blew out two tires on the rocky road. Normally I would walk the rest of the way, but I've got perishables in the truck, not to mention all my stuff."

Jake let out a low whistle. "Golly, sounds rough. I was worried about those roads, but there hasn't been much time to tidy them up. I'll send Cole your way in our truck. He can take you and your things the rest of the way. He ought to be there in about fifteen minutes."

"Thanks, Jake." Daniel hung up and groaned. He could make it to his new home in ten minutes at a steady pace, but not loaded down with his stuff. As much as he wanted to make it to the cabin and put his feet up, he resigned himself to waiting. It was yet another bit of bad luck to add to his recent streak.

It all began one chilly yet clear afternoon in mid-February when Daniel got a teary call from his mother. His dad had passed away unexpectedly. Daniel's dad already had two heart attacks under his belt, and claimed his heart was too strong from years of camping and hiking to give out so easily. Unfortunately, the third one turned out to be too much. Daniel had been close with his dad, and the news hit him like daggers to his chest.

Then, reevaluating his life in the city, Daniel told his at-the-time boyfriend, Troy, that he wanted to get away from the grind and the concrete jungle, revisit his childhood love of the great outdoors that his dad had instilled in him. However, he had said, he didn't want to drag Troy into this if he wasn't comfortable leaving Chicago, and he was willing to compromise for the sake of their relationship.

"Does this mean I can finally break up with you?" Troy had asked. "About time. You've been such a downer these past few weeks."

The heartless statement was enough to shatter the tenuous connection between them. Troy had been one of Daniel's best models, and while unearthly attractive, he was occasionally aloof and uncaring. Daniel stayed with him because the sex was good and working so closely together made flirting and teasing nigh unavoidable. Daniel broke up with him on the spot and cemented his plans to find something better.

Now here he was, stuck on a dirt road in the middle of Wyoming with half his tires in shreds and his mood souring more and more the longer he had to wait for Cole. Having only negotiated with Jake over the phone or via e-mail, Daniel had never met Cole before, but Jake had told him about their chief ranch-hand and maintenance man.

"Cole is like a Swiss army knife: doesn't look like much, but you can almost guarantee he'll be useful in any situation."

Daniel was grinding his teeth in impatience by the time the other truck arrived. He had been expecting a beat-up older model, but the Toyota Tundra that cruised up the road was nicer than the Dodge Daniel had bought. Furthermore, its driver was nothing like Daniel had expected either.

When Jake said Cole "doesn't look like much," Daniel assumed he meant Cole was plain, average, possibly on the older side like Jake. Cole wasn't exactly barrel-chested or beefy, but he was young with broad shoulders and black stubble that accentuated the perfect curves of his face. His eyes were so dark

Daniel first thought they were blue, but as Cole strode closer it became clear they were a deep and shining brown.

"You must be Daniel," Cole said. His voice was rich and strong with the hint of a southern accent. It caressed Daniel's ears like a river of chocolate. Daniel's mouth even watered slightly, and he had to concentrate hard to keep himself together while Cole inspected the damage. "Yyyep, they're both shot to Hell, like Jake said. I wasn't sure what you were driving, so sorry for not bringing spares. If you want to load your stuff into my truck, I'll get you to the cabin and I can come back and fix this soon as I can. Sound good?"

A few seconds of silence passed as Daniel broke out of his mesmerized state. "Yeah, yeah, good. Great. Thanks." He held out his hand. "I'm Daniel."

Cole smiled, his lips curving up more to the right. "So I figured. I'm Cole." He had a firm, warm handshake. Daniel took a deep breath, inhaling the scent of dusty leather and Old Spice. "What needs to go home with you right away?"

Daniel's first thought was *You*, but the sting of his break-up with Troy made him shy away from being so forward. He had mistaken instant lust for love-at-first-sight before, and Cole was most likely straight anyway. Using that thought to ground himself, Daniel said, "The food and my equipment, if not everything."

Fortunately, everything Daniel had deemed important enough to keep from his old apartment had fit into two duffel bags. Cole had to move some things from the truck cab to the bed, but they were able to fit it all, with Daniel holding his more delicate cameras in his lap. The interior of Cole's truck smelled like him, mixed with oil and hay. Daniel slumped into his seat and allowed himself to imagine getting even closer to Cole.

As the truck revved to life, the CD player switched on as well. Much to Daniel's surprise, the music coming from the speakers was neither country nor classic rock, as most of the stations out here played.

"I-Is this classical?"

Cole snorted. "Didn't think cowboys listened to Tchaikovsky? I'll admit, he's not my favorite, but with all the summer foliage in bloom, I figured it was the right day for 'Waltz of the Flowers'. This is my countryside mix CD. I've got some Beethoven and Chopin on here, too." He grinned. "Frankly, there's only so many times I can listen to songs about finding Jesus after my girlfriend shot my truck and stole my dog, or whatever," he joked. "And if I have to get a song stuck in my head while I'm working, I prefer one without lyrics. Helps me concentrate better."

"Oh." Jake was right. Cole seemed full of surprises. Daniel revised his fantasy from a romp in the hay with a stoic country boy to a romantic candlelit dinner and champagne by the fire. Trying to save face, Daniel said, "Yeah, I'm into less pop-ish music, too. Do you know Death Cab for Cutie?"

"Heard of them, couldn't tell you what they play."

"They've got a unique sound. If you knew them, you'd know their songs if you heard them. And—and some of their songs are sad and happy and soothing all at the same time. I've been listening to them a lot lately."

Cole nodded, but said nothing. Daniel didn't know if Cole could sense what the reason for listening to that sort of music meant, and he wasn't sure if he wanted to divulge so much about his personal life to someone he just met. The song on the CD ended and another piece, which Cole identified as Beethoven's "Awakening of Happy Feelings on Arriving in the Country," began. It was nice music, so Daniel didn't mind the lack of conversation.

It took two trips to get everything in the little house. The exterior was designed to look like an old log cabin, but inside everything had been fixed up and polished to look brand new. The main room acted as both living room and dining room for the small adjoined kitchen, which was only a woodstove, sink, microwave, and fridge packed against one wall with a set of cabinets next to the window above the sink. Daniel's bedroom took up a quarter of the floor space, and his work room another, with the single full bathroom between them. Another door by the study led into the garage, which Daniel knew contained his washer and dryer from the tour via Skype that Jake had given him.

"I hope you like it here," Cole said. "Took me and the guys a month to fix this place up, and I gotta say I'm damn proud of how it turned out."

"You should be," Daniel said. "It's gorgeous."

"Gonna feature it in any of your photos?"

"Jake told you, huh? Maybe. Get a fire going in the stove, snap a picture of the smoke rising from the chimney with the sun setting in the background. Yeah, I think I could."

Cole nodded in approval. "Speaking of which, Marcie told me I should show you around the ranch, like any places I think you would want to photograph."

Marcie was Jake's daughter, and she and her husband were both business school graduates who helped Jake with the administrative side of running a ranch. Daniel had initially spoken to her about renting the cabin, and his impression of her was all positive. If she wanted Daniel to spend more time with Cole, that was fine by him.

"Great! Let me know when you would want to do it. Give me a few days to settle in before—"

"Yeah, I figured." Cole nodded again. "I'll have your truck fixed up by the end of the day. Would you rather I drive it here or come get you?"

"I can walk there and pick it up myself. It's not too far, and you've already done plenty." Daniel smiled. "Thanks for coming to my rescue."

Cole smiled back and waved his hand. "Nah, wasn't much of a rescue. Just helped you save some time is all. On that note, I'd better get going if I'm gonna be finished by this evening. Can I get your number so I can call you when I'm done?"

Daniel couldn't contain his grin. It wasn't as though Cole were asking for his number so they could go on a date, but it was exciting all the same, knowing he could be in contact with Cole whenever he wished. "Absolutely!" he said, quickly pulling his phone from his pocket.

With their information exchanged, Cole gave a final fare-well nod and went on his way. Daniel sunk into the sofa chair by the fireplace and sighed. *Maybe, just maybe*, he thought, *I'm starting to turn my luck around.*

THE LANDSCAPE WAS as beautiful as Daniel had hoped. Over the next week, he went on short hikes around the property with his least expensive camera to take test shots. His cabin was near a shallow valley with a stream running through it that took up about a fifth of the ranch's total acreage. Daniel could stand on a ledge overlooking it all and take photo after photo of the horizon, the trees, the wildlife, the cattle grazing and slowly making their way to the stream to drink, and of the men watching over them.

Cole was hard to spot at first. All of the men on horseback looked much the same in their T-shirts and Stetsons, but once Daniel stopped paying attention to just the men, he noticed Cole always rode a chestnut horse with a white stripe on its nose and white forelegs. Daniel had to zoom in as much as his camera could manage, but within a few days he was able to spot Cole even from a distance.

When Daniel's phone finally showed Cole on the caller ID, Daniel nearly fell off the couch scrambling to answer it. "Hello?" he wheezed.

"...Daniel? You okay?"

"Huh? Oh, yeah. Yeah. Fine. I was, uh, exercising." Daniel winced at his own dopey lie and gritted his teeth in anticipation of Cole's response.

"That's cool. You too tired to take that tour? It's quiet up here, and I thought maybe if you weren't busy..." Cole trailed off, letting Daniel finish the question himself.

Daniel was delighted. He hadn't been up close and personal with Cole, or even spoken to him, since Cole helped him move in, despite going up to the main farmhouse to talk with Jake and Marcie a few times. Cole was almost always out doing errands or fixing something, and each time Daniel had hoped to at least say hi to the handsome cowboy. Without a heartbeat's hesitation, Daniel said, "No! That is, no I'm not busy, and no I'm not too tired. Are you coming over now?"

"If you want me to. Thought I'd give you a half-hour head start, y'know, if you wanted to finish exercising or whatever."

"Oh, I think I've exercised enough. Come on over!" By the time he hung up, Daniel was on his toes, ready to go. He dashed into his bedroom to put on something more suitable for a hike. Some of the clothes he bought earlier that week were piled in his laundry basket, which he unceremoniously dumped onto his bed. Gay, straight, or otherwise, Cole was the sort of person on whom Daniel wanted to make a good impression.

Daniel heard the knock at his door as he was brushing his teeth. Speeding to finish without gagging, he quickly spat and called out, "Be right there!" He rinsed and wiped the remaining toothpaste off his mouth, then grabbed his water bottle and camera bag and opened the door.

Outside stood Cole and two horses. One was the white-legged horse Cole usually rode, the other was a dappled gray with a black mane. Cole held out a Stetson nearly identical to the one he was wearing.

"Surprise," Cole said with a sheepishly hopeful smile. He had shaved recently, which made him look five years younger, but hot nonetheless. "I didn't know if you knew how to ride, but we have a lot of ground to cover and you can't reach some of it in the truck."

"No, I can ride. It's just...the last horse I ever rode had a pole in its back and only ran in circles."

Cole's eyes grew wide in alarm, then his face softened and

he laughed. "Oh! You mean a carousel. For a minute I wondered what sick bastard was letting people ride injured horses."

Daniel chuckled. "My bad. It wasn't that great of a joke."

"Don't sweat it. But you think you can handle Pepper here? She's not one for running in circles."

"I think I'll be fine," Daniel said with a smile. He took Cole's spare Stetson and tried it on. "How do I look?"

Cole nodded. "Like yourself, but with a bit more country charm."

"I'll take it."

Daniel climbed onto Pepper's saddle, with a little help from Cole. Cole then hopped onto his own horse, whom he introduced as Ziggy, as easily as though he were settling onto a chair. With a couple clicks of his tongue, Cole had the horses moving at a steady trot.

Pepper stayed alongside Ziggy even without Daniel tugging at the reins. "I chose Pepper for you because she's basically an oversized dog," Cole explained. "She's sweet and hardworking and she'll follow any of the ranchers anywhere if we ask her to."

It was definitely a new perspective, sitting on the back of a horse. Daniel pulled out his camera, securely fastened the wrist strap, and crouched as low in the saddle as he could go to snap a picture of the road ahead framed between Pepper's ears. He considered himself lucky for choosing the camera with the best motion stability, since the constant bouncing made it difficult to get everything squared up just right without any blur. The wide brim of the Stetson helped as well, since it kept the sun out of his eyes and he didn't need to squint as much.

As they neared the valley, Cole had their horses slow to a walk. He pointed out a pair of hawks hunting above them. "If we watch long enough, you might get to catch one diving after something."

Patience was not something Daniel was used to needing. Back in Chicago, he was the one calling the shots, telling the models how to pose or going out on foot to find the perfect picture amongst the streets and skylines. The hawks took their sweet time, and Daniel had his camera ready for so long his arms grew tired. One started flapping its wings strangely, and Cole excitedly whispered that it was about to strike. As if on cue, the hawk streaked toward the ground. Daniel took one photo after another as rapidly as his camera could manage until the hawk flew away, some fuzzy creature in its talons.

"Did you get it?" Cole asked, craning his neck to see Daniel's viewing screen.

"I don't know…" Even with the motion stabilization, the hawk was a blur in most of the photos, and off center in almost every one. By some miracle, Daniel had been in focus and on target right before the hawk hit the ground. It wasn't the best shot, but the hawk's wings were outstretched and its open talons were visible. "Well, it's not quite National Geographic material, but then again I'm not an experienced nature photographer, yet."

"So that's how you make money? Selling photos to big-name magazines?"

Daniel shrugged. "That's what I'm hoping, at least. Back in Chicago I knew a few indie art galleries that were always in the market for whatever, and sometimes private collectors would buy copies of my work. It wasn't glamorous or incredibly lucrative, but it was a living."

"What made you decide to move out here then?"

"My dad."

"Oh, does he live around here?"

Daniel swallowed hard. As much as he wanted to be good friends with Cole, he wasn't sure it was time to share such personal information. On the other hand, he had felt the need to talk about it with someone other than his grieving mother or unsympathetic ex. "No," he said. "We're both from Michigan. Yoopers." Noting Cole's confused expression, Daniel clarified, "From the Upper Peninsula. My family has been there for generations. I inherited Dad's wanderlust though, which is how I wound up in Chicago." Taking a deep breath to brace himself, he added. "Then he died, and I started questioning that choice."

Cole was silent for a moment. Daniel didn't want to look him in the eyes and see what he might be thinking, so instead he looked out over the valley. The cattle were in a different meadow at the time. The dark dotted patch of their hides was visible a mile or so to the west. Daniel wondered which of the ranch hands had taken charge while Cole was out here playing tour guide.

"I'm sorry about your dad," Cole said at last. "Was he sick?"

The dam that held all of Daniel's feelings cracked, but years of living among thick-skinned Yoopers made him hold back nonetheless. He shook his head. "Not in the slightest. He loved the outdoors. Co-owned a sporting goods store that specialized in hiking, kayaking, camping, you name it. Insisted on testing just about every product himself before he'd stock it, so he and I spent a lot of weekends in the wilderness together. Thought he'd live to be a hundred, but a heart attack got him. Af—when he died, I didn't want to go back home, but I wanted that freedom again, so here I am."

Cole nodded. "It's a good place to be free."

"Looks like it," Daniel agreed. "I want to see as much as I can today, so let's get going."

Daniel lightly dug his heels into Pepper's sides, nudging her onward. Cole followed, then took the lead again. The conversation revolved entirely around the landscape and wildlife from then on. They looped around the valley then came down to follow the river into its basin. They crossed at a series of large stepping stones. The horses knew the area well and deftly stepped from rock to rock until they reached the other side.

"There are two bridges, one upstream from here and one downstream," Cole said, "and usually it's shallow enough to cross on horseback, but if it's been raining or you're on foot for whatever reason, it's good to know these are here."

The other side of the river was much like where they had been, tall grasses and sparse short trees growing in clumps, until they climbed out of the valley and the land flattened out. The lusher green grass stopped in almost a straight line before giving way to sagebrush and sandy soil. Daniel wished he had a photo of himself, sitting on a horse, wearing a Stetson, looking out over a landscape like something from a Western movie. His dad would have liked to see it.

"Hey, would you mind taking my picture?" Daniel asked.

Cole glanced warily at Daniel's camera. "Uh...sure, but...are there any special buttons I would have to—"

"Oh! No, I meant with my phone." Daniel retrieved his phone from a pocket of his cargo khakis. "I want to send a picture to my mom." He opened the camera app and got it all set up. "Here, just push the button at the bottom of the screen."

"Ah, now *that* I can handle." Cole took the phone from Daniel's outstretched hand and backed Ziggy up a few steps to get a better shot. "Alright, say cheese!"

Daniel put on his best cowboy face, then asked to do another with a real smile. "Did you get them?"

"Yep, I can see it down in the little preview window."

"Great! Thanks!"

Cole moved Ziggy forward again, but as he reached out to give Daniel his phone back, Ziggy moved unexpectedly, causing Cole to lose his grip. The phone fell past Daniel's grasping fingers and landed with a dull thud in the loose soil below.

"Shit, sorry about that."

"No worries," Daniel said. "I don't think it would crack on this surface." With some difficulty, he swung his leg over the saddle and tried to jump down to retrieve his phone. Unfortunately, his foot caught in the stirrup, causing him to slip and fall backward, yanking his leg at an odd angle. He cried out in alarm and pain and struggled to orient himself.

"I got ya!" Cole was off Ziggy's back in a flash. Pepper nickered and shook her head, but Cole took the reins and calmed her. "Hold still," he said, grabbing hold of Daniel's stirrup. He carefully removed Daniel's foot and eased it to the ground. "They probably caught scent of a predator. We get coyotes and mountain lions up here, and the occasional bear, coming after our cattle or the mule deer who live nearby. If you're lucky, you might be able to get a picture of the deer, and if you're really lucky you might get a picture of a mountain lion and live to tell about it."

Daniel rolled over sluggishly, tenderly flexing his leg. "Yeah, well, luck and I haven't been getting along lately." In a panic, he checked his camera, which was still strapped to his right wrist. "No cracks...and it still turns on. Well, that's something." He tested weight on his foot, and a sharp pain encircled his ankle then shot up his leg. Gritting his teeth, he suppressed a yelp. "That, on the other hand, might be a problem..."

Cole crouched beside him. He furrowed his brow. "It's definitely swelling." He lightly felt around Daniel's ankle, causing Daniel to bite back another whimper of pain. "Doesn't feel broken, but best not to risk it." He looked up at the anxious horse. "Yeah, there's something nearby that has these guys nervous." He scratched at his shaved jaw pensively. "How much do you weigh?" he asked Daniel.

"Uh...one-sixty-five. Why?"

Cole shrugged. "I've lifted heavier. Brace yourself."

Daniel barely had time to do so before Cole put one arm under his shoulders and the other under his knees and scooped him off the ground. He reflexively clung to Cole, digging his fingers into Cole's back. "Sorry," he said, loosening his grip slightly.

"No worries. I've had calves kick me in the face when I pick them up. Now see if you can grab the pommels and pull yourself up with your arms."

That part was easy. It was getting his right leg over the saddle without relying on his left foot for assistance that challenged Daniel. Cole helped take the weight off by holding onto Daniel's left leg until Daniel had his right foot firmly in its stirrup. Cole fetched Daniel's phone and borrowed Stetson from the ground and handed them to him.

"Thanks for that," Daniel said, securing his phone back in

his pocket and donning the hat.

"Don't thank me just yet, we still have to get you back down when you get home." Cole climbed onto Ziggy, who was pacing nervously. "I wanted to take you out to our fence so you could see the edge of the ranch, but it's another half-mile away and we might run into whatever is spooking the horses. Let's see if we can catch up with the herd instead."

The horses were more than happy to canter back down around the valley. Cole led them over a bridge this time, and they met up with the rest of the Seyda Ranch workers and their cattle shortly after. Cole pointed out landmarks and anything else interesting along the way, including any tree or boulder he thought might be photogenic.

They wandered along with the herd for a little while. Cole chatted with his fellow cowboys and Daniel took a few pictures of the mass of cattle and the dogs running around their periphery.

Cole came and got Daniel when it was time to go. "I told them to keep an eye out for whatever's out there. Nothing new, but they'll be extra careful."

The two broke off from the group and headed for the farmhouse and barns. Daniel had to practically fall off the saddle again to get down, but Cole was there to catch him. Marcie and her husband fixed them up some lunch and drinks, gave Daniel an ice pack for his ankle, and they talked with him about his new home while Cole watered their horses. Daniel was glad when Cole rejoined them. He enjoyed the ranch hand's company, and he smiled to himself at the memory of being held in Cole's strong arms.

They rode the horses back to Daniel's cabin at an easy walking pace. Cole started humming something. Daniel strained his ears to listen, hoping he would recognize whatever classical piece it was and be able to remark on it. He was surprised when he did recognize it, but for a different reason.

"Are you humming 'Little Wanderer' by Death Cab for Cutie?"

Cole smiled sheepishly. "Yeah, I checked them out and that

one got stuck in my head. Don't remember most of the lyrics, but I like the chorus."

Daniel nodded. The dam around his emotions cracked again. "I—I've listened to that one a lot lately, too. Reminds me of my dad, 'cause he used to call me a wander-bug when I was a kid. But...the part about wandering back home..." He sniffled, then cleared his throat. "I went home when I could, but after Dad died I wondered if I went home enough, y'know? If I spent enough time with him."

"Well, I guarantee you saw him more than I've seen my dad."

"Oh? When's the last time you saw him?"

Cole's face settled into an expression of hesitance that Daniel understood well. "The last time? That'd be eleven years ago, when he threatened to kill me if I ever came home."

Daniel's jaw dropped. "*What?*"

"Yep. His exact words were, 'If I ever see your damned face 'round here again, I'll shoot you dead, boy'."

"Why? What did you do? Get a girl pregnant?"

Cole shook his head. "Worse. I came out of the closet."

Daniel thought he misheard at first, that it was some auditory hallucination based on what he hoped was true, but the look on Cole's face said it all. "Wow. Your dad sounds like a...a..."

"An uneducated, rotten, narrow-minded bastard. Yep. I think he was allergic to accepting new ideas or learning anything. Shoot, the only reason my siblings and I knew how to read was because our grandma taught us. She's the one who played classical records for us, too, hoped we'd absorb some culture." Cole shook his head. "The old man just wanted to raise cattle farmers to carry on the family legacy. It's the only thing I've ever really known how to do. Hitchhiked my way up here all the way from Texas and someone pointed me in Jake's direction. He's a good guy. Doesn't care about anything other than whether you're a good person and can do your job. Couple other guys here are gay, and all of us get along fine."

It was a lot to take in. Daniel stared ahead, wide-eyed but seeing nothing, as he considered why Cole would divulge his rocky past and the fact that he was gay. Daniel cleared his throat again. "Guess he likes keeping gay guys around, because, uh, I am, too."

"Yeah, I know."

Daniel's chest nearly exploded. "Y-You do?"

"Marcie told me. Said, 'Dad's bringing in another stray gay. We might as well turn this into a summer camp for wayward youths.' Then she got this look in her eyes like she was really considering that. Frankly, I think it'd be good to have kids come here and learn how to work or just have somewhere to get away, y'know?"

Daniel was speechless. All this time he had worried he was pining after just another straight guy. Yet, even though Cole knew they were both gay, he had literally swept Daniel off his feet. Daniel's heart sank a little. *If he were interested in me, he would have told me he was gay sooner.*

By the time they reached Daniel's cabin, Daniel had muddled through polite conversation and come to the conclusion that Cole wasn't truly interested in him like that. Cole had talked about the ranch and how they were going to move the cattle to the other side of their nine-thousand acre property for grazing rotation. That meant he wouldn't be around much for a couple months, which disappointed Daniel, but at the same time he felt it was best if he didn't have to wistfully watch Cole from a distance every day.

Cole helped Daniel ease himself off Pepper's back and get inside. "Go easy on that leg for the rest of the week, okay?" he said.

"I will. Thanks for taking me out today."

"My pleasure. If you need anything else, you have my number." Cole gave Daniel a farewell handshake, then hopped back on Ziggy and led Pepper back to the barns.

Daniel flopped onto his couch. *Terrific. I've got a gorgeous gay cowboy in my contacts list, but he probably wouldn't date me unless I were the only other single guy in the state. When is my bad luck going to end?*

❖

COLE OPENED HIS legs wider so Daniel could crouch between them. Daniel ran his hand over the denim-covered bulge, already as hard as a rock. He nuzzled his face against it, kissing the rough fabric and wishing he could reach the smooth skin beneath it. In an instant, Cole's jeans were gone. Daniel gratefully licked at Cole's heavy balls. Cole moaned and stroked Daniel's hair, urging him to continue.

The loud blaring of Daniel's alarm startled him out of the dream. He rolled over and tried to force himself back in, since he had been about to move onto Cole's taint and wanted to know how it all ended. His alarm went off again, however, and grudgingly Daniel sat up and pouted.

It was now mid-October. Daniel hadn't seen Cole in person for three months. Cole had texted him about his leg at first, then he sent the occasional photo message from out on the range. He even invited Daniel to come out and take real photos once or twice. Daniel politely declined. He had plenty of things to photograph around his cabin, like the fresh autumn foliage, or the family of chipmunks that lived behind his garage. Most of his time was spent on his computer trying to find someone to purchase his work, but he was gaining success with it and he had hope.

Daniel put on his good outdoor gear and grabbed his best water-resistant camera. A rare thunderstorm had rolled through the night before, and Daniel wanted to go out and take pictures of the aftermath. He especially wanted to check out the river, which was bound to still be swollen with run-off.

All the way to his truck and down into the valley, Daniel was caught between contradicting desires. He wanted to forget his steamy dream, like he tried with all the others he had about Cole, but at the same time he clung to each imagined moment because he knew it was the only way he would have a chance to experience his fantasies. *Don't think about how hot it was. Don't think about the ways he begged you. Don't think about how his cock felt in*

Daniel in Distress by Feral Sephrian   285

your hands...or mouth...or...

The truck beeped briefly as Daniel slumped against the wheel. He jumped back at the sound, then resumed his dejected puddle. *This is not a trashy romance novel and I am not a winsome lass falling for the charms of a rugged farmhand. Nor am I a sophisticated urbanite hoping to seduce a country girl. I am a rational man, and if Cole doesn't want to ask me out, it's not the end of the world. Dreams are dreams. Now I have to focus on work.*

Mist had settled in the valley like a shallow bowl of milk, tinged pink from the remnants of sunrise. Daniel inhaled deeply, filling his lungs with the rich smell of damp and decaying leaves and sodden earth. The air was cold and the breezes smelled of oncoming winter. It reminded Daniel of Michigan, where cold was another word for average when describing the weather. However, Daniel hadn't seen mist like this since his dad had taken him camping in the Poconos.

He had been out for an early jog several days prior when he spotted this in the valley, and didn't have a camera with him. Ever since, he checked weather conditions at night for the following morning to know if they would be right for this. At last he caught it. He took several photos on different settings, and even climbed on top of his truck for a better angle. By then, the mist was more pearly as the sky shifted to pale blue, and it was starting to disperse. Daniel got back in his truck and drove down to the river.

He searched for the stepping stones Cole had showed him. The river was indeed high, but Daniel was sure some of the rocks would be large enough to show above the water and would make for a great image. Someone might want them as part of a metaphor for standing true against the toughest conditions. If buyers didn't ascribe that meaning to it, Daniel could always say that's why he took the pictures in the first place, then he could call it art and he knew suddenly someone would *have* to have it.

The water splashed and rippled upward where Daniel knew there were other stones beneath the surface. The morning light reflected off the murky brown surge in a dazzling display. It was never the same pattern twice, so Daniel snapped numerous photos. As he was deciding on another angle, a thought occurred to him. A particularly large rock protruded out of the water enough that its top was still dry. Daniel noted a few other rocks he could step on to get there, though the ones on the other side were larger.

If I could get up there, I could get a shot of the water coming right at me. Plus the view upstream isn't bad either. But one slip and I could drop the camera, and I'd never find it again...

Daniel decided to test the water, so to speak. He left his camera in the truck, then found a rock about the same weight nearby. Holding onto that as though it were his camera, he set out to the edge of the river. He put one foot in the water. The current was fast, but Daniel and his dad had faced stronger. Daniel couldn't remember how large each stone had been when the water was at its normal level, but the horses had crossed with little problem and the rocks hadn't seemed remarkably large at the time.

It'll probably come up to my waist if I do fall in, but I can see where the stepping stones are. I'll be careful.

One rock near the shore protruded an inch above the water, and Daniel was able to balance on it well enough. The next one barely showed, but the way the water moved around it made it easy to find. Daniel planted his foot on it firmly, putting all his weight onto that leg. The third stone would require a larger step, but it was as visible as the first one, so Daniel was confident he could reach it.

As soon as he began to shift his weight, the foothold he had failed. The remaining stepping stones in the river bed only dazed him when he hit them. The river swallowed him immediately. The water was frigid. It was too early for the sun to have warmed it. Daniel's flailing limbs stung and stiffened. He struggled to stand, but the current was stronger here in the center than it had been on shore. It dragged him under at every attempt. He had been wrong about its depth. When he did feel his feet touch the ground, he knew he would be up past his elbows if he stood. He would never get enough leverage.

Even his attempts to swim for shore were fruitless. The water had made up its mind about where it was going, and anything in it was doomed to follow. Sticks and other bits of debris rushed along with him. Every gasp made him choke as water sprayed into his nose and open mouth. He was losing the ability to breathe, and losing hope.

Why couldn't I have taken that shot from one of the bridges instead?

That was it. The southern bridge. He was headed straight for it. That would catch him for sure, or he could at least grab hold of it and pull himself to safety. Daniel thought back to the times he and his dad had gone kayaking and river rafting. *Hold your breath and your natural buoyancy will keep you on the surface. Take breaths when you can, and I'll do my best to reach you quickly.* Except now his dad wasn't there to save him. *I can make it. I have to.*

The bridge came up fast. It was identical to the northern one, which Daniel had already used for a photo shoot. A frame of iron with thick wooden planks, it was broad enough to accommodate a truck or five cattle shoulder to shoulder. Daniel paddled towards it. The water had risen to lap around the edges of the bridge. At the center of the arch there was only a hand's breadth of space above the churning surface of the river. Daniel mustered all his strength to reach for the bridge, and he wanted to cry for joy when he caught it. The happiness was brief. The unrelenting current sucked his legs under the bridge, determined to continue dragging him downstream.

Daniel's fingers were already exhausted. He could barely keep his head above the water. He tried to reach up for a better hold, but couldn't support himself one-handed. More branches battered against him on their way downstream, making him flinch and lose focus. His torso was next to disappear under the bridge. He was hanging on by his fingertips. He sputtered and coughed up the water he inhaled with each stolen breath. This was it. He was dying. *All my bad luck has led to this. If I have any good luck left at all, they'll find my body before I get too far away.*

The dam around his emotions broke completely. He sobbed, the tears washed away as soon as they left his eyes. *Mom will be devastated, losing her husband and son in the same year. Cole...maybe Cole will care, but I'll never see him again. At least I'll be with Dad.*

He heard his name being called. *Dad? Have you come to take me to Heaven?* Some of his fear subsided, knowing he wouldn't be alone. *Okay, Dad. I'm coming.* With a heavy heart, Daniel let go of the bridge.

Someone shouted his name again. It didn't quite sound like his dad. There was a vague accent to it. Daniel told himself this must be what it was like to die, hearing Death itself beckoning. Then he heard it again, louder and accompanied by a softly rolling thunder. His head bobbed above the water in time to hear it one more time.

"DANIEL!"

The water burned his eyes, but Daniel opened them anyway. Running along the shore was a chestnut blur with white forelegs. "Daniel! Grab the rope!"

Vibrations in the water. Daniel sluggishly moved his hand toward them, but couldn't find anything. A moment later they were back, closer to him this time. His frozen fingers slipped past something more flexible than the other pieces of debris he passed. A loop tightened around his arm, and another force fought to drag him away, this one pulling him to shore. A mild pain wrenched his shoulder, but he was so numb he didn't care. He held onto the rope with what little strength he had left.

The current lessened and Daniel found himself on the muddy bank. He panted and gasped, overjoyed to finally breathe dry air. There was a thud on the ground beside him before strong arms enveloped him. "Oh God, Daniel. I spotted your truck in time to see you fall, and by the time I caught up you were already under the bridge, and I—Fuck!" Cole held Daniel at arm's length and looked him in the eyes, his face fraught with worry. "What were you even doing out there? You nearly got yourself killed!"

Daniel coughed, spewing murky saliva onto the ground. "Sisu," he mumbled.

"What?"

"Sisu. It's a term we use in the U.P. to describe someone's determination or courage, or thick-headed insanity, as the case may be." Daniel hacked and coughed, clearing his lungs. "My dad said it runs in the family."

"I'll say. It's a damn good thing Ike said he saw a mountain lion headed this way, or you could have—" Cole took a deep breath through his nose. "But you didn't, though you still could if you catch pneumonia. We gotta get you into dry clothes."

Daniel shrugged, although he was shivering. "I've been colder than this."

"Cold is one thing. Cold *and* wet is another. Hell, I'm freezing just from hugging you. Come on, get on the horse."

"But...my truck..."

"I'll get your damn truck later. The sooner you dry off and warm up, the better."

Strong as he wanted to seem, Daniel was a wreck. His nerves and emotions were fried, the parts of him that weren't numb ached and stung with the cold, and he was still having a hard time believing he hadn't died. The realization of what had happened was settling in, and Daniel was on the verge of tears again. He clumsily hauled himself onto Ziggy's saddle. Cole was up behind him a heartbeat later.

The horns on either end of the saddle meant Daniel and Cole were right up against each other. Daniel was grateful for the warmth, and the rescue. He had thought he would never see Cole again, or his mom. The mental image of his mother collapsed on the ground, bereaving his loss, filled Daniel with so much pain he broke down crying himself.

"Hey, it's okay," Cole said. "We'll get you home soon. You're gonna be fine. Hyah, Ziggy. Hyah!"

Ziggy took off at a gallop. Daniel gripped the saddle horn in front of him tightly, terrified he would lose his balance and fall. Cole wrapped a securing arm around him. Had Daniel not been soaked to the bone and still recovering, he would have been rock hard from having Cole lightly bouncing behind him, his groin pressed hard against Daniel's ass. *Guess the only way to get this close to him is to narrowly escape death. I can live with that.*

At Daniel's cabin, Cole tied Ziggy to a nearby tree using the same rope that had pulled Daniel from the river. Cole helped Daniel inside, just as he had after Daniel injured his leg. "I'll get the stove burning," he said. "You go get changed."

"Okay, I'll just—" Without Cole to hold him, Daniel didn't have the strength to stand. Two steps on his own and he fell to his knees.

"Shit," Cole hissed. He grabbed Daniel around the waist and brought him to his feet. "Did you hit your head? Are you going to pass out? Come on, Daniel, don't do this to me." He got Daniel to the couch. "Stay here, stay awake, I'll get you a towel and some dry clothes."

Daniel nodded. He didn't want to sleep. His brush with death had every cell of his body on edge, but his muscles were weary and twitchy as warmth returned to his core. *A cup of coffee would be nice. That'd perk me up again.*

When Cole came back from Daniel's bedroom, Daniel almost asked for that cup of coffee. However, Cole started rolling Daniel's sopping shirt up his torso. The warmth of his hands sent tingles through Daniel's nerves.

"Work with me here, Daniel. I need you to lift your arms."

Daniel did so willingly, despite his arms feeling like they weighed fifty pounds each. His vision was obscured for a moment as his shirt passed over his head, but once it was off Cole was right there, close enough for Daniel to feel his light panting breaths on his face. Cole noticed their proximity as well and stopped breathing altogether. Their eyes met, locked on each other like magnets, pulling them closer. In a flash, Cole had pressed his lips to Daniel's. He kissed him with fervor, then snapped back as quickly as he had come.

Cole bit his lips. "I—that—sorry if I—"

"Don't," Daniel said, grabbing Cole's shirt with both hands and yanking him back down. He had neither the strength nor the will to argue, but since Cole had started this, Daniel wanted to finish it.

With some effort, Daniel managed to wrap his arms around Cole's neck, holding him in place. Cole didn't seem to mind. He pried off Daniel's wet jeans while their tongues got acquainted. Daniel was too tired to be of much use, but he wasn't about to miss this for the world.

"I want you," he whispered.

"I noticed," Cole murmured. "I've been thinking about this every day since we met." He slipped out of Daniel's grasp to wrench his jeans all the way to the floor, yanking at his bootlaces so he could actually take everything off. Kneeling between Daniel's legs, Cole took Daniel's cock in his hand. "Not as thick as I imagined, but still, damn."

"Like it?"

"Oh yeah." Cole kissed up Daniel's thigh, gently rubbing Daniel's cock with his thumb.

Daniel bit his lip and exhaled sharply. All the new warmth in his body seemed to converge in his groin to fill Cole's hand. "I had a dream like this last night, except the other way around."

"What? You sucking me off?"

"Mmhmm."

Cole grinned. "Sounds hot, but right now you need the TLC more than I do, so..." He pulled off his shirt and got to his feet, unbuckling his belt along the way. "We need to get you warmed up. Best way to do that is by sharing body heat." His smile became cheeky as he pushed his own pants to the ground. "The sucking'll have to wait, for now." He straddled Daniel and kissed him from his nipple to his neck.

Daniel moaned softly and let his exhausted body relax into

the couch. "Nnnff, if I knew drowning was sure to get you to fuck me, I would have tried it sooner."

Cole stopped for a moment. He scowled. "You really scared me. Here I'd been trying to come up with the best way to ask you out, and you go and nearly die on me. Not saying I'd kill myself if you died, but I would have been *pissed*."

"Oh?"

"Yeah, *oh*. You know how much I've wanted to do this?"

"Then quit your bitchin' and do it already."

Cole's smile returned. "Don't worry. I'll go easy on you. You've been through enough already. What you really need—" he kissed below Daniel's left ear, "—is someone—" he kissed below Daniel's right ear, "—to take care of you."

Daniel put his hands on Cole's thighs. "I'm glad it's you. Wouldn't want it any other way."

Cole helped Daniel lie flat on the couch, then climbed on top of him. He had been right about the body heat. His skin burned pleasantly against Daniel's. Plus the way he had Daniel's heart pumping, Daniel could feel the life returning to him.

Their cocks nuzzled together. Cole wrapped his hand around them both, using his own precum as lubricant. Daniel dug his fingers into Cole's toned ass for leverage and thrust into Cole's hand. He moaned as Cole nipped at his jawline, licking the resulting bite marks with quick flicks of his tongue.

The freezing water was centuries away in Daniel's mind. All he knew was the heat and strength of Cole's body, the music of his moans and heavy breathing, followed by a warm spatter of cum on Daniel's flushed chest. "Unnngh, fuck," Daniel gasped. "Ohhh, Cole, faster, *faster*, I'm so close…"

Cole pumped Daniel's cock hard, not relenting until Daniel shot his load. He panted and reached for the towel he had brought from Daniel's room. "Didn't think we would need it for this," he said. He wiped up their mess, tossed the towel aside, and rested his head on Daniel's shoulder. "I don't know what got into me."

"Adrenaline," Daniel said, catching his breath. "It's one hell of an aphrodisiac."

"You can say that again." Cole suddenly tensed. "Crap! I gotta get back to the ranch, or they'll think that mountain lion got me." He pushed himself up, face-to-face with Daniel. "I can give you a ride back to your truck, if you want."

The mere thought of getting on his feet made Daniel dizzy. "I do, but now that I've used up all that adrenaline, I just want to pass out for a week. It's fine where it is. Not like that mountain lion will steal it or anything."

Cole smiled and laughed. "No, I guess not." He leaned forward to give Daniel another kiss. "Heads up, I'm gonna call you every half an hour if you don't text me to let me know you don't have a concussion. And you can text me whenever you feel well enough to go get your truck."

"Will do."

Without Cole's warmth, Daniel was left with only his aches and weariness. He lay like a sack of beans watching Cole get dressed. It gave him time to notice things he had missed in their rush, such as the way Cole's chest hair seemed to be an extension of his short beard, or how his tan stopped short at his waistline and gave way to the smooth white skin that was now riddled with Daniel's nail marks.

"Whether you're fully recovered or not, I could come by tonight," Cole said, tugging his jeans back up. "I could make you something to eat."

Daniel smiled. "That'd be...nice."

Cole paused with his shirt halfway up his arms. He looked Daniel up and down one more time, then smiled back. "I guess that's a date then." As he tied his boots, Cole said, "I've never been good at asking guys out. Back in Texas, one wrong word to the wrong guy could get you shunned for life, and out here it was the other guys asking *me* out, but I got so used to saying, 'No thanks, not interested,' I didn't know what to do when I *was* interested. Figured it'd be best to let you make the first move, if you wanted."

Daniel laughed. "I think this counts as making a move, don't you?"

"Only if it's moving in a direction you like."

"Absolutely." Daniel wriggled. "I'd get up and hug you goodbye, but I think you used up what little energy I had left."

"I'm sorry," Cole said.

"Don't be. You saved my life. Seems like you're always coming to my rescue, and I don't think I even thanked you properly."

Cole beamed. "You can thank me all you want tonight, how about that?"

"Sounds good," Daniel said with his best roguish grin.

Fully dressed, Cole ran and got a blanket from Daniel's room. Tucking Daniel into his couch, Cole said, "Warm up, get some rest, and for fuck's sake, don't die before I get back."

"I'll do my best," Daniel said with a tired smile. Cole gave him a farewell kiss, wished him well, then grabbed his jacket and ran out the door. Daniel could hear him talking to Ziggy, followed by the sound of beating hooves. When all was silent, Daniel heaved a sigh and allowed himself to melt into the couch.

All things considered, today was a good day. Daniel smiled to himself. *In fact, I get the feeling this is the first of many lucky days to come.*

SAVE A HORSE

BY J.D. WALKER

Drew, this one's for you.

NO. MORE. COWBOYS.

This was my new modus operandi. I'd had it with sexy, tight-assed hotties who winked in my direction, rode me like they were trying to round up stray cattle, then left me holding the lasso. I was over it.

It wasn't as though I hadn't enjoyed myself with each and every last wrangler, brawler, cow puncher, and ranch hand out there. But I was a romantic, and had just turned forty. The luster of finding that perfect, monogamous cowboy—who still had his own teeth—was decidedly tarnished. He didn't exist. And believe me, I'd tried to find him.

First, there'd been Billy Joe Raintree from Montana when I'd turned twenty-one. He'd taken me out behind the bar where we'd met. The blow job he'd given had made me see other universes. After making my knees weak, he'd taken me to his RV—I was a pit stop on his way to a rodeo—and popped my cherry. It was love at first fuck.

It didn't last, and I was mildly heartbroken when he'd headed out of town before the sun rose the next morning. That was okay, though. I was grateful for the night we'd had together, and the world he'd introduced to me.

A week later, Jeremiah Pinkett came roaring into my life. His body made me weak in the knees. Jeremiah was from Idaho and worked with sheep. He had arms and legs like boulders, and I was more than happy to be pinned by him, anywhere, anytime. The log between his legs had made my ass sing. That hookup had lasted a few days that time. See? I was improving.

On it went. The longest "relationship" I'd had over the years was for six months. That had been Grover Vasquez, when I was in my thirties. But it had been more of a fuck buddy thing. Whenever I'd bring up the idea of being exclusive, Grover would fuck monogamy out of my head until I forgot my own name.

All in all, in the nineteen years that I'd been sexually active and in search of my one-man cowboy, I'd washed out—every damn time. Was it because I'd wanted it too badly? At this point in my life, I just didn't know anymore.

Perhaps I was simply too starry-eyed to see the truth, but Daddy had always said that anything worth having required effort. Unfortunately, I'd expended a heck of a lot of that, to no avail.

After passing out drunk in a bar—alone—on my fortieth birthday, I decided to face the truth: I was too old to go trolling, and sex without love was for the young. Time to hang up those particular spurs.

"Lanice!" Whenever Ernie Trevine used that particular tone of voice, it meant trouble.

"Yeah?" I called out from where I worked on the ranch books in the back office. My ranch foreman of five years clomped across the faded rugs toward my desk, his heavy stride no doubt tracking in mud behind him. He didn't look happy.

"Jonah's gone missing again," Ernie said as he took off his hat and slapped it against his leg. The dust was plentiful, and his brow was sweaty. As weird as it may sound, it was a good look on him.

"Did you check all the usual places?"

Jonah Willett was sixty-nine years old and had been the foreman here for almost forty years before he retired. Ernie had made it a habit to check on Jonah's whereabouts daily because the man loved his alcohol. When he tied one on, he wandered. He was also half-blind, as well as deaf in one ear, which made things complicated. His disappearances had been happening more often lately.

When I could get Jonah to agree to go with me to a doctor—which was rare—I was told he would likely need to be put into an assisted living facility at some point. It was hard for me to think about doing such a thing. I'd known the man almost all my life, and he'd taught me so many things, he was like another parent.

"Yessir, boss," Ernie replied. "Me and a couple of the hands went searching the barns, but he wasn't there." He scratched his cheek, which was peppered with stubble. The sharp, sexy cut of his jaw was distracting. I needed to keep my mind on Jonah.

"Only thing I can figure is that he went off into the fields somewhere, something he's never done before today. You know we have a group to take on a dude tour this afternoon. You're gonna have to get the law involved."

Which meant I'd have to deal with Nicholas "Bulldog" McMurtry, the sheriff in these parts.

Younger than me by eight years, Nicholas had moved back to Wyoming to take over the sheriff's spot after our last lawman had made a spectacular ass of himself over a woman. Attempted murder of her husband, to be precise.

Our town was small—a couple blinks of the eye and you'd miss it while driving by. Nicholas was by the book, and solid. He also had the most piercing brown eyes I'd ever seen, and was built like Paul Bunyan. Our sheriff didn't hide the fact that he liked tight, male asses as opposed to women's curvy bits.

He had a small horse ranch which he'd taken over from his parents when they'd moved south to Arizona. Nicholas also employed an efficient foreman—Bo Clack—to run things. Bo was my age, tough as nails and as flamboyant as a peacock. No one had ever dared to get in his face about it, what with him being six-foot-six and solid muscle.

Bo had a devilish grin, light gray eyes and dirty blond hair—a total knockout. He didn't do plaid—not enough style, he'd told me once. Bright colors were his thing. If you needed to find him in town, just look for the brightest shirt out there.

We'd grown up together, Bo and I, aware of each other's sexual leanings, but had never hooked up. I assumed it was because a guy like Bo, who could have anyone he wanted—and probably did—wouldn't be interested in settling down with a homebody like me.

I grimaced. "Ah geez." I threw down my pen and rubbed the back of my neck. "Guess it has to be done. Thanks, Ernie. You and the others better get ready to earn our bread and butter, and I'll see about Jonah."

Ernie didn't move. He just stood there staring at me, his expression unreadable and his body tense. "You and the sheriff have a falling out, or something?"

"That would imply we had something out of which to fall."

He seemed to relax at my response, and snickered. "They should change his nickname from Bulldog to Horndog."

"Probably." I moved a stack of papers and repositioned the phone on my desk.

"You're not hung up on him, though, are you?" he asked.

I was surprised at the concern in his voice, since we'd never really talked about personal stuff much. Though I knew he was gay. "Not at all. But I will admit to Nicholas being very nice to look at."

Ernie snorted. "Guys like him always are, and I wouldn't want your heart to get trampled on."

I looked up when he said that and was surprised to see an expression on his face that could have been...longing. It disappeared so fast, I thought I'd imagined it.

He cleared his throat and put his hat back on. "Good luck with finding Jonah, and please keep me posted." He turned and practically sprinted out of the house.

Ernie was a nice guy, but not a pushover—he took shit from no one. He was my height, with hazel eyes and prematurely graying hair—the strands had started to silver when he was twenty-two—and pretty damn broad. He was hired at the ranch when I turned thirty.

About half of the men and women who worked for me were gay, and I made sure that my no-tolerance rules for discrimination of any kind were obeyed. Ernie was as firm as I was about that. Neither of us had any patience for bigots.

"WHAT'S UP, BOUDREAUX?" Deputy James Berry queried when he answered my call after the second ring.

James was a capable sort and about my age. We'd played football together in high school, with Bo as our quarterback.

"Caller ID, huh?" I replied, secretly relieved that McMurtry hadn't answered, as he sometimes did. That voice of his always made my dick leak, whether or not I wanted it to do so.

I heard him chuckle. "You know it. Saves time and frustration with sales calls."

"I bet. Look, Jonah's gone wandering off again, and I'm afraid he's out in the fields somewhere. He could be damn near the mountains by now, and the hands are busy with tourists."

"Shit. Well, the Sheriff is heading out your way right now. He's checking on an incident out at the Barnes place. I'll radio him and he'll be over by you as soon as he can."

"Appreciate it, James. How's the family?"

"How d'you think? I'm the only male in a household of women. God, six females." I heard him sigh but knew he wouldn't have it any other way. He loved his kids more than life itself and had been known to hold prospective suitors at gun point, with his wife right beside him.

I chuckled. "I feel your pain, buddy. Later."

❖

AN HOUR LATER, I watched from the porch as Nicholas McMurtry parked in front of the ranch house. I walked down the steps as he got out of his truck.

"Sheriff," I greeted him and shook his hand.

"Lanice." I manfully suppressed a shiver. His grip was firm and warm, and I ignored the way he filled out his uniform shirt and jeans to absolute, button-busting perfection. Well I tried to, anyway.

"Thanks for stopping by, Nicholas. Jonah usually stays around the ranch buildings but I'm a little worried that he's wandered off so far this time. Maybe he's getting senile."

"It happens, unfortunately. Got the horses ready?" he asked, and I nodded.

We made our way to where Peaches and Herb—I had a soft spot for the duo—were saddled and ready for action. I sent a quick text on my cell phone to Ernie so he'd know where I was, then Nicholas and I mounted our horses and headed out.

The ride through the fields was mostly silent, except for the sounds of nature around us. The Rockies before us were majestic, and it always hit me just how beautiful it was here, on this land.

"So, you seeing anybody lately?" Nicholas asked, and I almost fell off my horse.

Down, boy. It's probably not what you think.

"Why the interest?" I shifted in my saddle and silently apologized to Peaches for yanking too hard on the bridle.

"I haven't seen you at any of the bars within a two hour radius of this place in a while."

We used to frequent some of the same establishments. "If you must know, I've sworn off men, sex…the whole shebang."

I felt his stare burning holes into the side of my face. "Why on *earth* would you do that?"

"I'm too old to do the scene anymore, and I'd be a laughingstock if I tried. What I was searching for has eluded me at every turn."

"But," he sputtered, "You gotta know you're one of the best looking guys around, no matter how old you are."

"Well, it's nice of you to say that, but that doesn't take away from the reality of things. Take you, for example. I've noticed that you never choose guys over a certain age to hook up with. And we both know that gay men tend to have a short window of opportunity—in years—before we're passed over for fresher meat. Good looking or not, I'm now on the shelf with all the other middle-aged homos, and I need to accept that."

"That's depressing," he replied.

"It'll be your turn soon, you'll see."

He ignored my comment. "What were you searching for?" he prodded.

I shrugged. "I *was* looking for that special cowboy who'd be mine and mine alone, and not just use me for a quick fuck. After nineteen years and nothing to show for it, I think I'm better off alone."

AFTER AN HOUR had passed, we were about to change direction when my cell phone rang.

"Boudreaux."

"Lanice!" It was Ernie. "We found Jonah. He's over in the east pasture by that old abandoned barn, snoring to beat the band. Looks like he might have sprained his left ankle, too. It's swollen."

"Jesus." I was relieved and irritated at the same time. "Thank Christ. Call Mountain Medical, would you? And ask a couple of the hands to go back and get one of the trucks to transport Jonah to the hospital. I'll be there as soon as I can. Are the tourists freaked out?"

"Nah. They thought it was part of the tour."

I rolled my eyes. "Figures."

"Gotta go, boss." He hung up.

I stuck the phone in my pocket. "Sorry to waste your time, Sheriff, but Ernie found Jonah out in the east pasture. They're taking him to the hospital. We need to head back."

As we turned the horses around, McMurtry said, "It wasn't a waste, Lanice. I'm glad he was found before nightfall. I'll go with you to the hospital."

I looked at him. "Don't you have crimes to solve?"

He smirked. "In this town? Searching for Jonah is the most action I've had in a month."

"Well, if you're sure…" I said.

"I am."

"Okay."

Nicholas followed behind my truck as I headed to the hospital later that afternoon, and he was at my side as I stalked up to the front desk and demanded information on Jonah.

Marcy Slade, the doctor on call, just happened to arrive at the same time. We grew up together, as was true for most of the people still living in this tiny town.

"Jonah's in bad shape, Lanice," she said. "Aside from the issues that you already know about, he also has a weak heart, his liver is a mess…the list goes on. He needs around the clock care, and you know you can't keep up with him anymore. It will only get worse. He doesn't have many years left, I'm sorry to say."

I knew that, but it was still hard to accept. Is this what I would become when I was his age? It was a worry of mine. Jonah had never married, and ranching had been his life. Now all he had to show for it was a body that was failing him. He was the closest thing I had to family anymore, since everyone else was gone.

I sighed. "I understand."

Marcy led us to Jonah's room and left us alone. I stood beside Jonah's bed, and Nicholas stood on the other side of it. Jonah was asleep and hooked up to all kinds of monitors. He looked so frail against the pillows and sheets. The brown age spots were stark against the paleness of his weathered skin.

"I knew it would come to this," I said after a while. "I just didn't think it would happen this fast."

"Yeah." I looked up to see Nicholas' eyes focused on me. "You've done all you could, Lanice."

I wasn't sure about that, but Jonah deserved some peace of mind and a little dignity for his remaining years on this earth. It was the least I could do for someone I considered family.

By the time I got home, it was after nine and I was hungry. The place was pretty quiet since everybody had either gone to their homes in town, or retired to their bunks, for the hands who stayed on the ranch. Ernie lived in the foreman's house.

I went into my office to check the desk for messages. Ernie had left me a note that the hands wanted to know how Jonah was doing. Most of them had worked here for years and respected him. I'd update everyone in the morning.

I walked to the kitchen and grabbed a beer from the fridge before heading to the bedroom. It was Thursday night, which meant Martha would be coming in to do the housekeeping in the morning. I drank half of the bottle's contents before shedding my clothes and taking a shower.

The sheriff had stuck around with me at the hospital the whole time. When it was time to leave, he'd stopped me in the parking lot on the way to our trucks.

"I'm having a barbecue at the ranch on the weekend," he'd said. "It's my birthday, and a bunch of friends are visiting for a couple of days. I'll have to go to the office in the morning on Saturday, but James will take the afternoon shift. You should stop by. You could use the distraction."

We shook hands. "Thanks, I'll think about it. And I appreciate all you did today."

"Nothing to it." He tipped his hat and headed for his truck.

Drying off in the bathroom, I wondered if I really wanted to spend time with a bunch of younger guys who still had their lives ahead of them, whereas I felt stagnant. Maybe I was being maudlin. It would be nice to see Bo, though.

❖

SATURDAY AFTERNOON AROUND four, I pulled up in front of the McMurtry ranch and parked next to a Lexus SUV. Most of the cars around me were pretty expensive, making me think that Nicholas' friends were raking in the dough. Good for them.

I followed the smell of cooking meat around the back of the house. Bo was behind the grill wearing a searing yellow polo shirt that rivaled the sun. He looked up and smiled at my approach.

"Hey you." He set down his fork and leaned in to give me a hug and a kiss on the cheek. He smelled of hickory and citrus-scented cologne. "How are you, hon?"

"I've been better. Had to draw up the papers to put Jonah into assisted living."

Bo was sympathetic. "I'm sorry, sweetie. I know that must have hurt. Nicholas told me all about it."

"Yeah." To change the subject, I asked, "So who are all these young bucks anyway?" I gestured with my chin toward the rowdy group of men before us.

"Buddies from college, his old police squad, and some other guys he's met along the way. I'm sure he's slept with all of them at some point." His response was meant to be lighthearted, I was sure, but I heard a bitter undertone.

I turned to stare at Nicholas, who caught my eye and waved before continuing to flirt with a beefy, bear-like dude. Then I observed how tightly Bo's lips were pressed together. And it clicked.

"How long?" I asked.

Bo arched his brow. "How long…what?"

"That you've been in love with Nicholas?"

He turned a hamburger patty and added some seasoning. "Long enough."

"He knows?"

"Sure. It's an open secret between us. He's happy being a slut, and I've almost come to terms with that." I heard what he was saying, but I knew he was lying to himself.

It occurred to me then that I'd never seen Bo at any of the places I used to frequent to get laid.

"Have you been celibate this whole time?" I asked.

"Nah. I just never went to the same places he did. Had to protect my heart somehow."

Huh.

"What about you?" he asked before moving some of the cooked meat to a huge plate and setting it on the long table next to us where there were rolls, buns, potato salad and baked beans laid out in style. "Come and get it, you ingrates!"

Before I could answer Bo's question, a stampede of starving men converged upon our spot and the food was shared out onto paper plates. Within five minutes, the area was clear, and Bo started cooking again.

"Well?" he prompted.

"I decided I was too old to make a fool of myself for something that I may never find."

"True love, you mean?"

"Yes."

He poked a sausage. "I'm living proof of someone who's made a fool of himself for love. At some point, though, we have to decide what we're willing to live with, and whether it's worth all the heartache. You made the decision to change. I'm still working on that, but I'd like to think I'm getting closer to—"

I heard a wolf whistle and observed Bo's grimace. I followed his gaze and saw Nicholas grinding between two men, the one in front kissing him to death, and the one behind sucking on his neck.

"Why don't you grab a beer and take a break, Bo? I'll watch the grill for a while." Without another word, he handed me the fork, swiped a Budweiser from the cooler, and walked away.

I didn't have the corner on misery after all.

❖

"I SAVED YOU a hamburger, a hot dog, and a piece of chicken."
I handed a loaded plate to Bo and sat by him on the tree trunk
next to one of the horse barns. "Everything else is gone. You'd
think those guys had never had a meal in their lives."

It was late afternoon now, and the fire flies had begun to
show themselves. Nicholas and his buddies had become even
more amorous as the day went on, and I really wasn't interested
in watching an orgy.

"Thanks," Bo said. "How'd you know where to find me?"
He asked before taking a bite of his burger.

I pointed to his shirt. "Hard to miss."

He chuckled and shrugged, as if to say, "It's who I am."

"You feeling alright?" I asked as I leaned back on my
hands, watching the slow passage of the sun as it dipped lower
in the sky.

"I will be. It's not his fault he's the way he is. I'm the one
with the problem."

"You know, when he and I were searching for Jonah yes-
terday, he asked me if I was seeing anyone. Doesn't that seem a
little weird?"

Bo chewed on a piece of chicken. "Maybe he was trying to
hook up with you."

I laughed at that. "Nah, he's not interested. It just seemed
to be a strange question is all."

"Uh-oh."

I turned to look at him. "What?"

"He's tried to hook me up with guys before, and failed
spectacularly."

I smiled. "I don't know if that's sweet or…"

"He means well."

I wasn't convinced. "But if that's the case, why would he try
to hook us up? You would be the last person to look at me. I'm
not your type."

Bo's stare was incredulous. "How can you know what I like?"

"Well, why would you be interested in someone my age when you have your choice of all those young men out there, in spite of your unrequited feelings for Nicholas?"

"Clueless, that's what you are," was all Bo said before going back to his food.

"I beg your pardon?"

"You don't see it, do you?" he continued, wiping his hands on the napkins I'd provided.

I was confused. "See what?"

"You are a highly desirable man, Lanice Boudreaux. An upstanding citizen, giving more than you ever get in return, you wear your heart on your sleeve. Women and men fall all over themselves to get your attention, but you don't see it."

He ate the rest of his hot dog, then said, "I should know. I tried, when we were in high school, junior year. But you were oblivious to my interest, and I'm damned hard to miss, as you well know."

Shock went through me. "You were...but why?"

"Why not? Anyway, I gave up on that and then after a few years went to work for the McMurtry ranch. The rest is history."

"I had no idea."

He just shrugged.

A few minutes later, I helped Bo feed the horses and then got ready to leave. "I'm sorry, Bo."

"Nothing to be sorry for. You didn't know, and maybe I gave up too easily. I'm looking for the same things you are, Lanice, but with a man who's the furthest thing from monogamous. I've resigned myself to the way things are, though it hurts. Don't stop looking, man. The perfect guy could be right under your nose."

He gave me one last hug and patted my ass. "Have a safe trip home, sweetie."

As I drove back to the ranch, I thought to myself that this had indeed been a day for revelations. Bo had been interested in me in high school but I'd been too oblivious to notice, and now he was in love with Nicholas, a dead end street.

Bo said he shouldn't have given up on me so quickly, and I shouldn't stop looking. Maybe he was right.

❖

WHEN I GOT back home, I saw Ernie sitting on the porch swing. It swayed gently back and forth. I walked up the steps and sat beside him.

"You didn't want to go into town with the others?" I asked. It was Saturday night, after all.

"Nah. I rarely ever do. Thought I'd hang out here and wait for you."

Okay..."Why?"

"I thought you could use some company after the thing with Jonah."

"Well, I appreciate that, but—"

He cut me off. "Did you have fun this afternoon?" he asked, continuing to rock us in a soothing rhythm. I noticed in the dim porch light that Ernie had changed from the sweaty clothes I'd seen him in earlier into a faded T-shirt and jeans. His head was bare.

"It was eye-opening," I replied. "It turned into something of an orgy. Not for me, though."

"Bo still mooning over Bulldog?" he asked, staring up at the sky. The stars were pretty this time of night.

He knew about that? "Yup. Bo seems to be resigned to fate."

Ernie looked over at me. "What about you?"

"Me?"

"Yeah, *you*. You done running after men who won't give you what you deserve?"

I thought back to the expression I'd seen fleetingly on his face in my office a couple days back. Wow, it couldn't be. "Where are you going with this, Ernie?"

He shook his head. "Clueless."

Again with that word. "Okay, you're the second person to say that to me today. Care to explain?"

"Dude, I've been yanking my dick to thoughts of you since the day I came to work here. I've watched you head out on the weekends, year after year, searching for some cowpoke to plug your hole, like that would ever give you what you've always wanted."

"Why didn't you say something in all the time we've known each other?"

He shrugged. "I was willing to wait."

"But how could you know..."

"You're a romantic, Lanice. And I knew that eventually, you'd get tired of the meat market and then I could finally make my move." All I could do was stare at him.

Undeterred, he plunged on. "You want a guy to put you first, right? To take care of you and be there, no matter what. A guy who sees you as you are, flaws and all and still says 'hell, yeah, that's what I want, forever.' I'm that guy, Lanice. I've been here all along, waiting until the right time. Pick me."

And while I was still recovering from the shock of his words, Ernie reached over and pulled me into a kiss that silenced all the sounds around us.

As it went deeper, my swirling thoughts melted into a need so fierce, it almost frightened me. I hadn't had sex in months, and my libido was overruling my common sense, fast.

I tried one last time for sanity and pulled back a little. "But this is so sudden. How can you be sure...And since when do you..."

"Since always. Every time you came back from a tryst, you looked so sad, it hurt my heart. That one guy you spent six months with, I could have wrung his neck for the way he led you on. When it was over, you were so heartbroken, I was this close to beating him to a pulp." He ran a hand through my hair. "I've wanted you for so long, and I was willing to wait forever. I'm not saying I've been a monk or nothin'. But my heart is in your hands now, for as long as you're willing to hold it. Which

I'm hoping is for always."

As Ernie kissed my neck and licked my Adam's apple, I tried to gather my scattered thoughts. "It's way too soon to…"

"Shh…just let me make you feel good for a little while. We can talk about how I'll never leave your side after I've fucked you a thousand ways from Sunday."

I could barely think anyway, and all the blood was in my cock. "O-okay." Ernie went back to devouring my mouth and the swing jostled beneath us as he rearranged our bodies and pulled me on top of him.

"You know, there's a bed in the house," I offered before taking his mouth again.

I felt the hardness of his cock and relished the scents of horse, soap, and the outdoors on his skin. It made my dick leak.

"You can take us there in a minute. For now, I want to get you off with my hand. It's one of my hottest fantasies, where I imagine you writhing against me, utterly lost in bliss as I pump your dick dry."

"Shit," was all I had to offer as he reached between us and unzipped my jeans.

His hand made its way into my underwear and circled my cock, giving it a little squeeze. I jerked into Ernie's fist and kissed him harder, both our lips bruised and wet as I attacked his mouth like it held the secret of life itself.

"That's it, love, move with me," he said.

With one hand at the back my head and the other pumping my dick, I moved with Ernie, my arms around him as I fucked his fingers with very little to ease the way except the seeping fluid from my slit. The burn was so good.

"I'm, I'm almost there," I panted and licked his nose before nipping his chin. Then it hit me, and I cried out as I spilled seed all over his hand and moaned in release.

"God, you're even more beautiful than in my dreams," Ernie whispered, his voice awed as he kept pumping me through the shivers and jerks until I was spent. I collapsed against his chest, breathing hard and noticed the steel pole in his pants beneath me.

"Fuck, Ernie. That was…"

"I know. Wait 'til I fuck you. Come on, show me that bed of yours." Slowly, I stood on post-orgasmic legs, zipped up my jeans, and then pulled him up with me.

I kept his hand in mine and led him through the house to the back. I hadn't made my bed that morning so the sheets were still rumpled.

Apparently Ernie didn't care, because he quickly divested me of all my clothing, and his, and pushed me back on the mattress. "You don't even know how sexy a man you are, do you?"

He kneeled between my legs and sucked my sated cock clean. God, it felt good being in his mouth, and I hoped I could get it up again for another round. "How about you fuck me?" I suggested and turned over to give him my ass.

"That was the plan." Ernie proceeded to work my channel with his tongue, and for minutes on end he fucked me that way like he had all the time in the world. While moaning like a slut, I reached under one of my pillows to find a half-used tube of lube for him to finish preparing me.

"Here," I said and shoved the tube toward him on the bed. Two coated fingers plunged in seconds later, and then three, making my butt throb with need as he stroked my prostate. Hot damn, I was getting hard again. "Now, Ernie. I know you need it, and I can't stand the wait anymore. Please, take me."

"It will always be my pleasure to do so," he replied and I heard a condom rip. He must have had one in his jeans or something. Upstart Boy Scout cowboy.

"Come *on*!" I yelled.

"I've got you," he replied, and, hands firmly on my hips, he plunged into me, not stopping until his dick was fully seated.

"Oh mamma," was the best I could do while adjusting to his girth. "Damn, you're huge."

"Sweet talker," he said and pulled out, only to push back in.

Ernie kept it slow and steady, doing his best to make me beg, plead, and threaten until he gave me what I wanted, as hard as he dared, a fast fuck that made me forget the day of my birth.

"Lanice!" he cried out as he shortened his strokes and then keened on release, his hands digging into my hips, he came and came, no end in sight. I wished I could have seen it. It must have been a sight to behold.

When he was done, Ernie collapsed against my back, his furry chest tickling my skin. We ended up on our sides, his cock still inside my ass. He carefully pulled out and threw the rubber on the floor. My dick was now fully hard again, and I started to fuck my fist.

"No, let me," he offered. Throwing a leg over mine to hold me steady, he fisted my cock and worked me up and down while he kissed my lips, a languid exploration that made it even hotter to be taken by him this way.

"I know you can give it up again," he whispered as he nibbled on my neck and kept pumping. Ernie's pole was hard once more, and he positioned it between my legs, the leftover slick and semen from his earlier release lubricating his thrusts. Back and forth we went, a slow, sexy screw that took hours or minutes, I didn't really care.

When I came, it was on a sigh, and Ernie was close behind. We fell asleep, just like that.

SUNDAY AFTERNOON FOUND us on the swing again, and this time my head was in Ernie's lap. We'd talked a bit more after showering twice that morning. Apparently with the right partner, age and getting it up weren't even close to being issues.

Ernie was a bit of a surprise in the wasteland of hookups and trysts. I hadn't expected him at all. And maybe I wasn't too old to give true love a shot, if that's what this was.

It was worth saving a horse, after all, if I got to ride the cowboy.

THE GOOD, THE BAD, AND THE OJETE

BY SALOME WILDE

THE TOWN OF ESPAÑOLA was eerily silent as two figures on horseback rode in, soon after sunrise. Red removed his hat and ran a dusty hand through his namesake hair, a curling thatch that matched the parched earth beneath their horses galloping hooves almost as precisely as his eyes reflected the turquoise of the vast New Mexico sky. The man who rode beside him was called Justice, a name that suited far less well than Red's. It was bequeathed to him, as his only legacy by the woman who bore and raised him, a poor but beautiful Kentucky gal. His presumptive father had left them when the boy was only three, soon after he'd discovered her in bed with their twin farmhands. Despite or perhaps because of his beginnings, Justice had turned out equal parts handsome and ruthless. It was hard not to stare at the way his dark tan was set off by a mass of blonde, sun-streaked hair. Red and Justice made quite a memorable picture as they rode through the desert, especially surprising considering they were a couple of bounty hunters on the trail of a killer.

A dry wind set into motion a creaking hotel sign. It accompanied the muffled stamp of the horses' hooves on the dirt road into the little town. No one came out to greet the pair, who came to a stop in front of the dry goods store and dismounted.

Thick leather gun belts and the shine of the weapons they held would've made plain these men were not in town to shop, had anyone seemed to care. They dismounted quietly, taking in the empty street. Red wiped his brow with the back of his hand. Justice frowned and stomped his heels, shaking thick dust from his boots before looking up and pointing to the sheriff's office. His cactus-green eyes sparkled in the sunlight. Even from a distance they could see the worn door, painted with a dark smear of blood. The stain ended in a dried pool, indicating a body had clearly slumped there not too long before.

As they calmly approached, a squinting sheriff opened his door and gave the strangers a once-over. "That's close enough," he warned, voice sounding as if it was clogged with gravel. His pistol glinted in the sun, as did the dome of his balding head.

Red and Justice stopped in their tracks, raising their hands simultaneously in a gesture of peace. Justice spat out the butt of a well-chewed cigar. The ever-present dust rose again on the arid breeze, rustling the fringe on his coat sleeves.

"We're not here to make trouble," Red promised. He spoke with articulate precision, always. At the moment he also spoke the truth, though he knew the sheriff wouldn't believe him. He'd be a fool to trust outsiders after the violence the town had just evidently faced.

"Maybe you'd like to toss your gun belts my way, to prove you mean those words," answered the sheriff, waving his gun in the duo's direction.

Red pursed his lips. "Afraid we can't do that."

The sheriff pulled a second gun from his hip and cocked both.

Hands still held chest-high, Justice's fingers twitched, along with his cock. A bead of sweat trickled slowly down his stubbled cheek.

Red took a single step forward. "We've come to help, sheriff." He let the words sink in, watching as the tall, grizzled lawman weighed the likelihood he was telling the truth. Far away, a hawk's cry filled the silence.

Out of the corner of his narrow eyes, Justice spied a pair of rifles trained on them from behind a broken saloon window.

"Help how?" quizzed the sheriff.

Recognizing the change from command to question as a cue, Red lowered his arms, though he kept his hands away from his weapons. "We're after the man who shot up your town." His reply rang with the simplicity of truth, for truth it was.

Sucking his teeth in contemplation, the sheriff motioned with his gun, inviting the men into his office.

As they followed, Justice caught Red's eye and then gave a quick glance toward the saloon. Red had already seen the threat. He gave a tight nod before entering the dingy room.

The sheriff kept his pistols cocked as he kicked the door shut behind them. When his two guests were seated, the lawman leaned against his desk and offered them a choice of day-old coffee or cheap whiskey. Red helped himself to the latter, while Justice removed his wide-brimmed hat and asked for a basin of water.

Too pretty for his own good, thought Red, not for the first time.

"There's water in the pitcher," the sheriff told Justice, gazing toward a table just outside the single cell that served as the town jail.

"Much obliged," answered Justice with a nod, rising to leave the talking, as usual, to Red.

"I don't like your kind," the sheriff said, his opening bid in what both knew were inevitable negotiations.

"No doubt," agreed Red.

The older man cleared his throat and smoothed back the little hair he had. "Seen too much blood spilled when outlaws fight outlaws."

"Fighting's a dirty business," Red quipped before knocking back a healthy shot of the harsh liquor. He relished the way it burned, just as sure as the sun but to better effect when a man was of a mind to relax. Then he cocked his head toward the bent tin badge on the desk with a crimson-stained gun belt beside it. "But blood's already been spilled."

The sheriff frowned, deep furrows knotting between his wiry brows. "Emmett Farley," he said with feeling, eyes on the badge and hand on the belt. "A kid, practically, but the best deputy this town's ever had."

"Dead?"

The man sighed and shook his head. "Doc says he should pull through."

There was exhaustion rather than relief in the man's voice. Or maybe, thought Red, it was shame, shame because the blood spilled should've been his own. That made the man pliable, a factor in their favor.

Justice pulled his face from the basin of tepid water he'd poured from the pitcher and rubbed at it with a dingy kerchief he'd pulled from inside his coat.

The sheriff put his second pistol down beside him and poured from the half-empty bottle from which Red had drunk into his coffee cup.

"How'd it happen?" queried Red, opening the wound a little wider.

"Some pig of a bandit," the sheriff spat. "Rode into town, made himself cozy in a game of poker at the saloon, then held up the players for the measly few hundred in the pot and three bottles of good whiskey."

Red quirked an eyebrow. "Ain't much to get shot over."

Justice made a sound of derision as he walked back over to the others, rubbing at his wet head. Damned if the idiot didn't look even prettier wet than dry.

The sheriff continued. "Emmett was on duty and heard the commotion. Darn fool emptied his pistols at the renegade as he mounted his horse and rode off. Emmett was hit once in the shoulder and once in the thigh." He downed the contents of his mug and shuddered.

"Did he get any shots in before he went down?"

The sheriff grimaced. "He hasn't come to long enough to

say yet, but Jake, the bartender, says not."

"Shame," said Justice, returning to balance on a teetering stool.

"Sloppy," Red retorted, eyes on Justice.

The sheriff looked up, steel-eyed, hand on his gun. "What's that?"

"Sloppy," I said. "The criminal, I mean."

Scratching his chin with a horny thumbnail, the sheriff nodded.

"This Jake say what the man looked like?"

"Dark, mostly: hair, skin, eyes. Embroidered black hat that matched his boots. Went by the name of Bronco." The sheriff shrugged. "Hell, strangers come through here on the way to Santa Fe all the time. Usually, they don't make trouble." He sucked his teeth again. "Usually."

"Bronco, you say? Sheriff, that's our man," said Red. He pulled a crumpled piece of paper from his vest and shook it out. The defiant face of one Alejandro "Bronco" Vasquez glared up at them. "Been after him for months. Tricky devil. Travels all over, robbing and looting. No amount too small."

"Must have a death wish," said Justice.

The little paper promised five thousand dollars for his arrest on multiple counts, including the murder of a preacher in Montana. "If I had it, I'd pay that out of my own pocket for what that pig did to Emmett," grumbled the sheriff. He paused, looking at the small cluster of wanted posters on the back of the office door, none of which had Bronco's face on it. "Strange I haven't ever heard of him before."

Red and Justice looked, too. Red shrugged.

"You honestly think you can bring him in?"

"I'm sure of it. He'll be in Santa Fe tonight, maybe Albuquerque if he rides through. He's got to be headed for El Paso and then across the border into Mexico. Only plan that makes sense."

"We'll make sure he never makes it," added Justice, combing his fingers through his damp blond mop.

"And bring him back here?" prompted the sheriff.

Red took another swig from the bottle. "By rights to Montana, for the reward."

The sheriff nodded in understanding.

"Of course, if your town can pay..." Red let his words trail off. He knew that many a New Mexico prospector used Española's bank to stash his takings. Not too out-of-the-way, just enough so it wasn't a likely target for a hold up.

"Like I said, I don't like your kind," the sheriff replied to the unstated agreement. "But in this case, I'll make an exception."

Red could see the thirst for revenge glittering in the old lawman's eyes. If the man weren't so old, he'd have gone after Bronco himself. And had the victim been anyone other than the young deputy he was obviously so fond of? There'd probably have been no deal. As it was, the sheriff sent the bounty hunters on their way with a toast to their speedy success.

THE SHERIFF'S GOOD wishes were heartfelt, but it wasn't that which led the bounty hunters straight to their prey, only two days later. It was planning and experience. Red and Justice knew he'd have made his way to Santa Fe. They used the trail of drunks at the city's edge to find their way to the broken-down hideout where they discovered the wretch, snoring in the darkness after having shared his bottles of expensive whiskey with all and sundry and squandered every bit of the pittance he'd stolen from the Española poker table.

Kicking in the door of the creaking, windowless shack, bucket of water in hand, Red barked a welcome. "Wake up, you filthy mongrel!"

Justice strode in behind him, lighting a slender cigar. He used its glow to find a candle.

In the flickering light, a naked outlaw lay on a bare straw mattress. He groaned at the intrusion.

"This Bronco *hombre* looks like shit," said Red to Justice, picking up the gun belt lying beside the candle and slinging it over his shoulder.

"Smells like shit, too," answered Justice, blowing smoke.

Red hoisted the bucket and tossed its contents at the dark, sprawling mass.

Bronco roared as he rose to his knees. "Go to hell, *ojete*," he growled.

"Angry cuss, ain't he?" Justice said with a grin.

Red approached the bed and yanked Bronco's head back by his thick, black hair. "Listen up, *borracho*: there's five thousand bucks with your name on it waiting for us in Española. So get moving before we drag you there."

That seemed to sober Bronco up, and fast. "*Amigos,*" he said with what passed for a smile on his craggy face. "Perhaps we can...make a deal."

Justice sneered. Red, however, was listening. He released Bronco's hair with a shove. "What sort of deal?"

"I got money," murmured Bronco.

"You lyin' sonofabitch. You ain't got shit, *viejo*," answered Justice.

Calling him "old" seemed to enrage Bronco even more than being called a liar. "I'm talking to *him*, *cabrón*," he snarled, pointing. "To the man, not the boy."

Justice chomped his cigar as he reached for his gun.

Red held up a hand. "Hold on now, Justice. Bronco here says he's got money. We're reasonable fellas. You just fetch that money, *amigo*, and we'll see about letting you go."

Bronco scrambled off what passed for a bed and reached beneath it. He came up with a battered leather wallet and tossed it to Red.

"Well, look here. The thief is actually telling the truth." He rifled through a small rumpled wad of bills. "It's not five thousand, but it ain't hay either."

Justice exhaled a thick cloud of smoke as he peered over Red's shoulder. "What's say we keep this for our troubles, and take him in anyway?"

Red laughed. "I like the way you think, partner."

Bronco spluttered a string of cusswords in Spanish, some of which few north of the Mexican border had ever heard. "That's...not fair!" he finally shouted in English, perhaps the most outrageous words he'd uttered yet.

"You're right," answered Red, calmly. "It isn't fair at all." He tapped his bottom lip in thought. "But you know, Mr. Vasquez, today may still be your lucky day." Keeping his gun belt buckled, he reached below to unfasten his pants. "Why don't you show us a little of how grateful you'd be if we just take your money and forget we ever saw you?" He shook his half-hard shaft.

"*Hijo de perra,*" muttered Bronco, but he turned around and offered his ass, yielding without fuss to the coercion that might save his life.

Red spit down onto his cock and nudged Bronco's legs apart. He spit again between the smooth bronze cheeks before him. "Must be part Indian," he remarked to Justice. "Hairless as a baby down here."

Justice snickered.

Bronco hissed.

Taking hold of Bronco's hips, Red fell silent. He'd intentionally understated his appreciation of the firm flesh before him, but there was no need to talk more about it. Red had never had a taste for women, preferring a hard-living man with just enough hair on his body that he knew who he was fucking. Justice suited him well enough most of the time, but the eye-catching blond was a bit too pliant for Red's rougher tastes. Bronco Vasquez was a fine trophy despite the drunkenness. He was resisting just enough to make the claiming especially worthwhile, and when he arched his broad back, Red couldn't resist driving into him hard with a satisfied groan.

"You reckon he's making it easy 'cause he likes it?" Justice quipped, watching the scene and puffing on his cigar.

"I reckon," answered Red, jaw clamped and voice tight with pleasure as he pumped into his prey.

Justice strode over, sporting a toothy grin. "I reckon he might even like both ends filled." Walking around the creaking bed, he withdrew his own stiff prick. With his free hand, he took hold of Bronco's hair as Red had done, and stuffed himself into the gaping mouth. Bronco made an angry sound in his throat, but it was quickly stifled by cock.

Thrusting smoothly as they worked to match their pace, the pair of bounty hunters hungrily claimed their not unwilling quarry. Red's eyes closed as he held tightly to the dark slim hips. Justice watched his pale cock slide in and out of Bronco's red mouth, cigar gripped between his teeth. Then, always curious, Justice took his free hand to reach beneath, where he found the desperado nearly as hard as he was. The gesture brought forth a pretty whimper that hummed all through Justice. So he kept it up as he lifted his eyes to watch Red.

Red's harsh cry as he reached a sweaty climax urged Justice on. He bit down on his cigar and fucked Bronco's mouth like his own life depended on it rather than Bronco's. And Bronco took every inch. While Red filled one end with seed, Justice withdrew and proudly decorated the dark man's face.

Bronco collapsed as his accosters let their legs fold under them and sat on the floor, catching their breaths and reaching for the dregs of the whiskey Bronco had left beside the bed. After a few moments' panting respite, Red rose, stretched, and buttoned up. "All right, *amigo*. Enough fun. It's time to get dressed. We need to tie you up and get you back to Española."

Bronco narrowed his eyes and spat.

JUST AS RED had promised the sheriff, he delivered the fugitive the next day. He and Justice rode back into Española with the bound and gagged fugitive slung across the hindquarters of Justice's horse.

The lawman rose from the bench outside his office to greet

them. Red grinned as he dismounted and walked around to slap the captive Bronco on the ass. "We tried to pull him along on foot behind the horses for a while, but he kept falling. Didn't want him dragged to death before we got here."

Justice laughed. "Open the cage and we'll toss him right in."

"Right this way, fellas," said the sheriff.

Bronco moaned through his gag as Red and Justice roughly slung him onto the hard cot at the back of the barred cell.

The sheriff locked the door behind the prisoner, pausing to gaze into his red eyes long enough to be certain this was the right man. Then he pocketed the key.

A dusty, road-weary Justice looked longingly at the full pitcher in the corner.

"Mind if I . . .?"

"Why don't you head over to the hotel instead," the sheriff countered. "Get a real wash and rest up a bit while I make arrangements to bring in the county judge and fetch your reward."

Justice's wide mouth spread into a delighted grin. Red nodded his agreement.

MR. CALVIN T. Farley, owner and clerk at the small but tidy Española Hotel, was overjoyed to introduce himself and to thank his two new guests for bringing in the villain who'd laid his nephew low. Anything he could get for them would be his great pleasure. Red and Justice instantly took him up on the offer, one asking for a nice juicy steak and a bottle of brandy, while the other requested a bath, as hot as possible. Farley hinted that he might also be able to procure the hospitality of one or two of Miss Lena's gals for them, but was met with polite refusals. "Just as you say, gentlemen," replied the small, mustachioed man, no doubt surprised to find that the gunslingers were gentlemen.

Once the dining and bathing was accomplished, it wasn't

long before the sheriff was knocking on their door. He carried two hand-tooled saddlebags full of dollar bills and gold nuggets, which he laid carefully on an overstuffed chair.

"Thanks, Sheriff," said Red, pouring out a third or possibly fourth brandy for himself.

"Bill," corrected the sheriff. "Bill Thomson."

"Pleased to know you, Bill," said Red, lowering his hand for a shake.

"Right pleased," echoed Justice from the bed, happily pulling on a new pair of socks that Mr. Farley had been kind enough to provide him.

"Judge'll be here late tomorrow," Bill reported.

"That's good news," said Red.

The transaction complete, the three men fell silent.

Red downed the classy liquor in his glass in a single, satisfied gulp. "Can I offer you a drink, Bill?" He motioned with the empty glass at an ornately carved chair with a deep red velvet cushion in the corner.

Bill waved off the suggestion with a smile. "No, but thanks for the offer. Still on the job," he explained. "And I better be getting back to the office now. Got old Harry Parsons spelling me while I've been taking care of business, but can't leave that one alone too long." He chuckled low. "Probably asleep with his head on the desk this very minute." He turned to go.

"You'll be spending the night there with Bronco—the prisoner, I imagine?" asked Red, offhandedly. He was holding the half-full bottle of brandy up to the gas light, swirling its amber contents with appreciation.

"That's right," Bill said, about-facing to look Red squarely in his bloodshot eyes. "He'll stay put and face the law when the judge comes, rest assured." There was a determined pride in his posture and his promise.

"A sheriff's work is never done," affirmed Justice as Red rose to open the door for the older man.

Bill nodded as he left, and Red closed the door behind him

with a contented, mildly drunk sigh.

After unbuckling first one saddlebag and then the other, Red dug his hands into piles of neatly bound bills and hefty nuggets. "Now that's what I like to see," he told Justice. "A promise kept by a good honest sheriff in a good honest town."

Justice snickered and leaned back against a stack of pillows. "So long as it don't rub off on us." He watched Red at play, knowing his partner enjoyed money for money's sake—the smell of cash and the feel of gold. For Justice, wealth was only about what it could buy. He licked his lips, thinking about a saddle to match his jacket and costly cigars. Maybe even a new horse, a shiny black stallion, wild as the wind for everyone except Justice. That'd make quite a picture.

"Damn right," said Red, interrupting Justice's reverie by tossing a small chunk of gold at him.

Justice snatched it out of the air, just before it would have struck him in the face. He looked it over as Red joined him on the high bed.

"Only one thing I hate about this work," Red grumbled, sitting on the bed's edge.

"The waiting," answered Justice.

Red made a grunt of assent as he watched Justice's strong, nimble fingers toy with the glittering rock. "What say you put those hands to better use while we wait for this honest little town to lock its doors and go to sleep?"

Justice put the precious nugget beside him and helped Red undo his belt and unfasten his pants. Taking out his stiffening rod and bringing his mouth close, the younger man made a sound of annoyance. "Sure wisht you'd take a bath sometimes, Red."

"Tongue bath's good enough for me," Red replied, and shoved Justice down.

BY THE TIME the moon was high, a relaxed Red and a bored

Justice were ready to get the hell out of Española for good. With all dark and quiet in the town, there was just one final errand to manage before they made their discreet exit.

Justice headed for the stables. He picked three well-bred, well-kept horses that suited him better than the tired mounts they rode in on, then saddled and strapped the saddlebags of loot over the haunches of the bigger two. None was the black stallion he'd imagined, but that could wait. He wasn't one to let his fantasies get him into trouble, not since he'd joined up with Red.

Leading the horses quietly out of the stables, Justice smiled at how well things had turned out, even as he couldn't help but eye a tawny mare whose coat was a perfect match for his jacket and boots. Tying the trio loosely outside the sheriff's office, he slipped in to join Red and Bill in a farewell drink of the brandy Red had saved. A cuffed Bronco sat on the cot in his cell, hunched over his knees, glaring out at his captors with savage eyes so dark they seemed black rather than brown.

"Appreciate the hospitality, Sheriff—Bill, but we're hoping to reach Jicarilla by daybreak," Red was explaining. "Seems there's some crazy rustler up there, killing horses and Indians alike for sport. Not sure the reward's worth the risk, but we thought we'd take a look."

"A bounty hunter's work is never done," said Bill with a frown, savoring the brandy.

Justice leaned against the wall and crossed his arms, preferring to stand over the rickety stool available. He watched as Red clapped the sheriff on the back and laughed at his attempt at humor, then glanced at the man in the cell, who remained as still as death but for the dark, menacing eyes beneath thick, furrowed brows.

Bill yawned.

"Tired, sheriff?" asked Red.

"Guess so," Bill replied with a smile. "But don't worry about me. I'll be...I'll be..."

His thought was left unfinished as the sheriff slumped forward over his desk.

Red patted him gently on the back. "You have a good rest now. We'll see to everything, won't we, Justice?" With that, Red withdrew the cell and wrist-iron keys from the lawman's pocket and tossed them to Justice. As Justice went to work, Red carefully removed his gun belt from around his waist. "Got us some nice shiny new *pistolas, guapo*," he said over his shoulder as Bronco emerged from the cage, stretching and rolling his neck.

"*Vamanos*," beckoned Bronco, as he strapped the sheriff's belt around his waist and headed out the door. "I'm sick of this town."

"I don't know," offered Justice, lighting a fresh cigar. "Pretty friendly, I thought." Goading Bronco was irresistible, even if he'd pay for it later. By the time they reached Colorado, his ass would be so saddle sore he'd be numb. Bronco would bring the feeling back, he thought with a flush. No one fucked like the rough Mexican, especially when he was riled. And with the way they'd used him, he'd be plenty riled.

"*Pendejo*," growled Bronco, snagging the smoke from Justice's fingers and clamping it between his teeth as he made his way out the door.

"That's *Pendejo bonito*," Justice countered. The two snickered as Bronco claimed the biggest horse.

"Save the courting for later, you two," said Red, mounting up on and patting a full saddlebag. "I need to get somewhere I can spend this loot."

"And when it's gone," answered Bronco, watching Justice claim the remaining horse, "it's your turn to be the lawbreaker." Red grinned and spurred his mount, bringing up a thick trail of dust behind him. As the others followed, he wondered just how quickly he could spend five thousand dollars.

ABOUT THE AUTHORS

DALE CHASE has been writing male erotica for eighteen years with nearly two hundred stories published in magazines, anthologies, and collections. She has two erotic western novels in print: *Wyatt: Doc Holliday's Account of an Intimate Friendship*, and *Takedown: Taming John Wesley Hardin*. A California native, Chase lives near San Francisco. Online: dalechasestrokes.com.

R.W. CLINGER is the author of the Stockton County Cowboy series, also published by JMS Books. He writes gay romances and mysteries, and is currently working on a new cowboy-themed novel called *Bucking Cowboys*. Online: rwclinger.com.

LEE CRITTENDEN was born in Tennessee and grew up in farming country, dealing with plenty of cows and horses. After living in Florida for a long time, Lee returned to the mountains, and enjoys hiking and outdoor activities. Lee has been writing since the early nineties.

LANDON DIXON'S writing credits include *Sex by the Book, I Like It Like That, Boys Caught in the Act, Service with a Smile, Nerdvana, Boy Fun, Who's Your Daddy?, Brief Encounters, Hot Daddies, Hot Jocks, Uniforms Unzipped, Indecent Exposures, Best Gay Erotica 2009* and *2014; Hot Tales of Gay Lust 1, 2,* and *3.*

HUNTER FROST lost a bet at a blackjack table and begrudgingly traded temperate Southern California for the sweltering heat of Las Vegas. She adores reading and writing romance in all forms, but prefers her stories with two heroes that find their happily-ever-afters with each other. Online: hunterfrost.net.

DREW HUNT was fed up reading about the super-wealthy, impossibly handsome, and well-endowed, so he's determined to write more believable characters. He lives a quiet life in the north of England and someday hopes to meet the kind of man he writes about. Online: drew-hunt.co.uk.

REBECCA JAMES, an English major and avid reader, is passionate about writing and resides in the South with her husband, three children, and various pets.

KASSANDRA LEA lives in WI where she enjoys the bitter winters with long hours of writing. She shares her living space with cast of four-legged critters, her mom, and a friendly ghost. Online: facebook.com/pages/Kassandra-Lea.

GEORGINA LI lives in the South, loves Swiss meringue, and worries she's too tall for high heels. If you'd like to read more of her work, check out her Lambda Award-nominated short story collection, *Like They Always Been Free*, available now from Queer Young Cowboys. Online: Twitter @georginalives.

BOB MASTERS has published several short stories and is currently working on his first novel. Online: facebook.com/bobmasterswriter.

MICHAEL MCCLELLAND loves red wine, hot men, and history. After a decade as an ad man, during which he lived in England, South Africa, and Hong Kong, he has relocated to the American South, where he lives in the forest with his husband and a menagerie of rescue dogs. Online: magicmikewrites.com.

ROB ROSEN, award-winning author of eight novels and editor of the anthologies *Lust in Time*, *Men of the Manor*, *Best Gay Erotica 2015*, and *Warlords & Warriors*, has had short stories featured in over two hundred anthologies. Online: therobrosen.com.

❖

J.D. RYAN was a cowboy in a previous life. In this one, he's an avowed curmudgeon who enjoys having a stable of handsome men following his every command, even if they are fictional. Ryan lives in S.C. in a little house full of books and photographs. Online: jdryanbooks.com.

FERAL SEPHRIAN is a jack-of-all-writing-trades who scribbles anything and everything from poems to shorts stories to novels to screen and stage plays. She recently graduated from the University of Maryland with a double degree in Ancient Studies and English Literature and a minor in Theatre Design and Production.

J.D. WALKER likes to keep her stories short and sweet. A multi-published author, she is also a musician, artist, and lover of all things knit and crochet. Online: expressionsbyjo.com/jdwalker.

❖

SALOME WILDE has dozens of erotic stories in print across the orientation and gender spectrum, in genres from noir and Kaiju exotica to the secret sex lives of inanimate objects. Wilde is the editor of *Shakespearotica: Queering the Bard* and coeditor of *Desire Behind Bars: Lesbian Prison Erotica*. Online: salandtalerotica.com.

CPSIA information can be obtained
at www.ICGtesting.com
Printed in the USA
FSHW010501180619
59167FS

9 781517 158132